RE

7.4.11

Please return/renew this item by the last date shown

worcestershire
county council
Libraries & Learning

The Courtesan and the Samurai

The courtesan Usugumo of the Kadoebi-ro House in the
Yoshiwara with two child attendants, April 1914,
courtesy of Ichiyo Memorial Museum, Tokyo.

The Courtesan and the Samurai

LESLEY DOWNER

BANTAM PRESS

LONDON · TORONTO · SYDNEY · AUCKLAND · JOHANNESBURG

TRANSWORLD PUBLISHERS
61–63 Uxbridge Road, London W5 5SA
A Random House Group Company
www.rbooks.co.uk

First published in Great Britain
in 2010 by Bantam Press
an imprint of Transworld Publishers

A CIP catalogue record for this book
is available from the British Library.

ISBNs 9780593057933 (cased)
9780593057940 (tpb)

Addresses for Random House Group Ltd companies outside the UK
can be found at: www.randomhouse.co.uk
The Random House Group Ltd Reg. No. 954009

The Random House Group Limited supports the Forest Stewardship
Council (FSC), the leading international forest-certification organization.
All our titles that are printed on Greenpeace-approved FSC-certified
paper carry the FSC logo.
Our paper procurement policy can be found at
www.rbooks.co.uk/environment

Typeset in 11/14.5pt Sabon by
Falcon Oast Graphic Art Ltd
Printed and bound in Great Britain by
Clays Limited, Bungay, Suffolk

2 4 6 8 10 9 7 5 3 1

 Mixed Sources
Product group from well-managed
forests and other controlled sources
www.fsc.org Cert no. TT-COC-2139
© 1996 Forest Stewardship Council
FSC

To Arthur

Living only for the moment, giving all our time to the pleasures of the moon, the snow, the cherry blossoms and the maple leaves. Singing songs, drinking sake, caressing each other, just drifting, drifting. Never giving a care if we have no money, never sad in our hearts. Only like a gourd bobbing up and down on the river's current; that is what we call *ukiyo* – The Floating World.

Tales of the Floating World, Ryoi Asai,
written after 1661

JAPAN
1868–9

CHINA

RUSSIA

COREA
(KOREA)

JAPAN

N

0   200 km
0   200 miles

Ezo

Washinoki Bay

Esashi   Hakodate

Matsumae

Miyako Bay

Sendai

Aizu-Wakamatsu

Sea of Japan

Honshu

Kanazawa

Mt Fuji   Edo/ Tokyo

Kano   Yokohama

Shimoda

Kyoto

Kobe

Osaka

Shikoku

Pacific Ocean

Kyushu

Nagasaki

Acknowledgements

Huge thanks to Selina Walker at Transworld who was full of enthusiasm for this book and did a vast amount to encourage me and keep me pointing in the right direction. I'm much indebted to her and to her team – Deborah Adams, Claire Ward, and everyone else, who have been full of support, enthusiasm and patience when required.

Enormous thanks too to my agent, Bill Hamilton, who as always provided sterling support and, among much else, suggested I go and see HMS *Warrior*, and to Jennifer Custer and everyone at A. M. Heath.

I'm indebted to the Ichiyo Memorial Hall for their very generous permission to use the beautiful photograph of the courtesan Usugumo which forms the frontispiece. The Ichiyo Memorial Hall houses a collection of memorabilia of the celebrated novelist Ichiyo Higuchi who lived just outside the Yoshiwara and many of whose stories are set there.

Many thanks too to Kuniko Tamae, who negotiated the use of the photograph and was full of invaluable information on Edo-period Japan.

The beautiful calligraphy on the part titles was done by Sakiko Takada.

I owe a debt to the Japan historians whose work I've drawn on to write this book (though I've taken the odd liberty in the interests of telling a good story). Some are listed in the Bibliography at the end of this book; there are many more.

I was fortunate to be able to use the resources of several wonderful libraries, including the Diet Library in Tokyo, where I studied newspapers of the period, and the library of the School of Oriental and African Studies in London (SOAS). I was helped and inspired by the museums in Tokyo which recreate old Edo – the Edo-Tokyo Museum in Ryogoku, the Fukagawa Edo Museum and the Shitamachi Museum in Ueno, all of which were invaluable in helping me to recreate the period.

As always, last but most important of all is my husband, Arthur, without whose love, support, patience and good humour I couldn't possibly have written this book. He read and commented on each draft and, as an expert on military history, made sure I got the rifles and cannons right, visited HMS *Warrior* with me, and listened to endless harangues on the rights and wrongs of the civil war and on life in the Yoshiwara.

This book is dedicated to him.

Prologue

11th day of the 4th month, Year of the Dragon, Meiji 1
(3 May 1868)

The last of the cherry blossoms were falling, settling in drifts on the ground. Watching the pink petals float down, Hana wondered if her husband would be back in time to see the cherry tree bloom next year. She could hear him stamping up and down, then a crash as he slammed something on to the floor.

'The enemy taking the castle. It's too much to bear!' came his familiar tones, loud enough to set the servants trembling. 'Southerners inside the gates, polluting the great hall and the shogun's private quarters – and all we can do is run! But we'll be back, and we'll find a way to drive them out and kill the traitors.'

He burst out of the house and stood in the entranceway, tall and imposing in his dark uniform with his two swords at his side, staring round at the servants and at his young wife waiting nervously to wave him off.

There was a murmur of voices at the front gate. Some youths had gathered there, straw sandals crunching on the packed earth of the road as they shuffled their feet. Hana recognized them. Some lived in the barracks nearby, others in the apprentices' quarters, and they often came to the house to do cleaning and run errands. But now, in their bright blue uniforms and starched split skirts with swords bristling at their sides, they'd been transformed from boys into men. She could see the excitement on their faces.

They were going to war, all of them, leaving behind only herself, her elderly parents-in-law and the servants. Hana wished with all her heart that she could go too. She could fight every bit as well as any of them, she thought.

Hana was seventeen. As a married woman, she kept her eyebrows neatly shaved and her teeth polished black, and her long black hair, which, when loose, swept the floor, was oiled and coiled into a neat coiffure in the *marumage* style that young wives wore. She had put on her best formal kimono, as she always did to say goodbye to her husband. She did her best to behave in the proper way in all things, though sometimes she secretly wished her destiny might have been different.

She had been married for a couple of years; but in all that time her husband had almost always been away at war and she'd hardly had any chance to get to know him. This time he'd been home only a few days and already he had to leave again. He was a fierce taskmaster and when he was angry he beat her. But she'd never expected anything else; her marriage had been decided by her parents and it was not her place to question their decision.

In normal times, she would have been part of a huge household of in-laws, retainers, servants and apprentices, maybe aunts, uncles and cousins, and it would have been her task to keep the house and to serve them. But these were far from normal times. Edo was under attack – Edo itself, the greatest city on earth, a beautiful place of streams, rivers, pleasure gardens and leafy boulevards, where two hundred and sixty daimyos had their mansions and tens of thousands of townsfolk filled the bustling streets. Never within anyone's memory had the city ever been threatened and now it had been not only attacked but occupied, and hordes of southern soldiers were swarming in.

They had toppled His Lordship the shogun from power and this very day they were taking over the castle. Hana tried to imagine what the castle must be like – the echoing corridors with their creaking nightingale floors that sang out like birds, revealing the tread of the most light-footed intruder, the thousand-matted audience chambers and ranks of liveried servants, the priceless treasures and exquisite tea ceremony rooms and the beautiful ladies of the shogun's household sweeping along the corridors in their lavish robes. It was dreadful to think of the southerners with their coarse accents and rough manners tramping through the elegant rooms, destroying a culture they would never understand or appreciate.

All Edo knew it, all Edo was horrified. It was the talk of the city. The southerners had issued proclamations ordering people to stay in their houses while the takeover took place and declaring that any resistance would be brutally put down. Hana had heard the servants whispering that half the populace had fled.

'I'm proud that you're carrying on the fight, my son,' Hana's father-in-law said in his reedy voice. A gaunt old man with a wispy beard, he stood leaning on his sword like a battle-hardened veteran. 'If I were younger I'd be on the battlefield with you, shoulder to shoulder.'

'The north still holds out,' her husband said. 'At least we can stop the southern advance there. The people of Edo will have to endure occupation until we come back and win the city and the castle again.'

He turned to the youths at the gate and shouted, 'Ichimura!' A gawky big-boned lad, with hair flaring out like a bush, started and stepped forward. Glancing around nervously, his eyes met Hana's and he blushed to the tips of his large ears. She smiled and looked down, covering her mouth with her hands. Her husband pushed the youth towards her father-in-law.

'My trusty lieutenant,' he said, slapping him on the back so hard he staggered forward a couple of steps. Ichimura bowed until his back was nearly level with the ground. 'He's no beauty but he's a fine swordsman and he can hold his drink too. I trust him with everything.'

Watching him stumble awkwardly over a paving stone as he went back to join his comrades at the gate, Hana felt a pang of sadness. She bit her lip suddenly realizing she might never see any of them again.

The servants lined up along the path between the front door and the gate were in tears. Hana's husband was a fearsome master and they were all afraid of him, but they respected him too and knew what a great and famous warrior he was. He went down the line addressing each of them in turn.

'You, Kiku, make sure you keep the fires stoked, and, Jiro, bring in the firewood and water regularly. Oharu, take care of your mistress, and, Gensuké, watch out for fires and intruders.' Even crippled old Gensuké was rubbing his eyes.

Hana was near the front of the line, behind her mother-in-law, with Oharu, her maid, behind her. She smelt her husband's musky pomade as he came towards her. He raised her chin and she saw his strong face and piercing eyes, his furrowed brow and thick black hair oiled into a glossy topknot. There were streaks of grey in it she hadn't noticed before. She looked at him, realizing it might be the last time she ever saw him.

'You know your duty,' he said gruffly. 'Serve my mother faithfully and take care of the house.'

'Let me come with you!' she said fervently. 'There are battalions of women up north fighting with halberds. I can join them.'

Her husband gave a snort of laughter and the crease between his eyebrows deepened.

'The battlefield is no place for a woman,' he said. 'You'd soon discover that. Your job is to look after my parents and defend the house. You'll find as much excitement here, maybe more so. There'll be no menfolk here any more, no one but you, don't forget that. It's a heavy burden.'

She sighed and bent her head.

'Remember,' he continued, shaking a long, rather elegant finger at her. 'Keep the gates barricaded and the rain doors bolted and don't go out unless you have to. The city is in enemy hands now and there's no one policing the streets. The southerners know who I am and they may avenge themselves by attacking my family. Do you remember what I told you?'

'If all else fails, if I find myself in danger, go to Japan Bridge and ask for . . . the Chikuzenya.'

'They've served our family for generations.' His face softened and he cupped her chin in his hand. 'You're a good child and a brave one,' he said. 'I'm glad I married a samurai girl. You have a warrior's heart. I'll remember this lovely face when I'm on the battlefield and you'll bear me a son when I come back.'

He bowed to his father and asked for his blessing, then turned towards the gate. The men were already lined up there. They fell silent as he took his place at the head of the troop. Hana and her parents-in-law and the servants stood bowing until the last blue jacket had disappeared. The tramp of feet faded into the distance and all that could be heard was the chattering of insects, the cries of birds and the rustling of leaves.

Winter

1

10th month, Year of the Dragon, Meiji 1 (December 1868)

Hana was on her knees huddled close to the brazier in the great main room of the house, poring over a book by the light of a couple of candles, trying to absorb herself in the story and forget the silence and gloom around her. Then, somewhere in the distance, she heard a noise. She looked up sharply, her heart thundering, and listened, frowning, not daring to breathe. First it was a whisper, then it grew till it was like the roar of an avalanche – straw-sandalled feet, many of them, pounding along the road towards the house.

The footsteps were coming closer. There was a bang, echoing through the still air till it reached her, deep inside the darkened rooms. Whoever they were, they were beating on the hefty wooden gate. She kept it locked and barred as her husband had instructed, but they would break it down soon enough. She knew no one visited in times like this. It could only be enemy soldiers, come to take her away or kill her.

She clenched her fists, trying to calm the knot of panic in her stomach. Her husband had left a gun for her in the drawer of one of the great chests, but she'd never used it. She was better off with her halberd, she thought.

The halberd was the woman's weapon. It was light and long, twice as long as a woman was tall and three times as long as a samurai sword, which meant that if a man charged at her with his sword drawn, a woman would have a breath of time in which, if she was nimble, she could slash at his calves before he reaced her. Swordsmen instinctively protected their heads and throats and chests but a swipe at the calves always took them by surprise.

Hana had studied the halberd since she was a child. When she wielded it, it felt like part of her own body, and the different stances and five strokes – striking, slashing, thrusting, parrying and blocking – were as natural to her as breathing. But she had only ever fought with a wooden practice stick. She had never yet had the chance to use a real weapon.

Now she jumped up, raced to the entrance hall and lifted the halberd down from its rack across the lintel. It was heavy, heavier than a practice stick. She held it in her hands, feeling the weight of it, and her courage began to grow.

It was a beautiful weapon with a slim wooden shaft, with mother-of-pearl inlay at the top. Hana slid off the lacquered scabbard. The long elegant blade was curved like a scythe and as sharp as a razor. She was glad that she had kept it oiled and polished. She could see her reflection in it, small and slight; but beneath the fragile exterior she knew how to defend herself, she thought fiercely.

The thumping at the gate was growing louder. Oharu came charging out of the kitchen, a cleaver in her hand, her eyes wide and her forehead shiny. She was a thick-legged country girl, strong and loyal. A smell of burning wafted behind her, as if in her panic she had forgotten to take the rice off the fire. Gensuké, the old retainer, followed on her heels, hobbling on skinny bent legs, his eyes popping in alarm. He had taken the poker out of the stove and was holding it like a sword, the tip still glowing red. Oharu and Gensuké had come with Hana when she'd moved to her husband's house in the city and she knew they would do anything to protect her. Of all the servants, they were the only ones left.

Months had passed since Hana's father-in-law had sent for her.

He had been kneeling in his rooms bent over a letter and, when he'd looked up, there'd been a weary, resigned smile on his face. Hana had guessed straight away there was bad news.

'We have been ordered home to Kano,' he said quietly.

'Should I go and pack, Father?' she asked uncertainly. There was something disquieting about the way he was looking at her with his rheumy eyes. He pursed his lips and shook his head, scowling in a way that brooked no disagreement.

'You must stay here,' he said firmly. 'You belong in this house. Our son will return one day and you must be here to greet him.'

Hana had nodded, picturing the windswept plain and the streets of samurai houses clustered around the massive stone walls of Kano Castle. There'd been nothing but bad news from Kano in recent months, news of squabbles and internal dissent and of assassinations, neighbour killing neighbour. Nevertheless, both Hana's and her husband's families belonged to the Kano domain and had to obey the orders of the Lord of Kano, though her husband had also set up a residence here in Edo close to the shogun's castle, from which to pursue his military duties.

She remembered the servants weeping as they clattered about, packing trunks and baskets. They had set off that same day, her parents-in-law in palanquins and the rest on foot, leaving the rooms still smelling of tobacco smoke and the drawers lying open where they had packed in haste. With Oharu's help she had stored away cushions, low tables and armrests, piling them in cupboards alongside futons and lacquered wooden pillows. The grand reception rooms where her husband and father-in-law had entertained guests, the family quarters, the servants' areas and the kitchens which had once been full of people, chattering and laughing, eating and drinking, now fell silent.

A month after they left, dreadful news had filtered through of executions in Kano. It was said that everyone connected with the resistance had died – Hana's own parents as well as her parents-in-law. As she had suspected, they had left her behind to save her. She had wept for days, then steeled herself. They had ordered her to stay alive for a purpose and she must do so.

But she had lost everything. All that was left was the house and her memories of her husband. He at least was still alive. He had sent a letter saying he was on his way to Sendai, capital of one of the northern domains.

In the past, the wooden rain doors that formed the walls of the house would have been pushed right back, letting daylight fill the rooms. But now Hana kept them firmly closed and bolted and the big empty house was as dark and chilly as if the sun had never risen. Slivers of light shone through the gaps where the panels met and fell in pale lines across the tatami, like the bars of a cage. In the months that had passed since her parents-in-law had left, she'd had little to do but huddle beside the hearth and read by the light of a candle.

Even the street cries outside the gate had stopped. The tofu sellers and goldfish sellers, the hawkers of sweet potatoes and pedlars of clams no longer made their rounds. Hana hardly ever heard the clatter of feet or the babble of voices any more, or smelt roasting chestnuts or grilling octopus. Most of the neighbours had fled – though where they had gone and whether they had reached their destinations remained a mystery.

There were shouts of 'Open up or we'll break down the gate,' as Hana tucked up her skirts and tied back her sleeves. She knew the halberd was useless in a confined space, but outside she would have plenty of room to swing it. The great front door was barred and bolted, and she ran to the kitchen door at the side of the house and shoved it open, letting icy air flood in. In the sudden glare of daylight she could see the huge smoke-blackened beams and the smoke whirling over the hearth. She blinked, then darted outside, Oharu and Gensuké close behind her.

The sun was shining in a sky washed clear of colour and frost sparkled on the frozen earth. A few withered leaves still clung to the gnarled branches of the big cherry tree. Hana raced towards the gate at the front of the house and took up her position a good distance from it, one foot in front of the other, holding the shaft of her halberd firmly but loosely.

From the shuffle of feet, Hana could tell there were a lot of men on the other side of the gate. 'Open up. We know you're there,' a voice bellowed.

She heard scrambling and cursing and the clatter of falling stones and a man appeared, heaving himself on to the tiled roof of the high earthen wall, his breath puffing out like smoke. He must have climbed on to another man's shoulders to get there. Hana stared at his broad high-cheekboned face. Perched on the wall, he looked as huge and fearsome as an ogre, with bushy hair and long arms encased in a tight-sleeved black uniform.

He gave a guttural snort. 'No one here. Just two girls and an old serving man,' he called down to his companions. There were scornful laughs on the other side of the wall.

Hana took a deep breath and tried to focus but it was hard to hear anything except the blood pounding in her ears. She could see the hilts of the man's two swords sticking out of his belt. Her only chance would be to strike the moment he jumped down, but the thought of drawing blood and maybe even killing someone was terrifying. Shaking, she reminded herself that she was a samurai and she had to defend the house.

She pointed her halberd at the man. 'Stay where you are. I know how to use this and I will if I have to.' She tried to keep her voice firm but it sounded weak and quavery and sparked another burst of laughter from the other side of the gate.

Leering down at her, the man put his hand to his sword. Hana heard the screech of metal as he drew it from its scabbard and at the same moment he jumped. There were bangs on the other side of the wall as the men there battered again at the gate.

As the man hit the ground he stumbled and lost his footing. Before he could regain it, Hana lashed out with all her might. Light glinted from the blade of the halberd as it swung in a great arc, whistling through the air, and Hana felt it take on a momentum of its own. Quivering with horror, she staggered back, seeing the man's chest gape open like a mouth and a sheet of blood spray out. She had expected to feel resistance but there was none. The blade had cut through flesh and bone as easily as if they were water.

The man made a choking sound and flailed, lunging helplessly for his sword, then crumpled to his knees and keeled over. He looked shockingly small and young as he lay twitching on the ground, blood pumping from his mouth and chest. Oharu and Gensuké rushed over to him and wrenched his swords from his belt.

Hana was still staring at the man when more soldiers appeared on the top of the wall. Now she'd killed one of them they'd certainly kill her, she realized. Screaming at the top of her voice she stabbed at one with her halberd. She had to twist to get the blade out, then pushed the man until he fell backwards. Another jumped into the grounds but Oharu swung the big sword she'd picked up in both hands and managed to slice his thigh, sending the man staggering back, clutching his leg and yowling. A third man swung his sword at Gensuké but Hana knocked it out of his hands with her halberd and slashed at his calves.

More men were climbing the wall and blades burst through the wooden panels of the gate.

'Quickly, Oharu,' Hana said, panting. 'We must get inside and barricade the house.'

A moment later, Oharu was forcing the great wooden bolt through the rusty old hasps of the side door, her broad face clammy and her hands shaking.

'We've been lucky so far,' Hana gasped. 'But we can't fight them all.'

'It's you they're after,' said Oharu. 'You must get away.'

'And leave you behind? Never.'

'We're servants, they won't hurt us. We'll stay here and slow them down.'

Oharu tilted her head and put her finger to her lips. There were footsteps outside in the grounds. The men had broken through the gate and were racing towards the house. Heart thundering, Hana grabbed a quilted jacket and threw a scarf around her head and face, then picked up her skirts, pushing open the doors as she ran through one shadowy room after another, with their musty smell of damp.

Ever since her parents-in-law had left she'd kept a bundle of belongings ready at the back of the house, in case she had to leave in a hurry. Now she snatched up the bundle and wiggled the bolt that held the rain doors shut, but to her horror it wouldn't budge. She picked up a wooden bowl and whacked the bolt till it shot out, then shoved back the rain door. As daylight flooded in, she turned and looked for a moment at the huge porcelain vase in the alcove, the hanging scroll, the great wooden chests with their iron handles and hasps, the neatly patched paper doors and worn tatami mats, each with its ghostly memories of times gone by. She tried to fix the scene in her mind, realizing with a sob that she was seeing it for the last time.

Stepping on to the narrow veranda at the back of the house, she slammed the rain door shut behind her and tied on her straw sandals, fumbling clumsily with frozen fingers. Pine trees swaddled in straw ropes to protect them from the cold stood around the garden. The stone lantern and moss-covered rocks were laced with frost and the pond was frozen over.

The grounds of the house were a maze, but she knew them well. Clutching her bundle, she dodged along the paths and through the trellises to the gate in the back wall and pushed it open. Behind her there were crashes as the soldiers broke down the front door of the house, and the sound of chests being overturned.

Then Hana heard footsteps coming across the garden behind her. Heart thumping, she rushed out into the street and darted along the side of the house, down one tiny lane, then another and another. She ran on, gasping, not daring to stop until she was out of sight of the house, then bent over, panting, feeling the frosty air burning into her lungs.

She felt for her dagger, tucked securely in her sash, and tried to remember what her husband had told her. The ferry. She needed to get to the ferry.

2

By the time Hana reached the river her legs were shaking. The water stretched, dark and oily, in front of her, reflecting the lowering sky and the line of willows along the bank. In the past it had been crowded with cargo craft and passenger ferries jammed with travellers, but now it was almost empty.

Bobbing in the reeds was a small boat with a flat bottom and a pointed prow. There was a man squatting in the stern with a scarf wrapped around his head and a narrow-stemmed pipe poking from the folds, sending puffs of smoke coiling into the air. A pair of beady black eyes peered out at Hana, then a hand removed the pipe, holding the stem delicately between two stubby fingers.

'Where are you going so fast, young lady?' croaked a voice in a strong Edo burr.

A woman alone in a boat would be easy to spot, Hana knew. She needed to find a ferry where she would be hidden among other passengers, but she couldn't see any.

'Japan Bridge,' she whispered, trying to keep her voice from shaking. 'Can you take me there?'

She had never been that far by boat before and she was afraid to think how much it would cost, but she had no choice.

'Japan Bridge?' The old boatman nodded, staring at Hana like a frog eyeing a fly. 'One gold *ryo*,' he croaked, enunciating the syllables clearly.

Hana gasped. She didn't have anything like that much. Then she heard a commotion in the distance. Black-uniformed men were bursting from between the houses and charging across the grassland towards the river. Without a second thought she jumped into the boat with such haste that it plunged from side to side, sending water slapping against the hull.

The boatman climbed to his feet with infuriating slowness. His scrawny legs were encased in skinny black trousers and his shapeless cotton jacket barely protected him from the icy blasts that whipped across the surface of the water. With his pipe still jammed between his teeth, he took a pole from the side of the boat and dropped it into the water with a splash, then leaned on it so hard Hana was afraid he was going to fall in. The boat rocked as he gave a mighty heave and edged it away from the bank.

Hana stared straight ahead, the back of her neck prickling, convinced she could hear feet thudding along the towpath behind them, but when she steeled herself and looked around there was no one there. She slumped down in the boat and, with no one but the boatman to see her, buried her head in her arms. The world had never seemed so huge or she so small.

Hugging her bundle, she wondered what had happened to Oharu and Gensuké and her thoughts drifted back to the day she'd sorted through her kimonos with Oharu, deciding which ones to pack, even though it had seemed ridiculous to be packing when she probably wouldn't need to leave the house at all. In the end Oharu had carefully folded Hana's red silk wedding kimono together with another of her best kimonos and laid them in a wrapping cloth along with Hana's cosmetics set and her favourite book, *The Plum Calendar*.

The boat rocked, setting Hana thinking of another momentous boat ride, when she had knelt in a red-curtained palanquin and listened to the murmur of the river as it bore her to Edo and to the unknown man she was to marry. Oharu had been in the boat too and every now and then she had piped, 'Madam, are you all right? Is there anything you want?' It had been such a comfort to hear her voice. Oharu had been there on the day of the ceremony too, helping her into kimono after kimono, putting on the red silk kimono last and pulling the sash so tight Hana could hardly breathe.

Hana pictured her parents waving her off hopefully, thinking they had made the best possible match for her. None of them could ever have guessed that soon after she married, the disturbances that had racked the country would turn into full-scale civil war. And now her whole family was dead and she was alone and, with every stroke of his pole, the boatman was taking her further and further from all that she had left – the house, Oharu, Gensuké. She gave a sigh of despair. Whatever happened, she had to find a way to get back, she told herself.

For now, the most important thing was to stay alive. Go to Japan Bridge, her husband had told her, then ask for . . . Panic-stricken, she searched her memory, but she couldn't remember the name of the place she was supposed to ask for, where she would find people who could help her.

Soon Hana started to hear sawing, chopping and banging, and smelt the fragrance of freshly cut wood mingled with pungent odours of rotting fish, vegetables, human excrement and the rank smell of the river. She raised her head. They were gliding along between high stone-clad banks. In the past she'd seen children playing with balls and sticks, mountebanks selling their wares and couples snatching illicit meetings under the trees, but now there were only a few people hurrying along, shoulders hunched against the cold.

'We're supposed to call it Tokyo now,' said the boatman with a sniff. 'Edo was good enough for me, but now we're to call it Tokyo, or so our masters tell us.' He wrinkled his nose at the word 'masters', cleared his throat and spat. The gobbet of spittle glinted in the sun before it splashed into the murky water. 'To-kyo – Eastern Capital. Whose capital, that's what I'd like to know. Southern bullies. Give us back our city, I say, bring back His Lordship the shogun.'

He poled on a little way and pulled over to a landing stage

under an arched bridge straddling the river. On the other side was a fortified stone gate like the turret of a castle.

'Japan Bridge was what you wanted, wasn't it? This is Sujikai Bridge here and that's Sujikai Gate.' He waved a gnarled hand. 'Japan Bridge is through the gate and along the main road. It's a bit of a walk but you'll find it.'

Hana fumbled in her purse but to her surprise he shook his head.

'Keep it,' he said, scowling. 'You'll need it.' There was a kindly light in his black eyes.

He turned and waved as he poled away and Hana wrapped her scarf around her face and set off fearfully across the bridge. There was bound to be a checkpoint at the gate. In all her packing she hadn't thought to bring papers, and the guards would be on the lookout for lone women wandering the streets.

But there was no checkpoint, no guards armed with grappling irons, no stern officials checking papers. The walls of the gate were crumbling and the great stone blocks were overgrown with moss. People wandered through unhindered.

A pack of ragged women hung around the gate, their thin cheeks covered with make-up and their lips painted bright red. A man passed by and they ran after him, clinging on to his arms and shrieking, 'One copper *mon*, only one copper *mon*,' until he swung round, cursing, and shook them off. They turned on Hana as she went by, like dogs defending their territory. Perhaps it was because she was on her own, she thought. When she looked back they were still staring after her.

She hurried across the dusty windswept plaza and looked around, bewildered. 'Follow the main road,' the boatman had said, but there were roads leading in all directions. Hana took the widest, but she soon noticed that half the shops and houses were boarded up and many had doors missing and roofs falling in. She had expected a prosperous city, not these half-deserted ruins.

Then she heard shouts and raucous laughter. A gang of youths was swaggering towards her, completely filling the road. She was doing exactly what her husband had warned her against – walking alone through the city. Fearfully, she darted into the nearest side street and heaved a sigh of relief as the youths passed on.

But she was now completely lost. She was in a warren of alleys lined with tumbledown houses, crammed so close together that the eaves blotted out the sky. The walkways were slippery, the drainage channels clogged and the air stank of sewage. She stumbled over something soft and brown – a dead rat, left to rot in the middle of the path. In the past the gates at the ends of the streets would have been locked at dusk but now they hung loose on their hinges. She caught glimpses of young women hanging around in doorways, but they faded into the shadows when they saw her looking at them.

Trying not to panic, she turned into another street and came to a large well with a lid and a pump, bathed in a stray shaft of sunlight. There was a bathhouse in front of her, with light shining from the doorway and clouds of steam pouring out. A woman stepped out carrying a damp cloth full of towels. Her plump face was flushed and shiny and she had another towel draped over her head. Hana rushed up to her, relieved to see someone – anyone – she could approach.

'Excuse me,' she gasped. 'Can you tell me . . . ? Do you know . . .' She stopped, desperately trying to remember the name her husband had given her. Then it leaped into her mind: 'The Chikuzenya?' She said it again, as clearly as she could: 'The Chikuzenya.'

The woman stared at her. 'Of course, everyone knows the Chikuzenya. It's up there.' She waved a large red hand. 'Go right at the end of the lane, then left, then right again and you'll see the main road in front of you. The Chikuzenya's on your left, you can't miss it. The only thing is . . .'

But Hana was already on her way, remembering the clerk from the Chikuzenya with his round glasses, who used to arrive at the house with his anxious apprentices bent under huge bundles of silk. The Chikuzenya was one of the biggest dry goods stores in

Edo. There'd be people there who knew her and would take her in and her husband could come and fetch her when he got back from the war. She'd send a message straight away to Oharu and Gensuké, telling them where she was. Everything was going to be fine.

She quickly found the main road, a broad thoroughfare lined with two-storey wooden buildings, but to her dismay it too seemed deserted and all the houses she could see were boarded up. The largest one looked as if it had been empty for months. The rain doors were streaked with grime and the boards were cracked and rotten.

Then she saw a torn curtain flapping. It was so worn it was almost impossible to see what was painted on it. She peered hard, her heart in her mouth, and made out a faded circle with a character brushed in the middle: Chiku. It was the Chikuzenya.

Hana bowed her head, her last shred of hope gone. Night was falling, the streets would soon be even more dangerous, and she was overcome with exhaustion and hadn't eaten all day. Worst of all, it was beginning to snow.

Cold and shaking, she slumped down on the street, leaned against the rain doors, buried her face in her hands and started to sob.

3

Yozo Tajima opened the hatch and poked his head out into the gale.

Wind and snow beat on his face. He scrambled out, closed the hatch behind him and swung a canvas over it. It was only a few steps to the wheel but the wind was so strong he could hardly make any headway at all. Above the howl of the storm and the creak and groan of the great ship he could hear the ominous flap of a sail. Pushing back strands of hair that were flying loose and brushing off the shards of ice that blistered into his face, he peered up and saw that the main top gallant had torn loose.

Sleet lashed the deck, stinging his face and hands like showers of needles, and his straw cape flapped wildly, threatening to fly off. He grabbed at it with his big seaman's hands and for a moment found himself wondering what he was doing there. In all his life he would never have expected to be fighting a gale, sailing north through unknown seas in the worst season of the year.

Yet here he was, young, in his mid-twenties, adventurous and strong. And although he was different from the other sailors on board – wiry bow-legged characters from old pirate families of the Inland Sea, or hard-drinking seafarers from the Nagasaki dockyards – he was a sailor none the less, and a fine one. He prided himself on that.

The ship gave a lurch and the masts tipped towards the black waters. As the wind screeched through the rigging, the deck tilted till it was nearly vertical, and Yozo lunged for a rope and hung on until the ship righted herself. Seamen plastered in snow struggled past, leaning into the gale.

In front of him, the quartermasters were lashed to the helm, fighting to keep the ship heading into the wind. A couple had dog skins wrapped around their uniforms and the rest wore straw capes that, like Yozo's, flapped wildly. They were a miserable sight in their straw sandals, hanging on grimly to the wheel. One, a scrawny youth, small and slight, was not pulling his weight. His face, pitted with smallpox, was pinched and white, his eyes blank with exhaustion.

'What's your name, boy?' Yozo yelled, the wind whipping the words from his mouth.

'Gen, sir,' the boy answered, through chattering teeth.

'Get below decks, Gen, and find some warm clothes.' As Gen unlashed himself Yozo took his place at the wheel, his hands strong on the spokes. 'Hard 'a starboard!' he shouted. The eight men heaved together, straining every muscle as the great wheel began to turn. Yozo felt the judder of the ship as she bit into the wind. He was soaked to the skin, frozen to the core, his hands raw from gripping the wheel, but he felt a surge of satisfaction, of pure pleasure, as the mighty ship bowed to his will.

He knew the *Kaiyo Maru*, every curve and angle of her, as intimately as any lover. He knew her when she was at rest with her sails furled, tall and stately, or cutting across calm waters, the wake foaming behind her, or moving sullenly, laden down with men and cargo. He loved the feel of his hand on the helm, the vibration that rose from her rudder, the rhythms and creaks of her hull and rigging and the bite as she surged through stormy seas.

The *Kaiyo Maru* was the flagship, the finest, most modern warship in the shogun's navy. Employed in the service of the northern forces, she had won them a resounding victory at the naval battle of Awa. She was small as warships went, a ship-rigged three-master shipping 2,590 tons, fitted with a 400-horsepower auxiliary steam engine fuelled by coal. She carried a mere thirty-one guns and a crew of some three hundred and fifty sailors, rounded up from Japan's ports and dockyards. She had also taken on a tally of troops, some five or six hundred, as many as they had been able to pack in.

Together with the seven other ships that made up the shogun's fleet, they were sailing north. Everyone knew it was a foolhardy venture to sail north at this time of year, though no one had imagined quite how bad the weather would be, but they had little choice. They were on the wrong side of a bitter civil war, the losers in a revolution that had seen their liege lord, the shogun, toppled from power and replaced by his ancient enemies, the southern clansmen.

Most of the shogun's allies had capitulated to the southerners, but not Admiral Enomoto. He had been commanded to hand over the shogun's navy to the new masters of the country, but he was not a man to take orders from the enemy. He had refused, and along with Yozo and all those who remained loyal to the shogun had fled north, taking with him the shogun's eight ships. Now they were fighting not only for their ideals but for their very survival.

As Yozo leaned on the wheel, he remembered Enomoto pacing up and down his cabin. They had known they had to go somewhere, and urgently. But where?

'The island of Ezo!' Enomoto had cried, his face lighting up in a moment of inspiration. Ezo was a vast island on Japan's northern frontier, where Japan brushed up against the wilderness. Only the southernmost strip of coast had been settled; the rest was virtually uninhabited. All the northern armies had to do was set up a firm base there, gather their strength and when spring came march south again and take the country back for the shogun.

'The Star Fort is the key to the whole island,' Enomoto had exclaimed, spreading out a map. 'It's the main defence for the city of Hakodate. If we can capture the Star Fort then we'll have the city. It has a perfect harbour, very deep and sheltered by hills, so we'll anchor our fleet, then go to the foreign consulates in

Hakodate, explain our cause and get the support of the rest of the world. There are only two other towns on Ezo: Matsumae and Esashi. We'll easily capture those and the island will be ours. We'll establish the democratic republic of Ezo in the name of the shogun with Hakodate as our capital and from there we can move south and take back the rest of Japan.

'After all, we have the *Kaiyo Maru*,' Enomoto had declaimed, his voice rising. 'Whoever has the *Kaiyo Maru* has Japan. The war is not over yet!'

4

Yozo peered through the snow at the figure hunched over the binnacle. The officer of the watch straightened up and cupped his hands to his mouth, his words coming faintly through the blustering gale: 'East by north, a half east. Hold her on course.'

But Yozo was on another ship – on the *Calypso*, some six years earlier, heading for Europe. What an adventure that had been!

For as long as anyone had ever known, Japanese people had been forbidden to leave the country on pain of death, and the only western barbarians allowed in had been the Dutch, who lived in the tiny enclave of Deshima, just off Nagasaki. Ever since he was a boy, Yozo had been fascinated by western culture and his liberal-minded father had sent him to Dr Koan Ogata's school of Dutch learning. He had barely completed his studies there when the prohibition on foreign travel had finally been lifted and news had spread that the government was looking for fifteen loyal young men willing to go abroad for three or four years.

Standing now on the snow-swept deck, Yozo remembered the journey to Edo, the endless interviews with ancient courtiers in the audience chambers of the shogun's castle and how he had waited with bated breath for the decision to come through. He could hardly believe it when he was chosen.

Then on the eleventh day of the ninth month of the second year of Bunkyu, 2 November 1862 by the barbarian calendar, he'd finally been on his way. Along with Enomoto and thirteen others, he was to learn western languages and western science and study subjects like navigation, gunnery and engineering. Most important of all, they were to commission and oversee the building of a warship, the first Japan had ever commissioned, and sail it back.

After six long months at sea, Yozo arrived in Holland. Along with his colleagues he placed the order for the ship and from time to time went to the shipyards to oversee the construction, but he'd also travelled – to London, Paris and Berlin. He'd seen his first trains and ships, discovered how the telegraph worked, and soon stopped gawping at the way that water came out of a tap, not a well, and streets and wealthy houses were lit not with candles and lanterns but gaslights.

Then – three years after he arrived – the new warship, the *Kaiyo Maru*, was launched and along with his colleagues he set off on the voyage back to Japan. It had been a dreadful homecoming. Not long after he got back, the shogun was toppled from power. Determined to fight to the end for their liege lord, Yozo and his friend Enomoto had thrown in their lot with the northern resistance, bringing with them the *Kaiyo Maru* and the whole of the shogun's navy.

A crewman emerged, looming out of the driving snow like a ghost, slipping and sliding on the icy deck. He pressed his mouth to Yozo's ear.

'Captain's orders. You're wanted down below. I'm taking over.'

As Yozo opened the hatch, a blast of smoky air burst out, thick with coal dust and oil. He scrambled down the ladder into the darkness of the hold, fighting to keep his balance as the wind battered him from behind. He was chilled to the core and covered in snow from head to foot. He straightened his shoulders and flexed his hands, trying to get the feeling back, then fumbled with stiff fingers at his straw cape and loosened his hood. Snow showered off and scattered in icy lumps across the floor. His fine woollen-worsted uniform with its braiding and gold buttons was soaked through.

A tall, skinny man with long bony fingers and untidy black hair above a pale, hollow-cheeked face was standing at the foot of the ladder. Kitaro Okawa had been the youngest of the fifteen adventurers who had gone to Europe and was the intellectual of the group, though even now he looked too young to be a seasoned sailor. He had large sensitive eyes and his neck was so thin his throat Buddha – his 'Adam's apple', they called it in English – stuck out painfully. Yozo could see it bobbing up and down when he spoke. Even his hair was thin, tied in a scraggly knot on top of his head.

'They're waiting for us down there,' he said, handing Yozo a towel.

Yozo rubbed his head and face and pushed his hair back with his hands. He was in no shape to enter the captain's cabin. He glanced at Kitaro.

'It'll have to do,' Kitaro said with a shrug of his bony shoulders.

As they picked their way through the gloom of the gun deck, the howl of the gale and the crashing of waves outside faded away, drowned by the creaking of cannons shifting in their moorings and the clatter of plates and bowls tumbling around with every roll of the ship. A few oil lamps swung from hooks, casting a wavering yellow light, but most had been extinguished for fear of fire. Beneath the distant roar of the furnace, they could hear the faint squawk of chickens in their coop and the protesting bleat of goats.

The gun deck was crammed with men. The troops who had marched so jauntily on to the ship and lined up proudly on the forecastle now sprawled like casualties on a battlefield. Some swung in hammocks crammed together above the cannons and dining tables, wherever they could find a space. The rest lay on thin straw matting or directly on the wooden boards, their eyes closed and their faces pasty. The place stank of vomit.

'Like grains of rice in a sushi roll,' observed Kitaro as they stepped between the fallen bodies. 'Packed that tight.'

Ducking under the beams they made their way to the captain's cabin, grabbing the brass railings to keep their balance. There was a babble of voices inside and yellow light filtered out. Yozo pushed open the door.

Admiral Enomoto was there along with some of the higher-ranking officers and the nine Frenchmen, bent over maps spread across the table. They were all dapper in their uniforms, bow ties and watch chains in place, the braid on their cuffs glistening, buttons shining and hair gleaming. They fell silent as Yozo and Kitaro came in.

'*Merde*,' muttered one of the Frenchmen. 'What a horrible storm!'

Yozo grinned. Like all the Frenchmen on board, Sergeant Jean Marlin was a prickly, arrogant character. He spoke Japanese after a fashion, though he had an amusingly feminine turn of phrase; no doubt he had picked up his vocabulary in the pleasure quarters, Yozo thought. But underneath his arrogance, Marlin had a sense of humour. He had started as one of their instructors, drilling them until they had been transformed from a bunch of samurai who swung their swords whenever they felt like it to a disciplined, highly skilled army who marched in step, fought as one and could load and reload their Chassepot rifles three times a minute. Yozo knew that Marlin was as committed as they were to their cause.

The ship lurched and the men grabbed the table and slapped their hands on the maps and instruments to keep them in place. Enomoto stood impassive till the pitching eased, then looked across at Yozo, who stood dripping salt water on the fine Dutch carpet.

'Good job, Tajima,' he said. 'You could run this ship single-handed.'

The shadow of a grin flitted across his fine-boned face. Recently he had grown a moustache and taken to wearing his hair cut short and parted to one side in the western fashion. At first glance he looked the perfect gentleman, aloof and languid and clearly of aristocratic stock, but nothing could conceal the stubborn set of his jaw and the burning determination in his eyes. Yozo was the only person on the ship not in awe of him.

'If my readings are right we're just about here,' Enomoto said, pointing at one of the maps. 'Washinoki Bay. We'll swing the *Kaiyo Maru* to port, drop anchor and land the troops at dawn. Let's hope the weather's in our favour.'

'Tajima,' he went on, looking straight at Yozo. 'I want you to go with the land forces, with Commander Yamaguchi and the militia.'

Yozo was startled. 'Commander Yamaguchi?' The words were out before he could stop them, and the other officers exchanged glances. But orders were orders. Yozo bowed crisply, straightened and saluted in western style. 'Aye, aye, sir.'

'You too, Okawa,' said Enomoto to Kitaro. 'Now, listen carefully. Once you've landed at Washinoki Bay you'll be marching through Kawasui Pass across the peninsula, heading for the Star Fort just outside Hakodate. Remember, you'll be travelling fast and light. There'll be guides at the beach to lead you. Sergeant Marlin and Captain Cazeneuve are going with General Otori and taking the most direct route through the mountains, advancing from the north. With luck both detachments will converge on the fort at the same time. The garrison won't be expecting anyone to cross the mountains in this weather, so you'll take them by surprise. As for the fleet, we'll be sailing around to Hakodate Bay and will drop anchor once the fort is safely in our hands.'

When the meeting was over, Yozo and Kitaro scrambled down the ladder to the lower deck. Oil and coal fumes seeped from the stokehold as the ship chopped through the water and a couple of lanterns swung violently, lighting the darkness.

' "A hero holds the world in the palm of his hand," ' Kitaro mouthed above the roar of the boilers and the clangs and crashes of the stokers and trimmers working down below.

'The Commander, you mean?' Yozo sat himself down on a coil of rope. He could see that Kitaro was trying to look unconcerned but he knew him too well to be fooled. Kitaro was as dedicated to the cause as any of them, but he was a seaman and a scholar, not a soldier, and unlike Yozo had seen little action. While Yozo was perfectly at home with a rifle in his hands, Kitaro was more of a philosopher. Thinking was his métier.

Yozo took the flask off his belt and lifted it to his lips, enjoying the sensation of the fiery liquor burning down his throat. His hands were black.

'Commander Yamaguchi is a hero, but he's a brute too,' he said thoughtfully. 'The Demon Commander, they call him. Could be Enomoto wants us to keep an eye on him. I hear he's a bit too free and easy with his sword. Maybe that's why Enomoto's sending us with him and not with the regular army.'

Kitaro crouched beside him. 'You saw him at Sendai Castle, didn't you?'

Yozo nodded. 'The council of war.' He took another mouthful of rum and swilled it around his mouth, savouring the taste, as he thought back to the massive granite walls and towering battlements of the castle, the brilliant orange, red and yellow of the maple leaves in the grounds and the labyrinth of huge icy chambers and sunless passages. It had been some forty days earlier and the banner of the Northern Alliance, a five-pointed star, white on a black field, had fluttered over the citadel. Yozo had been there as Enomoto's right-hand man, instructed to listen but not to speak.

The vast audience hall had been dark and cold. Tall candles burned, throwing a yellow light on the tatami mats and gold screens that lined the walls, and smoke hung above the hearth and rose from the men's long-stemmed pipes. Officials of the shogun's former government were in attendance along with senior councillors representing the thirty-one warlords of the Northern Alliance, all in starched ceremonial dress. The commander of the northern armies, General Otori, and other military men, in uniform, took their places too. At first they had all – officials, councillors and military men – knelt formally in order of rank, but as their voices rose, echoing around the great hall, they forgot about precedence.

They wrangled for hours. Some of the senior councillors favoured giving up and pledging allegiance to the new government. They were well and truly beaten, they said. The southerners were advancing north, laying waste to their castles one after the other. It was madness to carry on. They should concede defeat.

Yozo listened in silent disgust to their complaints. Then Enomoto spoke up. 'We're not finished yet,' he argued. 'Winter's coming. Our men are hardy and used to hostile conditions and the southerners are weaklings, they don't know what our northern winter's like. We'll freeze them out. They'll never dare pursue us up north and if they do, they'll die.' His quiet, intense voice swelled until it filled the dusty corners of the great hall and made the cobwebs tremble. 'Don't forget, we have the toughest men in the land. Not only do we have the army, we have the Kyoto militia too.'

'What's left of them anyway,' grumbled a jowly florid-faced elder. 'The southerners have been hunting them down like dogs. Commander Yamaguchi's the only one of their leaders who's still got his head.'

'I agree with Admiral Enomoto,' barked General Otori, a short fiery man with a bullet head. 'If we consolidate all our forces we'll be unbeatable.'

'The Commander is with us right now,' Enomoto declared. 'Let's hear what he has to say.'

Yozo remembered the murmur that had run through the gathering and the stir as the legendary fighter strode in. He was quite tall, Yozo recalled, with strikingly pale skin, a handsome man in his greatcoat and breeches with his two swords bristling from his belt. He looked, Yozo thought, like someone who spent his time inside darkened rooms, plotting intrigue, not on the streets of Kyoto cutting down the enemy, though it was said he had killed hundreds. His long hair, black and shiny like lacquer, was pushed carelessly back from his face, and he stared insolently at the elders.

'The moment the Commander opened his mouth you could hear he was no samurai,' Yozo said to Kitaro. 'A peasant from Kano is what people say. He spoke out loud and clear. "I'll accept the joint command of the confederate troops." Then he stops and looks around, stares at all those great lords crouching there, huffing and puffing on their pipes.

' "But there's one condition," he says. You could have heard a feather drop. "My orders must be strictly obeyed. If any man defies orders, even a senior councillor of one of the great domains, I'll kill him myself." Those were his very words. They all looked at each other, those senior councillors. You could see what they were thinking. Who did he think he was, threatening them like that? And the way he said it, the menace in his voice. He had this look in his eye like he'd do exactly as he pleased.'

'When a man is stubborn enough and convinced he's right, there's no stopping him,' observed Kitaro. 'Put three stubborn men together and there's no knowing what may happem.'

Yozo nodded. Between them Otori, Enomoto and the Commander controlled the army, the navy and the Kyoto militia. They were all three loyal to the death to the shogun. And all three had that spark of madness in their eyes.

At dawn next morning Yozo was up on deck. The snow was still falling, so dense he could hardly see the coast, and icicles hung from the rigging and yardarms. When the weather cleared a little he made out a line of rocky outcrops and a few isolated shacks in the lee of snow-covered hills. The roiling sea was the colour of lead. In front of them, waves broke on the rocks, sending up a wall of water. It was going to be a treacherous landing in Washinoki Bay.

Around him, men stood hugging themselves. The unlucky ones had nothing but cotton uniforms; others had found straw raincoats, bear skins or dog skins and draped them around their shoulders. Yozo was wrapped in everything he could find but the cold still cut straight through.

A contingent of seamen uncovered the first launch, loaded it up and hooked it up to the yardarm. They pivoted the yardarm, tightening the ropes on one side and loosening them on the other, and lowered the launch. The coxswain, bosun and twelve rowers scrambled down and gingerly stepped in as the launch pitched and tossed and smacked against the side of the ship, sending up sheets of freezing spray twice the height of a man. The soldiers lined up on deck, bent under their heavy packs, rifles slung over their shoulders. The first peered over the side at the narrow steps protruding from the ship's hull, running straight down to the black water rolling far below. He hesitated, drawing a breath between his teeth with a hiss, then looked up and straightened as heavy footsteps approached.

Commander Yamaguchi's face was still pale from seasickness but he carried himself with the same awesome arrogance, his shoulders thrust back and his head held high. Frowning impatiently, he swung over the side and climbed down the steps in front of his troops, holding on to ropes at each side.

They followed, and as the last man stepped in and the launch tilted and nearly tipped, some of the soldiers yelped. The Commander's lip curled in disdain.

Yozo gripped his telescope and peered through the blizzard as the little boat tossed up and down on the waves. From time to time it teetered on a crest as if it was about to capsize. A second launch had already set out as the first came back.

Yozo and Kitaro joined the third group. The ship pitched as they stepped down into the launch. The rowers set about their oars and the wind sent the boat flying straight towards shore. When they were still a few yards out, Yozo jumped into the sea, gasping at the shock of icy water on his legs. Together with the oarsmen he gripped the launch and held it steady while the soldiers climbed ashore, wading to the beach, making a human chain to pass the boxes of equipment and supplies along.

The snow had stopped, the sky was clearing and from the shore Yozo could see the vast expanse of the ocean stretching grey to the horizon and the fleet of eight ships well out to sea, their masts bristling. Launches shuttled back and forth, conveying men from the ships to the shore. Then, as Yozo watched, one of the launches disappeared. When it bobbed back into sight the keel was in the air, tossing like driftwood. Tiny figures thrashed in the leaden water. Yozo headed for the shallows but Kitaro grabbed his arm.

'Don't be crazy. They're too far out,' he shouted above the roaring of the waves.

The troops were sombre as they picked up their kit. Some fine men lost, and not even in battle. But any death in the service of the shogun was glorious. Or was it, Yozo wondered, as he and Kitaro joined the others on the long hike through the pass towards the Star Fort and the city of Hakodate.

5

'Are you all right?'

Hana started as a finger prodded her arm. A woman was staring down at her. She had a scarf wrapped around her head, casting her face into shadow, but through the thick wool her voice sounded young.

'What are you doing here?' She spoke in a rapid high-pitched downtown patter. All Hana could see of her was a pair of black eyes, fixed on her.

'I was looking for the Chikuzenya. I was told they'd take care of me,' Hana whispered, her voice shaking. She was numb with cold.

The woman shook her head. 'It closed months ago. Everyone's left – everyone that could afford it, that is. They've all gone to Osaka. A nicely spoken girl like you shouldn't be out on the street alone like this. It's dangerous.'

Panic-stricken, Hana stared up and down the long empty street, suddenly realizing where she was. Rough shouts rang out not far away and she remembered the gang of youths she'd seen with their clenched fists and swords and threatening faces. A cold wind rattled the rain doors looming in a dark wall along the street and she gasped as the full horror of her situation struck her – her parents and parents-in-law dead, her husband long since gone to war. The last she had heard, he had been on his way to Sendai. She had no idea where that was but it sounded unimaginably far away.

The woman reached into her sleeve, took out a pipe and a tobacco box, filled the pipe and held it out. 'Here,' she said, adding with a bow, 'I'm Fuyu.'

Slowly Hana unwound her scarf and smiled gratefully at her new-found companion.

There was a sudden whiff of cheap powder and hair oil as Fuyu squatted beside her. She loosened her own scarf and Hana saw that she was indeed young, not much older than she was, with a round face covered in thick make-up and an upturned nose and shapely mouth. She had a down-to-earth quality about her that Hana found rather appealing. She struck a flint and pushed her face so close to Hana's that Hana could see the pores on her nose and the pits on her cheeks.

Hana took a long slow puff of the pipe, enjoying the taste and smell of the tobacco.

'You did well to get this far,' Fuyu observed. 'The place is swarming with riff-raff and out-of-work samurai.'

'I got completely lost,' said Hana, shaking her head. 'I was so sure I'd find someone at the Chikuzenya who'd take me in.'

'Your husband's a samurai, isn't he?' Fuyu was scrutinizing Hana's face in a way that made her uncomfortable. 'I expect he's gone to war and left you on your own. War is tough for women, isn't it?'

'Do you have a husband at the front?' Hana asked doubtfully. Fuyu certainly didn't look like a samurai's wife, or behave like one either.

But Fuyu didn't answer. They sat in silence as the raucous shouts from the youths Hana had seen earlier came closer.

'You need somewhere to stay, don't you?' said Fuyu suddenly. 'Somewhere warm and safe. I know the very place.'

'You do?' Hana said, surprised that this woman who had appeared so unexpectedly seemed to want to help her.

'No problem with business there,' said Fuyu. 'And it's guarded. Southern soldiers aren't allowed in, so you won't get any trouble from them. It's the best place to go if you want to steer clear of them.' Fuyu paused, her eyes still on Hana, and spread her lips in an ingratiating smile. 'They have jobs there too. You can sew, can't you? You could be a seamstress or a maid or an entertainer. You can read and write too, I expect. They're always looking for people like you.'

'But . . . where is this place?' Hana asked, beginning to feel uneasy.

'You only have to spend the night there; you won't have to stay any longer if you don't want to.'

Hana shook her head. 'Thank you, but I'm fine. I'll find somewhere myself.' But even as she spoke she knew she had nowhere to go.

Fuyu's face hardened. 'Do as you please,' she said, her mouth twisting in an ugly way. 'But I can tell you now, you'll end up selling yourself at the city gates if you don't follow my advice.' Hana closed her eyes, feeling panic well up as she pictured the women she had seen there.

Fuyu grabbed her hand. 'Come on. Let's go, before it gets dark.'

'But . . . but where is this place you're taking me?' Hana stammered.

'You've heard of the Five Streets, haven't you?' snapped Fuyu. 'You can make a good living there, the best there is.'

The Five Streets. Hana gasped. Everyone knew what that was – a colourful, noisy, raucous place where the lights never dimmed, full of brightly painted women, where men congregated in search of pleasure. Her husband had often bragged of how popular he was among the women there. It was said to be the worst of the Bad Places, a city in its own right a good hour's walk outside the walls of Edo, far enough away that decent folk would not be polluted by whatever went on in there. It was certainly not a place for someone like her.

'No, no,' she gasped. 'Wait, I have to think.'

'You can think on the way,' said Fuyu, pulling Hana to her feet.

*

The moon had risen and the road ahead unrolled long and straight, lined with slender lacquer trees with a few leaves still clinging to the skeletal branches, glinting like gold coins. Hana could see her small shadow stretching out in front of her along the frozen earth of the causeway. Far below them, on each side of the embankment, marshland patched with paddy disappeared into the blackness. Every now and then men pounded past, sometimes on horseback, sometimes on foot. Bearers raced by carrying palanquins and a heron swooped overhead.

They had long since left the low streets and drab slate-coloured roofs of Edo. Hana could feel Fuyu's hand on her elbow, propelling her along. She could easily have pulled away and run off in another direction, but where else was there for a lone woman to go? She knew they were going to a place of pleasure for men, but it was a whole city too, that was what people said. There must be plenty of other jobs to be found.

'There!' shrilled Fuyu, her voice high and excited. 'Look. Over there! Hurry, they've lit the lanterns already.'

In the distance, lighting up the blackness below the dyke, was a shimmer like a haze of glow-worms on a summer's night. The whisper of voices and laughter and faint scents of woodsmoke, grilling fish, incense and sewage drifted along on the breeze. The fabled Yoshiwara lay before them. Only it was not a fable, it was real, and Hana would soon be there. She stared into the darkness, her heart thumping.

Because, for all her qualms, the Yoshiwara pulled her and tugged at her and made her feet move faster. It almost made her forget the empty house, the banging on the door, the threatening figures pursuing her across the wasteland. The sounds and smells and glimmering lights drew her, promising an exotic new life which she could not yet even imagine.

Hana shivered in the icy wind and pulled her scarf closer around her face. Her legs were aching, stones dug into her feet and her straw sandals chafed with every step she took. But the lights ahead were growing brighter and brighter, and soon she began to make out the twang of shamisens and the sound of singing.

It was quite dark when they came to a solitary willow tree. Its leafless branches swayed and creaked in the wind.

'The Looking Back Willow!' said Fuyu.

Hana had read all about it. It was where men stopped for a last look at the walled city of the Yoshiwara before they set off for home in the morning. Below them the Five Streets spread, a square of light and colour in the darkness of the marshland.

Hana stared at the dyke stretching behind her towards Edo and her old life. She was about to enter a new world and she knew that when she left it – if she ever did – the dyke and the moon and the stars might still be the same, but she would not be.

6

Hana followed Fuyu as she hurried down the slope towards the walled city, past stalls crammed side by side and teahouses where waitresses lurked, grabbing at men as they passed, trying to drag them in, until finally they came to a bridge and crossed the murky waters of a moat. A huge gate loomed before them. On the other side were milling crowds and bright lights and all the roar and bustle of the city.

Hana stopped, trembling, as a guard stepped out and barred their path. His neck was like a tree trunk and his nose was squashed flat as if he'd walked into a wall, and in one enormous hand he had an iron staff with a hook on it.

He glowered down at them, but Fuyu smiled up at him coquettishly, waved a paper in his face and slipped a couple of coins into his hand. He opened his big mouth in a grin, revealing a jumble of missing and rotten teeth.

'On your way, ladies,' he grunted with a wink. 'Enjoy yourselves!'

And so they entered the Yoshiwara. At first Hana pattered along, keeping her eyes lowered, as people pushed past her, trailing fragrances sweeter and more subtle than any she'd ever smelt before. Silky garments brushed her hands. Kimono skirts swirled by with tiny feet in satin-thonged sandals peeking out from underneath, and wooden sandals clattered past bearing big feet with splayed toes sprouting black hairs. Men's voices chattered and shouted and women cooed and twittered like birds.

Then Hana recognized the enticing aroma of roasting sparrows and octopus and couldn't contain her curiosity any longer. She raised her eyes and gasped. People – so many it was almost impossible to move! She stared about her, wide-eyed. Merchants in silks and brocades strutted alongside samurai with shiny oiled topknots, tradesmen jostled by, servants darted about and squat, brown-skinned men peered around uncertainly as if they were on their first visit and didn't know how to behave. Old women crouched beside doorways, their wizened faces pressed together, gossiping; burly young men ran by, balancing trays of food piled one on top of the other; and little girls with white-painted faces and brilliant red lips walked solemnly by, carrying letters or holding hands.

Edo had been a ruined, fearful city, but the Yoshiwara was crammed with people looking for pleasure. Hana gazed around, enchanted by the smells and sights and sounds. But apprehension still gnawed at her belly. This was not a place for her.

Just as she had decided to tell Fuyu that she'd changed her mind and must leave at once, Fuyu clamped her fingers tightly around her arm and pushed her down a dark side street and through an open door. They had arrived.

An elderly maid in a shapeless brown jacket over an indigo kimono ran out to greet them, bringing a basin of water for them to wash their feet. As Hana stepped inside, she caught a glimpse of long corridors and men disappearing through doors from which came sounds of music and laughter. Fuyu hurried her along verandas lit with lanterns, past room after room, then slid open a door.

A woman knelt beside a low table, writing in a ledger by the light of an oil lamp. From the back she looked elegant and refined. She was wearing a plain black kimono tied with a red obi and her hair was coiled in a gleaming knot. She had a pipe and a cup next to her and there was a kettle humming on a ceramic stove.

But then she turned towards them and Hana had to stop herself recoiling as she saw that her face was a network of wrinkles, plastered with thick white powder that sank into every crack. Her lips were painted scarlet, her red-veined eyes were liverish, and there was a mole on her chin with a hair poking out of it; yet she still held herself as proudly as if she was a famous beauty.

The woman eyed her soiled kimono and the grimy shawl she had wrapped around her face, and Hana shuddered, realizing that she had been lured in by all the noise and colour and exoticism of the Yoshiwara. Now she felt its icy chill. She had allowed herself to be led into a trap.

'So sorry to intrude,' Fuyu whispered, her shoulders obsequiously rounded, pushing Hana to her knees.

'Not you again, Fuyu,' the woman said wearily. Her voice was deep and throaty and she spoke with a sing-song lilt, in a dialect that Hana had never heard before. 'How many times do I have to tell you, business is bad? You keep bringing me these women, but all they do is eat and sleep. They don't earn their keep. Now if you were to bring me a child I could train up, then we could talk business. But an untrained adult – they're more trouble than they're worth. Don't go bringing me any more.' She turned back to her ledger and picked up her brush.

Suddenly Hana was consumed with rage. She had no intention of kowtowing to this ugly old woman. 'I may be bedraggled but I'm not untrained,' she said fiercely, careless of the consequences. 'I'm a person of good family, I'm educated, I can read and write. I'm here to ask for sanctuary. I can teach and earn my keep in an honest way, but if you can't offer me a job that doesn't dishonour me I'll leave and try my luck elsewhere.'

The woman stared at her, her black eyes peering out from the painted folds of withered skin. 'So she has a voice,' she said in surprised tones. 'And pluck.'

A strand of Hana's hair had escaped from her shawl and was snaking around her face. The woman grabbed hold of it and tugged and Hana winced as it snagged against the rough skin of her fingers.

'Good hair,' said the woman. 'Good and thick. And black. No kinks.'

'Your shawl,' hissed Fuyu, snatching at Hana's scarf. Hana tried to hold on to it but Fuyu had already pulled it off.

The woman leaned forward sharply, peering at her hard. Her eyebrows rose and her eyes opened wide, then she reached out and gripped Hana's chin with a horny thumb and forefinger, breathing heavily. Shocked, Hana recoiled from the smell of stale make-up and sweaty clothes doused in perfume.

The woman sat back on her heels and narrowed her eyes, a cunning look on her face.

'Of course she's not a classic beauty,' she said to Fuyu, 'but that's no bad thing. Nice round face, slightly oval.' She drew back and called out, 'Father, Father.'

Footsteps shuffled across the tatami and the door slid open. A man with a square face and a belly that ballooned above his low-slung sash bustled into the room in a cloud of sake and tobacco fumes.

'A new one?' he enquired, clamping his mouth shut after each syllable. 'Not taking any more. Business is terrible, hardly a customer. Can't afford any more mouths to feed.'

The woman tilted her head and glanced up at the man through her lashes.

'You're quite right, Father,' she said in a girlish warble. 'But this one . . .'

'You do nothing but waste my time, woman,' he grumbled, lowering himself to his knees, taking out a pair of glasses from his sleeve and balancing them on his nose. He leaned over Hana and the woman took a candle from the low table where she had been sitting and held it close to Hana's face. The man's eyes, small behind the thick lenses, widened then narrowed. He sat back on his heels and stared at Hana as if he was appraising a painting or a tea ceremony bowl or a piece of fabric.

'Not bad at all,' he said finally. 'Almost melon-seed-shaped. Good skin too, white, no blemishes. Well, none that I can see. Wide eyes, fine nose, small mouth, slender neck. It's all there.'

Shocked, Hana stared back. She was opening her mouth to protest when the man grabbed her chin, gripping it so hard it hurt. He wrenched it down with one big hand and pulled back her lips with the other. Hana tried not to retch as she tasted the tobacco on his brown-stained fingers.

'Good teeth,' he grunted.

Fuyu was on her knees, her eyes darting back and forth as she took everything in.

'Off with your jacket,' she snapped.

The man gripped Hana's hand, turned it over and stroked the palm, then bent the fingers back until she thought they would break. Hana blinked hard, holding back tears.

'You won't get another one like this,' said Fuyu, hard-voiced. 'With a child you don't know how she'll turn out. With an adult you know what you're getting. I don't mean to contradict you, Auntie, but you can see for yourself. She really is a beauty, a classic beauty.'

Hana looked around at the heavy-jowled man, at the old woman with her painted face and at Fuyu, watching her with hungry eyes. It was no good trying to appeal to their better natures, she could see that only too clearly. But she would not give in without a fight. She took a deep breath. She had to remind them she was a person just like them, not an object to be bought and sold.

'This isn't why I came here,' she said, her voice shaking. 'My face has nothing to do with it. I can read and write. I can teach.'

'Listen to that, Father,' purred the woman. 'She's got spirit. And class. How she talks! Listen to that!'

The man put his glasses back in his sleeve and heaved himself to his feet.

'Too old,' he said, raising his shoulders in an expansive shrug and turning towards the door.

'Give her a chance, Father,' said the woman in wheedling tones. 'Singing and dancing, anyone can do. But reading and writing, those are rare skills. Let's see how she writes. Girl, come over here. Do us a sample.'

But Fuyu was already scrambling to her feet, her kimono skirts crumpled. 'I'll go somewhere else. This is an excellent young girl. I can easily find someone who'll take her,' she said in silky tones.

The candles sputtered and a globule of wax trickled slowly down the side of one. The man was staring at Hana with his small hard eyes.

'On your back,' he said abruptly.

Before Hana knew what was happening, the old woman had grabbed her by the shoulders and pushed her down. She screamed and fought but the woman was unexpectedly strong. Fuyu clamped her hand over her mouth to keep her quiet and helped hold her down.

The two women leaned on her hard while the man pushed up her kimono skirts and shoved her legs apart. Hana heard the tatami creak as he knelt between them. Then rough fingers were pulling and probing and pinching at her. She could hear the man's rasping breath and feel it hot on her thighs. There was a sharp pain as a thick finger prodded deep inside her and she shouted out and recoiled.

Finally the man released her and sat back on his heels.

'Good specimen,' he said. 'Firm, good colour. Rosy. Fresh-looking. Good shape.' He chuckled. 'Our customers will enjoy it.'

Hana sat up, pulling her clothes together around her bare legs. Breathless with shock, her face burning with humiliation, she swallowed hard as hot tears spilt down her cheeks.

'Well?' said Fuyu.

'We'll do you a favour,' said the man in measured tones. 'We'll take her off your hands.'

'You're too kind-hearted, Father,' said the woman, her lips curved coquettishly. 'No one else would take someone as old as this. Of course, it all depends on . . .'

Fuyu looked at one, then the other.

'Let's talk outside,' she said. 'I'm sure we can come to an arrangement. I'm sure you can find a way to offer this girl a job of some sort.'

Hana knelt, huddled, hardly daring to breathe, as the door closed and the footsteps pattered away. Too late, she saw how naive she'd been. She put her head on her knees and sobbed.

After a long while she looked up. The house echoed with singing, the jangle of shamisens and talk and laughter, but the sounds were muffled, as if they came from far away, through many walls. Steam puffed from the kettle and the charcoal in the brazier glowed. The teacups and writing brushes and vase of winter branches, the small things that lay around the room, shifted in the flickering lamplight as if they were alive. She drew a long shuddering breath and dabbed her face with her sleeve. It seemed she might have a chance – a small chance – to creep away. She picked up her bundle and pushed the door open a crack.

The veranda outside was empty. Lights glowed from behind the paper screens that walled the rooms around the courtyard and shadows moved about, plump rounded ones carrying trays and slender ones dancing with graceful gestures. Here and there the silhouette of a man jigged furiously. It all looked charmingly festive but Hana knew it wasn't. She glanced cautiously to left and right, checked a second time, then slipped out. For a moment she felt a surge of hope, then realized she had no idea even which way to go. Closing the door behind her, she crept along the veranda as softly as she could.

She had passed a couple of rooms when a door slid back and a figure glided out in a swirl of silk, wafting musky perfume. Hana stopped dead, her heart pounding. The woman's face hovered in the darkness. It was a white mask, smooth and flawless, glowing in the pale light that filtered through the screens. Her eyes, etched in black, were expressionless and there was a petal of red in the centre of each lip, making her mouth into a tiny pursed rosebud. She looked like a porcelain doll.

Stunned, Hana shrank back, staring, as the woman addressed some incomprehensible words to her in a breathy warble.

'Of course,' the woman said lazily, forming the syllables with care as if speaking a language she rarely used. 'You don't speak our tongue. That's the first thing you'll have to learn. Don't stand gawping. I was just coming to fetch you.'

As she spoke, Hana realized that beneath the thick make-up the woman was actually quite ordinary-looking. She had a pro-truding mouth and her hair was not straight but frizzy. Strands had come loose and hung round her face, and big thick-fingered hands poked from the sleeves of her dazzling red kimono.

But none of it mattered. The make-up transformed her into a mysterious apparition, a being from another world.

'I don't know who you think I am,' Hana blurted out. 'I don't live here. I'm . . . I'm on my way out.'

Even as she spoke she knew how ridiculous she sounded. There was only one reason women came to places like this, and it was not to visit.

'You fancy samurai wives – you're all the same,' said the woman. 'You think you're too good for us, but you're lucky to be here at all. A lot of girls get turned away. This is a good house. I've been told to take charge of you. You can call me Tama, that's my name.'

Ignoring Hana's protests, she took her elbow and shepherded her along the veranda and down a corridor. Through the gaps in the paper doors Hana caught glimpses of parties in full swing. She could hear singing and dancing and smell mouth-watering aromas that reminded her of how hungry she was.

A group of young women in magnificent kimonos came sweep-ing towards them like a flock of brightly coloured birds, their white-painted faces shimmering in the lamplight.

'I hate these southerners,' one was saying fiercely. She spoke in piercing high-pitched tones, but her accent was much like Hana's.

Hana gazed at her in surprise. 'I hate having to open my legs for them.'

'These days they're the only ones with money,' said another. 'They'll be gone soon, with any luck.'

They brushed past Hana without even noticing her, like a river flowing around a rock. Hana blushed, ashamed suddenly of her dirty travelling clothes.

'The southerner I've been entertaining keeps telling me that Edo's finished,' the first woman grumbled with a snort. 'He says the only thing that makes it bearable is the Yoshiwara. He calls our men rebels.' Her voice had become an angry growl. 'Rebels! The cheek of it! He says the "rebels" who are still alive went to Sendai and joined up with the navy, our navy.'

Hana's heart gave a leap. Sendai was where her husband had said he was going in his last letter.

The women were disappearing round a corner.

'They're headed north, a big force,' came the shrill voice, faint in the distance. 'Of course, I didn't tell my southerner what I really thought. I flattered him, I told him how clever he was. That way he'll be sure to tell me more. But I already know the most important thing: the ships have sailed. Our ships.'

Hana heard the words as clearly as if she'd been right next to her. Unless he'd been killed, her husband too was on one of those ships.

So there was still hope. She would just have to do her best to stay alive and pray that, when the war was over, he would come to the Yoshiwara and rescue her.

7

Yozo had never known such cold. One moment the sky was blue and the sun was glittering off the rocks, sparking shards of light from the spears and bayonets of the men trudging in front of him, the next it was as if night had fallen and snow was blowing in great flurries and gusts. The wind was so strong he could hardly keep his footing. The only sounds that broke the silence were the creak of branches as snow piled up more and more heavily and the occasional muffled thump as a mound fell from a branch and crashed to the ground.

By the end of the first day, Yozo was frozen to the core and wet through. His toes and fingers were numb and his teeth chattering. Grimly he plodded on up the mountain along with Kitaro and the other marchers, scrambling across the rocks, batting the damp snow off their clothing, on their painfully slow progress through the pass towards the Star Fort and the city of Hakodate.

As evening fell they began to make out the shadowy shapes of buildings, clustered beside an ice-covered lake, surrounded by trees. Around the village square were big houses with steep thatched roofs, from which came appetizing smells of woodsmoke and cooking. Scrawny dogs with thick white fur slunk around. The villagers cowered when they saw the soldiers and their guns. They were tall big-boned men with bushy hair and long beards, in thick quilted robes or bear skins – Ezo people, it seemed, native inhabitants of the island. As far as any of the soldiers knew, they were savages who fished for salmon and hunted bears.

Yozo heard the murmur going around the troops: 'The Commander says we're to billet here tonight.'

He stepped inside one of the houses with Kitaro on his heels. A strong fishy smell pervaded the place but at least it was sheltered and warm. As his eyes got used to the darkness, he made out a fire pit in the middle with rough straw mats spread over the damp earth floor and a couple of rolls of birch bark burning in holders, giving off a fitful light. Soon a good fifty men had piled in behind them and were squatted around the smouldering logs, blowing on their hands and rubbing them together. The smell of woodsmoke mingled with the stench of sweat and dirty uniforms.

Anxious to keep the soldiers happy, the Ezo ran about making food.

Yozo crouched on the rough mats, cradling a bowl of soup in his hands. It was a thick broth with an unfamiliar smell, oily and a little rancid, with fishbones floating in it. He wrinkled his nose, took a sip and was relieved to find that it was hot and filling. By now his companions were talking raucously and shouting with laughter.

'You remember that time we stormed the Ikedaya Inn?' came one voice. 'I cut down sixteen of the southern bastards. I counted them.'

'That's nothing,' yelled another, slamming his fist on the floor. 'My tally was twenty.'

'I'd like to feel my sword cutting through bone again,' grumbled another, a swarthy man with a broad nose and fleshy peasant's face.

'Tomorrow, with any luck,' said the first. 'When we get to the Star Fort.'

A woman was piling logs on to the fire. At first Yozo thought she was smiling, then realized she had a design tattooed around her mouth, like a moustache. Beneath the hubbub he heard a tuneless humming. One of the women had picked up an instrument and was twanging it and singing softly.

Through the smoke, in the dim light, Yozo could see Commander Yamaguchi. He was sitting very straight on a raised platform at the far end of the room, talking to a couple of his lieutenants. It was the strangest sight, this great military leader in a peasants' hut, holding himself as proudly as if he were in a king's palace.

Yozo glanced at Kitaro. He too was staring at the Commander with a bemused expression, as if, like Yozo, he was wondering what on earth they were all doing here, at the ends of the earth, in a land fit only for savages.

By early afternoon the following day Yozo was stumbling along, too frozen even to speak, trying to keep an eye on the Commander striding out in front. They were marching through a forest and the towering pine trees and silent white landscape made Yozo think of the great cathedrals of Europe. He'd never seen such magnificent buildings, soaring so high.

He let his mind wander back to the paddle steamer, the *Avalon*, which had taken him from Rotterdam to Harwich and the most powerful nation on earth. From there he had taken the train to London and had walked the streets, awestruck by the mighty stone buildings with their aura of wealth and history, the public squares and the places of worship, so tall it made his neck ache to look up at the pointed roofs dwindling into the sky.

But now that he was back in Japan, it was not the grand monuments he missed so much as the everyday sights – the hansom cabs, the men in shiny top hats and women in dresses shaped like temple bells, the modest streets of brick houses, the Metropolitan Railway which burrowed deep under the earth like a mole, the ear-shattering whistle of the trains, the choking coal dust that filled the air and the thick dank fogs – 'pea-soupers', they'd called them – which had blanketed the city in winter.

And above all there'd been the women, parading up and down the Haymarket with their smiles and painted faces and billowing bosoms. With their blue eyes and yellow hair and pinkish skin, they'd been so different from the ladies of the Yoshiwara, but they'd provided welcome and comfort all the same. What he wouldn't give to get back there one day, he thought.

Suddenly he found himself treading on the heels of the man in front of him. The Commander had stopped in a clearing, strode over to a rock, sprung on to it and pulled out a telescope. He stood staring down, then turned and beckoned imperiously.

Jerked back roughly into the present, Yozo raised his own telescope and focused it. They had reached the top of the pass, and below them, stretching as far as he could see, was a glittering plain of snow and ice, with hills in the distance and the lowering dome of the sky overhead. To one side was a web of streets criss-crossing the snow, dotted with houses, and in the distance lay the ocean, grey as lead. They'd crossed the peninsula. Directly below them, etched small but sharp against the dazzling white, was a perfect five-pointed star – the fort. Yozo could see smoke rising inside and the sparkle of ice on its moat.

'The Star Fort,' came a shout. Others took up the cry: 'The Star Fort! *Banzai!*'

Yozo's fingers and toes were like sticks of ice but he barely noticed. Quickly he and his companions crowded into the clearing, ducking under trees or finding rocks to perch on. The Commander stood straight and proud on a great overhang, shoulders thrown back. His western-style boots were encrusted with dirt and snow, his greatcoat stained. His gleaming black hair hung in wild strands around his face as he stared down at his troops.

'Men of the Kyoto militia,' he shouted, his voice loud in the silence. 'Volunteers, patriots.' He swept his arm towards the plain. 'The Star Fort, a five-pointed star, like the star of the Northern Alliance. It belongs to us, it's ours, it's our destiny!

'The southern traitors have driven our lord from Edo Castle and forced him into exile. They've murdered our families, destroyed our lands and seized our castles. But now the tide is beginning to turn. This is our chance.

'We all know that the Star Fort is designed to be impregnable. But the men of the garrison have only recently changed sides and they won't want to die for a cause they don't believe in. As for us, we are great warriors. We are fighting for our lord and we are not afraid of death.

'General Otori and the regular army are advancing through the pass on the other side of the hill. They will attack the fort from the north and take the northern bridge. Our job is to sneak down in twos and threes and take the bridge to the south. We'll keep well hidden and close in under cover of darkness. Once we have the fort, Hakodate will be ours and our fleet will anchor in Hakodate Bay. Today the Star Fort, tomorrow the whole island of Ezo! Long live the shogun! *Banzai!*'

The soldiers cheered so loudly it brought clumps of snow tumbling from the branches of the trees.

Yozo laughed aloud. He was ready to go, eager to have his rifle in his hands, to feel the recoil and the cut of his sword biting into flesh. Even Kitaro was beaming and cheering at the top of his voice.

The men swarmed down the hillside like a pack of wolves, then spread out and made their way silently across the plain. It was getting dark and the snow muffled the sound of their feet.

Keeping together, Yozo and Kitaro dodged through the snow, hiding behind trees, keeping the muzzles of their rifles covered and their ammunition dry. A couple of times one or other of them misjudged the depth of a pile of snow and floundered up to his neck in a drift. As twilight fell, they saw massive granite battlements looming out of the blanket of white not far in front of them and the shadows of gun emplacements along the walls. Yozo's mouth was dry. His heart beat hard and there was a knot in his stomach. The time had come.

There was a whistle like a bat's squeak and Yozo glanced around. Shadowy figures waved urgently. Huddling close to the ground, they crept nearer and nearer to the battlements, black specks against the snow. Yozo's breath came in quick shallow gasps. He had to stay alert, calm, focused, he told himself.

In twos and threes the men edged around the moat, doing their best to keep out of sight. Mounds of snow were piled against the walls and heaped along the ramparts. The moat was covered in ice.

The snow had been cleared on the bridge itself. Keeping light and low like a wild cat, Yozo padded silently across the icy boards, other men following close on his heels. He could see the sentries in their military greatcoats and straw sandals guarding the huge gates, their breath puffs of smoke in the frozen air. They stood awkwardly, as if they were uncomfortable in their foreign clothes. Drawing his dagger, Yozo grabbed one around the neck and pulled his knife across his throat. Hot blood sprayed out, soaking his hand. As the other sentry started forward, Yozo stepped across the body and thrust his dagger into the man's stomach.

With Kitaro, he dragged the sentries out of the way as silent figures raced past. Then the gates creaked open and the troops poured in, the Commander loping at their head. Yozo caught a glimpse of his eyes, like a wolf's in the darkness, darting from side to side, taking everything in.

Once inside, Yozo could see that the Star Fort was unlike any castle he had ever been in. It was a maze, a vast sprawl of barracks. Dodging from one building to the next, using them as cover, the men sprinted towards a massive wooden construction with steep roofs buried under a thick layer of snow and a watch-tower poking out at the top. Icicles like spears gleamed under the eaves. The wind whipped the snow into flurries, shimmering in the darkness, dusting the men and the buildings.

Suddenly there was a bang, deafeningly loud, and Yozo hurled himself to the ground, grabbing Kitaro, who was still on his feet, and pulling him down with him. After a moment he raised his head and looked around. There was another bang, and Yozo realized that it was coming from outside the fortress. Then came another, then another, followed by the crackle of gunfire. Flashes lit the sky, reflecting off the clouds, throwing the great fortress into silhouette.

'Our men. General Otori,' he muttered. Kitaro nodded. Yozo could hear him breathing out in relief.

An explosion split the sky, and for a moment the Commander's ragtag army, six hundred desperadoes, were lit up as they ran through the fort, rifles levelled. An alarm bell jangled wildly and there was a volley of shots from inside the building.

'Cover us,' barked the Commander.

Yozo scrambled up a tree in the grounds of the fort, wedging himself into a fork. He reached into his pack for a cartridge and loaded his Snider-Enfield. Seeing lights moving inside the fort, he aimed for the windows and fired. He reloaded and got in shot after shot as the Commander and the militia charged the door, yelling like a pack of wild animals.

He dodged as something whistled past his ear. A bullet. Another slammed into the tree trunk. Yozo ducked and half jumped, half tumbled, into a snowdrift. Dark figures raced towards him, swords flashing. Picking himself up, Yozo grabbed his rifle by the barrel and swung it. There was a rush of air and a crack as the butt made contact with a skull. Another man was sprinting towards him, yelling a war cry. Yozo swung his rifle on to his shoulder and put his hand on his sword hilt. With one movement he had it out of its scabbard and had clipped the man across the throat. He stepped out of the way as the man fell.

Footsteps padded towards him from behind. He swung round, deflected the blow, then hurled himself on his attacker and they rolled in the snow, punching and clawing at each other. Finally, Yozo twisted the man's arm behind his back, held him down with his knee and pressed his face in the snow.

'Why fight for traitors?' he yelled.

The man thrashed desperately. Yozo was holding him down when he heard the rattle of drums. He looked up. The light of many lanterns flickered through the trees. There was a sound, distant at first then growing louder and louder. Thousands of straw-sandalled feet were tramping across the northern bridge and the frozen moat, between the great granite ramparts, through the gates into the Star Fort. He caught a glimpse of something white fluttering above the trees. It was the five-pointed star of the Northern Alliance.

The surviving members of the garrison came stumbling out of the castle headquarters, their uniforms torn and bloodied, their hands above their heads.

Yozo released his opponent.

'Get up,' he said roughly. The man rolled on to his knees, gasping convulsively. He was a skinny youth, no more than sixteen, with acned skin and projecting teeth.

'You'll pay for this,' he snarled.

'Go home to your parents,' said Yozo wearily. 'And be thankful you're still alive.'

That night they celebrated. Inside the castle headquarters General Otori held court, commending men for their bravery.

The Commander sat outside with the militia. Gathered around campfires, the men ate and drank, then they stood up one by one and danced slow, stately Noh dances. Later, when enough rum and rice wine had been consumed, they sang nostalgic songs of their yearning for home, for wives and lovers left behind.

' "Ah, take me home, home to the north country, take me home," ' sang one. The rest swayed, softly joining in the chorus.

At least these men knew where their homes were, even though there was a good chance they no longer existed, thought Yozo. For many, their houses had been burned down and their wives and children were dead. But he . . . His family was dead, he knew that for sure. He had travelled so much, been away for so long, that the *Kaiyo Maru* had become the only home he had.

He glanced at the Commander, who was sitting in the shadows a little way away from the others, warming his hands, staring into the flames. The fire brought out the craggy contours of his face and its light seemed to burn in his eyes, and Yozo noticed an unexpected softness in them, as if the Commander was thinking of something or someone long ago. He looked away, feeling he'd intruded on some private thought.

'Hey, Tajima,' called one of the men. 'Sing us a Dutch song, something sad.'

Yozo scowled. The last thing he wanted was to draw attention to how different he and Kitaro were from the rest.

'I don't know any songs,' he muttered.

'A song, a song,' the men clamoured.

Kitaro was sitting next to Yozo.

'I know a song,' he announced. Yozo grabbed his arm and tugged him back but he shook it off and rose tipsily to his feet. In the firelight his neck with its jutting Adam's apple seemed longer and thinner than ever.

He stood for a moment looking into the fire, recalling the words, then launched into a shanty, swaying as he sang:

'I'll sing you a song, a good song of the sea,
With a way, hey, blow the man down . . .'

Yozo closed his eyes. The foreign words took him back to faraway places, to that long-ago journey to Europe. Suddenly he was on the high seas again, the smell of salt and sweat and oil and coal in his nostrils, hearing the seamen belt out the words as they heaved and strained on the ropes, unfurling the topsail little by little. But the soldiers were shuffling uncomfortably and he realized that to their ears the tune sounded jarring and discordant.

'What kind of song do you call that?' barked a voice. Kitaro's shanty tailed off and he stared at the ground.

'A sailor's song,' he muttered sullenly. 'We sing it when we're hoisting the topsail.'

'Is that so?' said the Commander, drawling the words sardonically. 'Sounds like a barbarian song to me. You two certainly know a lot about foreign parts, but if you hang around with barbarians too long you'll start to smell like them too. Don't forget that. We have enough to put up with already, what with foreigners invading our country, tramping our soil, interfering in our lives, selling arms to our enemies. But you – you look Japanese, you can fool us into thinking you belong here with us, but how are we to know you're not spying on us? We don't need your barbarian ways around here.'

There was a stunned silence, then a soldier picked up a shamisen and began to play a nostalgic melody.

'You're brave enough so we'll let it pass this time,' said the Commander, scowling at Yozo. 'But don't offend our ears with your ugly barbarian songs again.'

'Barbarians have hearts too,' said a gravelly voice in heavily accented Japanese. The Commander turned slowly. A tall, hefty figure with deep set eyes and a bushy moustache was squatting on a rock in the shadows. It was Jean Marlin, the dour heavy-jowled Frenchman who had accompanied General Otori's troops.

The men made a space by the fire. Marlin was a barbarian, there was no doubt about that, but he was also a friend, a fine soldier and a teacher. He was owed respect.

The Commander grunted and Yozo stiffened, feeling his eyes on him and Kitaro. In the firelight his face was as impenetrable as the masks that actors wore in the Noh dramas. The Commander had been made to look foolish and he would hold it against them, unfair though that was. They would have to be on their guard.

8

Early the next day Yozo and Kitaro set off for the port at the head of a contingent of soldiers. The city of Hakodate straggled across the plain and, as they strode along the broad streets between heaped walls of cleared snow, Yozo couldn't help noticing how small and miserable the wooden houses were. There were paving stones poking through the snow on the roofs to stop the tiles from being blown away by the relentless winds. Women bundled in thick clothing, with red-veined faces and swollen, chapped hands, stood unsmiling beside stalls with bear skins, otter skins, deer skins and deer horns laid out for sale. Salmon wriggled on other stalls and there were slabs of bear and deer meat on offer too. It was a desolate place.

He smiled as he caught the whiff of the sea and quickened his pace. They hurried along the road between the ocean and the steep flank of Mount Hakodate down to the port, where the water swirled grey and sullen beneath the leaden sky. Junks bobbed at anchor and seagulls screamed, swooping in to settle on the waves, rising and falling like black dots on the swell. Craggy snow-covered hills circled the bay. It was a perfect harbour, just as Enomoto had said, with land on three sides protecting it from the bitter winds and huge waves.

Yozo set the soldiers to work along with the crowds of dockworkers, shovelling away snow to clear the landing berths. Late in the afternoon some sixth sense made him look up. The hills across the bay were fading in the evening light, and a stray ray of sunshine lit the grey water. Edging shyly around the headland was the tip of a familiar bowsprit. Yozo felt his heart beat faster and his breath quicken.

'The *Kaiyo Maru*!' he cried. Kitaro straightened his back, yelling with delight as a sleek black prow and gleaming hull appeared, sails swelling. At the top of the mainmast fluttered the five-pointed star of the Northern Alliance, on the aftmost mast the red sun of Japan. In place of a figurehead, the hollyhock crest of the shogun was etched on her prow. The soldiers threw down their shovels and let out a cheer.

Yozo read out the hoist, strung from the masts in a colourful display of signal flags: 'All clear to land?'

He took his signalling mirror out of his fob pocket, focused the ray of sunlight on it and semaphored a message back in a series of long and short flashes: 'All clear.' A reply flashed from the upper deck: 'Coming in to land.' There was a barrage of ear-splitting booms and puffs of smoke billowed from the gunports. Cannonballs splashed into the water, sending up fountains of spray as reports reverberated off the hills.

The soldiers lined up on shore watched the salute, shading their eyes with their hands and slapping each other on the back as the ship swept in, like a great white swan. The other seven ships of the fleet glided into port in a long line behind her.

'*Banzai! Banzai!*' The men yelled until they were hoarse. They were home and dry. The Star Fort was theirs, and the city of Hakodate. There were only two more towns on the island – Matsumae and Esashi – and once they had captured those the whole of Ezo would be in northern hands. Their time had come at last.

Later that evening, Yozo sprang up the gangplank, delighted to feel the roll of the ship beneath his feet again. He headed for the captain's cabin, casting his eyes around as he went, taking everything in. He scrutinized every plank and nail, making sure everything was as it should be. The *Kaiyo Maru* was not his, never could be, nor any man's; she belonged to the shogun, to the country. Nevertheless every man who sailed in her loved her. But his love, he thought to himself, was greater. He had been there from her inception, when she was no more than a twinkle in the shogun's eye; he had been there when the order was placed and had overseen her construction; he had been there proudly at her launch and had sailed her halfway round the world back to Japan. Their fates were bound together.

Enomoto was in his cabin gathering up his papers. He glanced up as Yozo pushed open the door. The gold braid on his black uniform glittered as he drew himself up, every inch the aloof admiral. Then his stern face relaxed into a smile as his eyes lit on his friend.

'Just the man I wanted to see,' he said, beaming. 'We've had quite a job of it getting her round here. This weather is tough on the crew, but we had a good tail wind to bring her into harbour.'

He strolled across to a glass-fronted cabinet and studied the array of bottles inside.

'Have a seat,' he said, gesturing towards a chair with curved lion-claw legs, upholstered in red velvet. Yozo glanced around the room. With its rosewood writing desk, paintings of Dutch scenes, polished bookcase, plush red carpet, the dining table where Enomoto dined alone or with his officers and the shrine on the wall, it seemed palatial, particularly after the rigours of the long march across the snowbound pass to the fort. It was also more than a little disconcerting to find himself in this grand Dutch drawing room, this small corner of Holland, rocking gently on the water under the grey skies of Ezo.

As far as everyone else was concerned, Enomoto lived above and apart from his men. He was responsible for the lives and welfare of his crew and demanded of them total obedience and loyalty. It was only when he and Yozo were alone together that he could relax. Now he brought out a cut-glass decanter.

'You remember that cognac I brought back from France?' he said.

Yozo grinned. He knew the ritual.

'You've been eking it out.'

'I save it for special occasions.'

With a flourish Enomoto pulled out the stopper from the decanter and poured out a couple of glasses. Next he brought out a box of cigars and offered Yozo one, then lit one for himself. They sat for a while in companionable silence, wreaths of smoke wafting above their heads. The fragrance took Yozo back to the elegant drawing rooms of Europe, to men's clubs furnished with leather armchairs and large red-nosed men with coarse pale skin and booming voices.

'So you acquitted yourself well,' Enomoto said at last.

'I did my best,' said Yozo.

'And the Star Fort is ours.' Enomoto looked hard at Yozo, steely determination in his eyes. 'Tell me what happened. Give me the true story. I'll get the official version soon enough.'

'It's easy to tell,' said Yozo. 'They were nowhere near as well armed and well trained as us. More to the point, they were not prepared to die. They didn't hold out for long; in fact a lot of them ran away. If the garrisons at Matsumae and Esashi are anything like as half-hearted, we'll be able to walk straight in.'

Enomoto nodded, puffing at his cigar. 'Good man,' he said. 'And the Commander?'

Yozo knew that this was the question Enomoto really wanted to ask. He stared at the plush red carpet. 'It's not my place to judge the Commander,' he said at last.

'We've known each other a long time, Yozo, and there's no one else around,' said Enomoto. 'Tell me, is he good at strategy or only at swinging his sword? Can we trust him?'

'He's a formidable warrior,' said Yozo. 'What worries me is whether he'll accept your authority once we've taken the island.'

Ten days after they arrived in Hakodate, Yozo and Kitaro were back on board the *Kaiyo Maru* as she set off around the headland for the town of Esashi. The Commander had already taken

Matsumae – the other city loyal to the southerners – with the help of another ship in the northern fleet.

Yozo was on deck as Matsumae Castle came into view. It was a ruin. The massive stone ramparts were battered and smashed like a mouthful of broken teeth, the walls blistered and pocked with cannon fire and the roof tiles broken loose. Jagged timbers poked through the snow. Flapping at the top of the citadel was the five-pointed star of the Northern Alliance. The city itself had been destroyed by fire and threads of smoke still rose from the blackened buildings.

'The Demon Commander certainly made a thorough job of it,' Yozo observed. 'Looks like he laid into it with everything he had. He treats every battle like a personal vendetta. That castle was built so long ago, it wouldn't have withstood cannon and rifle fire for long. I shouldn't think we took too many casualties either.'

'With any luck the southerners will be packing their bags at Esashi,' said Kitaro. 'They'll want to be gone before the Commander arrives.'

The ruins of Matsumae faded into the distance as the *Kaiyo Maru* rounded the headland and turned due north, following the western edge of the island. But as she swept through the water, a wind blew up, whipping the waves and threatening to batter the ship against the rocks that littered the coastline.

Quickly Enomoto sent down the order, 'Up funnel and down screw.' The seamen furled the sails and the stokers fired the boilers to full capacity, but it was all the quartermasters could do to hold the ship steady.

Snow was falling heavily as Esashi came in view. It was a bleak, wind-beaten place, a scattering of meagre houses huddled in the lea of the hills, smothered in snow. The men loaded and primed the cannons and set the city walls in their sights, but the place was strangely silent. It looked like a ghost town.

Yozo and Kitaro were on the bridge with Enomoto, telescopes to their eyes.

'You were right,' Yozo said to Kitaro. 'The garrison's fled.'

'So it's ours without a fight,' said Kitaro, his face brightening.

'Looks like the land forces haven't arrived yet either,' said Enomoto, who was standing next to them. 'We'll send an occupation force to hold the town. With this weather we're better off getting as many men to shore as possible. Check the soundings. We'll drop anchor a safe distance from the coast.'

The seamen stowed the sails and battened down the hatches, while a launch set off for the town, bobbing precariously up and down across the waves. It sent back the all-clear and most of the three hundred and fifty seamen disembarked, together with the troops, shuttling across to the town on launches. Enomoto stayed on board along with Yozo, Kitaro and a small crew of some fifty men to man the ship.

Night fell early. Yozo strung up a hammock on the gun deck and closed his eyes and in a moment was fast asleep, lulled by the rocking and creaking of the great ship. Suddenly he woke with a start. His hammock was swinging so hard it seemed about to fling him to the ground. The ship was pitching wildly.

He scrambled up a ladder to the upper deck, where the eight quartermasters had lashed themselves to the wheel. Above the roar of the gale, he could hear the groaning of the chains that held the anchors as the ship bucked and reared. Sheets of lightning lit the sky, clouds scudded furiously and huge waves crashed across the deck, soaking Yozo in freezing water. The great ship bobbed like a toy, the wind tearing into her so violently it seemed that any moment she would rip from her moorings and slam into the shore.

Enomoto appeared from his cabin and gave the order to raise the anchors and put on more steam. Soon Yozo and Kitaro were taking their turn on the wheel, fighting to keep the ship steady as they tried to manoeuvre her further out to sea, away from the perilous coastline. The wind screamed across the deck, lashing their faces with ice and snow.

When the next watch came to relieve them, Yozo clambered down to the gun deck, frozen to the core. It was pitch dark;

Enomoto had ordered the lanterns extinguished for fear of fire. Lighting a single lantern, Yozo had started doing the rounds, making sure the gunports were sealed and the cannons roped in place, when a shock sent him flying across the deck. He shot forward and slammed into one of the cannons, sending his lantern crashing to the ground. He sprawled in pitch blackness, winded and dazed, then scrambled to his feet with more speed than he'd known he was capable of, shaking his head to clear the ringing in his ears. One thought rang in his mind with dreadful certainty: they had foundered.

He headed for the stokehold, feeling his way towards the hatch, staggering from side to side as the ship lurched and the deck rose crazily. He knew the oak hull was a solid fourteen inches thick; it would take a mighty crack to pierce it. The ship was made up of eight separate compartments and even if one was breached, it would take time for water to seep into the next. With any luck the break could be found and plugged before too much damage was done. But something about the way the ship was lurching made Yozo suspect that there was not much hope of that. He stumbled against the hatch and in his haste nearly fell down the ladder. Then a lantern bobbed towards him. It was Enomoto.

For a moment their eyes met.

'Looks like we hit a rock,' Enomoto yelled above the clank and roar of the ship. 'I've sent the order out to up anchor and reverse engines. One of the men's gone over the side to try and find the break and a couple more are below decks, assessing the damage.'

Yozo nodded grimly. In this weather it was a hopeless task to dive over the side – a death sentence, in fact; but they had to do whatever they could.

In the stokehold, ballast crashed from side to side as the stokers crowded towards the sturdy door that separated it off from the hull, their faces set and grim in the lantern light. Working frantically, they had located the damaged section of the hull and sealed off the first of the compartments. Yozo heard the crash as they slammed the next set of doors to seal off the adjoining compartment too and shoved the bolts into place. Some men had been trapped inside and he could hear their screams as the water level rose. But there was no time to waste. They had to save the ship.

Enomoto knelt and ran his fingers across the floor. Yozo too put his hand to the floor and his heart gave a lurch. There was no mistaking it. Water – seeping out from under the massive doors with their hefty iron bolts.

Yozo caught a glimpse of Enomoto's face in the lantern light. It was contorted, drawn and haggard, his eyes starting out of his head and beads of sweat glinting on his brow. Yozo knew he must look just as crazed himself.

There was a long silence. When Enomoto looked up, he had erased all trace of concern from his face.

'We'll ride out the storm,' he shouted over the roar of the engines. He was completely composed. Everyone calmed down at the sound of his voice. 'Then we'll get her into harbour.'

But Yozo knew – they all knew – that the odds on getting her into harbour in time to fix the damage were heavily against them. The storm was blowing so fiercely that they couldn't get off the ship at all. It was obvious she was doomed.

All night the men worked, manning the pumps and baling out the water that continued to seep under the great doors until finally they had to seal off another compartment. Yozo kept an eye on the water level in the stokehold, but despite all their efforts it continued to rise. The ship was listing alarmingly.

When daylight broke the storm was still raging. Waves lashed the ship, sending icy water sweeping across the decks, threatening to wash the men into the sea. The wind howled and screamed, picking up the ship and hurling her down again, and Yozo could see she was starting to break up under the violence of the wind and the waves.

The men staggered around the decks, gathering together equipment and arms. They unroped the thirty cannons and the Gatling gun and heaved them overboard, jettisoning cannonballs, arms and ammunition, doing all they could to lighten the ship.

Finally they lashed themselves down and sat, sometimes talking, mainly in grim silence. Even the most experienced seaman had no stomach for food. There was nothing more to be done, nothing but watch the ship break up before their eyes and try not to think about their own imminent deaths. They'd been too busy to be afraid but now they sat on the deck and waited for the end.

Yozo stared straight in front of him. If he had been confronted by an army of thousands at least he could have fought, he thought. That was a way for a man to die. But to sink into the ocean and be swallowed up by the waters, disappear into the freezing depths and leave nothing behind . . .

Beside him, Kitaro's Adam's apple bobbed convulsively in his throat. He was staring at the floor, running his prayer beads through his fingers, invoking the name of Amida Buddha again and again.

'You think too much,' said Yozo.

'Just as we'd made it,' groaned Kitaro. 'We're masters of Ezo and now . . .'

'We made it across the Atlantic,' said Yozo firmly. 'We can't die now; not when we're so close to home.'

It was four days before the wind died down. The men left on board were starved, frozen and numb. As the fourth day dawned they picked up whatever they could carry and crawled down the icy deck, which sloped like a snow-covered mountain. Weak and trembling, they managed to lower the launches. Yozo watched helplessly as one man slipped on the ice-encrusted rungs on the hull, clung to the ropes for a moment then lost his grip and tumbled into the black water. The others stood silently on deck watching him thrash in the waves for a few moments, then disappear. The water was so cold they knew he would freeze to death and as likely as not they would be the next to go.

Yozo and Kitaro were in the last launch. As Kitaro scrambled down the rungs he slipped and just managed to grab hold of the rope. He dangled for a moment, his thin legs scrabbling desperately at the hull before one quivering foot, then the other, found the rungs. The launch was so crowded it seemed it would surely sink if one more person climbed in.

Yozo was still on deck. When he looked around, Enomoto was on the captain's bridge, his face drawn and haggard, staring at the broken ship as if he couldn't bear to say goodbye. Yozo gestured wildly but Enomoto stood as if he was in a trance, gazing at the ship. Yozo raced up to the bridge, grabbed Enomoto's arm and pulled.

'Hurry,' he shouted. The ship was listing more and more. He almost had to push Enomoto over the side and down the rungs.

They cast off the ropes and left the *Kaiyo Maru* to her fate. As they lurched away across the waves Yozo turned for a last look at the ship he loved being broken to pieces on the ice-strewn sea. It felt as if all his hopes were going down with her.

9

Hana woke to the boom of a temple bell reverberating through the icy air. Crows were circling, their raucous caws fading into the distance, and feet pattered along the street outside.

For a moment she didn't know where she was; then, as the events of the previous day came flooding back, she shuddered with horror. Cautiously she opened her eyes. Brilliantly coloured kimonos hung around the walls and piles of bedding were strewn across the floor with heads, arms and legs poking out. Tama, the woman she'd met the previous night, lay near by, her huge oiled coiffure perched on a wooden pillow and her mouth open, snoring softly. In the harsh dawn light she didn't look like a mysterious beauty at all but a round-faced country girl.

Hana sat up. She had to escape, and quickly. She was sure there must be places in the Yoshiwara where she could find work, real work. She could sew, she could write, she could teach – she could do something.

Softly she picked up her bundle and stepped across the snoring bodies. She tripped over one and drew a sharp breath, afraid she must have woken her, but the woman just grunted and rolled over. Stepping between overturned sake bottles, ash-filled tobacco boxes and heaps of crumpled paper tissues, Hana crept through the next room, then another smaller room. The corridor outside was littered with spilt food and used chopsticks and stank of sake and tobacco. Loud male snores rumbled from behind closed doors. There were voices and noises in the distance and

Hana realized the whole house was astir. She hurried across the polished floor, starting and glancing around as the boards creaked, then reached a staircase and step by step crept down the steep stairs.

Her tattered straw sandals were on a shelf by the outer door, where she'd left them the previous night. She was stepping into them when footsteps came up behind her and she was engulfed in a cloud of stale perfume. A hand fastened on to her arm.

'Leaving us already, my dear?' enquired a throaty voice. 'But you've hardly had a chance to get to know us yet.'

Without her make-up the old woman's skin was as grey and withered as a paddy field in autumn and her hair, shockingly white, bushed out like a squirrel's tail.

'How dare you,' shouted Hana. 'Take your hands off me. You can't keep me here.'

She pushed the woman off with all her might and fled for the door. But feet came running and, before she could open it, strong hands had grabbed her and pinioned her arms to her sides. She struggled and kicked but she couldn't free herself. The next thing she knew, she was lifted off her feet and dumped in front of the old woman. Gasping, she scrambled to her knees.

'Let me go!' she shrieked.

'Don't play around with us, my dear,' said the woman. 'It doesn't work. Isn't that right, Father?'

The man from the previous night had come panting up, his broad face flushed and his cheeks mottled. His topknot was askew and he held his sleeping robe together with a thick-fingered hand. In the other he had a large stick. Without stopping to speak he raised it above his head. Hana caught a glimpse of a pale wobbling belly before he brought the stick down on her thigh. She leaped back, tears springing to her eyes. Above the commotion she could hear the woman's voice, speaking quietly, in level tones.

'Careful! Not her face. Don't mark her face.'

Hana flinched as he raised the stick again.

'You've no right to keep me here,' she shouted.

'Don't cause us trouble,' he growled, bringing the stick down on her back. Hana curled into a ball, trying to protect herself from the blows, crying as he hit her.

'Enough noise,' muttered the old woman. 'The customers will be out any moment now. We don't want her causing a scene.'

As the man and his young accomplices dragged Hana away from the entrance hall, she lashed out, kicking at the men's legs and grabbing at anything she could find, trying to scratch and bite, but they were far stronger than her. Somewhere along the way her bundle was ripped out of her hands. Half pulling, half carrying her, they ran along corridors and through rooms littered with sleeping bodies till they came to the back of the house. They pulled open the door of a storehouse and flung her down on the earthen floor.

One of the young men shoved her on to her back, ripped her kimono open and straddled her, fumbling with his clothes. Hana caught a glimpse of a veined erect penis and squirmed and kicked in horror. Then the old man appeared and pushed the youth aside.

'Not this one,' he snapped. 'You, stay here till you cool off.' He turned to the young men. 'Tie her up.'

'Please . . . don't leave me here,' Hana gasped.

There was a thud as the great doors slammed, leaving her alone in the dark and cold.

When her eyes had grown used to the blackness Hana looked around desperately. There had to be some way to escape, but there was nothing, only shelves stacked with sheets and pillows and piles of boxes and broken trunks, picked out in the thread of light that filtered between the massive doors. Slumping against a locked chest, she wept with rage and fury and terror.

As the line of light moved with agonizing slowness across the floor, she twisted and turned but the ropes were firmly knotted around her wrists and ankles. Finally she managed to wriggle into a sitting position and toss back the long strands of hair that tumbled across her face. She was bruised and covered in dust, her nails were broken and her fingers torn and bleeding.

Sobbing, she ran through the events of the day before, trying to work out the moment when she should have realized what was happening. She saw Fuyu's pinched face and hard eyes and heard her wheedling tones as she spoke to the old woman. '*I'm sure we can come to some arrangement*,' she had said. Some arrangement . . . The words sent a chill through her. Surely even Fuyu couldn't have done something quite so terrible? Surely she couldn't have sold her . . . The thought loomed like a monster in the darkness, pressing down on Hana, crushing her with its presence.

If it really was true, she was doomed, she thought. Her only hope now was to be docile. Then perhaps these people would let down their guard and give her a chance to escape.

She had daydreamed about the Yoshiwara so much and now she was here – but it was a dreadful place, entirely different from her imaginings. She remembered how she used to pore over the pages of *The Plum Calendar*, imagining herself walking the Five Streets. The characters in the story had seemed like old friends – sweet-natured Ocho, the ravishing geisha Yonehachi and the beautiful playboy Tanjiro, whom they both desired. She'd read the book so often she could recite whole passages from it.

Trapped with her ancient parents-in-law and a husband she didn't know and who was never there, she'd escaped into its fantasy world, filling her mind with stories of the fabulous walled city where night never fell. She'd even packed it in her bundle and brought it with her.

But at the back of her mind she'd always known that a samurai girl like herself could never be Ocho or Yonehachi, except in the pages of a romance. It had all been fine while it was just a day-dream. But now she was here, she realized how foolish she had been.

As the cold crept from the hard floor into her bones, Hana huddled into a ball and pressed her knees to her chin, shivering, too frozen even to think any more.

She had no idea how many hours had passed when she heard the slow grate of a bolt and the door creaked open. She'd been praying for someone to release her but now she was afraid to see who might step through the door. As a shaft of pale light flooded the room, falling on the shelves and dusty chests and piled-up boxes, Hana shrank back, dreading the crunch of heavy male feet. But instead she heard the patter of wooden clogs and caught a whiff of sandalwood and ambergris.

'There's no need to look so sorry for yourself.' Tama's voice was startlingly loud in the silence. 'I don't know why they've been so soft on you. They usually beat runaways to within an inch of their life.'

Framed in a square of light, Tama stood staring down at Hana, her large mouth open in a yawn, her words forming puffs of steam in the frozen air. She was wearing a plain indigo-blue cotton kimono with a thick collar, like a maid. It was hard to imagine that this heavy-featured girl was the same as the painted vision Hana had seen the night before.

'I'm not a runaway,' Hana gasped. 'They don't own me.'

Tama gave a snort of laughter.

'You wives, you're all so innocent,' she said. She crouched down and started to undo Hana's knots. 'Of course they own you. Or do you think your husband's suddenly going to turn up and repay your debt?'

As the last knot was untied Hana stretched, rubbing her frozen limbs. So Fuyu had sold her. Hot tears filled her eyes and trickled down her cheeks.

'What are you making such a fuss about?' demanded Tama, taking a quilt from a corner and bundling her up in it. 'It's a fine life here. Work hard and you'll make a good living. You might even be able to work your way out if you're so eager to leave. Just behave well and Auntie and Father will be like a real auntie and father to you. You'll be their favourite child, you'll see.'

'Silk crêpe,' said Tama, lifting the sleeve of a kimono to show off the design. 'Tenmei period. Been in this house for generations.'

It was an exquisite garment in an intense shade of blue with a crimson lining which flashed at the cuffs and around the hem. The skirts were embroidered with plum branches sprinkled with blossom, so realistic they could have been alive, and gold characters swirled across the back and sleeves.

Hana felt the weight of the garment and the softness of the fabric. She had heard that courtesans wore splendid kimonos but she had never before seen such lavish silks and satins. Her own family had been far from wealthy and her parents-in-law too had kept a modest household. Apart from her beloved red silk wedding robe, she had never worn anything but homespun cotton kimonos.

'You see?' said Tama. 'We live well here.'

Five days had passed and so far nothing terrible had happened. Hana had seen no more of the old woman and the old man. Rolled up in quilts, she had spent the days recovering from her ordeal. She had even been able to retrieve her bundle, which was now tucked away safely in a corner. When she was left alone for a moment, she checked that the contents – the kimonos, the cosmetics set and the precious book – were still intact.

But she hadn't forgotten that only a few days earlier she had been a samurai's wife, pacing the rooms of a silent house; nor could she forget the horrors she had seen as she fled across the city – the desolate streets and ruined houses, the cracked walls and doors gaping open, the ransacked warehouses and the haggard women who lurked, guarding their territory like wild dogs. Again and again in her dreams she saw the deserted streets and woke up gasping and covered in sweat, hearing footsteps pounding after her, seeing women's hungry faces rising from the ruins.

Often she dreamed of her parents and her beloved grandmother with her skin like parchment and her bony wrists. If they'd known where she was now they would have been horrified, she thought. But then tears would come to her eyes as she remembered that they were all dead, and her parents-in-law too. The only person who might still be alive was her husband, but he was far away.

Then she thought of the woman she had passed in the corridor, the woman with the shrill voice who had said that the ships had sailed. She was Hana's only link to that distant world where men were fighting and dying and where her husband was.

But as the days went by the memories became fainter, until they started to seem like dreams themselves. Perhaps life in the Yoshiwara was not so dreadful after all. For the time being, at least, Hana was required simply to watch and learn.

Tama, Hana now knew, was the house's star courtesan. She had a suite of three rooms – a parlour, a reception room and the sleeping chamber where Hana had slept along with Tama and some of her maids and attendants. The largest, the reception room, was splendidly furnished with an alcove in which stood a vase with plum branches arranged in it and above it a hanging scroll with a painting of a crane. Beside the alcove there were shelves of books and musical instruments propped along the wall. There was also a deep lacquered tray, the sort where one would lay guests' coats, a kimono rack and a six-panelled screen covered in gold leaf.

Hanging on the wall was a board with four words brushed on it: 'Pine, chrysanthemum, eternal, are.' Hana knew what the phrase meant: like the pine and the chrysanthemum that bloomed in winter when other flowers had died, a courtesan's charms endured for ever. Only it wasn't true, she thought. Even the ugly old woman must have been beautiful once.

'Auntie', Hana had discovered, was what everyone called the old woman and Hana too had to call her that, though it certainly didn't mean that anyone was related to anyone else. Auntie was the manager of the house and nothing escaped her gaze.

In Tama's sleeping chamber the bedding was so thick and piled so high it nearly touched the woven bamboo of the ceiling. There were tall rectangular mirrors on stands and tubs of creams, paints and powders scattered across the floor, together with lamps, a chest of drawers and a brazier with a kettle steaming on it. Silken kimonos embroidered with lavish designs, gleaming with gold and silver, hung along the wall and on kimono racks, filling the room with their jewel-like colours. Some were draped over incense burners. Hana had never seen such beautiful things in her whole life.

At first she gazed around, wide-eyed with delight, but little by little the opulence began to make her feel uncomfortable. It didn't seem right to be surrounded by luxury when there was so much hardship and suffering outside the gates.

Once Hana managed to peek outside Tama's suite and caught a glimpse of the closed doors of other rooms stretching along the corridor. In the evening she heard chatting and laughter as men were ushered in. From time to time she caught the sound of a pipe being tapped impatiently on a bamboo spittoon as a client waited for Tama to arrive. In the small hours Hana would be woken by ecstatic grunts and groans bursting through the thin paper walls. Tama's were particularly loud. Hana tried to sleep through it all but sometimes, despite herself, she was stirred to excitement by the yelps of pleasure.

As far as Hana could see, Tama entertained four or five clients a night, going from one room to the next. Sometimes she stayed for an hour or two, sometimes less, then she would come back looking perfectly composed, smoothing her hair and adjusting her kimono with a yawn.

'This is my home,' said Tama to Hana one morning, as they knelt together in the reception room, warming their hands at the brazier. All around was flurry and bustle as maids swept feverishly, poking brooms along the tops of the carved wooden lintels and into the corners of the ceiling.

'I was a little girl when I came here,' Tama went on. 'My parents were poor and I was pretty, so it made sense to sell me. I still visit them from time to time and give them money. They're doing well now. They have a big thatched house and grow so much rice they can sell it and make a profit. My brothers and sisters have married well too, and it's all thanks to me. So you see, I've been a good daughter, I've done my duty by them. I remember what a fuss I made when I first got here, just like you did, but do you really think I regret leaving that place? Do you think I'd rather be living in the mountains, hacking the soil with a hoe? I'd be an old lady already.'

Hana opened her mouth to protest that it was different for her, that she was a samurai, not a peasant; but then she remembered that everything had changed. Her family was dead and her husband had gone to war.

'From the moment Auntie saw me she knew I was something special,' said Tama. 'People told me she had been the most accomplished courtesan the quarter had ever known. She taught me the traditions and customs and how to dance and play the shamisen. I got punished too, worse than you, a lot worse. I had to go out on the roof of the house right in the middle of winter and stand there for hours, singing at the top of my voice. I got beaten, too, when I tried to run away. Once I got thrown downstairs so hard I broke my arm. But you have to be punished if you're going to learn anything. It takes time to understand how we do things here, but I got over it and you will too.'

'Can't you see?' Hana retorted. 'There's a war going on, that's why I'm here! Men are fighting and dying, and women too. How can you talk about something so trivial as your customs and your dancing when everything is going up in flames?'

Tama smiled grandly and patted Hana's arm.

'My dear girl, the only thing that matters here is whether we have customers or not. Peace is better than war, but now the north is losing, we have lots of southern customers coming in. You've heard of the floating world? That's us, we're just pond weed. It doesn't matter what sort of water it is, we float. The only difference the war makes is that we get another sort of woman turning up – quality women, like you, and that's good for business. As to who wins or loses, what difference do you think it makes to me? None!'

At the far side of the reception room, young women knelt playing cards, chattering like a flock of birds.

'My attendants,' said Tama, waving a large-fingered hand in their direction. Some Hana recognized. They'd run in and out as she lay in her quilts, shouting and laughing as if they had not a care in the world. In the evening they looked like birds of paradise in their brilliantly coloured kimonos with quilted hems layered one above the other. Now, in the daytime, with no guests around, they were bundled up in warm padded garments.

Hana listened to their lilting Yoshiwara brogue with its quaint turns of phrase. It was a coy, flirtatious, silvery language designed to wrap a man around one's little finger, quite different from the prim tones of a samurai wife. She wondered who they were, these girls, where they came from and why they were here. Some were plain with big mouths and fleshy cheeks, while others looked more refined, but the accent covered up all their differences. Well trained and well groomed, they knew how to preen and look coy. Their origins had entirely disappeared: they were Yoshiwara girls now.

Tama beckoned them imperiously and they came forward one by one to be introduced.

'Kawanoto,' said Tama, as a girl with a gentle face and big doe eyes pressed her forehead to her hands. 'My number one attendant. She had her début the year before last.'

'Kawagishi, Kawanagi.' Two girls knelt side by side and bowed, one short and smiling, the other long-limbed and willowy. Other young women knelt behind them.

'Kawayu, Kawasui . . . They're all Kawa something,' said Tama. 'I'm Tamagawa – Tama and Kawa. I've given them all part of my name to show they're my attendants. Anyone who meets them knows they belong to me, so they have to behave themselves!'

They were the strangest names Hana had ever heard, not ordinary women's names at all but more like the names of shops or kabuki actors. Kawanoto, the girl with the big innocent eyes – the name meant 'river mouth' – took a long iron-stemmed pipe from the tobacco box on the floor and filled the tiny clay bowl.

She held a piece of charcoal to it and took a couple of puffs until it glowed, then handed it to Tama with a bow. Tama raised it to her lips, little finger extended. She took a puff and blew a ring of blue smoke. It hung in the air, twisting and elongating before it disappeared.

She tilted her head. 'Now, what's all this about being able to write?' she said softly. 'How can that be, when you can barely talk properly? Auntie told me you bragged about it.'

Hana felt a spark of hope. Maybe they planned to use her as a scribe after all. She was about to say, 'Of course I can write, I'm a samurai, I'm well brought up,' but then she remembered and bit her lip. Doing her best to speak with a Yoshiwara lilt, she bowed her head and murmured, 'To tell you the truth, I can write, just a little. If I can be of any use . . .'

'Not bad,' said Tama. 'You're trying.'

She was handing the pipe back to Kawanoto when the door slid open with a bang and a child in a brilliant red kimono burst in, the bells on her sleeves tinkling and her under-kimonos rippling beneath the quilted hem. She skidded up to Tama, dropped to her knees, placed her hands neatly on the tatami and announced at the top of her voice, 'I saw him.'

'Softly, softly,' said Tama, beaming at the child. 'Here.' She waved to an elderly maid who gave the child a bean jam cake. The little girl smiled proudly. She was an exquisite child with a heart-shaped face, button nose and huge black eyes. Her hair was swept up and topped with a crown of silk flowers. She turned to Hana and bowed prettily.

'How long have you been here, Chidori? Three years? And how old are you? Seven? You see,' said Tama, turning to Hana, 'she already speaks nicely and knows how to behave. Chidori's one of my junior attendants. You can learn from her.'

Chidori meant 'plover'. The name suited her perfectly, Hana thought; she was like a bright-eyed bird, darting and skipping about.

'You're sure it was him?' Tama was saying.

'Yes, it was master Shojiro. Coming out of the Tsuruya.'

'The Tsuruya . . . ?' Tama wrinkled her forehead and her face darkened. 'And who might he have been seeing there, I wonder?'

'I stood right in the middle of the road. He came creeping out, looking to left and right. When he saw me, he went quite pale.'

'And so he should. How dare he think he can deceive me! That Yugao, she's cast a spell over him.' Tama paused for a moment. 'We'll deal with him first and take care of her later. Now, you. Can you write a love letter?' she asked, turning to Hana, who was waiting quietly on her knees.

'A love letter?' For a moment Hana was at a loss. Then she cast her mind back to the romantic poems she had learned as a child. She thought of *The Plum Calendar* and the words Ocho had used when she spoke to Tanjiro. 'To Shojiro?'

'Of course not,' said Tama with an exasperated sigh. 'I'm going to punish Shojiro, not favour him with a letter. No, to Mataemon. He's a southerner and hasn't been coming here long. He hasn't a clue how to behave, but a bit of encouragement will set him alight. We need to make him think I'm mad for him!'

There were writing materials on the tatami beside a candle with a square paper shade. Hana ground some ink, trying to conjure up *The Plum Calendar* as she rubbed the ink stick back and forth on the stone.

'What about this?' she asked. ' "Shall I have to sleep/All alone again tonight/On my narrow mat/Unable to meet again/The man for whom I long?" Something like that?'

'My, my,' said Tama, her voice rippling sarcastically. 'A girl with a classical education! It's a little high-flown for Mataemon. Write this: "Last night you were in my dreams but I woke to find you gone and now my pillow is wet with tears. I yearn to see you." Do several. I can use them for different clients.'

Unrolling a scroll of paper, Hana picked up a brush and wrote, forming the characters carefully. 'What's the address?'

Tama clicked her teeth. 'I don't know what's wrong with Auntie and Father,' she said. 'Ten-year-olds who've worked their way up the ranks have more idea than you. Mataemon works in some sort of government office; it would wreck his career if he started receiving letters addressed in a woman's hand. Chidori, run and catch the messenger. Get him to write the address.' Tama turned to Hana and sighed loudly. 'You've so much to learn.'

Hana looked at the tatami mats. There were worn patches, she noticed, and some of the silk edgings were threadbare. The luxury was just a veneer, as were Tama's ways. The letter writing had been a test, she saw now – a test in which she had not done badly.

10

Hana was warming her hands at the brazier in Tama's large reception room while Tama, who had just had her bath, knelt in front of a mirror. In a corner of the room a wispy old woman hunched over a shamisen, plucking out a tune. With her grey hair tugged into a bun and wearing the sombre colours of a geisha, she was so tiny and thin she seemed to merge into the shadows.

'If you were ten years younger we could give you a thorough training,' Tama was grumbling. 'But at your age there's no time to waste. Father will be wanting a return on his investment.' She beckoned Kawanoto over to massage her shoulders. 'I wanted to ease you in gradually but I've too many clients. You'll have to come along tonight and see how things are done.'

'But you don't need me,' said Hana, panicking. 'I can write. There must be letters to write.'

'Don't be a fool,' snapped Tama. 'How else are you going to survive? How else do you think you're going to repay your debt? All you'll have to do is watch, watch and be seen, that's all.'

Tama summoned an elderly maid, a tough old woman with work-roughened hands and frizzy white hair, who grumbled quietly in a Yoshiwara accent. She sat Hana in front of a mirror, pulled her kimono off her shoulders and tucked the top half round her waist. Beside her was a brass tray with a ewer and a small bowl on it. Hana wrinkled her nose as she smelt the familiar sour odour of sumac-leaf gall, vinegar and tea. Like every respectable woman she had blackened her teeth ever since she got married.

But Tama shook her head. 'No teeth-blackening for you,' she said. 'You're starting life all over again. You're worth more as a virgin. No one will know you're not until it's far too late.'

Hana opened her mouth to protest but Tama had already turned away.

A woman had come in, bent under a huge bundle. She opened it up and laid out combs, bottles of fragrant oils, tubs of pomade, sheaves of paper and rows of hair ornaments on the floor and put crimping irons on the brazier. The acrid smell of burning hair filled the room as the irons heated up.

'We have a new recruit,' said Tama. 'It'll be a job to get her hair into shape.'

Hana was used to putting her hair up by herself. As a girl she had practised until her arms ached, separating it into sections and folding each section up and forward and back, then tying it in place with gilt thread or coloured paper twine. She had become quite good at the elaborate *shimada* style that girls of her age wore, with a heavy coil of stiff glossy hair at the back of her head.

Now she knelt, gazing at her reflection in the tarnished silver rectangle while the woman set to work, wrenching and pulling with a fine-toothed comb. Soon tears were running down her cheeks. She let them flow. Let them think it was from the tugging, she thought. Only she must know it was for everything she'd lost.

'It's bad enough when you're a child,' murmured the woman, heating a block of wax and applying it to Hana's hair with the crimping irons. There was a sizzle and a sharp oily smell every time the wax touched the hot metal. 'But it's a lot worse when you're grown up and have known another life. You're not the only one, there's a lot of us here – wives, concubines, women who've lost their husbands or their lovers and have nowhere else to go.'

Startled, Hana looked in the mirror. The woman was dressed like a maid in a plain brown-check kimono with a purple collar, with her hair tied back in a bun. Something shiny sparkled on her hand and there was a metal clasp at her throat.

'It's best to forget the past,' the woman continued. 'That's the only way any of us survive. If you ever feel lonely, come and visit me. Ask for Otsuné. Everyone knows me here.' She tugged Hana's hair so hard Hana thought a clump would come out.

'They won't let me out.'

'They will, once they trust you. You're no use to them stuck here.'

Otsuné combed and crimped and waxed until Hana's hair gleamed like silk. She combed in globs of white pomade and musky-smelling camellia oil, then parted and sectioned it and tied, rolled, combed and folded it strand by strand until Hana's floor-length hair had been transformed into a towering pile of loops and coils, smooth and shiny as polished lacquer. Gingerly Hana raised her hand. Her hair was stiff and slightly sticky to the touch. She hardly dared breathe in case the enormous edifice came tumbling down.

For a moment Otsuné rested her fingers on Hana's shoulder.

'Here,' she whispered, pressing something into her hand. 'It's a charm. Tuck it backwards into your hair before you go out there, but make sure Auntie doesn't see it or she'll take it away. It's to protect against being chosen.'

Hana closed her hand around a small comb. She had no idea what Otsuné was talking about but she was grateful anyway.

As Otsuné moved on to the next attendant, the elderly maid-servant took a knob of soft white wax and kneaded it in her fingers. She rubbed it over Hana's face, then painted Hana's throat, chin, cheeks, nose and forehead chalky white, puffing clouds of white rice powder over the top. Hana watched in the mirror as her face became a perfect white oval with just a narrow line of flesh at the hairline.

Wielding her brush, the maid coated Hana's chest and shoulders and upper back with white, then held up a second mirror so that Hana could see the nape of her neck. There were three points of unpainted flesh there, stark against the matt white of her back, like a snake's forked tongue.

'It drives men wild,' the old woman said, chuckling, 'the nape of a woman's neck. The shape makes them think of . . . Well, you'll see.'

She painted in Hana's eyebrows, curving them like two crescent moons, and outlined her eyes in red, then in black, extending the line out at the corners. Then she puffed rouge on to her cheeks.

'Up you get,' she said. Naked and shivering, Hana stood like a statue while the maid laced her into a perfumed petticoat of scarlet crêpe, helped her into a white under-blouse with a red collar and long red sleeves, then tied another petticoat in place with silk ribbons. She laid a stiff embroidered collar around her neck and helped her into an embroidered red kimono with long sleeves and a quilted hem. On top of that went another kimono, then another and another, each tied in place with ribbons. Then she took a long brocade sash and wound it round and round her. Hana twirled round and turned her back to her. The old woman chuckled.

'What does she think she is – a virgin? An old maid? A stay-at-home housewife? She thinks I want to tie her obi at the back!' Everyone turned and there were peals of laughter. 'Things have changed, dear. Haven't you noticed?'

Silently Hana turned to face the maid. The woman tugged and tugged until the sash was so tight that Hana could hardly breathe. Then she brought the two ends together at the front and, fumbling, holding pins in her mouth, tying ribbons here and ribbons there and tucking in folds of fabric, shaped it into a huge ornate knot. The ends reached nearly to Hana's feet.

The red silk reminded Hana of her wedding day, when Oharu had done her hair and helped her dress, and her throat tightened. She was dressed like a bride, as if she was to be married all over again. The only thing that was wrong was the obi. Even geishas tied their obis at the back. Only one sort of woman tied her obi at the front in an ostentatious bow, as if daring any man who crossed her path to try to untie it. She shivered as she thought what sort of woman that was.

The maid clicked her teeth and dabbed at Hana's face, then adjusted her collar, checked that the hems and cuffs of her kimonos were evenly aligned, tucked a sandalwood comb into the front of her hair and studded it with hairpins. Finally she put a crown of silk flowers on the top.

'You'd better put that charm in,' she muttered. Hana handed the small curved comb Otsuné had given her to the maid and felt her tuck it firmly into the back of her hair. Then the maid took a stick of safflower paste, moistened a thin brush with it and painted a petal of red in the centre of Hana's lower lip, leaving her upper lip white.

Everyone turned – the attendants, naked-breasted, their kimonos tucked around their waists, Otsuné, comb in mouth and crimping irons in hand, and Tama, who was tying her obi in place. Even the wispy old geisha stopped strumming her shamisen and looked up.

Voices murmured, 'Lovely. Beautiful!'

Hana took a few uncertain steps. Not even on her wedding day had she been so encumbered with heavy garments. Awkwardly she turned, hardly daring to look at herself in the mirror. When she did, she gasped. She had become a painted doll. It was not her at all – and yet it was. She had become a woodblock print of herself, not a person but a painted image.

Behind the mask she was still Hana, she told herself fiercely. But despite everything, she couldn't help being just a little enchanted. It was almost as if she had sloughed off her old self and left it behind, like a butterfly emerging from a chrysalis. She was not Hana any more, no, she was not Hana at all. She was a brand-new person.

'We'll find a new name for you,' said Tama, as if reading her thoughts. 'I'll talk to Auntie about it. Now, walk. Pick up your skirts with your left hand and walk. From over there to over here.'

Hana took hold of the heavy fabric and took a few steps in her bare feet, trying not to trip over her skirts. The ungainly train and the huge knot of her obi pulled her off balance. She was not used to carrying so much weight. She stumbled and nearly fell.

'Kick,' said Tama. 'Kick your skirts out of the way. Nothing wrong with showing your ankles.'

Tama too had been transformed and had become the mysterious creature Hana had seen the first time she met her. Her hair was divided into two gleaming wings on which rested a crown studded with gilt and tortoiseshell hairpins like the rays of the sun, decorated with silk flowers and foliage, dangling mother-of-pearl ornaments and strings of coral weighted with gold leaf blossoms. The bow of her magnificent brocade obi, tied flamboyantly at the front, all but concealed her thick quilted kimonos.

'That's all you have to do this evening,' said Tama. 'Walk, then sit. Concentrate on doing that as well as you can. Don't speak. Watch and listen, that's all.'

It was nearing dusk, the hour of the monkey. In the distance a deep-toned bell tolled, the melancholy sound booming out across the hills of the city. As if in answer, small bells began to peal, some further away, some close at hand. One was so loud it sounded as if it must be right in the house itself.

Tama rose grandly to her feet. With her magnificent pompadour and hairpins radiating like a halo, she was more a divine being than a woman. It would take a brave man to try to undo her obi, Hana thought to herself.

'They will be surprised,' Tama announced archly, raising her eyebrows and glancing in a mirror with a nod of satisfaction.

'You're not coming with us, are you, Big Sister?' clamoured the attendants.

'I am indeed,' said Tama, smiling just enough to reveal the black lacquer glinting on her teeth. 'They're in for a treat tonight.'

The attendants crowded around her, lining up in pairs in height order. Little Chidori was looking crestfallen. Together with Namiji, the other child attendant, she had to stay behind.

Kawanoto, the attendant with the large innocent eyes, grabbed Hana's hand and pulled her next to her at the front of the line. The eight were like dolls in matching red kimonos, with matching white faces and crowns of flowers on their hair. The older ones had sleeves that hung to the waist to mark their adult status, while the younger ones wore kimonos with sleeves that hung nearly to the ground.

'That's my place,' said a sulky voice. The girl who spoke was about sixteen, the same age as Kawanoto. Her face was painted whiter, her eyes blacker, her lips redder and her hair piled higher than anyone else's. She wore the same kimono as everyone else, but hers was more loosely tied, revealing a glimpse of a white-painted bosom, and the bow of her obi dangled invitingly.

'I don't know why I have to go,' she complained. 'I'm booked up this evening already.'

'You go because I tell you to, Kawayu,' snapped Tama.

The door to the corridor opened and a swell of music and singing surged into the room as a mask-like face appeared, accompanied by a swirl of perfume.

'Auntie!'

Everyone, even Tama, tumbled to their knees and pressed their faces to the floor. Remembering the storehouse, Hana glanced fearfully at the old woman.

Auntie was in an elegant pale blue kimono with a glossy black wig fitted over her hair. She carried herself tall, as if in her mind she was still the proud beauty she had once been, but her thick white make-up threw every wrinkle into hideous relief. Her black-rimmed eyes sank into her cheeks and the scarlet paint on her lips seeped into the lines that surrounded them. She walked straight over to Hana.

'On your feet,' she said. She tugged at Hana's kimonos and tucked in a hair. Then she spun Hana round and her hand sought out the charm tucked into the back of Hana's coiffure. Hana froze, fearful that she would take it, but Auntie gave a knowing smile.

'Let's wait awhile with this one,' she announced. Tama bowed and nodded. 'We'll see what offers we get. We might have something good here.' Auntie bent towards Hana. 'Come,' she said in kindly tones. 'It's time for the world to see you.'

As they filed out into the corridor, the sound of music, voices and laughter grew until the house was throbbing with it. The maids led them along corridor after corridor, holding up lamps and candles to drive back the encroaching shadows. Darkness licked at the edges of the pool of light as doors slid open and women glided out, moving like sleepwalkers drawn by the music. The corridor was filled with the rustling of kimonos and the mingling of perfumes. Hana kicked out her bare feet, so concerned with not tripping over her skirts that she barely noticed where they were going.

They pattered down a staircase and around a veranda. Then Hana felt a draught of cold air and smelt dust and roasting foods and woodsmoke – the smells of the street. She looked up and realized they were near the entrance. They stopped outside a door. Shamisens twanged somewhere near by, a young clear voice was singing a ballad and wooden sticks beat a tattoo, like in a kabuki theatre when the play is about to start.

Then a voice gave a yell, the door slid back and light flooded out, so brilliant that Hana hesitated and covered her eyes.

Hands on her waist, Kawanoto steered her forward. Hana stumbled out into the brightness, feeling icy air swirl around her as Kawanoto shoved her to her knees. She heard breathing and felt the warmth and perfumes of women's bodies crowding in around her. There was a moment's silence, then a roar went up, like the roar that greets an actor when he steps out on stage.

Hana raised her eyes and gasped. She was not on stage at all but in a cage, a huge cage with wooden bars along the front, like the cages she had seen when she arrived at the Yoshiwara. Then she had been outside, staring in at the occupants. Now she was inside. She was one of them.

The roar died down and a man's voice sang out, 'A new girl! A beauty! Hey, darling, look over here!'

Another voice butted in, 'She's mine. Hey, new girl, what's your name?'

A chorus of voices demanded, 'New girl, what's your name?'

Beyond the bars the darkness was alive with eyes, some big, some small, some round, some almond-shaped, all staring – staring at her. Hana made out the shadowy figures of men, some with their noses pressed between the bars, others lurking behind, stopping to peer. Horrified, she edged back, glad of all the other women around her, and put her hand on the charm in the back of her hair. She knew now what it was for.

Like wax figures, gorgeous in their silk and gold and silver, the women knelt, silent and still, as men strolled by, gathered round, peered in. Some stayed, their noses glued to the bars, trying to attract the girls' attention, while others moved on.

Tama was at the back of the cage, facing the audience, along with a couple of other women as extravagantly dressed as she. As Hana turned to look at her, she took a long-stemmed pipe and began to puff, as cool and relaxed as if she was in the privacy of her own rooms. Casually she blew a smoke ring, as if unaware of the men a few steps away who shuffled their feet, blew on their hands and gawped at her.

She took a scroll from her sleeve, unrolled it and slowly ran her eyes across it as if it was a letter from an adoring admirer, smiling every now and then, narrowing her eyes and running her tongue across her lips. Then she turned and whispered to a fellow courtesan, gracefully bending her head and hiding her face in her sleeve as if stifling a peal of laughter.

She glanced slyly towards the men and inclined her head ever so slightly. A murmur rose from the crowd as she turned back languidly and took a puff on her pipe.

Hana watched, mesmerized. Tama was like the puppet master

controlling the crowd, making them do whatever she wanted.

As the time dragged by, the attendants started whispering together and giggling.

'Ooh, look at him, he's handsome.'

'That's Jiro. Don't you know him? He's always here.'

'Disowned by his father, wasn't he? Disinherited?'

'He's got no money. No point wasting your charms on him.'

'What a jacket, so old-fashioned, and what a dreadful colour. He's got no idea. What a bumpkin!'

'I don't like him at all. I hope he doesn't ask for me.'

A couple of the attendants pushed to the front of the cage and preened. Others beckoned to the men and winked. Kawagishi, with her plump little-girl face and big smile, and willowy Kawanagi, who were always together, were reading each other's palms.

'It used to be only the poor ones who came to look at us,' Kawanoto whispered to Hana. 'That was all they could afford to do – to look. The rich ones already knew who they wanted. But nowadays, with all these new clients, it's a good way to get customers. You never know who might see you.'

'Kawanoto-sama, Kawanoto-sama,' came a voice. A young man had pushed his way up to the bars. Kawanoto slipped to the front of the cage and pressed her face close to his. He nodded and disappeared.

Kawayu, the sulky overpainted girl, sidled up to the bars. She arched her back, tilted her head and fluttered her eyelashes, but no one paid the slightest attention. Instead there was a shout, 'Hey, new girl, what's your name? Tell us your name!'

Kawayu threw Hana a venomous look. Hana smiled at her serenely and bowed her head with exaggerated politeness. This girl, at least, couldn't do her any harm.

Suddenly everyone was looking at her. The men had been chatting and shuffling their feet, but now, on the other side of the bars, utter silence fell.

Overcome with shyness, Hana put her hands over her mouth

and, as she did so, her kimono sleeve slipped back to reveal her arm. There was a hungry murmur in the crowd. Hastily she put her hands back in her lap and adjusted her sleeve. A young man was gazing at her through the bars. Their eyes met and he shuffled and looked down, blushing till the top of his shaven pate was purple.

Trying not to draw any more attention to herself, Hana turned away from the staring eyes. There was a rustle in the crowd behind her. She stared down at her hands in her lap, wishing she could disappear. But the murmur grew – a tremulous sigh, a long-drawn-out moan of desire, rippling through the mob. Suddenly she realized what they could see – the back of her neck and the three points of unpainted flesh there. The elderly maid's words flashed into her mind – '*The shape makes them think of . . .* ' Under the white paint her face glowed until she was sure every-one could see her ears burning.

She raised her head and adjusted her collar, aware that Tama was watching her. Tama nodded and a smile crossed her face. She looked positively exultant.

11

As the bell tolled the hour, Tama and her fellow courtesans swayed to their feet. Maids scurried in to tug the courtesans' collars, tidy the layers of fabric, adjust the massive bows of their obis and straighten their hairpins. From outside the open door of the cage a high-pitched voice floated by. Hana started. It was the fluting tones she had heard the first night she'd arrived, saying the ships had set sail. She'd been waiting for a chance to find the speaker ever since.

Forgetting everything, she slipped through the crowd of young women. Kawanoto was at her heels, plucking at her sleeve as Hana caught a glimpse of quilted hems swirling out of the main door of the house.

'We have to get back,' Kawanoto was saying anxiously behind her. 'The clients will be waiting.'

Men were crowding into the earthen-floored vestibule, blowing on their hands, their breath steaming in the cold air. Some were old, some young, but they all looked prosperous. Smartly turned out in starched hakama trousers, haori jackets and thick woollen capes, they were quite different from the hungry-eyed men who had gathered outside the cage. Jostling elbows, greeting each other and bowing, they stepped out of their clogs and handed them to menservants, who gave them wooden tickets for their footwear. Geishas, carrying shamisens wrapped in silk, and grinning cheeky-faced jesters pressed in behind them.

The only thing Hana knew was that she had to find the woman with the bell-like voice. Nothing else mattered.

She wrenched her sleeve from Kawanoto's grasp and, picking up her heavy robes in both hands, burst through the crowds and ran out of the door into the night, chasing after the voice and swirling skirts. She gasped as she felt the cold air on her skin. Then she caught a glimpse of a gleaming head slipping between the men crowding into the neighbouring house. She darted inside and looked up and down the lamp-lit corridor, then saw a door sliding closed and rushed up to it, panting.

As she put her hand to it, she was suddenly aware of what an outrageous act she was about to commit. To open the door of a prostitute's rooms and walk in uninvited – who knew what might be going on inside? But there was nothing else she could do.

Taking a deep breath, she slid the door open.

She was in a parlour almost as large and luxurious as Tama's. Through the open doors leading to the adjoining room she could see a charcoal fire blazing in an enormous brazier and a table laid out with dishes. Tall candles on stands burned with huge yellow flames. In the centre of the room a group of geishas strummed shamisens, beat drums and sang. A couple of geishas were dancing, casting long undulating shadows. A party was in full swing.

At the back men lounged, clapping to the music and gulping down sake in tiny cups. Women sat among them, some snuggled against them, looking up at them and pouting, others disdainful and aloof. A couple of doll-like children, as exquisitely dressed as little Chidori, ran about, topping up sake cups.

With their white-painted faces, brilliant kimonos and enormous obis, the women all looked much the same. Dumbfounded, Hana stared. She had no idea which was the woman she was looking for or whether she'd even come to the right place. The music and clapping and laughter were so loud that the revellers didn't even notice she was there.

A youth in the blue cotton jacket of a manservant and an ancient maid scuttled out.

'Who called you?' hissed the maid. 'One of our guests? I don't have any note of it.' She looked Hana up and down. 'You're lost, aren't you? Be off with you, quickly.'

Doing her best to speak in the Yoshiwara lilt, Hana murmured, 'I'm so sorry. I have a message for . . . for one of the ladies.'

'Give it to me and I'll pass it on.'

'I have to give it to her personally,' said Hana desperately.

The manservant started bundling Hana towards the door. Wriggling away from him, she pulled up her skirts and darted towards the room where the party was going on. She was at the threshold when the maid and manservant grabbed her arms.

Above the music a man's voice boomed. 'My dear Kaoru, who's your protégée? What's this secret you've been keeping from us?'

The music faltered and stopped, and the geishas froze in their dancing. Everyone – men, courtesans and geishas – swung round and stared at Hana.

The maid crumpled to her knees. 'So sorry,' she whispered. 'I'll get rid of her.'

'No, let her stay,' said the man who had spoken. 'Who is she?'

'Yes, who is she, Kaoru-sama?' chorused the other men. 'She must stay!'

'I can't say I've ever seen her before,' said a high-pitched voice that Hana recognized.

In the middle of the group, kneeling straight-backed with an air of reserve, was a woman. Her stiff white obi, tied in a bow, was embroidered with a delicate pattern of pine, plum and bamboo sprigs. Her topmost kimono too was white. Instead of a crown, her hair bristled with hairpins, tastefully arranged. Her face was as perfect and blank as a mask in a Noh play. She pursed her lips and gazed at Hana with a puzzled air. 'What is it?' she asked.

For a moment Hana was struck dumb, but then she remembered that she had only this one chance. Keeping her voice soft and trying to remember the dulcet Yoshiwara dialect, she spoke. 'I'm sorry. I wanted to know if there was any news from . . . from outside. From the front.'

The woman's eyes opened wide and a frown creased her brow; then, quickly recovering her poise, she laughed, a tinkling silvery laugh. The other women, who Hana now saw were youthful attendants, covered their mouths with their sleeves and giggled as if they would never stop.

'Foolish child,' said Kaoru, her voice shriller than ever. 'Whatever makes you think I know anything about what happens outside? We don't talk about such dull things here. We have fun, don't we, gentlemen? That's all we do.' She turned to the maid. 'Give her some coins and see her out.'

She gestured to the geishas. The ragged notes of a shamisen rang out and the geishas began to dance again.

'Let her stay.' It was the man who had spoken before. Hana looked at him, surprised. He was young and slender, with tawny skin, slanting black eyes and a full, sensual mouth. 'We need young girls. She can be my guest.' He turned to Hana. 'Come and join us, have a drink!'

Hana took a few steps forward. As a samurai wife she had led a confined life. She was used to serving guests with food and drink, but the only men she had ever exchanged words with were her family members and her husband. Now she was surrounded by strange men, all looking her up and down and smiling at her.

'What's your name?' the man asked. 'Come and sit here.' He stretched out his hand and Hana noticed his long slender fingers. She took a step towards him, then stopped, horrified by his accent – harsh and guttural, like nothing she'd ever heard before. He must be a southerner, she realized. They were all southerners. How else could they afford a party like this?

She looked again at his hand. There were brown marks on the inside of his fingers – calluses, as if he'd held a sword or a gun. How did he come to be here, in Edo, the northern capital?

The man was looking at her kindly still. Kaoru smiled coldly. 'Of course you may join us, my dear, don't be shy.'

Then the door slid open and Tama swept in in a cloud of fragrance, with Kawanoto just behind her. She looked around, took in the situation, then knelt ceremoniously and bowed with a great rustling of silk.

'I'm Tamagawa. This' – gesturing to Hana – 'is my attendant. Do forgive her, she's still young and must have got lost. Come now, my dear, we have to leave.'

Hana turned, utterly deflated. She had had no answer to her question. All she had managed to do was antagonize Kaoru, her only link to the real world.

'Wait. She hasn't done anything wrong. Tell me, my dear, what's your name?' said the man.

Before Hana could answer, Tama straightened her back and looked around proudly. The glittering colours and vast bulk of her kimonos seemed to fill the room.

'Hanaogi,' she announced. 'Her name is Hanaogi. She will be the next star courtesan of the Corner Tamaya.'

There was silence.

'Does she have a patron?' asked the man.

'Not yet, sir. You're welcome to place your bid if you wish. I'm sure you know the procedure.'

'Hanaogi,' said the man slowly, revolving the syllables around his tongue as if he found them particularly musical. 'Hanaogi. Well, Hanaogi, you asked if there was news. I can tell you that there'll soon be peace. There's a new government now that will treat you girls very kindly.' His face changed and for a moment he sounded less sure of himself. 'We're still dealing with the rebels in the north, but we'll take care of them.'

Hana nodded, careful to keep her face impassive. 'We'll take care of them' meant they hadn't taken care of them yet, which also meant that the northerners were still holding out. She had to stop herself from smiling triumphantly. She had a hundred more questions – about her husband, and whether there was any news of him – but that would be going too far. She turned away, ready to leave.

'Let me hear your voice once more, lovely Hanaogi. Where are you from? What part of the country?'

'She . . .' Tama was about to answer for her but Hana wanted to speak for herself.

'Nowhere,' she said in the lilting tones she found hard to identify as her own. 'I've made up my mind to forget everything from before I came here.'

And, with a swirl of silk, she followed Tama and Kawanoto out of the room.

Spring

12

2nd month, Year of the Snake, Meiji 2 (March 1869)

Yozo sat cross-legged on the tatami, warming his hands at the brazier in the presidential quarters at the Star Fort. Despite the grand name, the presidential quarters were every bit as smoke-filled and freezing as anywhere in the land of Ezo. Draughts rattled the wooden rain doors and flimsy window frames and Yozo's breath puffed out in icy clouds.

It was late in the second month, spring according to the calendar, but here in Ezo the ground was still covered in a thick layer of packed snow. It was some four months since they'd taken the Star Fort and three since they'd lost the *Kaiyo Maru*.

Outside, Yozo could hear the shuffle of feet and a gruff voice barking orders in a strong French accent: 'At the double. Quick march!' Then came the tramp of men marching across the parade ground. Horses whinnied and there was a distant rattle of shots from the firing range, but inside all was peace and tranquillity.

Enomoto stood, legs apart, hands behind his back, studying the contents of the glass-fronted drinks cabinet which, fortunately, had been transferred to the fort before the *Kaiyo Maru* went down. Inside was a splendid array of bottles. Now that he was in his private apartments and in the company of friends, he had discarded his uncomfortable western uniform and was relaxing in thick cotton kimonos and a padded jacket. With his gleaming hair and delicately boned face, he looked every inch the aristocrat. He reached in and brought out a bottle of Scotch.

'Glendronach 1856,' he pronounced. 'This should warm us up.'

'Excellent year,' said Yozo, affecting the air of a connoisseur. He raised the cut-glass tumbler in his big sailor's fingers. 'Well, we've certainly come a long way, especially you, Mr Governor General of Ezo. I always knew you'd do great things.'

'And look what we've achieved!' said Enomoto, laughing. 'We've had elections and we've created Japan's first republic – the Republic of Ezo. We're a young nation like America, and we're carving out a new path. Those southern bastards might be able to win battles with the cannons and rifles the English sell them, but that's the only way they'll ever be able to lay their hands on power. They wouldn't dare organize elections because they know no one would vote for them. They're still in the feudal age, they can only get their way through brute force. The law of the jungle, isn't that what they call it?'

Yozo swirled the translucent golden liquor in his glass and took a sip, holding it in his mouth for a moment before letting it trickle slowly down his throat. He paused, enjoying the malty flavour.

'The law of the jungle,' he repeated with a slow grin. 'Survival of the fittest – at least that's what it said in that book everyone was talking about in Europe.'

'*On the Origin of Species*,' said Kitaro. He had wrapped his thin frame in a thick padded jacket and sat huddled close to the fire. 'By Charles Darwin.' He framed the words very precisely, savouring the foreign syllables.

'You read it, Kitaro,' said Yozo. 'You actually read it, a whole book, in English. I couldn't have done that. If those southern baboons only knew that, or the Commander and those militia brutes who fight for him up here, for that matter. All they're interested in is whether you can wield a sword.'

Kitaro pushed his glasses down his nose with a bony finger and looked over the top with a comical air.

'The best adapted to survive win,' he said, frowning in mock severity. 'But bear in mind that that doesn't necessarily mean the strongest. It could be the most intelligent. In fact, it usually is, in the end.'

The others laughed.

'Do you remember that coffeehouse where we used to sit and argue?' asked Enomoto. 'You know, the one with the big glass windows and leather seats.'

Yozo shook his head, smiling. 'We had arguments everywhere. London, Berlin, Paris, Rotterdam . . .'

'It was Dordrecht,' said Kitaro. Dordrecht. They all fell silent. From outside came the thunder of marching feet, punctuated by fierce yells and the rattle of side drums.

'Do you remember how the sun came out that day?' said Enomoto, gazing into the distance. He was no longer the Governor General of Ezo but a youth swept up in a glorious adventure.

It had been the third day of the eleventh month of the year 1866 by the barbarian calendar, when fourteen of the fifteen men chosen to go to Europe had met in Dordrecht to celebrate the launch of the magnificent ship they'd commissioned, the *Kaiyo Maru*. (The fifteenth man, who had gone out to Holland as a blacksmith, had drunk himself to death. Yozo had not been close to him and had never found out why.) In honour of the occasion they set aside their trousers, jackets and neckties and put on formal Japanese wear of starched pleated kimono skirts and jerkins with shoulders that jutted out like wings. They stood proudly, shoulders thrust back, with their two swords in leather scabbards pushed into their belts. They were samurai again, though they'd long since cut off their topknots and wore their hair western style.

'They'd set braziers alongside her hull,' remembered Yozo. He could see it all clearly – the great ship with her gleaming black hull resting on the slipway, dwarfing the windmills and the cathedral, and the spectators crowding the banks and bobbing about in little boats on the water, waving their hats and cheering. 'But the weather was perfect. She didn't even ice up.'

'The Lord of the Admiralty made a speech,' said Enomoto. 'Then he smashed the bottle of wine against her bows.'

'Do you remember the roar as she started to move . . . ?'

'The creaking and grinding, and all the people cheering and clapping . . .'

'And off she glided . . .'

'And the splash as she hit the water, like a tidal wave! I thought the boats would all capsize.'

'What a ship!' said Enomoto. They bowed their heads and stared at the fire. Sitting cross-legged in the presidential quarters at the Star Fort in the freezing land of Ezo, it was hard to believe any of it had happened. Even as Yozo tried to picture Dordrecht the image was beginning to fade in his mind.

'And that storm just after we left Rio, when you nearly fell off the mast,' said Kitaro, looking up and grinning. 'I thought we'd lost you for sure.'

'Lots of times I thought we'd had it, and the ship too. But we always made it through,' said Yozo.

A hundred and fifty days it had taken, the journey back to Japan. They had had a Dutch crew, mainly Dordrecht men, to sail the ship. They had coaled up in Rio, sailed round the Cape of Good Hope and across the Indian Ocean, and coaled up again in Batavia. They had been through storms and across wild oceans and had chopped their way through waves as high as mountains, and they had never lost her.

But when they got back to Japan, nothing was as they remembered. Little by little they began to find out what had gone on in the four and a half years they'd been away – treason, murders, assassinations and finally full-scale civil war. A few months after their arrival the shogun had been toppled from power, and Yozo and Kitaro had joined Enomoto, all three determined to fight to the end for their beliefs.

The *Kaiyo Maru* had been their home. Every plank of wood, every creak of the hull, every swell of the sails had reminded them of the happy days in the West. And now she too was gone.

For a while they sat in silence, thinking of their beautiful ship. Yozo pictured the sweep of her bows, the power as she'd surged through the water, the luxury of the captain's cabin, the gleaming cannons, the brasswork that they'd kept lovingly polished, the sheer size of her, large enough to house 350 sailors and 600 soldiers. Then he remembered his last sight of her, battered and broken, a lonely black hull on an ice-strewn sea, sinking under the waves as they left her behind. He brushed his hand across his eyes and swallowed hard.

Enomoto straightened his back, frowning. He was the Governor General again.

'This is our home now,' he said firmly. 'The land of Ezo. I've been speaking to the foreign representatives here in the city of Hakodate, explaining our plans to establish a liberal republic and improve people's living conditions. The Americans, the French and the English have all undertaken to recognize our government.'

He paused for a moment, his fine features darkening. 'There's something else,' he said. 'There's news of the *Stonewall* . . .'

Yozo looked up sharply. He had seen the *Stonewall* in Yokohama Harbour. She was an ironclad, the most up-to-the-minute, powerful warship the world had ever seen, with a huge engine and walls twice as thick as a man's thigh, covered in massive iron plates. Cannonballs simply bounced off her. Powered by steam and sail, she moved far faster than the *Kaiyo Maru*. She wasn't even shaped like a ship. Sitting low in the water with her sinister black prow, she looked like some fearsome predatory fish.

The shogun's government had ordered her from the Americans and paid most of the cost; but by the time she arrived the shogun had been deposed and his government overthrown. Before they left Edo, Enomoto had visited the American minister, Van Valkenburgh, and demanded that he hand her over; after all, the shogun had already paid for her. But Van Valkenburgh was adamant. The shogun's government no longer existed and the new government was not yet established, he had said. All the foreign representatives had agreed to maintain strict neutrality while the country remained in a state of war. He was not at liberty to hand her over to either side.

'You won't be surprised to hear that when the southerners heard that the *Kaiyo Maru* had sunk, they set to work on Van Valkenburgh to convince him that without our flagship our government didn't stand a chance. They gave him their word that the war was over.'

Yozo slammed his glass on the floor and clenched his fists. So the southerners had told the American minister the war was over, in order to persuade him to hand over the *Stonewall*. But it was all lies. The war was far from over, and the moment the southerners got their hands on the ironclad they'd be steaming north to attack them. If it was a case of the survival of the fittest, their chances were worsening by the day. The more Yozo heard of the southerners' treachery, the more he wanted to kill them all. He would fight to the end, no matter how bloody that was, and take as many of the enemy with him as he could.

'The southerners will be here in their tens of thousands,' Enomoto told them sombrely. 'They're just waiting for spring. We have to do everything we can to make sure we're ready. The defences are nearly in place – Captain Brunet is overseeing them – and we have some three thousand men, training night and day. But they're an ill-matched lot. There's the professional soldiers for a start – the French officers have trained them well and they've seen a lot of action. Then there's recruits who've joined because they're loyal or because they'd be executed if the southerners caught them. Some are not even military men. Some can barely shoot.'

'Me, for example,' said Kitaro.

'As for Commander Yamaguchi's Kyoto militia, they're brilliant fighters and totally fearless, but they're swordsmen in the main. Marlin and Cazeneuve are trying to turn them into riflemen but they're living in another era. They leave the fort at night and pick fights with the locals and kill them, just to keep their hand in, and think that's an acceptable way to behave. They call themselves samurai but most of them never were samurai and never will be. There's only one person they take orders from, and that is the Commander.' Enomoto frowned and poured another round of whisky. 'If we can't meld these men together into one army we'll be in real trouble when the southerners arrive.'

13

The following morning the parade ground was bustling with activity. A squadron of soldiers in black uniforms and crested leather helmets swung out, marching crisply in tight formation with a couple of drummer boys at their head, rattling out a jaunty rhythm.

At the edge of the grounds, men were clustering around the huge wheels of a shiny cannon. It was one of the new breech-loaders Yozo and Enomoto and their colleagues had brought back with them from Prussia. As Yozo watched, the men started to run, scuttling off in all directions like startled rabbits. The next moment there was a boom like a thunderclap and the cannon leaped backwards as a shell careered through the air and smashed into the earth, throwing up an eruption of sand and gravel. Horses tied up not far away whinnied and reared in terror.

There was one thing missing. There was not a single blue-coated militiaman among them.

'They refuse to train with our men because they think they know it all already,' Kitaro said.

'It's time we saw for ourselves what kind of training they're doing,' said Yozo. 'Swords won't protect them against bullets, no matter how brilliant their technique.'

'The Commander doesn't trust us or Enomoto either,' said Kitaro nervously. 'He thinks we're polluted because we've been with foreigners.'

'From the moment we left the country we were outsiders,' said Yozo. 'But it's wartime now and we're up against overwhelming odds. If the commander has any sense he'll save his opinions till the fight is over. Enomoto wanted me to keep an eye on him and I will.'

The Commander's militia occupied a large wooden building a little way from the collection of barracks where the regular army was housed. As Yozo and Kitaro approached they could hear fierce yells and the thwack of wood on wood.

No one seemed remotely surprised to see them. The Commander himself was sitting on a raised platform under a banner displaying the hollyhock crest of the shogun. He was in his militia uniform of sky-blue haori jacket and striped kimono skirts, his long oiled hair swept back from his handsome face. He nodded to Yozo and Kitaro as they came in, then turned his attention back to the arena in the centre of the hall where a couple of men were duelling with practice sticks.

Other members of the militia clustered round the arena, all in uniform. Some wore their hair in sleek ponytails, others in spiky clumps which bushed out on top of their heads, making them look like wild men. Most were familiar faces from the march across the mountains, but they looked cleaner now, more settled, more of a tight group. Yozo glanced around the lower ranks and noticed pretty soft-featured youths among them, their lips provocatively curved – pageboys, who traditionally performed the women's roles in an all-male society like this; though it would be a mistake to underestimate their swordsmanship, he thought to himself. Often the prettiest youths were the most formidable swordsmen.

A few steely-eyed warriors stood behind, arms disdainfully crossed. Yozo could see that they were used to prowling the streets, crossing swords with the enemy, and were no doubt spoiling for a fight. There was something about them all that made him feel as if he'd strayed into a blood brotherhood. His skin prickled with the hostility as they turned to stare at the newcomers.

Prominently displayed along one wall was a noticeboard with the words 'Code of Conduct' brushed in muscular characters. Laid out alongside was a set of prohibitions: 'Betraying the samurai code. Deserting the militia. Borrowing money. Fighting for personal reasons. Being struck from behind. Failing to kill your opponent.' Following each of these was the punishment: 'Seppuku' – execution by ritual suicide. There was one rule which made Yozo's blood run cold: 'When a captain falls in battle all his men must follow him to the grave.' He'd never come across a creed before which focused so obsessively on death. Outside he could hear the yells of the French drill sergeants barking orders. Here, as Enomoto had said, they were in another era.

At first glance the duellers seemed to be equally matched, but it soon became clear that they were teacher and student. The student dodged and darted, trying to get in blows, occasionally somersaulting his way out of trouble, while the teacher effortlessly fended off every attack, then caught the student off guard, put him into an indefensible position and forced him to concede. Another student stepped up, then another, and the teacher trounced them all, barely breaking a sweat.

Yozo recognized the teacher's face, his sunburnt cheeks and full mouth. He had fought alongside him during the capture of the fort and had thought then how young he was to be such an accomplished warrior. Only his eyes were old and there was a deep frown mark between them. He looked at the world wearily, as if he'd seen so much he was not afraid of anything, certainly not of death, and he took on one student after the next with an air of complete indifference. But every now and then, when one of his opponents briefly gained the advantage, a look of fury crossed his face, as if he was fighting not the young man in front of him but an implacable enemy out to destroy him.

Watching him, Yozo thought with a sinking heart of the southerners and their Gatling guns which fired a continuous stream of bullets, far more lethal even than the French manually operated mitrailleuses that their own side had. Against those even this brilliant swordsman wouldn't stand a chance. He'd be mown down long before he had time to draw his sword. All this bravado was just so much wasted effort.

The last bout came to an end and the opponents bowed to each other. The Commander pushed back strands of oiled hair with a large swordsman's hand and looked hard at Yozo and Kitaro. There was a flame in his eyes, a dancing madness that Yozo found disconcerting.

Kitaro shuffled awkwardly as the Commander glared at them from under his brows.

'So it's the world travellers again,' the Commander said with a twist of his lip, 'come to find out how we do things in Japan and gawp at our quaint practices. Or are you keeping an eye on us, making sure everything's just as Governor General Enomoto likes it? You've probably forgotten what a samurai sword looks like.' There was a burst of laughter from the militia and his face relaxed into a grin. 'No matter, you're welcome. You're brave lads, even you, Okawa.' He nodded at Kitaro, then turned to Yozo, his eyes narrowing. 'Tajima. You're a fine marksman, as good as a barbarian with that rifle of yours. But I wonder . . . Can you still fight like a samurai or have you forgotten how, after all that time in the West?'

He gestured to the fencing master. 'What do you think, Tatsu? Fancy a round or two with our friend here? Will you take him on?'

'Sure,' said Tatsu, with his habitual look of indifference.

Yozo had trained at Jinzaemon Udono's school of swordsmanship in Edo several years earlier and had learned a few techniques, but he doubted if he stood much chance against Tatsu. But he knew that if he backed down he would shame Enomoto and all his men. He nodded his agreement.

The Commander chuckled as if he had had an amusing idea. 'This time we'll use swords,' he said.

Swords. A chill ran down Yozo's spine. Swords, razor-sharp, with a curved blade as long as a man's leg, that could sever a limb or cut through a human body as effortlessly as a knife slicing tofu. That was a very different proposition from wooden sticks.

The militiamen leaned forward, derisive smiles on their lips. A whisper of excitement went round the hall.

Kitaro was doing his best to look indifferent, but Yozo could see his Adam's apple bobbing in his thin throat. He grinned at him reassuringly.

'They think there's going to be a show,' he said softly. 'They think they're going to see blood or, better still, me on my knees pleading for mercy. But I won't give them that pleasure.'

'Better wear this just in case,' said the Commander cheerfully. A headband with a protective iron plate skidded across the polished wooden floor to Yozo's feet. He bowed, picked it up and tied it in place with the guard across his forehead.

'Tatsu-sama,' Yozo said politely. 'You might want one too, just in case.'

Tatsu jerked his chin dismissively.

Yozo drew his sword and held it for a moment, caressing the hilt, feeling its reassuring weight in his hand. It was a fine weapon, made in the Bizen smithies and marked with the seal of a master swordsmith. All he could do now was try to hold his own. It would be up to the Commander to call a halt if it seemed either he or Tatsu was likely to be injured.

He gripped the hilt in both hands and crouched in the centre of the arena, facing Tatsu, trying to see through his eyes to the man inside. But all he could see was darkness. In spirit Tatsu was already dead, with no fear and nothing to lose. Unlike Tatsu, Yozo had every intention of staying alive, and he knew this put him at a disadvantage.

The tips of their swords touched and Yozo felt the energy quivering in Tatsu's blade. The world dwindled away until he was aware of nothing but Tatsu's blank face and the sound of his breath in the silence.

They rose to their feet, swords still touching, and circled slowly, never relaxing their gaze. Yozo was wide awake, every sense alert.

He was aware of the walls hung with banners and the crowds of blue-jacketed men, watching beady-eyed like vultures. He edged closer. Then Tatsu's sword flashed and he leaped back and caught the blow on his blade, near the hilt, with a deafening clang. The force of the blow sent him staggering back. He regained his balance, raised his sword, stepped forward and swung out in a cross-cut. Tatsu parried. Steel rang on steel as they let fly a barrage of blows, lunging, feinting, dodging and parrying, yelling at the top of their voices with each stroke.

Yozo had fought in battles and single combat, but this was different. Tatsu was relentless. Nothing and no one would stop him from beating Yozo. It was a fight to the death – Yozo's death.

The blow seemed to come out of nowhere. One moment they were crouching, eyes locked, the next Yozo staggered back, his arm tingling. His shoulder had been cut and hot blood was streaming down his arm. He was beginning to lose sensation in his fingers and he was panting and moist with sweat despite the chilly air. Tatsu was still fresh.

In the silence he heard a clink and a stifled laugh. The men were gambling on who would win and the odds on Tatsu had just increased. Again he heard the chink of coins. He caught a glimpse of the Commander's face, watching him, lips curled in disdain. For a moment Yozo was filled with rage so blinding he could hardly see, but then his anger was replaced by icy determination. He was not going to lose this fight.

Tatsu circled like a wolf preparing to spring. Yozo watched him as he prowled. He had thick, slightly wavy hair which grew straight up and a sprinkling of moles on the right-hand side of his face. He swung his sword again. He was out to finish this off as quickly as possible. Yozo parried, resisting as Tatsu tried to force down his sword arm. Tussling, they raced, blades locked, kimono skirts swirling, towards the side of the hall. Yozo kept his concentration, never losing his hold on Tatsu's eyes.

Perhaps it was the flurry of blue as the spectators scattered or perhaps he sensed Yozo's renewed determination, but for the space of a breath Tatsu wavered. Yozo was ready. He twisted his sword free and took a swipe at Tatsu's calves, cutting through his kimono skirts. It was an underhand move but in war a man had to be ready for anything. Tatsu fought by the book, keeping his head and arms and chest shielded, but he hadn't thought to guard his legs. Taken by surprise, he stumbled over the torn fabric and Yozo saw with satisfaction that he'd drawn blood.

With a yell Yozo spun on his toes and sprang towards his adversary. They locked blades but instead of releasing his grip, Yozo used his body weight to slam Tatsu against the wall. He could hear the hiss of breath from the watching militiamen. The odds had changed. He had Tatsu on the run.

Swiftly, before Tatsu had a chance to regain his balance, Yozo drew back and took up his position, right leg forward, knees loose, weight low to the ground, and raised his sword in both hands. Grimacing in concentration, he lowered it until the hilt was in front of his face, blade pointing to the ceiling.

He could hear his own breath. He was ready. He would never be readier. He knew with absolute certainty that in one more breath he'd have split Tatsu's head and he could see the same knowledge in Tatsu's eyes. Calmly, he swung his sword back.

A voice barked, 'Enough!'

It was the Commander. The two men froze. For a moment they stood like statues, caught in mid-motion, then lowered their swords, slid them back into their scabbards and bowed to each other.

The Commander had been leaning forward, watching intently. Now he straightened up and looked at one, then the other, from under his eyebrows. 'You've picked up foreign ways, my friend,' he said. 'You fight dirty, but you won fair and square. Our friend certainly gave you a run for your money, Tatsu,' he added, grinning uncertainly.

Yozo bowed. He could see the Commander was trying to make light of Tatsu's defeat, but it was a humiliation for the fencing master all the same. The only way Yozo could have won was by using unorthodox methods, but, unorthodox or not, he had beaten the Commander's best swordsman and by doing so had made the Commander look foolish too, both in the eyes of his own men and of Enomoto's. From now on he'd have to watch his back.

14

'We'd better get you back to the barracks and get that wound bandaged up,' Kitaro said.

Yozo nodded, wincing as he tried to move his arm. He had forgotten his shoulder in the heat of the fight but now it was on fire and stiffening rapidly. He probed it gingerly, easing away his shirt, which was stuck to his skin with congealed blood. It was only a flesh wound, but a deep one.

The barracks were deserted, so Yozo and Kitaro went in search of the doctor, a bulky young man who had been with them on board the *Kaiyo Maru* and had travelled with them in Europe. Young though he was, he had mastered both western and Chinese forms of medicine and had set up a makeshift surgery at one end of the barracks with an assortment of western medicines in bottles, along with pickled ginseng root, deer antler and an impressive array of knives. There was even an operating table.

He bandaged Yozo's wound then put a large brown ball of Chinese herbs into a clay teapot, poured in water and set it to brew over the hearth.

'Here, drink this,' he said, giving Yozo a cup of the bitter liquid. 'It'll make you sleep for a while.'

'I'll go and find Enomoto,' said Kitaro. 'He needs to know what's happened. I'll come back and check on you in a couple of hours.'

*

When Yozo woke up it was dusk, and the pain in his shoulder had turned into a dull throb. A voice was calling his name in a sing-song French accent.

Yozo sat up slowly. 'Here!'

Stockinged feet clumped across the barracks as he pushed aside the bedclothes and stumbled out into the great hall. The lamps around the walls had been lit and soldiers were crowding in for their evening meal. Savoury aromas drifted from the kitchens, mixed with smells of sweat and grime.

Sergeant Marlin's burly frame appeared, stomping across the tatami. In his own country, Yozo knew, he would not have been considered particularly tall but here he was a giant. He filled the hall with his bulk and had to bend his head to get through the doorway. Yozo grinned as he saw his heavy features and drooping moustache, but his smile quickly faded. He could see by the Frenchman's face there was something badly wrong.

'There's been a casualty,' said Marlin. There was an edge to his voice. 'By the rifle range. An accident.' There was a long pause. 'I'm sorry, sir.'

The pain in Yozo's shoulder was beginning to return and his head was still befuddled from the potion. He tried to focus on what Marlin was saying. Men got killed from time to time; it couldn't be helped. Why was Marlin coming to tell him personally?

'You'd better come and have a look, sir. It looks like . . .'

A fearful suspicion stirred Yozo out of his daze. Where was Kitaro?

Without stopping for a coat, Yozo ran out into the freezing night and headed for the rifle range. The grounds seemed to stretch for ever and no matter how fast he ran, he couldn't seem to get any closer. For a moment he wondered if he was still asleep and it was all some kind of nightmare, but the icy wind pummelling his face and cutting through his thin uniform told him it couldn't be. The moon was rising, casting a bleak light across the distant buildings and ramparts, and the endless expanse of bare earth was heaped with grubby mounds of snow. Outside the walls of the fort, a wolf howled, a melancholy sound that echoed around the hills.

The rifle range was on the far side of the grounds, well away from the barracks. Yozo could just make out the line of targets in the distance. Then he noticed a dark shape crumpled on the ground near one of the firing positions. He stopped short, his heart thumping. Shaking, he put his hands on his knees and gasped for breath. Then, very slowly, he walked towards it.

Kitaro was lying on his back, his jaw agape, his eyes open. His glasses glinted a little way away, the lenses broken, and his large bony hands were flung out to his sides, as if he had fallen over backwards and hadn't had time to save himself. There was a great black stain spreading across his shirt.

Yozo dropped to his knees and stared at his friend, trying to take in what he was seeing. Shuddering, he stretched out his hand and touched Kitaro's cold cheek. Then he put his fingers on his eyelids and gently closed them.

Leaning across, he ripped Kitaro's shirt open and ran his hand across his bony chest. There was a single wound there, a long narrow cut – a sword, not a gunshot wound. Kitaro had been murdered with a single stroke before he had had a chance to put up a fight.

Yozo sat back on his heels. He had seen battlefields heaped with corpses, people killed before his eyes more times than he cared to remember. But this was different – this was his friend, with whom he'd been through so much. With a groan he grabbed Kitaro and lifted his shoulders off the ground. Kitaro's head fell back and Yozo cradled it to his chest, then laid it back down. The first time they'd met, Kitaro had been a gawky hollow-cheeked seventeen-year-old with unruly black hair and absurdly thick glasses. Yozo had covered for him on shipboard when there were difficult jobs to be done, such as climbing the rigging. But in Holland Kitaro had been quicker than anyone at fitting in. He was like a jackdaw, snapping up nuggets of information.

All that travelling, all that knowledge, the long journey back to Japan and up to the land of Ezo – and all for this, to die so brutally, so casually, with a single sword-stroke, at the age of twenty-four.

Yozo rubbed his eyes. Someone would pay for this.

'I give you my word,' he promised Kitaro, his voice hollow in the silence. 'If I make it back, I'll find your family and tell them you died honourably. I'll make sure they are well provided for. And I will find your killer and make sure you are avenged. This I swear.'

A hand touched his shoulder and Yozo jumped. Marlin was looking down at him, his face full of concern. Yozo shook the hand off and rose to his feet.

By the time he realized where he was, he was in front of the militia headquarters. He felt strangely calm, every sense poised. It was obvious who had killed Kitaro. It was a swordsman – Tatsu, surely, or one of his cronies – and it had been done with the Commander's knowledge and approval, in retaliation for what had happened that morning. It might even have been the Commander himself. After all, he had a reputation for cutting down men without a second thought if they displeased him.

Whoever had been responsible, Yozo would find them, all of them, and exact his revenge. But he had no coat and his clothes were stained with Kitaro's blood. He wiped his face with a handkerchief and straightened his uniform. He would have to be cunning.

The militiamen loitering in groups gawped as he walked briskly through the hall towards the section of the building where he guessed the Commander's private rooms must be. Voices shouted: 'Hey, you can't go there! Out of bounds!'

'I have a message for the Commander,' Yozo snapped. 'From the Governor General. It's urgent. I have to deliver it direct.'

The men followed as he padded through the silent rooms, sliding open one set of doors after another. Light filtered around the edges of a last set of doors. A couple of blue-jacketed youths grabbed his arms but he shook them off and pushed the doors open, then blinked for a moment, dazzled by the sudden brightness. He was standing outside a small tatami-matted room. Quivering with panic the men laid heavy hands on his shoulders and shoved him to his knees.

The Commander was kneeling in the centre of the room, strands of oiled hair hanging around his cheeks. He was holding a brush between two fingers, poised above a large sheet of paper spread on a cloth on the floor, held in place with paperweights. The fragrance of fresh-ground ink filled the room. In the lamplight Yozo caught a glimpse of his pale complexion, broad nose and stern brow, his hooded eyes and sensual mouth. He could see the pores in the Commander's skin and smell the musty scent of his pomade.

There were two retainers kneeling opposite. They jerked their heads up when Yozo appeared. Yozo's skin prickled as he saw Tatsu's face and the moles on his cheek.

The Commander must have heard the clunk of the doors sliding back, but he paid not the slightest attention as he dipped his brush into the pool of ink on the ink stone and brought it down on the paper in a flowing black line, lifting it to make the line more delicate, lowering it to make it fatter and ending with a flourish. Yozo watched, mesmerized. Much though he hated the Commander, it was impossible not to be in awe of him as well.

From where Yozo knelt he could read the first words: 'Though my body may decay on the island of Ezo . . .' The words glowed on the page, burning into his mind. He saw Kitaro's body bathed in moonlight. In the end they were all going to die on this accursed island.

The Commander rinsed his brush, wiped it and laid it on a rest. He sprinkled sand on the paper, shook it, and knelt for a moment studying his handiwork. Then he turned slowly and looked from beneath his brows at the three men kneeling on the threshold.

'Tajima,' he said mildly, as if he was not remotely surprised at

Yozo's sudden appearance. 'Have you written your death poem yet?'

Yozo couldn't speak. The blood was booming in his ears.

'We are fighting a losing battle for a government that no longer exists,' the Commander said, his face stern. 'With the shogun gone, it would be a disgrace if no one was willing to go down with him. I will fight the best battle of my life and die for my country. What greater glory could a man ask?'

Yozo gripped the hilt of his short sword so tightly he could feel the binding cutting into his palm. Now was his chance to avenge Kitaro. Summoning up all his energy, he took a deep breath and was about to spring forward when a bulky figure appeared in the doorway beside him.

'Begging your pardon, sir.' Marlin put a hand on Yozo's arm, addressing the Commander in his quaint French accent. 'My friend here came to tell you the news. It seems the southerners have taken possession of the ironclad and they'll be sending a fleet here as soon as the weather improves. If we all pull together, sir, we have a good chance of defeating them. The French army is the best in the world and the southerners only have English arms. No need to despair yet, sir. We'll destroy those bastards!'

Yozo stared at the Commander. 'Watch out, Yamaguchi, you're not immortal,' he thought. 'You're a man like any other. I'll wait my chance but my time will come; and I will find a way to avenge the death of my friend.'

Trembling with rage and hatred, he stood up and, with Marlin's hand on his good shoulder, left the Commander's room.

15

Hana woke with an inexplicable feeling of excitement. It was dawn and the scent of spring was in the air, yet in Tama's rooms in the Yoshiwara everyone was still fast asleep. Maids and attendants sprawled around the reception room and Tama herself was in her bedroom with the last of her lovers for the night.

It was too good an opportunity to miss. Hana had been in the Yoshiwara long enough to know that she would not get away with simply sitting in the cage for much longer. She would soon be expected to do more – far more. It was time to take her chances and try once more to escape, no matter what the consequences.

She pulled on a plain jacket and cotton socks to hide her feet, stepped across the creaky rung and hurried down the stairs. At the front entrance she hesitated, trembling, remembering the last time she had stood there, the footsteps pounding along the corridor towards her and the stick coming down on her back. But today there was no one around and the entranceway was dark and empty, lined with racks of sandals. She slipped on a pair and pushed aside the curtains that hung across the doorway.

Outside, the sky was a brilliant blue, birds were singing and a balmy breeze rustled her skirts. A manservant was on his haunches beside the door, snoring softly. Hana looked around, thrilled to be free, if only for a moment.

Morning people loitered – scrawny cleaners wielding brooms,

porters staggering under bundles on poles across their shoulders and bandy-legged characters bent under buckets swilling with night soil from the toilets. A man stumbled out of a door as if he'd only just realized how late it was and, as he turned and gawked, she caught a glimpse of bleary eyes and dark stubble on a pallid face. She shrank into the shadows, feeling every eye on her.

Suddenly there was a bang like a thunderclap. Hana jumped and looked up, sure it must be someone coming after her, but it was only maids pushing back the shutters of the house opposite. It was the first time she had seen the street in daylight and she stared around in amazement. The buildings were palaces, huge and splendid with slatted wooden walls, grander by far than any house she'd ever seen before. Curtains swung like banners outside the enormous entrances and along the upper floors were balconies, where faces were already beginning to appear. The street looked washed-out, as if even the houses were exhausted from the partying of the night before.

Blazoned across the pale brown curtains of the establishment Hana had just crept out of was the name: the Corner Tamaya.

Glancing back, stopping to listen for footsteps, she half walked, half ran the few steps to the end of the street. Around the corner was a broad avenue yet more splendid than the one she had just come from, with a line of cherry trees down the middle just bursting into bud. Smoke spiralled from the food stalls and smells of grilling fish and sparrows and simmering vegetable stew filled the air. She was in the grand boulevard she had walked along with Fuyu when she had first arrived a few months ago, though it felt like a lifetime now.

She could see the city wall at the far end, too high even to think of climbing over. The massive doors of the Great Gate were pushed right back and a guard was squatting in the sunshine, dozing, tattoos mottling his massive thighs. She knew there were four guards there night and day, to make sure women didn't escape and men didn't sneak out without paying their bills, but he seemed to be the only one around. Glancing to left and right, she sauntered towards the gate as casually as she could.

She was nearly there when a woman burst out of one of the houses, setting the dark red curtains over the doorway flapping like wings. Startled, Hana jumped back but the woman was beaming.

'Welcome to the Chrysanthemum Teahouse!' she cried. 'Come in, come in! I'm Mitsu, and this is my teahouse. I'm so happy to make your acquaintance at last!'

Hana bowed, bewildered. She had never seen the woman before in her life.

'Hanaogi-sama, isn't it? The young lady everyone's talking about?' gushed the woman. She was tiny and birdlike with a delicately sculpted face that was still quite beautiful and white hair smoothed back into an immaculate chignon. 'I'm swamped with enquiries about you.'

Hana was shocked. She hadn't realized news travelled so fast. Another woman pushed through the curtains of the neighbouring house, quickly followed by others from other houses, and they clustered around Hana, introducing themselves in a babble of voices.

Mitsu laughed, a high-pitched fluting laugh, and flapped her hand dismissively at all of them.

'The Chrysanthemum is the best teahouse in the Yoshiwara,' she said firmly, in tones that brooked no disagreement. 'You can be sure that any guest I recommend will be of the highest quality. Now, come in and have a smoke and a cup of tea!'

Any hope of slipping away had been foiled, for today at least, yet Hana felt strangely relieved. After all, if she had been caught, Father would only have given her another beating and, in any case, she didn't know where she would have gone. Suddenly she thought of the sweet-faced woman who did her hair and had given her the comb to protect her before she went into the cage.

'I'd love to come and see you another time,' she said, smiling. 'But actually, I was looking for Otsuné, the hairdresser. Do you know where she lives?'

*

The houses on Otsuné's alley were small and humble, packed so tight not a single ray of sunlight could get through. Hana picked her way along the dirt path to the door marked with Otsuné's name, slid it open and peeped inside. Piled in corners and on shelves were boxes overflowing with combs, hairpins, curling irons and clumps of bear's hair, along with tubs of camellia oil and bintsuké wax. Pungent smells of burnt hair, hair dye and charcoal smoke filled the small room.

Otsuné was kneeling at a low table with a swag of hair in her thin hands, working on a hairpiece. She looked up and beamed with delight when she saw Hana. She was in a striped indigo kimono with a padded collar. Charcoal burned in a ceramic brazier in the middle of the room and a couple of candles lit the shadows.

She filled a teapot and gave Hana a cup. As she did so, a ray of light caught her face, picking out the lines on her forehead and at the corners of her mouth. She had rather a sad face, Hana thought.

Sipping her tea, Hana started to tell Otsuné about the extraordinary encounter she had had with Mitsu and the teahouse owners.

'You're doing very well,' Otsuné said when she had finished. 'The Corner Tamaya auntie will be very pleased.'

Hana held her breath, wondering if Otsuné might ask how she came to be roaming the streets, but she didn't seem at all concerned.

'The teahouses are very important,' Otsuné continued. 'They're where men go to arrange meetings. Some always visit the same woman, some try lots of different ones and some are eager to book a famous courtesan. They'll need plenty of money if that's what they want. If they don't know who to ask for, the teahouse owner recommends someone. Even men who see you in the cage still have to book you through a teahouse. Mitsu used to be the most famous courtesan in the entire district and she's still a legend. After she retired, her patron set her up in her own business and the Chrysanthemum Teahouse is the most popular in town now, with the best customers and the best connections. If Mitsu likes you, you'll be fine.'

Spring breezes wafted through the cracks in the walls and around the door frame and Hana pulled her jacket closer round her. If she was going to stay in the Yoshiwara, she would have to find a way to make it bearable. Tama for one didn't seem to lead a bad life.

'I've noticed Tama doesn't lie with every client even if they're paying her,' she said thoughtfully. 'I've seen her sit and drink sake with someone and chat to him and tease him, then pack him off after an hour without anything else.'

'Ah, but Tama's been here a long time, ever since she was a child, and she's very clever. She's mastered everything – how to talk, how to behave, how to please the old ladies who run things here; she can dance and write poetry and sing and do tea ceremony. But in the end none of that makes any difference. She still has a huge debt and she'd give anything for someone to buy her freedom. She sleeps with rich clients, I can tell you that. Women in our profession can't afford to be too fussy.'

'In our profession . . .' Hana stared at her.

The door slid open and a thin face poked round, grinning enquiringly, followed by a scrawny neck and a thin chest. Otsuné jumped to her feet, took out her purse and gave the boy some coins. He disappeared and returned a moment later with a couple of bowls of steaming noodles.

'I read that in the olden days some courtesans never slept with anyone at all unless they liked them,' Hana said, cradling the bowl in her hands and inhaling the savoury aroma. If she had to stay in the Yoshiwara, she thought, she'd like to be that sort of courtesan.

Otsuné put down her bowl and rocked with laughter.

'That's what everyone hopes for and with your face you might just manage it, but the chances are small. Most of us accept whatever clients come our way. You remind yourself it's just a job and keep topping up his sake cup and hope he'll fall asleep before anything happens. That's always a good ploy. There are plenty of ways to get it over with quickly. Tama's an expert on those and even I can teach you.'

She put her thin hand on the shiny clasp she wore on her kimono collar and stroked it, smiling quietly, as if at some secret thought that pleased her.

'The key thing is, never forget it's just a job, that's what we always tell the new girls. Above all, don't ever give your heart away. The big danger is not the awful men you have to lie with sometimes, but when you lose your heart to someone. It's always the wrong fellow – the young handsome one who can't afford your fees. That's when you'll come crying to me, asking what to do. As for sleeping with a client, you might even start to enjoy it. You had a husband and slept with him, didn't you?'

Hana shifted uncomfortably. 'I . . . I hardly even knew him,' she whispered. 'All he ever said to me was, "Run my bath! Bring my tea!"'

She pictured his face, dark and angry. She could almost smell the pomade he wore on his hair and thought of how her heart used to sink when she caught a whiff of it. She heard his voice barking, 'Bath!' 'Tea!' 'Dinner! What? Not ready?' and remembered how she had pressed her forehead to the floor while he slapped and kicked her. At night he had thrust his body against hers so fiercely she had to grit her teeth to stop herself crying out in pain, and whenever he was home for a day or two he would demand if she was with child and explode with rage that she had not produced a son for him yet.

She had been nothing but a servant in his house, Hana could see that now. She had cleaned and cooked and been scolded and beaten by his mother, until war had erupted, as if a god had ground his heel on their small ants' nest and put an end to that world and all its certainties. Treacherous though it had seemed at the time to think such a thing, it had been a blessed relief when he had gone off to fight. Being a courtesan could not be worse than being his wife.

'He didn't care about me at all,' she muttered.

'Mine did,' Otsuné murmured, stroking her clasp. Hana was startled to see tears glistening in her eyes. 'He cared about me.'

Footsteps pattered up and down the alley and women's voices broke the silence of the little house, chattering shrilly. The lid of the kettle hanging over the brazier jiggled.

'Your husband, Otsuné?' Hana asked softly.

'My patron.' Otsuné took off the clasp and showed it to her. It was a small faded square of fabric, ragged at the edges, embroidered with a black bird with a green snake in its beak, and a silver coin hanging from it with a wreath embossed around the edge. On one side were words, too worn to read; on the other, the profile of a man with a sharp nose and pointed beard. Hana had never seen anything like it.

'He gave it to me to remember him by,' said Otsuné, her voice muffled. She spoke so softly that Hana had to lean forward to hear her. There was a long silence. 'Before I came here I was the concubine of a man who worked for the Lord of Okudono. I hated him but my parents were poor and had sold me to him. It was the only way we managed to survive.'

Hana stared at the clasp, listening to Otsuné's soft tones. She'd never in her life heard so much pain in a voice.

'Three years ago my master was ordered to move back to the country and left me in Edo, with no money and nothing to eat. I wandered around for three days, then found an empty house and curled up and waited to die.'

Otsuné's face was small and white in the shadowy room. 'A man saw me and gave me some rice balls. He said he'd give me more if I slept with him, so I did, and I ended up here. I was a lower-class whore at the Yamatoya on Kyomachi 2 – a cheap place, not like the Corner Tamaya. I used to sit in the cage like you do, but all the men wanted younger girls. I wasn't like Tama; I didn't know how to make them desire me.

'Then one day a man came along. He was . . .' She hesitated.

'He was . . . ?' prompted Hana breathlessly.

Otsuné shook her head, took the clasp and held it for a moment, then pinned it back on her collar. 'He asked for me again and again, then he said he didn't want me to lie with anyone except him. He bought me my freedom and bought this house for me. Everything I have he gave me.' She wiped her eyes with her sleeve and refilled the teapot.

Hana stroked her arm. How thin she was, a frail bundle of bones inside the wadding of her jacket. She was burning to ask what had become of her patron and, if he had cared for her so much, why he was no longer there, but Otsuné was silent. Perhaps he too had been caught up in the war, Hana thought. She looked around. Now her eyes were accustomed to the gloom she could see signs of a man's presence – an enormous pair of boots pushed to the back of the shoe rack and a dark blue obi that looked as if it must have been a man's.

There were fates worse than being a star courtesan at the Corner Tamaya, she was beginning to see that now. She thought of the ruined buildings she'd passed in the city and the women offering themselves to every man that went by. Here, inside the Great Gate, at least business was thriving.

She remembered how she used to collect woodblock prints of the courtesans of the Yoshiwara, how she'd read about their love affairs and fashions and hairstyles, admired them and even tried to imitate them. She thought of her favourite romance, *The Plum Calendar*, of that intense world of feeling in which Ocho and Yonehachi lived, and how she had yearned for a life as romantic as theirs. That was how she had always imagined the Yoshiwara to be.

And now she was here.

There was another thing too – the man at Kaoru's. She knew he was a southerner and an enemy but, like Otsuné's patron, he had been kind to her. She could still see his broad face and full mouth curved in a smile and his delicate long-fingered hand. She'd met so few men in her young life and had imagined that any client she had to lie with would be a monster; but it wouldn't be so terrible to lie with this one, surely.

Hana took a deep breath and straightened her shoulders. This was her life now, at least for the time being. Perhaps she could even find a way to be happy.

16

By the time Hana slid open the door of Otsuné's house and stepped out into the narrow lane, the shadows were beginning to lengthen. On the grand boulevard the lanterns were already lit and early visitors were strolling up and down or disappearing through the curtains of teahouses. Men turned to stare curiously after Hana as she passed and she quickly lowered her head and shrank away from their gaze.

As she reached the Corner Tamaya, a hand with pink-tinted nails pushed the curtains apart and a mask-like face appeared. Black eyes glinted behind the white paint as Kaoru brushed through with a rustle of fabric, kimono hems swirling at her feet.

'I'm so sorry I intruded,' Hana whispered, bowing as low as she could, remembering how she had burst uninvited into Kaoru's rooms a few months earlier. She hadn't seen her since then.

Kaoru gazed haughtily past her. In her lavishly embroidered kimonos with her hair piled into a gleaming coil, crowned with combs, jewels and hairpins, she was a magnificent spectacle. The high clogs she wore made her taller than everyone else, like a goddess on an altar commanding reverence. Men stopped to stare, keeping a respectful distance.

Her red-painted lips opened, revealing immaculately polished black teeth, like a dark well in her mouth. 'You wanted news from the front, you said?'

'The first night I arrived here I heard you say the ships had sailed,' Hana whispered, aware that Kaoru's face had softened. Kaoru carried herself like the wife or concubine of a daimyo warlord, as if she had once commanded a great household, and Hana wondered if she might even have been one of the shogun's ladies. To have fallen from such high station and ended up in the Yoshiwara must be hard to bear. If that really was the case, the only thing she could possibly have left was her pride, which perhaps was why she clung to it so fiercely now.

'Well, I can tell you something else,' Kaoru said. 'They've landed in Ezo and taken over half the island. They may even come back one day to look for us.' A spasm of pain crossed her beautiful face. 'And what do you think they'll do when they find us? When they find we've been making love to their enemies? Whether we win or lose, we're finished. Our lives are over, yours and mine.' She composed her face and drew herself up disdainfully. 'From now on, stay on your own side of the house and keep away from my clients. If you're lucky you might even find some of your own.'

Miserably Hana trailed through the house to Tama's rooms. As she slid open the door she was engulfed in a cloud of perfume, make-up, wax and the vinegary tang of teeth-blackening lacquer. Charcoal glowed in the huge brazier in the middle and candles and lamps burned. Tama's most splendid kimonos were spread on racks along the walls with the thick quilted hems fanned out to display the exquisite embroidery. The luxurious brocades threaded with gold and silver glimmered in the flickering light, making the room look breathtakingly opulent.

Hana smiled. To samurai taste it was shockingly vulgar and showy. She remembered how dark and austere the rooms had been in even the grandest samurai residences she'd visited. Even the shogun's palace, she thought, could not be as luxurious as this. It was like nothing she'd ever seen before she came to the Yoshiwara, more like the dragon king's palace under the sea than any earthly dwelling. But now, unexpectedly, she'd come to like it.

The attendants were getting ready for the evening, chatting cheerfully to each other. When they saw Hana they moved up to make space in front of one of the mirrors. She fancied they glanced at her strangely but no one asked where she'd been.

Tama was sipping a cup of tea, a robe flung casually around her shoulders. Her large-boned, rather plain face was flushed as if she had just come from the bath. She yawned and took a puff on her pipe as if she hadn't even noticed Hana had been away.

'So you met Mitsu,' she said.

Hana got down on her hands and knees and bowed. Tama was her ally, she saw that now. She needed desperately to keep her on her side.

'You certainly weren't made to be a wife,' Tama said, looking at her hard. 'I knew it as soon as I saw you. You look like a domestic pussy cat, but you're not. You have claws, like me. That's what'll make you a good courtesan.'

Hana took a breath. Tama was cunning and wily. It wouldn't do to speak to her too directly.

'I know I can never be as good a courtesan as you,' she said, knowing she had to be cunning too if she was to survive in this new world. 'But I'd like to learn. Will you teach me?'

Tama looked at her out of the corner of her eye and smiled.

'I'm so glad you're coming round to my way of thinking.' She took another puff on her pipe. 'But I thought you were supposed to be the clever one. You can read and write, can't you? Anything else?'

'I can dance, well enough, and sing and play the koto. I can do tea ceremony and play the incense game . . .'

'What else do you need?' said Tama nastily. 'There's nothing else I can teach you.'

A vendor shouted outside and she called to Chidori to run out and buy some medicine.

'Aren't there special things a courtesan needs to know?' Hana whispered, her face blazing.

Tama tapped her pipe out on the tobacco box and gave her a knowing look.

'You want to learn how to sing in the night, is that it?' Hana nodded. 'Well, we caged birds certainly know a bit about that. Shosaburo has booked me tonight. Take a peek through the bedroom doors. He's a skilled lover, very passionate, a real adept. You can watch all night if you like. That's what all the other girls do.' She narrowed her eyes until they were two slits in her face and ran her tongue around her lips. 'And you're right, there are techniques that I can teach you. How the Jade Stalk moves through the Lute Strings, the forty-eight positions, all the secrets of the way of love. You can become an adept. And even if you don't, I can certainly show you how to enjoy yourself.'

She took a wad of tobacco and moulded it between her fingers, then pressed it into the tiny bowl of her long-stemmed pipe, picked up the tongs, took a piece of charcoal from the brazier and lit it.

'But what most men want is just to dream,' she said.

In the light of the fire her face was serious, almost sad. Hana could see the lines appearing in her brow, the heaviness in her cheeks, the sagging flesh around her eyes. Tama was already losing her looks, she realized.

'They want to feel young and handsome and desirable, no matter how old and ugly they really are. They want to believe that they're brilliant and witty, the most irresistible men on earth. They want you to gaze into their eyes as if you can't bear to be apart from them, as if you'd give anything just to be with them for one moment. Make a man feel that and he's yours for ever.' She puffed reflectively on her pipe. 'You'll learn fast and with your face and that way you have about you, men will be fighting over you. But a little polish will make you even more desirable.'

Footsteps padded towards the door and Tama's eyes widened and her forehead wrinkled. Hana recognized the tread and panic lurched in her stomach. Father must have discovered she had been roaming the streets and was coming to punish her.

As the door slid open, the women fell to their hands and knees, faces pressed to the ground.

'Wasting time again!' growled a familiar voice.

Trembling, Hana looked up, trying not to recoil as she saw the paunch, jowly face and small greedy eyes encased in folds of skin.

'Not dressed yet, young lady?' He was looking straight at her. 'We have several gentlemen eager to make your acquaintance.'

Hana threw a desperate glance at Tama, but Tama was staring at the floor. Even she seemed cowed.

'We've told them you're a virgin,' said Father with a lascivious grin.

Hana's heart was banging hard. She tried to speak but her mouth was dry. 'But . . .' she croaked. 'But . . . I'm not.'

'No one worries about that,' snapped Father. 'It's standard practice.'

Tama sat back on her heels, lifted her pipe to her mouth, took a defiant puff and blew a smoke ring. It hung above her head, slowly dissolving into the air.

'She's my protégée,' she said, looking Father in the eye. 'You put her in my care and I've just begun her training. We can charge a lot more if we wait a while.'

'But she's not a child. Who's going to believe she's still a virgin if we wait any longer?'

With Tama on her side Hana could face anyone, even Father. She thought of what Tama had said about men wanting to dream.

'Let me entertain these gentlemen,' she said softly. 'Let me drink and talk and dance and sing and do tea ceremony. I can make them feel I really want to get to know them, and then if I decide to lie with them it'll make them feel much more special. If they can't lie with me straight away, they'll want to come back again and again till they can. Can't I be properly introduced to the district? Isn't that the usual way?'

A withered face had appeared behind Father's shoulder. The candlelight flickered, picking out the sunken cheeks and hollow eyes, hideously painted. Then the light changed and for a moment Hana caught a glimpse of the beauty Auntie had once been.

'I told you, Father, she's got spirit, this one,' the old woman purred. 'She's quite right, she needs a proper début. Business is down, right down. We need something to bring back the sparkle, to remind customers of the days when the Corner Tamaya was the glory of the Yoshiwara. With a bit of training she'll be our star courtesan. We'll find an excellent patron for her, who'll pay a lot.'

Father scowled at Hana suspiciously. 'If you can make money without sleeping with anyone, all well and good. But if you're not getting repeat bookings in a couple of days, then it's into the cage with you.'

Hana nodded, grateful for the reprieve. She thought of the young man with the broad face and delicate hands. If they put her virginity up for sale, she hoped he would bid the highest.

17

Kitaro had been in his grave a month when the cherry trees flowered. Clouds of pale pink blossom filled the grounds of the Star Fort, wafting through the air and lying in great drifts on the ground. Flocks of seagulls wheeled and screamed, buzzards soared, larks trilled and huge crows with beady yellow eyes opened their black beaks and cawed. The island of Ezo had become somewhere Yozo could call home, somewhere worth fighting for.

With the cherry blossoms came news that eight warships had left Edo, steaming north. Lookouts kept watch night and day, scouring the horizon, training their telescopes on the harbour mouth, but nothing happened, no enemy fleet appeared, guns blazing.

One balmy spring morning Enomoto called a meeting in the presidential quarters. When Yozo arrived, straw sandals were lined up side by side with leather boots in the entranceway to the building. The leaders of the new republic had all gathered in their high-collared uniforms with burnished buttons and swords in their belts. The quiet, intense General Otori, now Minister of the Army, stood beside Navy Minister Arai, a gangly man with prematurely thinning hair and eyes that popped out when he was excited. Three of the nine French military advisers were there too, resplendent in belted blue jackets with gold epaulettes and red trousers – the dapper Captain Jules Brunet, now second-in-command of the army, and Sergeants Marlin and

Cazeneuve, who headed a battalion each. Japanese and French, they were all in their early thirties and talked loudly and eagerly, eyes blazing, full of ardour for their cause.

Commander Yamaguchi stood a little apart from the rest, looking around and taking everything in. Yozo watched him, eyes narrowed. It was the first time he had been in his presence since Kitaro died. He turned away abruptly. In the centre of the room, maps were spread on the table alongside a pile of books, including two precious volumes of naval tactics which Enomoto had brought back from Holland and saved from the *Kaiyo Maru*. Another thick volume, the *Règles Internationales et Diplomatie de la Mer*, lay open.

Enomoto raised his hand and the room fell silent.

'Gentlemen,' he said. 'We have news.' He spoke gravely and seriously as befitted the Governor General of the Republic of Ezo but there was a twinkle in his eye and a hint of a smile at the corners of his mouth. 'As you know, the southern forces are on their way but it seems they've been having trouble navigating the *Stonewall*. They got into difficulties as soon as they left Edo, put in at Miyako Bay and haven't moved since. Their crews have gone on shore leave.'

The men looked at him, then at each other. Navy Minister Arai hooted with laughter and the others too began to chuckle. Even the Commander smiled.

'Waiting for the weather to improve, no doubt,' said Arai when the hubbub had died down.

'Fine sailors they are!' said Captain Brunet sarcastically. 'We managed to make it up here in the middle of winter!'

'No doubt the crews are enjoying the local brothels,' added Arai. 'We won't be hearing from them for a while!'

'Hear me out, gentlemen,' Enomoto persisted. 'We're not going to sit around any longer waiting for the southerners to come and get us. We're going to take the fight to the enemy. Arai and the Commander have cooked up a plan.'

'We have only six ships left now we've lost the *Kaiyo Maru* and the *Shinsoku* and none of them are as strong as the *Stonewall*,' General Otori interjected soberly.

'The *Stonewall*'s the key,' said the Commander. He glanced around the room, eyes glittering. 'All we have to do is get her back and the war's won. And even if we fail, we'll have done the enemy some real damage.'

The room was silent.

'The southerners think we're cowering up here,' the Commander went on. 'We'll show them they're wrong. We'll take the *Kaiten*, the *Banryu* and the *Takao* and sail into Miyako Bay . . .'

'. . . flying the American flag!' shouted Arai. 'It's allowed by international law.' He slapped his hand on the *Règles Internationales*, sending a cloud of dust puffing from the yellowing pages.

'At the last minute we hoist our colours,' the Commander continued, his voice rising. 'The *Banryu* and *Takao* pull in alongside the *Stonewall* and the *Kaiten* gives covering fire. We board, capture the crew, take the ship and we're back in Hakodate before anyone knows what's happened.'

It was a reckless plan, Yozo thought, there was no doubt about that, but the best plans always were. For all their merriment, the men were well aware that the southerners massively outnumbered them and would soon be sailing north to drive them off the island and destroy them – unless, that is, they could make the first move and intercept them. In any case, they were eager for action, and the idea of taking the southerners by surprise was a brilliant one.

And the troops too were more than ready. They'd been training for so long, practising at the firing range, honing their swordsmanship, and they were desperate for a glimpse of the enemy. A sneak attack might just work and even if it didn't – well, they had to do something. It was unbearable to sit around any longer, waiting to be flushed out of their lair. Let the hunted become the hunter! They would show the southerners that they were a force to be reckoned with. And if they actually succeeded in laying their hands on the *Stonewall*, they would have command of the seas around Ezo. Yes, thought Yozo, it was a risk worth taking. With a bit of luck they could turn the odds on their head and put the southerners out of business once and for all.

For a moment the Commander's words hung in the air. Then the men started laughing and cheering and slapping each other on the back.

The only person looking sceptical was General Otori. 'They have eight ships,' he said, measuring his words. 'And we send three?'

'We have surprise on our side,' said Enomoto, his eyes shining. 'The *Stonewall*'s gun deck will be packed with provisions and fire-wood. They won't be able to get to their guns and their boilers won't be lit. By the time they're ready to fight we'll be halfway home.'

After the others had left, Yozo stayed behind. Enomoto took off his swords and threw down a couple of cushions, then opened a bottle of vintage Glendronach and poured them each a glass.

'You'll be wanting to join them,' he said as they clinked glasses.

Yozo settled on one of the cushions, legs crossed, and took a sip of the fiery liquor, swilling it thoughtfully around his mouth. Sunlight filtered through the paper screens on to the Dutch carpet and rosewood furniture and for a moment he forgot he was on the island of Ezo and imagined he was with his friend back in Holland. 'I could do with some action,' he said. 'We haven't seen any serious fighting yet, not what I'd call a real engagement. Sure, we captured the Star Fort and Matsumae, but those were skirmishes, and Esashi was a walkover. I'd like to take the measure of this mighty southern navy of theirs and find out what's the worst they have to offer.'

'I wish I could go myself,' Enomoto said.

'That's the price of success,' said Yozo. 'The Governor General of Ezo can't just leave his post and set off on some madcap expedition. What about General Otori?'

'He's in command of the garrison and it'll be a sea battle, added to which he's not fully behind the plan.' Enomoto emptied his glass and looked at Yozo. 'I'd like you to go on the *Kaiten*. No one knows more about the Krupp breech-loaders than you do.'

Yozo nodded. The Prussian breech-loaders they'd brought back from Europe were the most advanced cannons in the world, far more lethal and effective than the old muzzle-loaders, but they were also less reliable and a lot more dangerous and there were frequent accidents. Apart from Enomoto, Yozo was the only man among the northern forces who had detailed knowledge of how they functioned and could keep them in good working order.

Enomoto was staring into the distance. 'Remember Herr Krupp and that mansion of his in Essen?' he asked.

Yozo pictured the long-nosed industrialist with his grey spade-shaped beard and extravagant residence and grinned. 'I'd call Villa Hugel a castle, not a mansion.'

Of all their adventures, visiting Alfred Krupp had been one of the most extraordinary. When they and their thirteen colleagues had first arrived, crowds had followed them wherever they went, gawping at their samurai skirts, oiled topknots and curved swords, and they'd quickly had their hair cut and started wearing western clothes so they could blend in. But they'd soon discovered that when they needed a favour, if they put on their samurai out-fits and their swords, no one seemed to realize that they were mere students and treated them as if they were high-ranking emissaries of their country.

Together with one of their colleagues named Akamatsu, Yozo and Enomoto had been taken to observe the Schleswig-Holstein War and had toured the front lines, where they'd seen the new Prussian breech-loading field guns in action. They'd also asked to visit the Krupp armaments factory in Essen but were told they couldn't do so in wartime for reasons of security. Instead, they had been invited to lunch with the legendary Alfred Krupp.

'The size of the place!' said Yozo, as he remembered bowling through the grounds in a horse-drawn carriage and seeing the vast expanses of lawn, the liveried guards lined up outside the front doors, the cavernous entrance and hallway and the grey-bearded magnate and his buxom wife, Bertha, coming out to greet them. 'Didn't Herr Krupp tell us there were three hundred rooms?'

'I was more nervous than that time we had an audience with the shogun, before we left,' said Enomoto, chuckling.

'And that huge high-ceilinged dining room, and all the cutlery,' said Yozo. 'I was terrified I'd use the wrong knife and fork.'

He remembered how his heart had sunk as the servants came trooping in, bent under platter after platter laden with enormous sides of meat. Until they'd arrived in the West they'd hardly eaten meat at all – the Japanese diet was mainly fish – and they had had to struggle manfully to show their appreciation of the rich German food. But they'd managed to converse in simple German with the great industrialist and his formidable wife and later with some of his lackeys, and had acquired considerable knowledge of the cannons.

'So I'm to go on the *Kaiten*,' said Yozo, coming back to the present. He grimaced, suddenly realizing there might be a snag. 'The Commander's travelling on the *Kaiten* too, isn't he? I'm not on the best of terms with him, as you know.'

Enomoto drew himself up and looked at Yozo sharply, no longer his friend but his commanding officer. 'Commander Yamaguchi and Navy Minister Arai will be in charge of the operation. They're an excitable pair. I need you there as a steadying influence – and to be my eyes and ears.'

When Yozo went down to the docks that afternoon, he found the seamen already on board, making final checks on the ships and going through their jobs again and again, ensuring everyone knew exactly what they had to do and where they should be.

He paced the *Kaiten*'s decks, getting to know the feel of the ship. Raised to flagship after the demise of the *Kaiyo Maru*, she was a paddle steamer with two masts and a funnel, a little smaller than the *Kaiyo Maru* had been but not by much, and equipped with thirteen of the new Prussian breech-loaders. He went from cannon to cannon, checking that all the parts were in good order, that there was an ample supply of shells and powder, that each man knew his job and that the rifling was not clogged up with lead.

When the three ships steamed out of Hakodate Bay the following day, the weather was mild but the wind was as strong as ever. Huge gusts whipped the waves into billows and it was all the men could do to keep the *Kaiten* on course as they sailed along, hugging the coast. A few hours into their journey, the *Banryu* and the *Takao* started to fall behind and finally the *Takao* hoisted a signal flag, a red diamond on a white square: 'Ship disabled. Engine trouble.' The *Banryu* had been driven out to sea by the wind and had disappeared from view.

On the *Kaiten*, the seamen turned and looked and a silence fell across the decks.

'What now?' muttered one young fellow. His skin was already leathery but beneath the tan Yozo could see he was not a day over sixteen. 'They expect us to carry on on our own?'

'Sure they do,' grunted another, jerking his head towards the officers standing on the captain's bridge. 'Those fellows don't turn back once they've set their minds on something.'

Yozo screwed up his eyes and peered up at the bridge. Captain Koga, the ship's captain, was there, conferring with the Commander and Navy Minister Arai. A moment later the Commander strode across the deck to where the militia were gathered in their sky-blue coats.

'Are you with me, lads?' he shouted. 'We'll show the southerners how to take back what's ours. It'll be a tough battle but we've fought tougher. We'll give those cowards something to think about!'

One against eight. The odds had worsened quite a bit, Yozo knew, but that only made the men all the more determined. He wished Enomoto were on board. With the Commander in charge there would be no turning back, no matter how great the odds.

At first light next morning, the *Kaiten* steamed into Miyako Bay, the American flag flying high on her mainmast. Eight great black warships lay there at anchor, bobbing gently on the calm blue water, each far bigger than the tiny ship Yozo was on. Among them the *Stonewall* lurked, long and low, like a sinister sea monster. Yozo looked at her and felt a stab of foreboding. She was a floating fortress, even more formidable than he remembered. Fast and deadly, 'like a snake among rabbits', he thought, remembering how the Dutch sailors he'd known had spoken of the fearsome ironclads.

But there was no life on the ships, no steam coming out of the funnels. Their sails were stowed, and there was not a single sailor at work on the decks. It was like a scene in a painting.

Yozo was relieved to see several ships flying foreign flags in the harbour as well. Maybe their ruse would work. He held his breath as the *Kaiten* nudged between the ships, heading straight for the *Stonewall*. Amazingly, no one seemed to pay them the slightest attention.

They were approaching the *Stonewall* at breakneck speed. Then, at the last moment, the men at the mainmast hauled down the American flag and ran up the flag of Ezo.

'*Banzai!*' the men shouted. '*Banzai! Banzai!*'

By now they were so close that Yozo could see the faces of the men who had rushed out on to the *Stonewall*'s deck. They were waving and pointing, opening their mouths to shout, though their yells were drowned by the thunder of the *Kaiten*'s engines. Then, as the *Kaiten* bore down on them, they scattered and ran.

'Now!' Yozo yelled, leaning over the bulwarks and thumping the railing in excitement. All they needed was to give the *Stonewall* a good blast of cannon fire, then her crew would flee and they'd be able to take her without a fight. He looked around, slapping his fist into his hand in impatience, waiting for the order to fire. But no order came. He cursed aloud. What the hell was the Commander doing?

The next moment there was a deafening crunch and the sound of metal ripping and wood cracking and Yozo was thrown with stunning force halfway across the deck. Around him, sailors and militiamen slammed into masts, cannons and launches. Gasping for breath, he scrambled to his feet and stumbled towards the bow. The *Kaiten* had smashed headlong into the massive iron hull of the *Stonewall* and her wooden bow was half stoved in, bristling with shards of torn metal and splinters of wood. Yozo leaned over the mangled bulwark. The bowsprit was entirely destroyed but as far as he could see the damage was above water level. At least she was still seaworthy.

Now at last came the order to fire. Half the men raced to the bulwarks and peppered the *Stonewall*'s deck with rifle fire. Militia and soldiers scrambled on to the bow, shouting, 'Let's go! Let's get 'em!'

Yozo could see at a glance that boarding the *Stonewall* was going to be far more difficult than they'd thought. In all their planning no one had foreseen that the *Stonewall*'s deck would be well below the *Kaiten*'s, added to which the men had to jump from the damaged prow, which meant that only a few could leap at a time. Above the crackle of rifle fire, alarm bells rang out on the *Stonewall* as southern soldiers burst out of the hatches and charged across her deck, some still pulling on their uniforms. Through the smoke Yozo saw the first group of boarders jump, but the southerners cut them all down before they had a chance to draw their swords or ready their rifles.

Another wave of men jumped, only to fall straight on to the spears and swords of the southerners. Yozo could hear Arai and Captain Koga on the captain's bridge, yelling, 'On! On! Board! Board!' The Commander was striding up and down the deck, his eyes burning, his hair flying, urging the men on.

Yozo ran across the deck from cannon to cannon, checking that the men were all at their places and everything was in good order, then put his hands to his mouth and yelled, 'Fire!' There was an enormous boom and a pall of smoke covered the *Stonewall*'s deck. When it cleared he could see that it was strewn with dead and wounded. Then the *Kaiten* turned her cannons on the other warships. By now the enemy warships were beginning to return fire. The sky was black with smoke, the sea pocked with falling cannonballs and shot and the air was full of the choking smell of gunpowder.

Shells smashed across the *Kaiten*'s decks. Men fell silently, eyes glazing; others staggered about with arms or shoulders spurting blood. The young lad who had hung on to the wheel of the *Kaiyo Maru* so bravely in the storm when they were on their way to Ezo was standing near Yozo. There was a boom and he staggered back, clutching his belly, blood oozing between his fingers. Yozo put his arm around him and held him as he gave a sigh, went limp and slipped to the ground. Another youth stumbled by, half his shoulder blown off. Deafened by the incessant noise, closing his ears to the boom and crackle of gunfire and the screams of the dying men behind him, Yozo focused on doing what he was trained to do – checking on the cannons, helping to load the shells, stepping in to take over whenever a man fell.

They battled on for a full hour until they saw steam beginning to drift from the funnels of the enemy warships as the crews stoked their engines. Before they were ready to give chase, the *Kaiten* gave a last blast of cannon fire, backed away from the *Stonewall*, then swept round and steamed out of the harbour.

Hugging the coast, they headed back towards Ezo. Listing heavily, the damaged ship limped through the waves but the wind filled their sails and the engines were running at full steam. The men still on their feet stared around in relief, panting, breaking into smiles and slapping each other on the back, their faces streaked with sweat and dirt and gunpowder. Half were bloodied but they grinned and cheered. Every enemy soldier killed was a reason to rejoice. They had taken on eight warships and managed to get out of the harbour without being sunk, defeated or captured. The enemy had not even managed to get up enough steam to pursue them. There was good cause for celebration.

The Commander strutted up and down the deck in his leather boots. He was wearing a black jerkin that flew out in the wind, revealing the crimson lining, and his oiled locks blew around his face. 'Well done, boys,' he shouted, his eyes sparkling. 'We showed them what we could do!'

Yozo wiped his sleeve across his forehead. The wounded were strewn across the deck, sprawled among the corpses, some in black jackets, some in blue, with human flesh scattered around them like chunks of meat. The wooden planks were sticky with blood and the air full of the dreadful stench of death. Worst of all, they had had to leave their brave comrades, the survivors among those who had boarded the *Stonewall*, in the hands of the enemy.

He shook his head. They'd made an all-out effort to take the offensive, instead of sitting and waiting for the southerners to come and pick them off. Had they succeeded in capturing the *Stonewall* they would have had a fighting chance of turning the tide and keeping the enemy at bay. But they'd failed, and now there was nothing for it but to return to Ezo, shore up their defences and wait for the enemy fleet to arrive.

The *Kaiten* had barely dropped anchor in Hakodate Bay the next morning when Yozo was summoned to report to Enomoto. He could hear him pacing up and down before he even reached the presidential quarters. He slid open the door. Enomoto was in military uniform, his hair gleaming, his buttons glinting and his sword jutting out at his side.

'So the Commander failed us,' he snapped, a vein bulging on his temple. 'The great warrior forgot to give the order to fire till it was too late. Forgot to give the order . . . !'

He reached into the drinks cabinet and poured Yozo a whisky. Their eyes met for a moment, then Enomoto's face softened and he shook his head. 'So what happened? It's not like the Commander to make a mistake – certainly not one as costly as this.'

Yozo had thought through the events of the previous day again and again, trying to work out why the Commander had failed to give the vital command to fire when the *Kaiten* was charging towards the *Stonewall*. Then he'd remembered how he'd burst into the Commander's rooms on the night Kitaro died and found him writing his death poem. '*I will fight the best battle of my life and die for my country*,' he had told him. '*What greater glory could a man ask?*'

'He's convinced that we'll lose,' Yozo said slowly. 'He doesn't think we've got a chance, so he's not even trying any more.'

'In that case why in the name of all the gods did he propose this fools' expedition?'

Yozo shrugged. 'Maybe he wasn't thinking in terms of gaining command of the seas; maybe he saw it more as a suicide charge and that's why he didn't give the order to fire. He wanted us to ram the *Stonewall* and die gloriously.'

Enomoto breathed out hard. 'A *banzai* attack in the great samurai tradition,' he said. 'Charge out, yelling like madmen, take on the enemy against overwhelming odds and die with honour.' He frowned, thinking it through. 'But we have bigger ambitions than just to die. We've established the Republic of Ezo. The southerners have the numbers and the might, but we have ideas and ideals.'

'Yes, but it's survival of the fittest, and the southerners are fitter and have far greater numbers than we do.' Yozo stared at the Dutch carpet, remembering how he and Enomoto had sat here with Kitaro, reminiscing about their travels abroad. And the next day Kitaro had been killed. He still thought about his friend and missed his good humour and bitterly resented his death – and he hadn't forgotten his promise to avenge him one day, when the war was over.

'He was a good man, young Kitaro,' Enomoto said quietly, nodding. 'I miss him too. We have to make sure we win this war so he won't have died for nothing.'

18

The last of the cherry blossoms had fallen and the wild lilies and azaleas were bursting into bloom. The hills around the Star Fort had turned brilliant green, splashed with clumps of wild flowers blazing pink, yellow, blue and purple. Flocks of geese filled the sky, sea eagles swooped and innumerable birds, of varieties Yozo had never seen before, warbled, twittered and peeped.

But there was little time to marvel at Ezo's vast skies and the wildlife that roamed its hills and forests. Along with everyone else, he was busy night and day, directing operations as squads of men shovelled earth to shore up the city's defences, set up gun emplacements overlooking the harbour and built a stockade fence across the isthmus, preparing for the invasion which they all knew was coming. Enomoto had sent troops along the coast to bolster the garrisons at Esashi, where the *Kaiyo Maru* had sunk, and at Matsumae with its burnt-out castle, which the Commander had captured with chilling efficiency five months earlier. But the largest concentration of troops was posted at the Star Fort to defend the bay and the city of Hakodate. The city was like a ghost town. Everyone who could had fled.

Then, as spring turned into summer, reports began to arrive that the southern fleet was on its way. Not long afterwards, news came that the enemy had taken Esashi.

Yozo was on his way back to the fort one fine morning after his daily tour of the defences, when a soldier galloped past him, his ragged uniform flying in the wind. Yozo hurried after him to Enomoto's office and was taking off his straw sandals when his friend came out, waving a dispatch. Yozo could tell by his face the news was bad.

'So Matsumae's fallen,' he said.

Enomoto nodded grimly. 'Our men put up a brave struggle. They ran out of cannonballs and ended up filling the eighteen-pounder guns with twelve-pound shot, but none of it did any good.'

'Did we lose a lot of men?'

'Too many. The survivors fled to the next village along the coast and set up their line of defence there, but they won't be able to hold out for ever. It won't be long now before the fleet arrives.'

Six days later, on a warm summer morning, alarm bells rang out across the town. Eight warships had been seen on the horizon, steaming straight for the city. Enomoto had left the Star Fort, which was inland, and set up his headquarters in Kamida Fort, strategically placed right at the mouth of the harbour. Yozo was there with him, watching through his telescope as the eight ships approached, led by the *Stonewall*, a long grey sliver surging low in the water. The three surviving ships of the northern fleet – the *Kaiten*, the *Chiyoda* and the *Banryu*, which had managed to return safely – shuttled back and forth, guns blazing, trying to keep the enemy fleet from entering the bay. The *Takao* had put in to land after she suffered engine failure and her crew had been captured, and two other ships had been lost in the battles to defend Matsumae and Esashi.

'I should be out there with them,' said Yozo, scowling and clenching his fists.

'I need you here with me,' said Enomoto. 'We have to plan our strategy.'

As evening closed in, Yozo watched as a white flash ripped open the sky, followed by a boom like thunder. A pall of black smoke spread across the water as one of their three ships staggered to a halt.

'The *Chiyoda*'s disabled,' yelled Yozo. 'Looks like she's taken a shot to her engines.'

'We'll have the other ships tug her in close to the fort,' said Enomoto. 'As long as the guns still work we can use her for defence.'

The two looked at each other. They'd lost a lot of their men already and now one of their ships was out of action. Then there was a boom right overhead and a shell slammed into the grounds of Kamida Fort. Men raced around with buckets of water putting out fires.

Enomoto and Yozo and their men managed to keep the enemy at bay for another couple of days but finally the southern fleet laid siege to the town. Enemy warships filled the harbour, spewing fire and destruction. For the ragged remnants of the northern army, the only strategy now was to defend themselves to the last gasp as the net closed tighter and tighter.

It was a glorious afternoon in early summer as Yozo ducked behind an earthwork overlooking the harbour and took cover there. His face was black with soot and his hands were burnt. There was a taste of gunpowder in his mouth and a thick growth of beard on his chin. He hadn't washed for days. He had become a fighting machine. He aimed, he fired, he reloaded. He aimed, he fired, he reloaded. When his rifle barrel became too hot to hold, he dunked it in a bucket of water to cool it.

The men jammed in beside him fired round after round. Shell after shell shrieked over their heads and smashed into the grounds of the fort, while around them the pile of mangled limbs and bodies grew ever larger. No one could take breath long enough to bury the dead and the stench of decaying corpses filled the air and stuck in everyone's nostrils. Yozo flung himself down as another shell screamed over his head, then clambered to his feet and carried on firing.

When night fell, he stayed where he was, snatching a few hours' sleep on the ground beside his fellow soldiers. Then, as the sun rose the following morning, casting a brilliant light on the ruined battlements and the blades of grass poking out of the trampled mud around him, he saw that some of his comrades had taken advantage of the lull to begin hastily digging a mass grave and realized something strange had happened. The harbour was completely silent.

Looking over the earthworks, he saw that the enemy warships had pulled back as if by some prearranged plan. He straightened up and watched, puzzled, as a ship flying the French flag appeared at the harbour mouth. As far as he knew, the French were on their side, but the ship steamed straight in without any interference from the southern ships occupying the bay.

He turned as Marlin pushed in beside him, put his telescope to his eye, then lowered it, scowling. '*Merde!*' he muttered. 'Cowards.'

A series of messages flashed back and forth between the ships and the land, then a launch left the French ship and sped across the bay. From where Yozo stood, it looked like a water bug.

Of the nine French officers, three had been killed or captured and Sergeant Cazeneuve was gravely wounded. Incredulous, Yozo looked on as Captain Brunet and three French colleagues pushed their way through the soldiers crowding the waterfront, stepping on corpses as they went. One held the French flag aloft, another waved a large white flag. As they carried Sergeant Cazeneuve across on a stretcher, Yozo caught a glimpse of his white face and long limbs swathed in grubby bandages. They loaded him into the launch, then climbed in themselves.

Yozo watched with a mixture of rage and foreboding. So their French friends had given up on them and were fleeing. In that case, their cause must be truly hopeless.

Captain Brunet stood up in the stern, a small, elegant, moustachioed figure, swaying back and forth as the boat gently rocked. Facing the earthworks where Yozo and Marlin stood, he waved, then put his hands to his mouth and shouted. His words drifted clearly across the water.

'Marlin! *Venez! Vite, vite!*'

Marlin turned his head firmly from side to side.

'Go on! It's your chance,' said Yozo. 'Why should you die for our cause? There's no dishonour. Leave, take your chance. Go!'

Marlin put his hand on Yozo's shoulder. 'I belong here,' he said. 'Those bastards – let them flee. There's nothing for me in France, just the guillotine.'

Yozo swallowed. Marlin was stubborn, as stubborn as any Japanese, he thought, and as driven by honour. The two men stood side by side and watched as the launch shuttled across the bay and the tiny black figures climbed on to the French ship.

With the French gone, the northerners prepared themselves for the end. Yozo had lost track of how long they'd been fighting. He only knew that as long as he was alive he had to carry on. In the grounds of the fort a single azalea bush bloomed, fragile clumps of pink blossom on the rocky terrain. What had been a grassy knoll had turned into a field of churned earth. The sun blistered down on his leather helmet. Summer had come with a vengeance.

On the twentieth day of the siege, the enemy attacked before dawn, hammering the city and the forts with shell fire. By now there was little left of the town apart from charred wooden beams jutting from piles of rubble.

Suddenly Yozo noticed that the great gun at the eastern angle of Kamida Fort was silent. The soldiers manning it had fallen and lay crumpled on the ground.

'Marlin! Over here!' he shouted.

Together he and Marlin climbed over the broken wall of the fort, stumbled towards the cannon, loaded it and turned it on the ironclad and the other warships. The ships turned their fire full on the small fort but they carried on loading and firing, ignoring the shells that rained down on them, somehow managing to fight on.

Yozo had sent a shell screaming out across the water when there was a boom like a thunderclap, resounding off the mountains. Out in the bay a plume of flame shot high into the air, followed by a column of dense black smoke laden with fragments and debris. He stared, baffled, then laughed out loud. He'd managed a direct hit, right into the magazine of an enemy ship.

He watched in amazement as the ship went straight down, sucking water around her in a massive bubbling whirlpool that swung like a serpent's tail, threatening to drag the other ships down with her, and tossing up huge waves that smashed on to the shore. Only her bowsprit and foremast were left poking out of the water. Bodies bobbed in the swell. Some of the crew, still alive, clung on to spars and rigging or struck out for shore, thrashing desperately. Smoke filled the sky, casting harbour and town into darkness as black as if twilight had fallen.

Yozo and Marlin slapped each other on the back and their yells of triumph were taken up by the men watching from the shore.

But their joy was short-lived. Not long afterwards there was a roar from behind them. Enemy troops had scaled the near-vertical flank of Mount Hakodate, which formed a natural defence behind the town, and were swarming down its slopes. The northerners were hemmed in on all sides. For a while they managed to keep the enemy at bay, but the southerners closed in tighter and tighter until they had pushed Yozo, Marlin and the remnants of the northern army right to the waterfront. There they fought hand to hand with swords, pikes and bayonets, anything they could find, until the ground was slippery with blood. There were corpses everywhere – northerners, southerners, some freshly dead, some already bloated. Men lay on the ground or flopped across rocks and walls wherever they had fallen.

Through the smoke Yozo caught a glimpse of Commander Yamaguchi striding through the enemy ranks with an expression so fearsome that even the hardened southern soldiers hesitated and drew back in fear. One after another they stepped into his path to intercept him, but with a sweep of his sword he cut them down. No one seemed to dare shoot at him, or if they did the bullets went wide of the mark.

As evening fell there was a massive boom as the *Kaiten*, the only one of the northerners' ships still afloat, exploded. She glowed white like the belly of a furnace, blazing with a ferocious heat and casting a garish light across the broken houses and ruined streets of the city. Fires dotted the town and Mount Hakodate, rising behind, was completely hidden in a dense pall of smoke.

Deafened by the gunfire and the clash and clang of swords, the thunder of shells exploding and the war cries mingled with the screams of the dying, Yozo laid about him with his sword and rifle butt. Finally he broke through the southerners' ranks and, trampling on corpses as he went, stumbled through the empty streets in pursuit of a sniper.

The crumbling ruins cast long shadows as he ducked between them, climbing over piles of rubble. Flies buzzed and the air was thick with ash. Yozo's clothes were in rags and he was covered in cuts and bruises, his ears ringing from the noise of battle, but he was aware of nothing but the need to find and kill the sniper.

Catching a glimpse of a shadow loping between two broken walls, he raced around the corner to confront him then stopped, his heart thundering, as he came face to face with the man and realized it was not the enemy sniper after all. The two stood looking at each other on the deserted street.

'Tajima!'

Yozo heard Commander Yamaguchi's hoarse shout clearly above the roar of the battle. The Commander's face was contorted and filthy, streaked with blood and blackened with dirt and gunpowder, and Yozo knew that he must look just as demented himself.

'Our time has come, Tajima,' the Commander growled. 'Today we die in the service of the shogun. We may as well have it out like men and go to the next world together.' He stared at him disdainfully. 'I should cut you down for the way you humiliated my man with your foreign trickery, but you're not even worth bloodying my sword for.'

The sun was setting, huge and red, and bats swooped low over Yozo's head. He could see the street with its ruined buildings stretching away behind the Commander, silhouetted there with his burning eyes. The explosions and gunfire faded into the distance.

Blinded with rage and hatred, he pictured Kitaro's body on the moonlit ground. His blood was roaring in his ears. He knew that if the Commander went for his sword he would kill him instantly and Kitaro would never be avenged. He fumbled for a cartridge, pushed it into his rifle and set it to his shoulder.

For a moment he hesitated, his finger on the trigger. To fire on one of his own commanding officers was a capital offence. He'd be shamed, court-martialled and sentenced to death. But the war was over and they were all going to die anyway. He reminded himself that the Commander had executed many of his own men. He saw the list of rules in the training hall, all ending with death by ritual suicide. If the Commander fell, all his men had to go down with him; that had been the most blood-chilling of all.

Still Yozo couldn't bring himself to pull the trigger. But then Kitaro's dead face swam before his eyes. He had promised to avenge him, he had given his word, and the duty of revenge took priority over all others. It was a matter of honour. He would shoot the Commander down like a dog, as brutally as Kitaro had been killed.

Yozo tightened his finger on the trigger. There was a bang, deafeningly loud, a plume of smoke puffed out of the barrel and the butt slammed into his shoulder as the rifle recoiled.

Through the smoke he saw the Commander lurch, his eyes and mouth open and blood spurting from his stomach. Slowly he stumbled backwards and his arms flew out. For a moment his eyes met Yozo's and Yozo fancied he saw a look on the Commander's face, a look almost of surprise. Then he staggered and crashed to the ground. Yozo heard the thump as he fell.

Shaking, Yozo ran towards him. He wanted to check that he was really dead. Then a bullet whistled past Yozo's ear and he swung round and caught a glimpse of a black uniform and a conical helmet. It was the southern sniper he'd been searching for.

Yozo knew he should raise his rifle, but he no longer cared whether he lived or died. The Commander's death poem echoed in his ears: *'Though my body may decay on the island of Ezo . . .'* He'd stayed alive all these months knowing that he had to avenge Kitaro's death. But he'd done that now and he could die with honour.

Yozo turned to face the enemy guns and, as he did so, he saw the events of his life pass before his eyes. Yes, he thought, this was how it was meant to be. He would die here beside the Commander and his body too would decay on the island of Ezo.

Summer

19

Hana braced the toes of her right foot against the thong of her clog and lifted it a little, testing the weight. The huge heavy clogs were like shiny black hooves, raising her so tall she could see over the heads of everyone around her. Outside she heard the murmur of the crowd, the chink of the iron rings at the top of the firemen's staffs as they struck them on the ground and their hoarse shouts, 'Stand back, stand back! Make way for Hanaogi of the Corner Tamaya!'

She was perfectly painted, from the petal of red on her lower lip to her white-powdered hands and feet. Her toenails were stained with safflower juice a delicate shade of pink, her hair was oiled and padded and moulded into an enormous halo, split like a peach, with silken tassels swinging at the back, and her head-dress, spiked with tortoiseshell and silver hairpins and dangling mother-of-pearl ornaments, was so heavy it made her neck ache. Inside the sumptuous kimonos her chest prickled with the heat, but she was barely aware of it. There was something else on her mind.

'Are you sure it'll be all right?' she whispered, throwing a last desperate glance at Tama, who was straightening her obi. Tama was dressed in lavish kimonos exactly like Hana's, with a brocade coat over the top embroidered with a white crane on the shoulder and a silver and gold tortoise across the back and skirts.

'Yes, of course. Just concentrate on your figure eight.' Tama smiled, momentarily revealing the black-painted teeth in the white face. 'Do exactly as I taught you.'

'What is it?' wheezed Auntie. She too was in her best kimono, an elegant black silk affair with a red obi. Her eyes were startlingly yellow in her chalky face, her lips a livid slash of red.

'As always,' said Tama. 'What to do when he finds out . . .'

The old woman drew back her lips in a smile and patted Hana's arm.

'Don't you worry about that, my dear,' she cooed. 'He'll be so excited he won't even notice. They never do.'

'Just make sure he has a good time,' said Tama. 'Do everything I taught you and you'll do well. Enough worrying. It's time to go.'

The door slid open and a hot damp breeze wafted in, bringing with it enticing smells of grilling sparrows and roasting eel, charcoal and woodsmoke, and the scent of the purple irises that bloomed along the central boulevard. The child attendants adjusted their faces and stepped solemnly out, Chidori carrying Hana's smoking set in a silk cloth in her plump hand and Namiji holding her writing materials. The four attendants, Kawanoto and Kawayu, plump smiling Kawagishi and willowy Kawanagi, followed in height order, smallest first, in identical red kimonos. After a suitable pause Tama strutted out on her enormous clogs, quilted hems swinging.

Auntie tugged Hana's collars, straightened the bow of her obi and adjusted the hems of her kimonos. 'Remember, take your time,' she said. 'Keep your head high. Make them look up to you!'

Lifting her skirts with her left hand, Hana rested her right on the shoulder of one of the menservants, took a breath and stepped out into the steamy air. There were gasps and the sound of breath being drawn in, then utter silence. The men gazed at her, rapt. Hana surveyed them through her lashes – the shiny shaven pates, the gleaming topknots, the wide eyes and jaws gaping open. She might be a chattel to be sold to the highest bidder, she thought, but she would never let them see the smallest hint of anger or pain. She would make them look up to her, just as Auntie had said. She drew herself up and looked straight ahead. Every movement, every gesture, had to be perfect.

Hana had practised the figure-eight walk until her legs were aching and her feet rubbed raw by the thongs of her clogs. It had been hard enough to learn to balance on the tall unwieldy footwear, let alone to make every step graceful and seductive, to swivel her foot provocatively and let her body sway as she moved; and this was the first time she'd had to do it for real.

Now she tilted her right foot till the clog was nearly on its side, kicked it out and traced a wide semicircle in the dust. In the silence she could hear the inner edge scraping along the ground. Her skirts opened, allowing the onlookers a glimpse of a slim white ankle and a flash of crimson crêpe de chine, before the heavy fabric fell back into place. She planted her foot in front of her, turning it out like the character for eight. Then she took a breath, rocked delicately back and forward, and, with a toss of her shoulder and hip, she kicked out her left clog, dragged it around in an arc and brought it up to join the right.

Beside her, Tama promenaded with the same fantastic gait. Chidori and Namiji progressed in front like two little boats tugging two great ships, with a flotilla of attendants and servants bringing up the rear. There were menservants in front and behind. One carried a huge lantern with the peony crest of the Corner Tamaya, two held oiled parasols over Hana's and Tama's heads, while others pushed back the crowd and scurried about clearing twigs and dead leaves from the path.

Hana breathed the moist air of the summer evening, lost herself in the beat of the drum, the jangle of the rings on the firemen's staffs, the murmur of the crowd. Raised on her clogs, she could look out over the sea of heads to the rows of red lanterns glowing along the eaves, making the street as bright as day. From below came awed whispers. 'It's Hanaogi, Hanaogi. As beautiful as a dream.'

The procession made its way from the Corner Tamaya along Edo-cho 1 through the gate at the end of the street, then along the grand boulevard to the Chrysanthemum Teahouse, by the Great Gate. On a normal day Hana could run there in a moment or two but today it took her an hour.

From the teahouses along the boulevard came the twang of shamisens, the chink of sake cups and the sound of singing and laughter. Men's voices mingled with the high-pitched tones of women and people crowded the balconies, staring down at the procession.

At the door of the Chrysanthemum Teahouse servants helped Hana down from her clogs. Mitsu was waiting on her hands and knees. 'Welcome, welcome,' she cried.

Hana smiled at her. In the months since they had first met, Hana had attended many parties at the teahouse and often sat on the bench outside in the daytime when there were no clients around, enjoying a pipe. They were old friends now.

Ushering the party into the shady hallway, Mitsu slid open a door. Chidori and Namiji went in first, bobbing politely. The attendants filed in next, then Tama swept in. Kneeling outside in the hallway, Hana heard her voice, loud and clear: 'Gentlemen, please welcome our new star courtesan: Hanaogi!'

Keeping her eyes lowered, Hana slipped in.

She was in a banqueting hall glimmering with gold and lit by sputtering candles in huge golden candlesticks. Men sat cross-legged at low tables overflowing with dishes of food and flasks of sake, their faces flushed. Geishas and a couple of jesters sat among them.

Right in the middle was the man who had paid for the whole celebration, the man who would be her patron for the night. Hana smiled as she saw the broad face and sensual mouth. His slanting eyes were fixed on her with a look of naked desire.

It was strange to think that she knew him far better than she ever had her own husband. They had sat together over sake and talked; he had told her she was beautiful and had been kind to her and brought her presents – rolls of kimono fabric, luxurious bedding. He had even asked her about herself, though she had been careful to give only the vaguest of answers. He was not handsome in a classical way, she realized, but he was obviously brilliant and ambitious. He had an appealing energy about him and he was young, only a few years older than her. And as she knew, he was a southerner, though little by little his dialect had begun to sound softer to her ears.

Until now, Hana had always thought of the conquerors of their city as brutish uncultured men. She had told herself that the war would soon come to an end and they would all be gone. But the news only grew worse and worse. No one came looking for her; no one arrived to claim her, redeem her debt and take her away. And they were good clients, these southerners. They booked her; they paid their bills.

There was only one worry. This man had paid for her virginity, but he would soon discover that she was not a virgin at all. 'It's the same with everyone,' Tama had told her. 'Women sell their virginity again and again. For him it's enough to be known as the first patron of a famous courtesan.' Still, she wondered how he would feel when he discovered; and she hoped she would remember everything Tama had taught her.

It seemed an interminable length of time before Tama finished smoothing her skirts and raised a red-lacquered saucer full to the brim with sake. 'Well, gentlemen, this is indeed an auspicious day,' she trilled. 'Here's to Masaharu-sama, our host, and the new courtesan of the Corner Tamaya, Hanaogi!'

Men, courtesans, geishas and jesters raised red saucers and downed the cold sake. 'Masaharu-sama! Lucky fellow!' one shouted. 'Make the best of it!' yelled another.

One of the guests stood up and made a speech about how Masaharu's military exploits and brilliant career faded to nothing when compared to his conquest of the loveliest courtesan ever to be seen in the Yoshiwara. He rambled on, swaying and slurring his words, his eyes like slits in his puffy face.

Masaharu shuffled impatiently. He too was flushed. Perhaps he had drunk so much he would fall asleep as soon as the meal was over, Hana thought. She didn't know if she would be pleased or sorry.

At long last the banquet was over and Hana was back in her chamber at the Corner Tamaya. Her attendants removed her headdress and hairpins and dressed her in a thin, almost transparent night garment, tying the silken obi so that it would come undone easily, and tucking sheets of folded paper tissues into the belt.

She hesitated for a moment and took a deep breath, then slid open the door of the bedroom. Masaharu was leaning on an armrest, sipping sake and smoking a pipe with a long silver stem. The kimonos she had worn that evening were draped on racks around the room, shimmering with gold and silver, and the wadded damask bedding and black velvet coverlet were laid out. A couple of lamps burned. He held out his hand as she closed the door behind her.

'Never has a man persisted so long with only the reward of seeing your beautiful face!' he said, stretching out his long slender fingers. She was aware of the faint scent of his skin, his tawny high-boned face, the excitement that burned in his eyes. 'You've enchanted me.'

She stood looking down at him, aware of the picture she made with her slender body enfolded not by layers of heavy fabric but only the diaphanous silk gauze of the long, loose night robe.

'I know how it is with you men,' she said teasingly. 'You love to hunt but once you've captured the deer . . .'

'Ah, but you're not just any deer . . .'

He reached up and tugged her obi and her robe fell open, then grabbed her hands and pulled her down on top of him. Laughing, she tried to resist but he was too powerful for her. He rolled over and put his mouth to hers and she felt a tingle run through her, as of something awakening deep inside her. She realized she'd never before felt the soft touch of lips on hers or known how arousing it could be. Whenever she had lain with her husband it had been a peremptory affair which took place late at night, in the dark. She'd always hoped it would be over quickly and lain waiting for him to slump on top of her and push her aside. She had never imagined it could be like this.

'Let me look at you,' said Masaharu. He tugged down the collar of her robe and began to lick and nibble the soft skin at the nape of her neck.

'I can't believe I have you to myself,' he whispered. He licked her throat and chest, then put his lips to her nipple. She quivered and closed her eyes as he brushed his hand along the inside of her soft white thighs. Tama had taught her how to fake pleasure but tonight she knew she wouldn't need to.

Gently he pushed her legs apart. She was glad she kept her hair neatly plucked and clipped. Tama had told her that a man could tell the degree of a woman's sexual skill by the way her hair was trimmed and she knew by the sureness of his touch that Masaharu was an adept.

She felt the warmth of his breath as he gazed, murmuring, 'Beautiful, like a rose,' then began softly stroking and tugging and pressing, exploring every crevice until he found her tenderest place, which no one but she had ever touched before.

'The precious jewel,' he whispered, and as she felt his tongue lapping, licking up the juices that welled out, she remembered Tama saying that men thought of a woman's juices as the elixir of life. Then a spasm overtook her, blotting out her thoughts, surging through her until she no longer knew what he was doing and making her cry out in a voice she hardly recognized as her own.

After a while she raised herself on her elbow and brushed her fingers across Masaharu's slim young body, admiring his smooth skin and firm muscles. Remembering Tama's lessons, she ran her tongue down his chest and across his nipples, tasting the salt, enjoying his groans of delight. Then she took his penis in her mouth – the Jade Stalk, Tama had called it – and began to lick and suck it, playing it like an instrument, drawing out his pleasure, hearing him groan as she brought him close to release, then pausing before bringing him close again.

Finally she climbed on top of him and began to move and felt the hot spurt inside her as his body arched and he let out a shout.

'You're too cruel,' he groaned, panting. 'I wanted to conserve my seed. Now we'll just have to start all over again.'

Laughing, she flung her arms around him. The night was just beginning.

20

A month had passed since Hana had made her début. She was expected to accept clients for more than just sake and chit-chat now, but there were other more subtle changes. People treated her differently and she felt different too. She carried herself with a new confidence. Admittedly she was a prisoner with a debt to repay and there were clients she would have preferred not to sleep with, but that was a woman's lot. There had been no delight in sleeping with her husband either. Now, when she looked back at her old life, she felt as if she had been even more of a prisoner then.

Hana loved the early afternoons when there were no clients around and she could sit with her hair carelessly tied in a knot, in a thin summer kimono, fanning herself and smoking a pipe or sipping iced tea from a thick ceramic beaker. As soon as she had bathed and dressed on this steamy summer day, she strolled around the corner to Otsuné's house. As she ambled along she thought back to what Otsuné had said the day after her début.

They had been downing chilled buckwheat noodles which Otsuné had bought from a passing vendor, dunking them by the chopstickful into small cups of dipping sauce spiced with horse-radish and scallions and consuming them with a slurp.

'Auntie's proud of you,' she had said. 'Business had gone down badly at the Corner Tamaya – all over the quarter, in fact – but now you've brought it back to life. Men love you, that's what

Tama says. You were wasted being a wife and hiding your talents away.'

'I only have a few clients,' Hana had replied, smiling. 'Auntie said I was to say No as often as I liked and make them wait as long as I liked.'

'That way they'll want you more and more, so your price will rise and Auntie'll make more and more money,' Otsuné reminded her sternly. 'It's all to do with money, don't forget that.'

Hana smiled to herself. The air was hot and humid and the sun beat down on her. Bamboo screens hung all along the upper storeys to keep the interiors shady and cool. She could hear the tinkle of wind chimes and smell the flowers planted along the Yoshiwara's lanes. On the street everyone bowed to her as she passed.

She had been fortunate, she realized that now, but she knew that her success as a courtesan depended on maintaining her mystique. As long as she remained out of reach, she could enjoy the sort of life Tama had, but the moment her allure faded her life would be over. To bob along like a paper boat on a stream, oblivious to the sludge on the bottom – to the grimness of life outside the city walls: that was the floating world. Here in the Nightless City, she and her fellow courtesans lived a gilded storybook existence where time stood still. That was the reason men came, to forget the harsh reality on the other side of the wall, beyond the Moat of Black Teeth.

There were plenty of men eager to spend whatever it cost for a few hours with the new star courtesan. Some were old with seamed faces and floppy bodies, but so witty and amusing that she saw them again and again. Others just wanted to chat or have her hold them and cuddle them as if she was their mother. One high-flying government official told her his woes and cried like a baby.

Hana picked and chose among them and a few became her lovers. Some were sexual virtuosos, eager to try different techniques, energetically twisting their limbs into every possible position, determined at all costs not to spill their seed. Others wanted to explore every orifice or ordered an extra woman or a boy. Some brought manuals and made sure they tried everything. But most just wanted to enjoy themselves.

She was careful to follow Tama's instructions to avoid conceiving a child. She knew the times of month when she was most likely to fall pregnant and refused to sleep with customers on those days, or put folded paper tissues inside herself as a protection. She had also had moxa herbs burnt on her belly for two successive days, a procedure which was supposed to provide protection for the following year. She knew that most of the serving staff and many of the courtesans were children of women of the quarter; but she also heard of women who died in childbirth or in clumsy attempts to terminate the pregnancy and, all in all, pregnancy was to be avoided as far as possible.

Some of her lovers Hana liked more, some she liked less, but she never forgot Otsuné's warning that it was just a game, nothing to do with romance or deep-seated feeling but only with fun, with sensation; and above all she remembered never, never, to lose her heart to anyone. It was all to do with bodies, not hearts, she told herself. And of course it was always a commercial transaction and the exchange of money coloured the whole relationship.

The men who paid to spend time with her – the older ones among them, at least – knew as well as she did that when she said she loved and adored them and that they were the only man for her, they were paying her to say so. They knew that she was acting and she said the same to every man. Nevertheless, some of the younger men were so dazzled by her that they fell entirely under her spell and bankrupted themselves in order to see her as often as they could.

Hana knew that for all these men the Yoshiwara was a fantasy place, where they could escape from the dull world of wife, children, house and job. All the men had wives, of course; but with her they could behave entirely differently. Their wives were chosen for them by their families and they had to keep a proper distance, but with her they could relax – tease, laugh, flirt and behave like little boys. They didn't have to maintain their dignity or worry about how they appeared in public. They were paying for the freedom to be anything they wanted. No one was under any illusion, which was what made the game so perfect.

When Masaharu asked for her, she always made sure she was available and reminded herself that for him too it was only a game – though sometimes she caught herself wishing that things could have been different.

Now Hana slid open the door of Otsuné's little house, making the flimsy wooden slats grind and judder in their grooves, and stepped inside, snuffing the smells of burnt hair and dye appreciatively. Otsuné was always busy about something. She had a spinning wheel and a loom at the back of the house and when she was not cleaning her tools or working on a wig she would be carding or spinning or weaving.

But today the house was silent. The loom was not clacking and the charcoal in the brazier had gone out. Otsuné was at her table in the middle of the room, her head in her hands. She looked up as Hana came in. Her face was pale and her eyes swollen and red.

'What is it?' gasped Hana, rushing to her side, then stopped as she saw the newspaper on the table. She knew the new government had outlawed newspapers because they supported the northern side and that the most outspoken editor had been arrested and put into prison. No one had any idea any more what was going on.

For a moment Hana dared not even look, then she knelt, gripping the edge of the table to support her, and stared at the tiny characters uncomprehendingly.

'A French ship has arrived at Yokohama,' whispered Otsuné, dabbing her eyes with her sleeve.

Hana looked at her in astonishment.

'Does that mean . . . it's all over?'

Though it was a hot day, she shivered. If the war really was over, it could only mean that their men had lost and the southerners had won. It would also mean that she'd find out what had become of her husband. The thought of him made her recoil with fear. Suppose he came looking for her and found her here in the Yoshiwara? He wouldn't stop to ask why she had ended up here. He would kill her, that was for sure.

Otsuné's hands were shaking. She looked helpless and lost, so unlike herself that Hana felt even more afraid.

'These names are so difficult.' Otsuné's voice was dull with despair. 'I've been trying to decipher them. It says there are prisoners on board – the French who fought with our men. Not all were captured; some were killed.' She was staring at the tiny print. 'No, not captured, they surrendered. They say terrible things about them. See, it says here: "The French cowards abandoned the northern troops . . ." How could they say that? It's not true. They're brave, loyal men: they stayed with their men and fought with them when they could easily have left and gone back to their own country. Now it says they're to be sent back to France and put on trial. I suppose they'll be ordered to commit harakiri or whatever they do in France.'

She laid her head on her arms. 'I keep going through this list of names but I can't find his. It's so terrible not to know,' she whispered.

'Your patron . . .' Hana gasped, suddenly realizing why Otsuné was so distressed.

'If he's dead I want to know,' Otsuné sobbed. 'I can't bear to think that he's somewhere in Ezo being eaten by animals. If he's dead he should be brought back here to be buried.'

'Your patron was a foreigner?'

'Yes.'

Hana stifled a gasp. She'd seen tall, gawky foreign sailors with pinkish faces and huge noses lumbering down the central boulevard in outlandish uniforms and turning off into the back alleys. They had a reputation for trouble-making and tended to head for the cheapest houses. She'd always thought it was only the lowest-class girls who accepted their business and she'd certainly never heard of anyone taking a foreigner as a patron.

Otsuné opened a drawer in one of the large chests along the wall of the room and brought out a small wooden box. She put it on the table, opened it up and took out a lock of pale brown hair. It lay on her palm like a skein of silk, not robust and strong like Japanese hair but rather fine and delicate.

'When I was at the Yamatoya foreigners used to come sometimes, though there weren't so many then. Military types, sailors. I remember I was in the cage one day – I'll never forget that day – and this man appeared, a big man with big round eyes. He was staring at me. I thought, Why me? All the men gawped at the other girls, the young ones, but he seemed to like me. Then he booked me. The other girls used to refuse foreigners because they were afraid of them and they didn't want to run the risk of their regular clients refusing to bed them because they'd been with a foreigner. But I wasn't in great demand so I said I'd lie with him. At first I was afraid too, but he was kind and gentle.

'After that, every time he came he asked for me. He looked grotesque to me too till I got used to him. It wasn't so much sex he wanted, but comfort and tenderness. He wanted to feel someone cared about him. And he could speak our language. He didn't bark at me or boss me around or hit me, he didn't behave like a man at all, and that made me like him more and more.

'Then he bought me my freedom. He said I should find a small house and he'd buy it for me. But then things got bad, as you know, and he was ordered to go back to his country, but he refused. He said he wanted to stay with the men he'd been training.'

Otsuné reached up to her collar and undid her clasp, then rested her elbows on the table and gazed at it, her hands trembling. For a moment she held it to her lips.

'One day he came to me and told me he was going away for a while. And he gave me this, the clasp he used to wear on his jacket. Then he cut off a lock of his hair and told me to keep it too. He also gave me money – all the money he had. And that was it. I never saw him again. And now I can't even find out whether he's alive or dead. I miss him so much – his big hands, his funny nose. I wish I could find his name here . . .'

She turned away, her face glistening with tears, and started fumbling with the teapot.

'Maybe he escaped,' Hana said. 'Maybe he's on his way back. Don't despair yet.'

'But they're tightening up on security,' Otsuné said, looking fearful. 'Haven't you noticed? People are being stopped outside the Great Gate. It can only mean that the war really is over and northern soldiers are on the run. You know as well as I do there's only one place where the police don't come – here, in the Yoshiwara. It's where everyone comes when they need somewhere to hide.'

Hana took her hands and stroked them. Perhaps Otsuné's patron was on his way here too. She hoped so.

Hana hurried through the gate at the entrance to Edo-cho 1, her eyes on the ground, her thoughts far away. By now it was late afternoon and the street was teeming with people. Women were already filing into the latticed parlours and here and there shamisens jangled. Men surged along the boulevard, gawping and whispering as she slipped by. Then little Chidori burst out of the Corner Tamaya, red sleeves flying, carrying a letter in her hand. She saw Hana and bowed, then flew off through the gate towards one of the teahouses, the bells on her sleeves tinkling.

The crowd fell silent and drew back as a couple of foreigners ambled by in their outlandish costumes. Hana looked at them curiously, remembering everything Otsuné had told her. It was hard to imagine lying with such strange-looking creatures, let alone coming to care for one.

She was about to push between the curtains of the Corner Tamaya when she noticed a young woman perching nervously on the bench outside. Her dress and hairstyle were those of a townswoman, though her kimono was rather bright and showy and her hair studded with hairpins. The woman turned towards her and blanched as if she had seen a ghost. Hana stared at her, puzzled. There was something familiar about her.

Then it all came rushing back and Hana turned and fled in horror. Footsteps pattered behind her and a hand gripped her sleeve. She gasped, back in the nightmare, on the Japan Dyke causeway, being dragged down the slope to the Yoshiwara.

'What do you want?' she cried, her voice shrill with panic. 'Leave me alone.'

'Hana-sama, Hana-sama,' said the woman. 'It's me, Fuyu.'

Hana shuddered, remembering the look Fuyu had given Auntie. She could still hear her words: '*I'm sure we can come to an arrangement.*' Then there had been the storehouse, the ropes, and the horror of realizing she'd been sold.

She swung round. The full face, wide-spaced eyes and shapely mouth were almost pretty, but Hana couldn't help seeing the cunning glint in Fuyu's eyes and the way she twisted her lips.

'Don't you remember me?' Fuyu demanded. 'It was me who brought you here.'

Hana wrenched her sleeve out of Fuyu's grip. 'You sold me!' she said. 'You took money!'

Fuyu stared at the ground. 'I didn't take money,' she mumbled. 'I helped you.'

Hana scowled in disbelief. 'I have nothing to say to you,' she said, beginning to walk towards the Corner Tamaya. But Fuyu pattered along beside her, chattering breathlessly.

'Don't you want to hear how things are in Edo? My master's a pawnbroker. People pawn things when times are hard, so he does OK, and he hears a lot of news too.'

Hana walked faster, trying to shake her off. She couldn't imagine why Fuyu was pursuing her.

'The city's half empty,' said Fuyu. 'It's not easy living under the occupation. You're better off out here in the paddies, where business is booming. You must get plenty of people coming here, wanting your services.'

Hana was nearly at the door of the Corner Tamaya, but Fuyu was still at her heels, still talking.

'The government's pretty well installed now. I can't see our men doing much to dislodge it. There was talk of a Republic of Ezo, but no one thinks they're going to put the shogun back in the castle, so it looks like we'll have to live with the southerners. I hear you're popular with them.'

As Hana pushed aside the curtains, Fuyu stepped in front of her. 'Isn't there anything I can do for you to make up for everything I did? Anyone I can take a message to?'

With a pang Hana thought of the big empty mansion she had left behind in the city and of Oharu, her maid, and Gensuké, the elderly retainer. She needed desperately to get a message to them, to let them know that she was all right and find out if they were. She knew she would be taking a risk. If her husband was still alive he would undoubtedly go home and ask them where she was. But she had a responsibility to Oharu and Gensuké, she couldn't just let them go on thinking she was dead.

'Come inside,' she said at last. 'I'll write something if you promise you will deliver it safely.'

21

Yozo opened his eyes and moved his lips. There was a bitter taste in his mouth. His limbs were stiff and sore, his clothes were soiled, his hair felt matted and filthy and he was sticky with sweat from head to toe. But he was alive, that was the main thing. He was alive.

He was in a bamboo cage, that much he knew, so small that when he tried to straighten his back he hit his head on the top. Outside he could hear the shuffle of feet and porters grunting in unison with the sway of the cage. Shadows flickered on the other side of the slats and light burst through a slit in the bamboo wall. He leaned forward and put his eye to it. Figures in black jackets with straw hats, bristling with swords and spears, marched along silhouetted against the sun, framed in fuzzy halos of light. Dazed though he was, he knew those southern uniforms all too well. He scowled and clenched his fists, feeling the ropes he was bound with cut into his wrists. Beyond the soldiers, tree trunks faded into the distance, tall and straight like prison bars.

He tried to work out where he was and where he was being taken – in a train of cages somewhere in the mountains on the northern part of the mainland, he guessed, heading for Kodenmacho Prison in Edo, then trial and the execution grounds soon after that. With luck he would die before they got there.

A mosquito settled on his cheek. Yozo shook his head fiercely and fixed his eyes on the triangular weave of the bamboo and the tiny dots of light dancing through the gaps. Even under the trees the heat felt stifling.

At least the terrible pain that had seared through his head had sunk to a dull ache and the throbbing in his arm and shoulder was bearable. He thought back to the last battle, how in his fever he had rounded the corner of the ruined house again and again, and seen the Commander ducking along the street. He saw him turn, saw recognition flash across the dark face, heard his rough tones challenging him. He remembered raising his rifle, hearing the gunshot, seeing the Commander fall. Then he had realized there was another man there. He recalled seeing a black uniform and a conical helmet, and not caring that he himself was going to die too.

But what had happened after that? That was the real nightmare. What had become of Enomoto and his comrades-in-arms, all those friends with whom he had fought shoulder to shoulder? All dead, he supposed, or in cages like him, heading for Edo and the execution grounds. He thought of the years he had spent in Europe working and studying, acquiring knowledge for his country – only to end up here, caged like an animal, crouched in his own dirt.

He growled and shuffled, lashing out furiously with his foot, trying to shake the porters off balance. A spear whacked against the side of the cage and there was a barked roar and he slumped back in the dappled twilight.

Gradually the light on the bamboo changed. Outside the opening, the tree trunks grew denser and the shadows longer. The cage began to tilt, at first a little, then more and more steeply, until Yozo was pressed up against the back wall. He could hear the porters' groans and curses and their laboured breathing as their steps grew slower and slower. After a while they seemed to be stopping after each step to lift and heave the cage. It was strangely quiet, as if the rest of the convoy had moved on and they'd been left behind.

There was a rustle and a faint snap, as if some creature, a deer perhaps, was moving through the woods. Something shrieked – it could have been a monkey – and the whole forest came alive. There was a great cawing and flapping of wings and branches creaked and groaned.

Then out of nowhere came a rush, more a wind than a sound, and suddenly the cage crashed to the ground. It bounced then smashed up against something hard. Yozo had curled into a ball to protect himself and cautiously raised his head. In the silence he heard dull thuds, a strange gurgling and a soft deep snarl. Then a monstrous shadow appeared, looming above him. The creature moved closer – too large for a man but too small for a bear. Yozo stared at it in numb fascination: it seemed a cruel way to die, to be ripped apart by some wild beast.

Then to his utter amazement he heard a voice. 'Watch out!'

A blade sliced through the bamboo hasp and the door of the cage lifted. A face like a mountain demon's with a long nose and huge round eyes appeared. Yozo broke into a grin so broad it hurt his bruised face and tore his cracked lips. He knew those steely blue eyes and that pallid skin, though the square jaw was now covered in light brown stubble.

'Marlin!' he gasped.

The Frenchman put a grimy finger to his lips. Other faces crowded round the cage and then hands were grabbing Yozo, pulling him out and cutting his bonds. He sprawled on the ground and feebly shook his arms and legs, trying to get the feeling back into them. His wrists were red and raw and his hair was gummed together with dirt and sweat, with something hard and scabby on one side. He fingered it gingerly and felt a stab of pain. It seemed like an old wound that was healing on its own.

Slowly he sat up and looked around. Black-jacketed figures sprawled in the bushes, limbs bent and broken. Blood gushed from the throat of one and trickled in a dark stream from the arm of another. A severed hand lay nearby. A bearded man wearing a broad-brimmed straw hat was running a cloth up and down the blade of a large knife, while another collected up fallen swords and spears. One came up to Yozo and said something in a gruff northern burr, then slapped his shoulder reassuringly. Small, wiry fellows, they moved as lightly as deer. Bear hunters, Yozo thought; this was bear country.

A soft snarling came from behind him where a couple of dogs, fangs bared, white fur bristling, held four porters at bay, pinioned against a tree. Yozo turned to look at Marlin as he strode towards him up the path. Instead of his neat French uniform he had on a cotton jacket like a Japanese peasant and his big rough heels were bursting out of straw sandals. His hair had grown over his ears and his face was covered with a bristly beard. He was different somehow, Yozo thought, different from before. It wasn't just the way he was dressed. He looked younger, more cheerful. There was a brightness in his eyes and a spring to his step as if he'd cast off a weight of responsibility along with his uniform.

He walked over to the porters, who were quivering with fear, their lips drawn so far back Yozo could see their gums.

'Sorry, lads,' he said airily. 'Either you come with us or I slit your throats. Can't risk you giving us away.'

'We're northerners, sir,' squawked one in a terrified tremor. It was obvious the southerners had press-ganged the locals into portering. Marlin frowned as if he was considering the options.

'OK,' he said, shrugging. 'I'll let you go. But remember, if there's any trouble, the dogs will find you, wherever you are.'

Marlin took a last look around the clearing, then he and one of the hunters looped their arms under Yozo's. Yozo groaned in protest, feeling the wrench on his damaged arm as they lifted him up and plunged into the woods.

The hunters led the way, darting between trees, dodging rocks and jumping over streams as if they knew every leaf and stone in the forest. They cut across a valley, loping between ferns and bushes with great trees soaring overhead, and scrambled up a rise dotted with huge rocks. Tucked around the side of a knoll was a makeshift hut, covered in branches and twigs, which almost looked like part of the forest. They pushed through the doorway and crouched inside, panting, listening for pursuers. There was silence, only the twittering of birds and the rushing of wind through the trees.

Marlin pulled a metal flask from his belt and held it to Yozo's mouth. Water. He drank greedily, feeling strength return to his limbs.

The hunters had taken off their hats. Their faces were like bark, lined and weathered, and their eyes glittered like berries, half hidden in their hair.

Yozo nodded his thanks. He was probably a lot more filthy and wild-looking than they were, he realized.

'My brother wrestles bears single-handed,' said one, jerking his chin towards his companion. Yozo could see that he had a bear's claw on a string hanging round his neck. 'A few soldiers are no problem.'

'You want something to eat?' said the other. He took some foul-smelling brown strips from his pouch and held them out. 'Mountain whale,' he said. He grinned, revealing a mouthful of decaying teeth. 'That's what you lowlanders call it, isn't it?'

Yozo groaned and shook his head.

'I have rice balls,' said Marlin, digging into his pack and bringing out a bamboo-leaf package. Yozo folded back the leaves and took a cautious bite, then another.

The hut was hot and sticky inside, with rough wooden walls and a doorway made of branches, and a musty smell emanated from something black and furry in one corner. A bear skin. One of the hunters stood in the doorway and whistled, a long low note that might have been a bird call or an animal cry.

'How . . . How did you get here?' Yozo croaked. 'What happened to Enomoto and . . . and the rest?'

Marlin stared at the ground and rubbed at it with his straw sandal.

'Later,' he mumbled. 'When you're stronger.'

'No, now,' said Yozo fiercely.

Marlin took a knife from his belt and started to whittle a chunk of wood, turning it over and over in his hands.

'It was after you disappeared,' he said slowly. 'The Commander had gone too. We'd lost half our men, we were nearly out of ammunition and we knew that if the fighting went on much longer we'd all be dead. Enomoto was in his rooms. The windows were shattered and the place was a ruin but that drinks cabinet of his had somehow made it through. He got out some of the whisky he was so fond of and poured us all a glass.'

He stopped and Yozo heard branches creaking and twigs snapping as something huge padded by outside.

'And then?' he demanded.

'Then General Otori called me in. He wanted me to help persuade Enomoto to surrender.'

'Surrender?' Yozo echoed in outraged disbelief. 'Enomoto?'

Marlin nodded. 'It was the last thing he wanted to do, that was obvious. The southerners were a bunch of cowards, he said. It was only because the Americans had handed over the *Stonewall* that they'd made any headway at all – that and sheer force of numbers. He was determined to go down fighting. If he had to, he said, he'd die by his own hand.'

Yozo was picturing the room, remembering the last time he had seen Enomoto.

'You Japanese and your samurai pride,' Marlin said with a snort of admiration or disbelief – Yozo didn't know which. 'Then Otori spoke up. "If it's dying you want, you can do it any time." Those were his words. We've got work to do still, that was what he meant. There was no need to be in a rush to die.'

Marlin paused and his face grew dark as he remembered what had happened. 'I could see he'd hit the mark. Enomoto paced up and down for a while, then he said, "Our men have been loyal to the death. They deserve to live. I'll hand myself over on condition they let our men go free." So that's what he did. Otori surrendered too.'

So Enomoto had surrendered. In that case they really were finished. Yozo put his head in his hands. All those times he and Enomoto had sat together sipping whisky, the intense conversations they'd had about how they'd set things to rights when they got back to Japan. It had been Enomoto who had insisted on defying the southerners and making off with the fleet and sailing for Ezo, Enomoto who had created the glorious Republic of Ezo in which all men were to be equal, Enomoto who had organized democratic elections. If anyone deserved to live, it was him.

'You should have rescued him!' he groaned. 'Not me. What use am I?'

'Enomoto's a proud man,' said Marlin. 'I doubt if he'd have agreed to be rescued. In any case, there were only three of us and the front of the convoy was bristling with soldiers. We couldn't have got anywhere near Enomoto, so my decision was to come after you. You're my brother-in-arms, after all.'

'How many of our men did the southerners take?' Yozo demanded.

'They let the lower ranks go free and just took the leaders. I was watching from behind a wall when they loaded up the cages. One of the injured men looked like you, so I decided to take my chances and follow.'

He carried on whittling. Yozo had a feeling he was avoiding his gaze. Perhaps someone had seen him gun down the Commander and rumours had spread. Everyone knew there had been bad blood between them. Once again he was back in the ruined town, seeing his face, remembering Kitaro, raising his gun . . .

'As for Commander Yamaguchi,' Marlin said, as if he could read Yozo's mind, 'no one knows what happened to him. He disappeared halfway through the battle. He's probably under a pile of corpses somewhere.'

'And you?' Yozo asked slowly. 'How did you escape?'

'The southerners didn't seem eager to catch me. You can kill a foreigner but if you arrest one you have to explain yourself to the powers back in Edo. Anyway, they wouldn't have had a cage big enough to hold me.'

One of the hunters struck a flint and lit a candle and set it in an alcove in the wall. In the flickering light Marlin's huge nose and deep-set eyes made him look more like a demon than ever.

'I saw them load the cages on to boats and found a boat to take me to the mainland. I started following the convoy but I soon realized I was drawing too much attention to myself. People up here have never seen a foreigner before and crowds kept gathering wherever I went, so I decided I'd better avoid the towns and stick to the mountains and keep a lookout for the convoy from there. I knew the soldiers would have to take the main road south. Then I fell in with my friends here and we waited our chance.'

'Thank you,' said Yozo, bowing. 'You saved my life.' Weak and feverish though he was, it was entirely clear what he had to do. He looked Marlin in the eye. 'Now we must do the same for Enomoto and Otori.'

Marlin nodded grimly. 'I knew you'd say that,' he said, 'but it won't be easy.'

'We've been through so much together, Enomoto and I,' Yozo said. 'There's no way I can stand by and see him put on trial and executed.'

'They're very closely guarded, him and Otori, which means we'll need more men. And you're on the run yourself now, don't forget that. But if you're determined to take a chance and follow the convoy to Edo, I'm with you all the way.'

Heavy bodies came crashing down the hillside and the two dogs hurtled in and stood panting, tongues lolling, tails lashing feverishly. The hunters patted and hugged them and threw them strips of dried bear meat.

'For now, let's turn you back into a human being,' Marlin said to Yozo. 'We'll get down to a river so you can have a wash. You need cleaning up.'

22

Yozo wriggled through the bushes, keeping low to the ground. After being on the road for more than a month he could disappear into the landscape nearly as easily as a bear hunter. A bullet whizzed over his head and buried itself harmlessly in a tree trunk as the sounds of stumbling feet and breaking branches faded behind him. Then the scrub thinned and he scrambled uphill, beating his way through the close-packed trees and plunging through mounds of dusty foliage under a dark canopy of leaves. He stopped for a moment to swab his brow and catch his breath. A large shadow darted through the woods not far away: Marlin.

Pinpricks of light penetrated the leaves at the top of the hill. Yozo clambered over branches and roots and shoved his way through bushes, then burst out into sunlight and threw himself down, gasping for breath. He was high above a brilliant yellow plain, on a broad sill of land thickly carpeted with grasses and wild flowers. Marlin thumped down next to him and they lay for a while, panting, while the sun blazed down out of a hazy blue sky.

As his breathing eased, Yozo pressed his ear to the ground and listened hard. Silence. Cautiously he raised his head. The air was full of floating thistledown and the scent of flowers. Birds swooped and soared, and wild geese honked overhead.

'We lost them,' he said, with a laugh of triumph.

'They'll be back,' said Marlin. 'They'll track us down. We're not hard to spot. You'd be better off on your own, my friend.' His big face creased into a grin.

Yozo grinned back. In his cotton jacket, with the front of his head shaved and his hair combed into a rough topknot, Yozo could pass for a peasant, but Marlin towered above everyone. Here in the north Yozo and Marlin were in friendly territory. Villagers and farmers welcomed them like heroes and fed them and hid them wherever they went. Whenever southern soldiers came knocking, they were given false information and sent off in the wrong direction.

As much as they could the two men kept to the mountains to avoid border posts, and whenever they were forced to take to the road, Marlin hid his head inside a straw hat as deep as a basket, like a mendicant monk. They drew stares all the same.

'No one's ever seen a monk as huge or as well fed as you,' Yozo told him.

Below them, the plain stretched far into the distance, a sea of golden rice ready for harvesting, laid out in a patchwork of ragged squares. A thin line snaked across, edged with trees and dotted with moving figures. Yozo peered down, searching for a convoy of cages, but there was nothing.

Then he made out a dark smudge on the horizon with a haze of smoke floating above it.

'Over there,' he exclaimed, narrowing his eyes. 'Isn't that . . . Edo?'

Marlin heaved himself up on an elbow and shaded his eyes with a large hand.

'Too bad you lost that telescope of yours,' he said.

Yozo nodded. 'It's Edo, I'm sure of it. The only question is what to do when we get there. We'll have to start looking for men and making plans.'

'Enomoto's probably in prison by now, awaiting trial.'

'Unless he's managed to escape, which, knowing him, is quite possible.' Yozo didn't want to tempt fate by saying so, but he knew there was also a good chance that Enomoto was dead.

Nevertheless, at the very least they had to find out what had happened.

Pacing their shelf of land, he found a goat path that led down the cliffside. Marlin followed as he edged along it, looking out for handholds, clambering from one crumbling outcrop to the next. The shadows were lengthening by the time they jumped down the last slopes to the bottom. The paddies began almost at the foot of the hills, slotting into the contours, and they followed the narrow paths that wound between them, keeping the road in their sights, then, when it was too dark to walk any further, found a copse and curled up under a tree, their stomachs rumbling, resigning themselves to a long night.

Suddenly a small grey rabbit hopped out of the bushes and looked at them, nose twitching. Marlin made a lunge for it, grabbed it by the ears and held it up, prancing about in triumph. They both knew lighting a fire would be risky but they were a long way from the road or any town and well hidden in the trees and, in any case, much too hungry to care. Yozo cleared the ground and collected brushwood while Marlin slit the rabbit's throat and skinned it and, when it was cooked, they wolfed it down greedily. It was the first good meal they'd had in days.

The following day they came to a river and followed it downstream till they found a place where the water was shallow and waded across it. The opposite bank was a wilderness of silver plume grass, the feathery fronds towering high above their heads.

'Looks marshy,' said Marlin. 'If we're not careful, we'll be up to our waists.'

Yozo took a few steps between the clumps of grass, stamping his feet. The soil was dried out and firm.

'We've got no choice,' he said. 'At least we won't leave any tracks. So long as it doesn't rain we'll be able to make it through.'

They threaded their way single file through the tall grass, tramping down stalks and beating back the swaying fronds. There was no sound except for the rustle of the leaves, the crunch of their straw sandals and the warble of tiny birds flitting from stem to stem. Yozo kept an eye on the sun, hoping they were heading westward.

They were deep in the marshland when the land started to become damp, then boggy. Yozo took off his straw sandals and walked barefoot, feeling his feet sinking into the ground with each step and the mud sucking at them as he pulled them out. The sun beat down. He wiped away the sweat that ran into his eyes, his legs aching with the effort of dragging them out of the cling-ing mud. Marlin squelched behind him, cursing volubly.

'We'll be out of this in no time,' said Yozo, trying to sound more cheerful than he felt. Looking around at the sea of grass, he realized with a shock of fear that they'd lost their bearings. At least in battle he knew where the enemy were and how to fight them, but here, in this wilderness of swaying white fronds, he had no idea which way to turn.

Peering between the stalks, he noticed a rise in the land not far away.

'Looks like dry ground over there,' he said lightly, trying to conceal his relief.

They were exhausted by the time they got to the bottom of the slope. As he climbed, Yozo started to hear a noise. At first it was a whisper, barely audible beneath the rustle of the grass and the rattle of pebbles tumbling down behind them. Then it grew into a distinct hum – voices, and the clatter and tramp of feet.

Keeping his head low, Yozo peered over the top and gave a groan of dismay. There was an enormous earthen wall in front of them, cutting right across the plain, entirely blocking their path. It was a massive rampart, many times higher than a man. They were so close that he could see the pale straw walls of stalls at the top and people moving along it. As for the road, they'd lost it completely.

'Whatever that is, it's between us and Edo,' he said grimly. 'One way or another, we'll just have to get across it.'

He turned to Marlin and stared at him in disbelief. The big

Frenchman was beaming as broadly as if he'd just defeated an army single-handed.

'It's the Japan Dyke, my friend,' he shouted, as if he could barely contain his excitement. Smoke rose from the stalls at the top of the wall and tantalizing smells of food drifted across.

Yozo glared at him and hit him on the shoulder. They needed to keep quiet.

'Don't you understand?' said Marlin. 'It's the Yoshiwara. We're nearly there. We can hide out there.'

Yozo's jaw dropped. Then the words sank in and he too began to laugh. The Yoshiwara, the walled city. It was years since he had even thought of it. Marlin was right; it was another country in there, with its own laws and its own law-keepers. Once inside they'd be fine – if only they managed to get in, that was. He frowned, thinking it through, trying to picture the layout.

'We'll have to get past the guards first, but they'll never let us by,' he said. 'We look like beggars. So in that case the only way is to get as close as we can to the bottom of the dyke then skirt along it till we get to the edge of the stockade. Then we'll have to cross the Moat of Black Teeth and get over the wall. It won't be easy, but we've got this far. We'll manage somehow.'

'Why not just wait till evening and walk in with everyone else?' said Marlin. He was twitching with impatience. 'All we have to do is get to the top of the dyke.'

Yozo looked at his friend, at his huge square face, lank brown hair and moustache and his long arms and legs poking incongruously out of his cotton jacket and leggings. It was the most preposterous thing he'd ever heard.

'Merge with the crowd? You? There'll be soldiers up there checking papers, and we haven't got any.'

'They know me,' Marlin said airily.

'They know you?' Yozo laughed aloud.

'Of course.' Marlin was still grinning. 'If anyone challenges us, I'll say you're my servant. Leave it to me.'

Yozo sighed. It was the craziest plan he'd ever heard but Marlin seemed sure of himself and he had never failed him yet. 'We'd better lie low till nightfall,' he said reluctantly.

They edged back from the top of the hummock, trying not to give themselves away by making the grass ripple, and found a patch of shade under a clump of fronds, then curled up there and waited while the sun beat down overhead.

The Yoshiwara. Yozo was a man of the world, he'd been to the West, but even so he couldn't help feeling a thrill of excitement. When he was a boy it had been the most glamorous of places. Everyone had talked of its courtesans and geishas and bandied about the names of the most celebrated. Like every young man, Yozo had dreamed of being seen with a beautiful courtesan on his arm and admired as someone who knew his way around there.

'So you know the Yoshiwara,' he said to Marlin.

'No better than you know the Pigalle or the Amsterdam red light district.'

'My father first took me when I was thirteen,' said Yozo. He closed his eyes. He could hear his father's deep tones. 'You have to learn how to be a man,' he had said. Yozo had gone abroad after that and become part of a different world and since he'd been back he'd never once even thought of the Yoshiwara. There had been a war to fight.

But now, as the sun crawled across the sky, he let himself dream. What a place it had been for a young lad to see – the women in their gorgeous silks smiling and waving and beckoning, looking at him with knowing glances that made him blush to the roots of his hair. Then there had been that first encounter with a courtesan with trailing red skirts, wafting clouds of perfume. He remembered her smile and her soft white hands. Since then he'd known many women of her profession, but none so gentle and so consummately skilled. Dreamily he wondered what had become of her – and what the Yoshiwara could be like now. Surely the war must have touched it too.

Yet Marlin was right: it was the perfect place to hide. As a samurai he had had to leave his swords at the gate, he remembered, and his status along with them. As for merchants, outside the Yoshiwara samurai had looked down on them as vulgar creatures who soiled their hands with money, but inside they had all swum together. In fact, in the Yoshiwara, the merchants had been kings and flaunted themselves like nobles, hosting feasts and entertaining courtesans. Even peasants were welcomed if they had money to spend.

As dusk was falling Yozo and Marlin picked their way across the last stretch of marshland to the foot of the dyke. Yozo took a good look at the rough earthen wall, then started to scramble up it as nimbly as he could, searching for handholds and footholds. He was halfway up when there was a crash. Marlin had slithered to the bottom, taking with him an avalanche of rocks and earth. Yozo raised his head, expecting to see rows of eyes staring down at him, but there was so much bustle and tramping of feet above them that it drowned any noise the two of them could make.

At the top was a road lined with stalls, with food, woodblock prints, souvenirs and books laid out on display, along with any disguise a man might want, from a doctor's robes to a false topknot. Lanterns lit the way. Men hurried by, sashes slung fashionably low around their hips, and bearers raced along carrying palanquins.

Shimmering in the distance was a huddle of buildings with banners of smoke rising from the close-packed roofs: the Yoshiwara. It rose out of the plain like a fairy city, floating in the darkness, dancing with lights, drawing men towards it like moths to a flame, as alluring as Amida Buddha's western paradise. Above the tramp of feet, the tinkle of music and sounds of roistering drifted towards them.

Yozo brushed the dirt off his clothes and smoothed his hair. 'It's lucky it's night time,' he muttered. He wrapped a scarf around his head to conceal his face, so that only his eyes and nose were visible. He was expecting Marlin to put his hat over his head, but the Frenchman strutted off as arrogantly as any rake heading for a night on the town. 'Remember, not a word,' he said over his shoulder. 'Leave the talking to me.'

They joined the crowd of men hurrying along the road. Covertly Yozo surveyed them – southerners, most of them, from their accents, and bumpkins, for all their showy robes. The thought of these men not only occupying his country but sleeping with its women made him crazy with rage. He fingered the knife tucked in his sash. Then he felt Marlin's touch on his arm. The big Frenchman sensed his fury.

They were nearly at the turning that led to the Yoshiwara when they saw a group of soldiers blocking the road, stopping everyone who went by. Marlin brushed through them as if they weren't even there. Yozo bowed his head and was following when an ugly man with a round head and black uniform stepped into his path.

'Papers,' he barked in a thick southern accent.

Yozo gripped his knife but before he could move Marlin had swung round and grabbed him by the collar. 'Idiot!' he barked in English, giving him a shake. 'You're too damn slow. Get a move on.'

The guards' jaws dropped. 'Bloody halfwit,' said Marlin, and cuffed Yozo round the head.

The guards backed off, bowing nervously, clearly in awe of the gigantic foreigner, and Marlin swaggered on. Yozo followed, grinning inwardly, rubbing his head and shuffling his feet like the most dim-witted of servants.

He was congratulating himself on their lucky escape when a couple of lanky foreigners strode up from behind and flanked them, one to each side. Yozo recognized their uniforms. English sailors, rough-looking characters with ruddy faces and that meaty smell that foreigners had.

They moved in close to Marlin and stepped right in front of him. It was obvious that for them Yozo and the guards didn't even exist. Marlin moved to one side, then the other, but the sailors did too, blocking his path.

'Frenchie, aren't you?' demanded one in English. 'I thought they threw you lot out.'

'What are you doing here, dressed like one of those monkeys?' drawled the other.

He gave Marlin a shove and Marlin took a couple of steps back. It was too dangerous to start a fight here and Yozo knew that if they drew attention to themselves the guards would discover who they were.

'You want to go to the Yoshiwara?' Marlin snarled at the Englishmen. 'They don't let you in if you cause trouble.'

He stepped around them and headed quickly down the zigzag slope towards the Great Gate. Yozo followed at his heels. As if in a dream, he passed the swaying willow tree and saw the familiar tiled roof of the gate, the massive wooden doors pushed wide open and the huge red lanterns hanging on each side. The guard, a burly fellow with a neck as thick as a bull's and massive arms covered in ornate tattoos, stepped forward as he saw Marlin and broke into a huge grin.

'Shirobei,' said Marlin. 'You still here?'

'Monsieur,' said the guard. 'Welcome back. We've been waiting for you. These men causing you trouble, are they?'

Suddenly Yozo was through the gate. Swept up in the crowd, he stared around at the glittering buildings and the rows of red lanterns. He breathed in sweet perfumes and felt the touch of silken fabric as delicate creatures with white-painted faces floated past and lavishly dressed children threaded their way through the throng.

Ahead of him he could see Marlin's brown head poking up way above the crowd as he pushed straight up the main street and swung down a back alley. Stunned, Yozo followed him.

23

Hana stood at the Great Gate of the Yoshiwara, bowing gracefully as she said farewell to a heavy-browed young man who was
clambering into a palanquin. He poked his head in, then pulled it
out again, turning to gaze at her with a look of almost comical
despair while his attendants stood around exhorting him to hurry.
People said he was a rising figure in the new bureaucracy and had
an important position in the Ministry of Finance, but with her he
behaved like a sulky little boy.

Ordinarily she saw her clients off at the house but he had
begged her so pathetically to come to the gate that in the
end she'd agreed. Thinking that it was early and there would
be few men around to see her, she had thrown an old haori
jacket over her night robes and run out with only the lightest of
make-up.

Until now Hana had taken care not to look through the Great
Gate. She belonged in the Yoshiwara and she knew all too well
that the outside world was closed to her. But today she glanced
through, wondering if she might see a messenger running down
the slope with a letter from Oharu and Gensuké. More than a
month had passed since she had given Fuyu a note for them but
still there'd been no reply.

Beyond the trees on the other side of the gate she could see the
winding track that led up to the Japan Dyke. In the distance
the embankment loomed like a great wall cutting across the plain.
Figures hurried along the top, silhouetted against the pale sky,

appearing and disappearing between the straw-walled stalls which shimmered in the sun. A cock crowed, breaking the morning hush. The weather had turned refreshingly cool.

The wind that blew through the gate brought smells of the city, scents she'd almost forgotten, and odd clatterings and bangings and children's voices. Geese wheeled above the marshes, shrieking. Here in the Yoshiwara she was confined to a grid of five streets, but she remembered now with a pang of longing that out there beyond the Great Gate the world went on and on for ever. An hour's march across marshland and paddy fields would bring her to the city of Edo, which she now had to remember to call Tokyo, and, several days beyond that, across endless hills and valleys, to Kano, where she had grown up. Unexpectedly she found herself picturing her parents' house with its ramshackle gate and big entrance porch and huge shady rooms. At this time of year the rain doors would still be pushed back, leaving the house open to the breezes.

It had been on a sunlit morning like this that she had said goodbye to her parents. She remembered them waving as she peeped out of the wedding palanquin, her father tall and stern, her mother small and round, huddling in his shadow, blinking back tears. She was so proud, she had said, that Hana had made such a good marriage, and Hana had replied that she'd do her best not to make them ashamed of her. She remembered how she'd watched them growing smaller in the distance. She thought of them now with such longing that tears came to her eyes.

A crow landed on the stockade beside her with a harsh caw, bringing her back to earth with a start. Around her, women were bowing to their lovers who were scuffling up the slope, dragging their feet with a great show of reluctance, kicking up clouds of dust, turning at the Looking Back Willow for a last look at the woman they'd spent the night with. The young man stepping into his palanquin had turned once more to gaze at her.

'I can't bear it,' he said fretfully. To Hana's eyes his western-style tight-fitting trousers and jacket looked incongruous above his neatly tied straw sandals and white tabi socks. 'You'll forget me the moment I'm gone, I know you will. You'll be busy with all those other lovers of yours.'

She smiled at him like a mother at a recalcitrant child. 'You're such a silly,' she said, laughing. 'You know you're the only one I love. I have to see the rest, it's my job, but you're the only one I care for. I won't sleep a wink till I see you again. I'll be thinking about you all the time.'

'You say that to everyone,' he said ruefully but he smiled all the same. She watched as he bent down and clambered into the wooden box, taking off his sandals and folding his legs underneath him. Porters heaved the palanquin on to their shoulders and set off up the slope at a trot. Hana stood bowing till it disappeared.

With the last of their clients gone, the women at the gate looked at each other and smiled. For a few precious hours they could be themselves. Hana yawned and turned towards the Corner Tamaya. She was looking forward to a couple of hours of undisturbed sleep. A bell tolled in the distance and the shrill of the cicadas swelled then faded then rose to a clamour again. There was an autumnal tone to their burr now. From the houses along the alleys came the rhythmic thump of the papermakers' mallets. The whole of the Yoshiwara seemed ready to sink into slumber.

Hana was passing the Chrysanthemum Teahouse when the curtains over the door flew open.

'Hanaogi-sama! Hanaogi-sama!' called a voice.

Hana stifled a gasp. Mitsu had on a shabby cotton kimono and jacket. She was usually immaculate, even in the morning, but today she wore not a speck of make-up. Her ageing face was the colour of parchment, her eyes half hidden inside folds of skin and her hair bushed out in a white mane around her head, but to Hana's amazement she was positively dancing with excitement. She glanced up and down the street as if to check that no one was within hearing distance then scurried up to Hana with tiny pigeon-toed steps.

'I have wonderful news,' she said, hiding her smile with her hand. 'Saburo has returned!'

Hana looked at her, puzzled, wondering what news could be so thrilling as to make Mitsu behave in such an extraordinary fashion. 'Saburo?' she repeated.

'Saburosuké of the House of Kashima,' said Mitsu, emphasizing each syllable with a nod of her head. She laughed her high-pitched, fluting laugh. 'The quarter's coming back to life! We're in business again!'

'Saburosuké Kashima . . .'

Even in the countryside Hana had heard of the Kashimas. Before she married, her mother had sent a servant to the Kashima store in Osaka to order the red silk for her wedding dress. No one had finer silks, she had said firmly. The Kashimas were said to be rich beyond imagining and hugely powerful. She had heard that they had funnelled money to both sides in the civil war to make sure that no matter who won, they would come out on top.

'Naturally his clerk came straight to me, to the Chrysanthemum Teahouse,' Mitsu crowed, patting Hana's arm. 'He's a man of taste, you see. He knows which is the best teahouse in town.'

She beamed at Hana, her eyes sparkling. 'He was our best patron before the war began. He once booked every girl in the Yoshiwara, all three thousand of them, and had the Great Gate closed for the night so he could have a party. Our chefs were busy for days! He sampled all the top girls and always said he was looking for the perfect woman. But then the war came and he went down to Osaka like all our best clients. And now he's back. And you know what his clerk said to me? The very first thing?'

Hana shook her head.

'He said, "Mitsu-sama, who is this Hanaogi we keep hearing about? The master wants to meet her. You must book her for him straight away." You see, even in wartime your fame has spread right across the country.'

A hush seemed to fall over the street. Hana felt a surge of apprehension. 'But I'm fully booked,' she said slowly. 'I've been booked up for months.'

'I've moved your appointments around,' said Mitsu briskly. 'You're to see him tonight.'

Two children in bright kimonos darted by, chasing each other, shrieking and giggling.

'But . . .' Masaharu, her favourite customer and the man who had paid for her début, had booked her that night. Hana always reminded herself of Otsuné's advice: never to forget that for him she was just a plaything. He paid for his pleasure and that was all there was to it and she always took care to maintain a distance and not to lose her heart to him. But despite all her efforts she couldn't help looking forward to his visits. 'What will my clients say when they arrive and find their appointments cancelled?'

'Not cancelled, postponed. It's good to make them wait; it makes them hungrier for you.'

'But Masaharu's my long-standing client.'

'That's as it may be. Masaharu is a newcomer to the quarter and although he has plenty of money to splash around, Saburo is a far more important customer. Your Auntie and Father know Saburo very well and Tama does too. They'll be delighted.' She laughed shrilly. 'Saburo back! It'll be like old times. It makes me feel young again!'

Hana had a sinking feeling in the pit of her stomach. 'I don't have to lie with him if I don't like him,' she muttered. 'He'll have to woo me like all the others.'

Mitsu wrinkled her forehead. Like all the women she had no eyebrows, only a shadow where they had been shaved off.

'Don't be a fool,' she said. 'Liking doesn't come into it. You haven't been here long, I always forget that. He's a very important man.'

Hana swallowed. 'Is he old or young?' she demanded. 'Is he handsome? Is he clever?'

'He's rich, that's all you need to know. Go home and sleep. You're going to need all your energy tonight.'

Before Hana could say another word Mitsu had pattered back into her teahouse, leaving the curtains flapping.

Reluctantly Hana took a few steps towards the Corner Tamaya. She could imagine the excitement there. Auntie and Father would be insisting she lie with this man; Tama would be telling her what a great opportunity it was. She kicked at the dust. Just as she had begun to imagine she was mistress of her destiny, something always happened to remind her that she was still a slave. For all her fine clothes, she belonged to these people.

She had reached the gate that led to Edo-cho 1 and the Corner Tamaya when she paused, playing with her fan. She would go and see Otsuné. She would know what to do.

A few moments later, Hana was outside Otsuné's door, trying to slide it open. But it was locked. She stopped, puzzled. No one ever locked their door, especially not Otsuné. She shoved at it again, wondering if it was jammed, then shook it and rattled it.

Thinking that perhaps her friend had fallen ill, she hammered at the door and shouted, 'Otsuné! Are you there?'

Then she heard footsteps inside and the sound of something heavy being shifted and heaved a sigh of relief. The door slid open a crack.

'What's the matter? Were you sleeping?' Hana demanded, pushing the door back.

A shaft of pale sunlight lit the sandals that littered the entrance and the step up to Otsuné's little room, throwing them into relief. Hana's shadow lay across them, black and sharp-edged. But as she stepped inside she realized that outside that narrow oblong of light the place was in darkness and as humid and close as a bathhouse. Otsuné must have shut the rain doors, Hana thought, puzzled.

Then a pair of hands grabbed her roughly by the shoulders. Hana cried out in shock as her attacker twisted her round and thrust her to one side. She stumbled forward, putting out her hands to try to save herself, then tripped over some sandals, lost her balance and fell. She heard the crash of a shoe rack falling over as the door slammed, throwing her into total darkness, and there was the thunk of a bolt being thrust into place.

Still dazzled from the light outside, she fumbled around, shaking with shock and fear, feeling for something familiar, then sprang back with a gasp of horror as her hand brushed against coarse fabric. She could hear breathing, smell male sweat and the stench of dirty clothing, and feel the heat of someone close to her. As her eyes adjusted to the darkness, she saw a shadowy figure.

A madman or a beggar, she thought, hearing her heart pounding in her ears. He must have burst in and killed Otsuné and now she was trapped here alone with him. She screamed, but the man grabbed her and clamped his hand across her mouth so hard that she tasted the sweat and dirt on it. She felt his body pressed against hers and struggled, trying to wriggle out of his grasp, but he only held her tighter. Panic rose in her chest as she kicked and fought, gasping for breath, sure he would have her down on the floor and be ripping off her kimonos in a moment. He wrestled her on to her knees, keeping his hand pressed tightly across her mouth.

'Don't be afraid. I won't hurt you,' he said quietly. 'Please don't make any noise.'

She stared up at him and shrank back as she caught a glimpse of unkempt hair, a dark growth of beard and glittering eyes in the thread of light that filtered through the gap between the rain doors.

'Forgive me,' he said. 'Please don't scream.'

She nodded, shaking, and he released her. She clenched her fists as she remembered the dagger in her obi. If he moved an inch she would stab him.

'Where is Otsuné? What have you done to her?' she whispered fiercely.

'She'll be back soon,' he said. 'I'm a . . . a visitor. I'm sorry I frightened you.'

He knelt opposite her, keeping his eyes fixed on her warily, and she noticed that he held himself like a military man, knees apart and back very straight. His face was scarred and streaked with dirt but perfectly calm. He was looking at her appraisingly, eyebrows lifted, as if wondering what sort of creature it was that he had captured.

Then she realized. He was probably a fugitive, a soldier of the northern army. That must be why the door was locked and the rain doors in place. He was on the run. He had more reason to be afraid than she did.

'I won't betray you,' she said softly, her fear ebbing away. 'We're all from Edo here and loyal to the northern cause.'

The man breathed out sharply and glowered at her from under his thatch of hair.

'There is no northern cause,' he said, his voice bitter. 'It's finished.'

So he had fought up north, she thought. He might even have fought side by side with her husband. Perhaps he knew what had become of him. But the thought of her husband reminded her that that part of her life was over. Now she was a courtesan, her husband would never accept her back, no matter what happened.

The man's mouth twisted into a scowl. 'I saw southern faces on the street out there,' he muttered. 'I heard their voices. You women sell your bodies to the enemy.'

Hana recoiled as if she'd been hit. 'We've all had to find ways to survive,' she said at last, her voice shaking. 'I'm alive, you're alive. It's best not to ask how.'

The man's shoulders slumped. 'Forgive me,' he said, and Hana felt a surge of sympathy. He had fought for their cause and been defeated. He might have been wounded, he might have had to commit all manner of terrible acts, and to return to Edo in rags, unable to hold his head high – it was impossible to imagine how he must feel. She reached out and laid her hand on his.

'We've both suffered,' she said gently. 'But we've made it through, somehow. That's all that matters.'

He looked up at her and suddenly she was glad that she was dressed in a simple robe, like a maid, not in the gorgeous garments of a courtesan.

'My name is Hana,' she said, and smiled.

24

Yozo's spine tingled as he felt the girl's hand on his. In the gloom all he could see was the oval of her face, pale like the moon, and the black hair that hung loose down her back. He was aware of her softness, her gentle tones and calm presence, and the scent of her sleeves and hair. She was young – he could tell by her voice – and small, for when he had taken hold of her it had been like holding a bird.

Her touch filled him with feelings he had forgotten existed. He had had another life once, he remembered now, where men did not fight and die and where there were soft-skinned women with gentle voices. Then his existence had seemed full of possibilities; now it had shrunk until it was just a matter of surviving.

He had been trapped in this house for a good part of a day now and it was beginning to seem even worse than being locked in the bamboo cage. It was cramped and cluttered and, worst of all, that morning Marlin had insisted on closing the rain doors before he disappeared with his woman, leaving him stumbling in the dark, choking on charcoal smoke and the odour of singed hair. Yozo felt as if he'd been pitched into hell. He belonged on the ocean navigating a ship, or in Ezo battling the enemy alongside his men, or in the mountains with bear hunters; not here, stuck in a tiny house awaiting slaughter.

He had been pacing up and down, cursing, when the banging started. Soldiers, he'd thought, pulling his dagger from his belt.

Then he'd heard a woman's voice and put it aside. His first thought had been to bundle her into the house before she alerted the neighbours, but it was only when he had her inside that he had begun to wonder who she was. Too refined to be a Yoshiwara girl had been his first thought, though he had only the haziest recollection of the women he'd met when his father had brought him here as a boy.

And then she had put her hand on his. He knew he looked like a wild man and he'd behaved like one, yet she was not afraid of him.

There was a rap at the door, then another – it was the signal he'd agreed on with Marlin. Yozo slid out the bolt and the big Frenchman stumbled through the door, bending nearly in half to avoid hitting his head on the lintel. His woman pattered in behind him, a bundle in each hand.

'Ara! There's no air in here!' Otsuné cried, putting down her packages, unfurling her fan and flapping furiously. 'Big brother, you must be suffocating! Hana, is that you?'

Marlin stomped across the room and shoved back the rain doors. As air and light flooded in, Yozo turned, curious to see the girl's face. She had run to greet Otsuné and as she knelt, bowing, sunlight etched her slender body and the black hair that tumbled down her back and lit up the design of white chrysanthemums on her indigo kimono.

Yozo drew a breath as he took in the tilt of the eyes, the delicate nose and small full mouth. He had been wrong; she was indeed a Yoshiwara girl. He could see it straight away in the confidence with which she carried herself and the carefree way she behaved around men. Far from kneeling in silence or running away and hiding at the back of the house like a samurai wife, she seemed to enjoy his attention; yet she had an innocence about her too, as if she had not been long in this profession.

She turned to Marlin as if it was the first time she'd noticed him, then clapped her hands to her mouth and sprang back, wide-eyed, as though she'd seen a monster. The men started to laugh.

For a moment Yozo saw his friend through her eyes – a huge-limbed figure with brawny hands, an enormous nose, startling blue eyes and tree-trunk legs, Marlin really did seem a giant in this doll's house.

Otsuné opened one of her bundles and took out rice wrapped in bamboo leaves and dishes of pickles, stewed aubergine and slabs of fried tofu. Twisting her hair into a knot, revealing the soft white flesh at the nape of her neck, Hana went to a trunk at the side of the room and brought out trays, chopsticks and condiments. The women laid the dishes on the trays and set them in front of Yozo and Marlin and the two men ate greedily, savouring each mouthful. It was months since they had had such a delicious meal.

'You need a wash, my friend,' said Marlin, wiping his moustache with the back of a hairy hand. 'A wash and a shave. Then you'll be civilized again.'

Otsuné was darting around as if she'd been born for nothing else than to take care of her man and his friend. Now she threw herself on her knees in front of Yozo and leaned forward, studying his face.

'Hana,' she said. 'Our Yozo needs to fit into the crowd so no one will notice him. He has to have a haircut. What do you think? Should he be a samurai or a merchant? Or should he have a western-style haircut like the southerners have?'

Hana tilted her head to one side. 'Well, he certainly has plenty of hair,' she said. 'Enough to do practically anything with.' She turned to Yozo. 'Otsuné knows all about cutting hair.'

'I usually do women's hair,' said Otsuné, laughing. 'But I'm sure I can manage.'

Hana frowned. 'I don't think anyone would ever take you for a merchant.' She was pretending to be serious but Yozo could see the smile lurking at the corners of her mouth. 'You're too lean. All the merchants I've ever met are fat and pale with wobbly stomachs because they spend so much time indoors counting their money. And you certainly shouldn't be a samurai. You'd be getting into fights all the time. No,' she said, sitting back on her heels. 'I think you should be one of those lads who do guard duty and chase customers who don't pay up. The locals will know you're new but the clients won't notice, and it's the clients we need to worry about. Otsuné, you should introduce him to Auntie at the Corner Tamaya and she'll give him a job. You could say he's your cousin just up from the country – that'll explain why he hasn't been around before.'

Otsuné gave Yozo a basin which she'd filled with warm water. He went outside to the back of the house, stripped down to his loincloth and washed as best he could.

'And when you're presentable you must go straight to the bathhouse,' Hana added sternly when he came back in. Yozo scowled and looked away, infuriated at the hold she had over him already, the way she effortlessly charmed him, the way he couldn't stop looking at her.

He sat down and Otsuné trimmed his beard, then sharpened a razor on a stone and shaved his chin and cheeks, expertly wielding the long blade. Finally she set to work on his hair. He sat quietly as thick black tufts fell in piles on the cloth she had spread on the wooden floor, enjoying her soft touch as she bustled around, kneading his scalp and pushing him this way and that, creating unaccustomed lightness and coolness around his ears. And then there was Hana, in her cotton kimono, flitting about refilling their teacups. Yozo tried to ignore her, yet noticed how curiously she watched him, how her eyes widened as the last scraps of beard and locks of dusty hair disappeared and his young face was revealed, and how she grew shy when he met her eye, and looked away.

As Otsuné stepped back to admire her work, Hana slipped over and knelt beside Yozo.

'One day, big brother,' she said, looking up at him, 'you must tell me where you've been and what you've done. I want to know everything.'

Her voice was soft and low. When she had been helping

Otsuné, she had chattered in playful high-pitched tones like a Yoshiwara girl, but now she spoke so seriously that he had to answer.

'I'll tell you, I promise,' he said. 'One day.'

He straightened his shoulders. He had to be careful, he told himself. This was no time to be sidetracked by a woman. He needed to find Enomoto and his other comrades.

Otsuné's second bundle contained neatly folded clothes and Yozo threw on a dark blue workman's jacket, tucked his dagger in his belt, then rolled up a towel and knotted it round his head. The women sat back on their heels and looked at him, then at each other, and smiled.

'Perfect,' Otsuné said, turning to Marlin, who was lying on his back like a fallen tree trunk, filling half the room, his head propped on a pillow.

Yozo sprang to his feet and took a step towards the door.

'Not so fast, my friend,' said Marlin, reaching up and grabbing his sleeve. 'There are spies in the Yoshiwara and you're a wanted man. Give me time to investigate before you start roaming around. People know me here.'

'Please be careful,' said Otsuné, looking up at Yozo with big eyes. 'Don't bring trouble down on us – not now that I've got my Jean back. Now the war's over, the southerners know this is the first place fugitives will come. People say there are police on the street already, dressed as customers, mingling in the crowds.' Tears glittered in her eyes.

'I missed him so much,' she said softly, laying her hand on Marlin's massive thigh. 'The Yoshiwara used to be a world to itself and the shogun's men never came in, but these new men in power don't respect the old ways.'

Yozo sighed. He was touched that his friend, this gruff foreigner whom he had always thought of as a lonely exile in their land, should turn out to have a woman waiting for him – and such a devoted one.

'I doubt if the police will pay the slightest attention to a mere servant when a gigantic Frenchman has turned up in town,' he said. He patted Otsuné's shoulder. 'But don't worry, I'll wait an hour or two before I leave.'

From the distance came the muffled boom of a temple bell, floating across the fields towards the small houses that lined the back alleys of the Yoshiwara. The sound reverberated through the small room, setting the paper doors clattering in their frames. Hana went pale.

'I hadn't realized it was so late,' she whispered. 'I wanted to talk to you so badly, Otsuné, but there's no time now.'

Otsuné stroked her hand. 'I know what it was you wanted to ask me.' She glanced around at the two men, leaned closer to Hana and lowered her voice. 'This man everyone's talking about – people say he's a monster, but he's just a man, richer than the others but with the same appetites. Make sure he has lots of food and lots of drink and everything will be fine. Come back tomorrow and tell me how it was.'

Yozo looked from one to the other. He had no idea what they were talking about but Hana looked hunted suddenly, like a wild creature caught in a trap.

'You don't have to do anything you don't want to,' he said to her. 'We're here now, Marlin and I. We can protect you.'

Marlin sat up. 'Of course. We won't let anyone hurt you,' he declared in his deep bass voice.

'I have to do what I'm told,' Hana said sadly. 'You were in the army, you men. You had to obey orders whether you wanted to or not. It's the same for me.' Yozo felt the touch of her fingers on his hand again. 'But thank you,' she added, as she bowed and made her farewells.

On the threshold she paused, graceful in her indigo kimono, her hair swirling loose down her back, then slipped her bare feet into clogs and slid open the door. For a moment she was bathed in sunlight. Then the murmur of insects filled the room and she was gone.

'She's a beauty,' Yozo said, shaking his head with a rueful smile.

Marlin put his arm around Otsuné. Otsuné glanced at Yozo as if to check whether he was shocked at such a display of affection, then leaned against Marlin, turning her face to gaze up at him.

'I have all the beauty I could want right here,' Marlin said, smiling down at her.

25

Holding her parasol over her head with one hand and lifting her skirts with the other, Hana hurried along the grand boulevard. Since morning, red curtains had appeared over the doors of the houses and red lanterns had blossomed along the eaves, proclaiming the name 'Saburosuké Kashima'. Wherever Hana looked she saw the grim brushed characters and they made her heart thump with foreboding.

Every step she took was a step closer to the moment when she was to meet this Saburo. She tried to remember Otsuné's advice but all she could think about was the events of the morning. She had never seen any man treat a woman as Marlin treated Otsuné, with such affection and tenderness. And then there was Yozo. She found herself smiling as she thought of him. She could tell he was brave, yet he was gentle too, so familiar in the way he looked yet utterly foreign in the way he behaved.

She remembered how his face had changed as Otsuné shaved his beard and cut his hair. It was a manly face, muscular and deeply tanned with a wide brow and intelligent eyes – the face of a man she could trust. His words echoed in her mind: '*I can protect you.*' To her husband she had been a chattel; to her clients, nothing but a plaything. No one before had ever offered to protect her.

But he had also said that the Yoshiwara women sold their bodies to the enemy. The thought sent a chill down her spine. It was true; she had slept with the enemy, and she still did. She had even allowed herself to care for Masaharu. What greater treachery could there be than that?

The afternoon sun beat down and the scents of flowers and grilling fish and sewage filled the air, so intense she thought she would suffocate. Outside one house the street was jammed from wall to wall with men, staring at the girls who had just filed into the cage there. Hana threaded her way through the crowd, shrinking as she brushed against one sweaty body after another. Lurking among the clients in their fine clothes were thin-faced men with hungry eyes, most likely northern soldiers on the run, like Yozo. Then she came nose to nose with a couple of heavy-set, thick-necked characters who were pushing their way through, no doubt looking out for fugitives. She felt a knot of fear like an iron fist in her stomach and slipped past as quickly as she could.

A stick-like figure in a glittering black kimono was hovering outside the Corner Tamaya, staring up and down. It was Auntie, her white-painted face contorted with rage. Little Chidori raced up to Hana, her plump cheeks glistening with sweat under the heavy make-up, and grabbed her sleeve. 'Hurry, big sister, hurry,' she panted. From the kitchens came the thump of cooks pounding fish for fishcakes and refining rice.

'What a time to be late,' Auntie hissed as Hana bowed, apologizing. 'You know perfectly well what an important day this is. Go inside and get ready. Saburo'll be at the Chrysanthemum Teahouse any moment now.'

Like the rest of the Yoshiwara, Edo-cho 1 was decked with bunting and lanterns. Girls scurried about twittering with excitement, geishas hurried past followed by their servants carrying their shamisens, jesters practised their acts and lads ran out of restaurants balancing trays of food piled one on top of the other. Everyone was even more magnificently dressed than usual and all, Hana knew, were hoping to catch Saburo's eye as he promenaded through the Yoshiwara. But while the younger girls, who had never met Saburo, were burbling with excitement, the older women seemed oddly subdued.

Hana was stepping through the curtains at the door of the Corner Tamaya when Auntie turned. 'Oh, I forgot,' she said carelessly. 'There was something I was supposed to tell you. Do you remember that Fuyu? She was here, asking for you.'

Hana gasped. Fuyu must have had a letter from Oharu and Gensuké and had brought it herself to make sure of a generous tip. That was why Auntie had been avoiding her gaze.

'Where is she?' she demanded.

'You weren't here, so I told her to come back tomorrow.'

Hana sat down heavily on the step. 'She didn't . . . leave anything for me?' she said, close to tears.

'No,' Auntie said, pulling her to her feet. 'She had someone with her – a man.'

Hana snatched her arm out of Auntie's grasp. 'What sort of man?' she asked eagerly.

'He certainly didn't look as if he had any money,' said Auntie, sniffing disdainfully.

'But was he young? Was he old?' If he was old and crippled, then it was surely Gensuké.

The mole on Auntie's chin quivered. 'I can't say I paid much attention,' she said. 'Young, I suppose, and shabbily dressed. Not the sort of person we want around here.'

Young . . . So it had not been Gensuké. A dreadful possibility began to dawn on Hana. She had assumed her husband was dead and had been so eager to discover what had become of Oharu and Gensuké that she had given Fuyu her address – Fuyu, of all people. But supposing her husband was not dead – supposing he was alive – and Fuyu had gone to the house, met him and he had insisted Fuyu bring him straight here. Filled with one of his terrible rages, he would drag Hana home, take her out to the wood pile and cut her head off.

Shaking with terror, she put her hand on the wall to steady herself.

'When . . . when were they here?' she whispered.

'A while ago,' said Auntie. 'Don't waste time, we must go upstairs.'

Hana stood up, stumbling as Auntie hurried her inside and along the polished floors to her rooms, where the maids were busy laying out her bedding and the box for guests' clothes, straightening the hanging scrolls and putting the last touches to the flower arrangements.

Her only chance, Hana thought, was to find someone to protect her, someone so powerful that even her husband dared not oppose him. For a moment she thought of Yozo, then shook her head. Even Masaharu was not that powerful and in any case she was not so foolish as to imagine that he would do anything that might jeopardize his career.

Yet there was someone who could protect her, someone rich and powerful, who was obliged to no one and who everyone told her always got what he wanted: Saburosuké Kashima. Maybe the famous Saburo would turn out to be her salvation.

26

In her room Hana was applying her make-up herself, putting it on more sparingly than usual. Instead of an opaque white mask she made it a pale sheen through which her delicate features were clearly visible. Her maids had combed her hair into a towering coiffure, set an elegant crown of corals on it and studded it with a few gilt and tortoiseshell hairpins. Even her kimonos were less elaborate than usual, somewhat filmy as befitted a warm evening on the cusp of autumn, with the topmost one a delicate shade of peach. The lavishness was left for the obi, a magnificent brocade embroidered with lions and peonies.

When she looked at herself in the mirror, the Hana she knew had disappeared. She had become Hanaogi, an enchantress presiding over an immense charade where men could do whatever they wanted, confident there would be no consequences.

She caught herself wishing that Yozo could see her now, when she was at her most beautiful. She pictured his face, remembering the way he had looked at her – and then shook her head, frowning at her own folly.

Her parlour had been polished, dusted and filled with hangings and decorations which exuded luxury and sensuality. The air was rich with fragrances of aloe, sandalwood, cinnamon and musk, and at the far end of the room were three damask cushions in front of a six-fold gilded screen, one for Hana, one for Kawanoto, Hana's favourite attendant, who was to be the mistress of the revels, and one for the honoured guest, with a lacquered tobacco box beside each. Musical instruments had been propped against the walls, exquisitely embroidered kimonos were draped over kimono racks, obis heavy with gold thread were prominently displayed and a painted scroll hung in the alcove depicting a stork against the rising sun. It was far more lavish than any daimyo's palace could ever be.

As the time for Saburo's arrival grew near, Auntie scuttled in and looked Hana up and down, straightening her kimono collars and adjusting the crown on her hair with a gnarled finger. Maids trooped in bringing trays of food – simmered vegetables artfully cut, whole baby squid, platters of thin white noodles and small purple aubergines pickled in sake lees. They spread them on a low table along with flagons of sake, flasks of plum wine and a large glass bowl filled with water, in which tiny transparent fish darted about.

'Whitebait,' said Auntie, beaming proudly. 'We had them sent specially from Kyushu. They certainly weren't cheap.' She smacked her lips as if anticipating the huge amount of money that she would charge her guest for this feast. 'Saburo-sama has very demanding tastes.'

Hana took a deep breath and forced herself to remain calm. She needed to bewitch Saburo to make sure he became her patron, but to do that she would have to sleep with him; there would be no escaping that.

Tama had given her some advice when she was new to the quarter: 'Encourage the client to drink as much as possible, then, when you retire to bed, let him have his way immediately. Then make him do it again. Remember to squeeze your buttocks and grind your hips to left and right. That will tighten the jade gate and make him reach satisfaction quickly. He'll be exhausted and fall asleep and you'll be able to get some sleep yourself.'

Until that evening she had lain only with clients she liked and had never needed Tama's advice; tonight would be the night to apply it.

With a twinge of panic she heard clogs clattering along the street towards the Corner Tamaya, first soft then louder, shuffling and clacking as if a line of people were dancing along in a carnival parade. As the singing and clapping grew, Hana slipped out of the room into a side chamber. Through the thin paper doors she made out the high-pitched chatter of geishas and the shuffle of feet across the tatami as people came trooping in.

She closed her eyes, but to her horror found Yozo's words running through her mind like a mantra: '*I will protect you.*' Furious with herself, and with him for distracting her, she clenched her fists and forced herself to concentrate.

Auntie glanced at her to make sure she was ready, then slid open the door with a flourish and Hana stepped forward into the light. She saw her room and the people in it frozen as if lit by a flash of lightning – the jester in his beige robe with a handkerchief on his head, toes coyly turned in, mimicking a courtesan; smiling black-toothed geishas fluttering fans; and at the far side of the room, next to Kawanoto, a large bulky presence – the man who would be paying for these festivities.

Hana lifted her skirts and revealed her bare foot, well aware of the effect it had as, peeping from beneath the froth of silk and brocade, it conjured up the woman concealed inside. Swinging her train, she glided across the room and took her place on her knees opposite her guest. She lifted a sake cup, drank, then peeked through her lashes at Saburo.

He was fat, grossly so, a great dumpling of a man – but rich men tended to be fat, she told herself. He was old, too, but that was not unusual either. He was expensively dressed, his vast bulk swathed in a robe of finest purple and black silk with a poem beautifully calligraphed in gold thread across the sleeves and collar, but it was stained with sake and there were sweat marks across the chest and under the arms. On top of his large round body, like a tangerine balanced on top of a pumpkin-sized rice cake, was a small round head, with bulging eyes surrounded by folds of skin. All in all, he looked like an enormous toad.

Hana looked him up and down. He was clearly a man used to getting his own way, but she knew that to yield to him immediately would be a bad move. The best strategy would be to make him wait, to stoke his desire to a blaze until the statutory third visit at least, so that when he finally got what he wanted, it would be all the more of a thrill for him. Nevertheless she couldn't put him off for ever. A man like him had the power to protect her from her husband and for that she needed to keep him under her spell.

She arranged her skirts and looked at Saburo demurely. It was customary to spar with a customer, to play with him as a cat plays with a mouse. Remembering Tama's lessons, she turned away from him a little and inclined her head so that he could glimpse the unpainted nape of her neck.

'So you're Saburo-sama,' she said in silky tones. 'You've neglected us for so long, it's quite unforgivable. And now you reappear and book me, of all people, when you don't even know me.'

'Our older sister Tama has been dying of love for you, did you know that?' piped Kawanoto, joining in, all wide-eyed innocence. 'She hasn't been able to sleep a wink ever since you left. But now, after crying and weeping for months, she's found a new favourite. But I suppose you found someone down in Osaka that you cared for more than us.'

'That's not true,' Saburo said, simpering, a purple flush suffusing his ugly cheeks. 'How could I care for anyone except all of you at the Corner Tamaya?' His face creased into a grin, revealing several missing front teeth. 'The moment I heard about the famous Hanaogi, I rushed straight back from Osaka. And you really are as beautiful as everyone says – more so, in fact.'

The dancing had started. A troupe of geishas beat out a haunting melody on shamisens, shoulder drums and flute while one warbled a song; then a pair performed a dance, gesturing with their fans while the jester minced about playing a courtesan. He glanced towards the guest but Saburo was staring at Hana through half-closed eyes.

'More sake?' Hana said, topping up his cup. She wanted to be sure there would be no evening fumbles tonight, at least.

Saburo picked up his cup, emptied it in one gulp, then beckoned to one of his attendants, a sharp-eyed fellow kneeling at the side of the room. The man slid forward on his knees holding several lengths of fine red damask and laid them out in front of Hana.

'What makes you think I'm for sale?' she asked, pretending to be offended as she refilled his sake cup. She was taking care to drink as little as possible herself.

'Hanaogi never loses her heart to anyone,' prattled Kawanoto. 'All the rest of us have favourites but she never does. Men say she has a heart of ice and no one can melt it. Every man who comes to the quarter is eager to be her patron but she won't have any of them.'

'I'm not every man,' growled Saburo. His face had turned dark red and his eyes and mouth were narrow slits. He was staring at Hana again, as if he was picturing what lay beneath her many kimonos.

There was a commotion outside the room as the door slid open and Auntie crept in on her hands and knees and pressed her face to the tatami matting, then raised her head. In the candlelight her face was a white mask and her wig glistened with oil.

'Yodo River carp!' she crowed.

A maid paraded in bearing aloft a large cypress-wood cutting board on which was a whole carp. Its body had been transformed into slices of pale pink flesh laced with red and piled on top of the skeleton with such lightning speed that the head, which was still attached, was twitching with life. The whole creation was laid on a bed of white radish and dark green kelp so skilfully arranged that it looked as if it was swimming through the sea. There was a roar of appreciation from the jester and geishas as the maid placed it on the table in front of Saburo.

Saburo licked his lips. 'Where's the chef?' he roared. 'Why didn't he cut it before our eyes? That would have been a show.'

The attendant put a sake cup to the carp's lips, tilted it up and poured in a few drops. Saburo watched intently as the fish's throat convulsed as it swallowed, then he began to laugh, clutching his stomach and rocking to and fro. The attendants, the jester and the geishas looked at him nervously for a moment, then joined in. Finally he turned to Hana, wiping his eyes and looking at her. His face had become stony.

'You can play all the games you like, my beauty,' he said, 'but I'll have you in the end. You'll dance to my tune.'

A chill ran down Hana's spine. 'I can see you're a man who knows what he wants.' She gestured towards the glass bowl of splashing fish. 'Even whitebait. It's out of season, isn't it?'

'Of course,' he said. 'But not in Kyushu.'

Kawanoto scooped out a few of the darting fish and put them into a small bowl. She poured in soy sauce and the fish thrashed madly, turning the sauce into foam. Hana took a pair of chopsticks but before she had time to pick out a fish for him, Saburo had grabbed the bowl in both hands, put it to his mouth and tipped the whole lot in. He clamped his lips shut and held the fish in his mouth, his cheeks puffed out. Hana could almost hear the fish thrashing, beating against his teeth and tongue and cheeks. Then he swallowed, his eyes bulging, and grasped his huge stomach, grinning idiotically.

'What a feeling!' he grunted. 'They're squirming. I can feel them squirming!'

There was a long silence, then the jester and attendants started to laugh and the geishas to titter. Finally they all applauded and Hana smiled and put her hands together too.

Saburo had turned an intense shade of puce which spread until it entirely covered his bald head. Very slowly, like a great tree in a forest glen, he toppled over on to his side, gave a long sigh and began to snore.

Hana waited for a while to make sure he was really asleep, watching his great stomach rising and falling, then stood up slowly and, still feeling a little nervous, crept out of the room. At least she would not have to worry about entertaining Saburo tonight.

27

The quarter was quiet when Hana stepped outside. The flames in the paper lanterns along the eaves and in front of the doors had been snuffed out and when she looked up she could see hundreds of stars twinkling in the dark sky. She had had a lucky escape, she thought.

Out of the corner of her eye she caught a movement in the gloom. There was someone there, a man. She spun round.

Even in the darkness she could see that he was not a client. He was too young and had the starved, half-crazed look of a northern fugitive. She shrank back into the shadows. He was big, a lot bigger than her, and had a hefty staff and a bundle, with a smell about him of dirty clothes and stale bedding.

He bowed brusquely like a soldier.

'Excuse me,' he said in a clear, loud voice. 'I'm looking for the courtesan Hanaogi.'

Hana glanced around, relieved she had changed out of her robes and loosened her hair. 'What do you want with her?' she asked.

'I have a message.'

'Go inside and ask for Auntie and give it to her.'

He shook his head. 'I'm under orders to give it to Hanaogi personally.'

Puzzled, Hana looked at him more carefully. He spoke with the soft burr and flat vowels of central Japan. He was from Kano, she realized, like she and her husband were. It was not just his accent that was familiar; there was something about the way he held himself, legs apart as if braced for an attack. His face was gaunt and half hidden under a thick layer of stubble and there was a livid scar under his ear, but she was sure she had seen his squashed nose and bunched forehead before.

Then it came back. It had been the day her husband left. Waiting outside the house she had seen a group of young men in blue jackets standing silently at the gate. Her husband had barked an order and one had stepped forward. Hana had looked up and for a moment had locked eyes with a tall, big-boned youth with a ferocious scowl and hair flaring like a bush around his head. To her amusement he had blushed to the tips of his ears. Her husband had pushed the youth over to her father-in-law, who was leaning on his sword like a battle-hardened veteran.

'*My trusty lieutenant*,' her husband had said, slapping the youth on the back so hard he had staggered forward a couple of steps. '*He's no beauty but he's a fine swordsman and he can hold his drink too. I trust him with everything.*'

She swallowed hard, trying to stop her voice from shaking. 'Ichimura?'

'Madam.' He bowed, recognition dawning in his eyes too.

Doors slammed in the house behind them and people came clattering down the stairs. It was a party of geishas, taking with them the clients who couldn't afford to stay the night. As they burst out of the door one of the guests tripped then scrambled to his feet, cursing volubly and sending the geishas into squeals of high-pitched laughter. They disappeared round the corner into the grand boulevard, singing cheerfully.

Ichimura stared at the ground as though horrified to find his master's wife in such a place.

'Everyone is dead, Ichimura,' Hana whispered, her voice faltering, as the singing faded into the distance.

'I know,' said Ichimura. 'I went to your house.'

Hana breathed in sharply, recalling the darkened rooms empty even of cushions, the closed rain doors, the embers glowing in the hearth. She remembered desperately running, wrestling with the rain door with the sounds of crashing and baying just behind, and how she'd run through the woods towards the river, leaving Oharu and Gensuké to fend for themselves.

'It's not the same any more, madam; it doesn't look well cared for.' He stopped and wiped his sleeve across his eyes. 'The servants told me what had happened. There was a girl there and a crippled old man.'

'Oharu and Gensuké! And they were not hurt?' Even to think of them gave Hana a feeling of comfort.

'I was supposed to deliver my message to the master's father,' Ichimura said, frowning. 'They told me what had happened in Kano and said the southerners had come for you too and you had had to flee. They hadn't heard from you since then. They guessed you were dead too, so I gave up and went to the city.' He glanced around and lowered his voice. 'We've formed a resistance movement now, madam. We're going to drive out the southerners and put the shogun back where he belongs. Some of my comrades ended up in Edo and they took me in. I kept asking around, just in case you might still be alive, but then I ran out of money. It was a few days ago.'

'And you went to a pawnbroker and met . . .'

'A woman called Fuyu. She said you sounded very much like the runaway she had met last winter and that she would make some checks.'

So that was why Fuyu had come in search of her and had tricked her into revealing the address of her house. She probably hadn't even delivered the letter, Hana realized with a surge of anger, and Oharu and Gensuké still didn't know she was alive.

'When I went back Fuyu said she had found you and brought me here straight away. I didn't think it could really be you, madam – but then I saw that it was.'

In the starlight Hana could see Ichimura's jaw trembling.

'And my husband?' she whispered. 'My husband?'

'I'm sorry, madam,' Ichimura said, swallowing hard.

Hana took his arm. 'Come inside,' she said gently. 'I'll send to the kitchens for food and tobacco.'

As Ichimura untied his sandals and wiped his feet, Hana remembered that Saburo was in her parlour, sleeping. The house's grand reception room was empty and she ushered Ichimura in there instead. He knelt in the huge room with its painted ceiling, among the lacquered tobacco boxes, hangings, scrolls and blazing candles, sitting straight-backed as a soldier despite his ragged clothes. When she had seen him last he had been a brawny fellow with a broad face, but now his cheeks were sunken and there were black circles around his eyes. He put his bundle on the floor and fumbled with the knot.

There were two boxes inside, a wooden scroll box and a metal box with a tightly fitting lid, the sort an ordinary soldier might use to carry provisions. The youth bowed and handed the boxes to her, holding them out reverently in both hands. They were unexpectedly light. She put them down beside her.

'Please,' she said. 'Tell me. My husband.'

Ichimura sat back on his heels and stared at the ground. When he looked up his face was grim.

'I'll tell you what I can, madam,' he said slowly. 'We had been fighting for months but we were heavily outnumbered and by the fifth month we knew we were beaten. It was unbearably hot. It should have been raining but in Ezo there is no rainy season. Men lay where they died. There were too many to bury and the wounded just got bandaged up and went out to fight some more.

'The master was right in front, leading every battle, but he didn't say much any more. In the evenings he kept to his rooms. Then one day he summoned me. It was the fifth day of the fifth month. He had these boxes. He said, "Ichimura, go to Edo and deliver these to my father. If he is dead, give them to my brothers; if they're dead, to my mother; and if she's dead, to my wife."

'I didn't want to leave him. I wanted to die alongside everyone else and begged him to send someone else but he had that look on his face. He said, "Do as I say or I'll cut you down right now." '

Hana could hear her husband's ferocious bark and see the servants running like chickens to obey his orders. She remembered how she used to run too.

'I waited till there was a lull in the fighting before leaving the fort and as I was leaving I looked back. He was watching me through the gate, making sure I went. I cut through the town to the docks, then got across to the mainland, then walked. It was a long way, madam, and the enemy were all around. Sometimes I had to fight them off, but I always reminded myself that I had my orders and a job to do.'

'And my husband?'

'When I got to Edo, I heard that the enemy had attacked at dawn and closed in on the fort and bombarded it. In the end our leaders surrendered and were arrested and brought down here in cages. I tried to find out what had happened to the master. I knew he would never have let them take him alive but I prayed he might have managed to escape. But then I met men who had seen him fall.'

'He could have been wounded, not killed,' Hana whispered.

'But he's not here, madam, and no one has seen him, and no one knows where he is.'

'But what happened to his body? Shouldn't it be brought down here for burial?'

'You don't understand how many men died, madam,' Ichimura said. 'If the master died in Ezo, then that's where he's buried. Myself, I give prayers for his spirit every day.'

He looked at her as if he was seeing her for the first time.

'Madam, let me help you,' he said quietly. 'The war is over, you are the last of my master's family and I want to do what I can. Let me get you out of here.'

Hana shook her head. 'It's too late for that. But there's one thing I have to ask of you.' She leaned forward and lowered her voice. 'Here we never talk about the past. My husband died a rebel to the new order – to the emperor – and there are a lot of southerners here. Please, I beg you, keep my secret. Don't tell anyone who I am. My safety depends on it.'

Ichimura nodded.

'I served your husband, madam, and I will serve you. I won't betray you.'

Hana drew back as a couple of servants came in. She told them to take Ichimura to the kitchens and carried the two boxes upstairs to her rooms.

She crept through the parlour, casting a sidelong glance at Saburo to check that he was still snoring, then went into her bedroom, sent the maids away and slid the door shut. She took a deep breath and with trembling hands lifted the lid of the scroll box and unrolled the scroll.

She read the first word: 'Greetings.' It was her husband's hand. Peasant though he was, he had swaggered like the most arrogant of samurai and had read and written like one too. Her eyes filled with tears. It was a while before she could focus on the brushstrokes.

'My revered father,' he had written. 'The end is approaching, but we will fight on to defend the shogun's name and honour even if our deaths prove futile. It is the right and proper course. Rest assured that I will not bring shame on you or on the family name.

'I send you with this some mementoes. When peace returns, place them in our family tomb in Kano. It is my destiny to rot in this northern land but I want these mementoes to rest alongside my ancestors. These are my last orders. Think of me as one already dead.'

At the bottom her husband had signed it and marked it with his stamp in faded red ink. Brushing away tears, she prised off the lid of the tin box. A faint scent wafted out: the pungent smell of pomade. Inside was a piece of mulberry paper, neatly folded, containing a hank of black hair streaked with grey, long, glossy and tied with a ribbon. His hair, his smell. Hana held it in her hand, remembering his weight when he lay on her, his salty odour and the sake on his breath. The knot of hair rested in her palm like a dead thing, cold and heavy. When she put it back there was oil on her fingers.

Underneath it, folded in another piece of paper, was a photograph. The grey and white image seemed to fade in the candlelight even as she looked at it. A grown man, as old as her father. She knew the broad forehead, the strong jaw and powerful mouth, the fierce eyes and glossy hair swept back from the angular face. She looked at the crease between his eyebrows and the lines beside his mouth. It was an angry face, a face that frightened her.

The first time she had seen that face had been on their wedding day. That night she had stared shyly at his big toes and broad flat toenails as he opened her robes layer by layer, trying not to recoil at the rough touch of his hands and the ripe smell of his body. 'Let me look at you, my beautiful bride, let me feast my eyes on you,' he had muttered. Then he had climbed on top of her. She remembered the rasp of his breathing and his skin, hot and sweaty, sliding against hers.

And now he was dead. He had packed this box with his own hands, knowing that it would be his last act on this earth. But it was not his father or his brother who'd opened it or even his mother, but his wife – his wife, who had betrayed him, lain with other men and felt disgust for him in her heart.

There was a noise outside in the parlour. Auntie had come to check on Saburo. Frantically Hana threw everything back into the box, pushed it away in a drawer and piled kimonos over it. She would look through it later when everyone had gone.

28

Yozo slid the door of Otsuné's house shut behind him and looked cautiously up and down the narrow lane. Weeds pushed between the stones and along the walls of the rickety houses, a rooster crowed and a half-bald dog was scratching itself in a patch of sunlight. There was no one around as he set off, enjoying the morning hush, the cool air in his lungs and the earth and stones under his feet.

It was his second day in the Yoshiwara and he had managed to persuade Otsuné and Marlin to let him go out, nodding when they reminded them that he was a wanted man and if he did something stupid it would put them in danger too. He was eager to start work on a plan to rescue Enomoto and there were bound to be comrades here, northern soldiers making themselves at home in this lawless place.

He turned on to the great boulevard and stared up at the opulent buildings with their curtained entrances, elegant wooden walls, parlours fronted with latticework caging and balconies with women flitting to and fro. He hadn't seen such magnificence since he'd walked the streets of Europe. Daimyos probably lived in palaces as splendid as these, he thought, but they were hidden behind high walls and closed doors, as everything always was in Japan – except here in the Yoshiwara, where the riches were on display for everyone to see. The place was awash with money – southern money.

The day was still dawning but the street was not entirely

empty. Outside some of the smaller brothels beggars were gathering like carrion, clawing through piles of half-eaten food. Yozo felt a prickling on the skin at the back of his neck and glanced round. In the shadows across the road, a group of tattooed men with oiled topknots was staring at him, narrow-eyed. Bodyguards, he guessed, keeping watch over their pleasure-seeking masters. For them this town was enemy territory. He stared back defiantly; he had every bit as much right to be here as they did.

He was scrutinizing the sweepers, wondering if any of them might straighten up and prove to be a northern soldier, when he caught a whiff of something familiar – the pungent sweetish smell of opium smoke. It had followed him everywhere, from the teeming alleys of Batavia, in Java, to the brothels of Pigalle. Now it took him back to the streets of London, Paris and Amsterdam, where languid young men chewed balls of the potent brown gum and ladies drank laudanum for their nerves. He'd thought Japan was another world, but the Yoshiwara, it seemed, was not. The dream-inducing drug of Europe, China and the Dutch East Indies could be had here too – and here too men were indulging in their first pipe of the day.

The seductive smell set him dreaming, thinking back to the days when he had hung around his teacher's house as a young man, poring with growing fury over news reports of the opium wars, as Britain forced the Chinese to legalize opium and open Chinese ports to British trade so the East India Company could sell it there. The second opium war had finished scarcely two years before Yozo left for the West, in 1860 by the western calendar.

That same year the British had destroyed the emperor's Summer Palace in Peking. Yozo remembered discussing the news with his friends, eager young students all, as they realized that their country too could be vulnerable – that Japan might be invaded, its buildings destroyed and its way of life overturned. He knew that was one of the chief reasons he and his fourteen companions had been sent to the West – to commission warships and learn western ways so that Japan would have a better chance of beating the westerners at their own game. And in the end his countrymen had played their cards better than the Chinese, far better, and had managed to keep the foreigners at bay, for a while, at least.

A thick-set man came puffing towards Yozo, stomach jiggling above his sash.

'He'll be leaving any moment now,' the man panted.

'Who?' asked Yozo, but the man had already padded on up the street and was shouting to the women who leaned over the balconies of the brothels.

Curtains parted and people began to emerge from houses, yawning. Young girls with eager faces painted white, making them look as if they were wearing masks, ancient pinch-faced crones, laughing children and surly youths poured out, sweeping Yozo up in a mass of perfumed bodies. With a great clattering of clogs, the crowd moved down the boulevard, through a tiled and gabled gate and along a side street, then gathered in front of the biggest and most palatial house of all. On the curtains across the doorway were the words 'Corner Tamaya'. Yozo scowled as he recognized the name. It was the place where Hana had told him to go and look for a job. He had thought he had put her out of his mind, but he had ended up here despite himself.

Drawn up outside the entrance was an enormous lacquered palanquin, its gold finishings glinting in the sun. A battalion of servants, porters and guards stood by in silken livery, chests puffed out proudly. Maids in indigo kimonos came hurrying out of the house and formed two long lines flanking the path from the door to the palanquin.

Yozo kept to the back of the crowd while the mob scuffled and shuffled, elbowing each other, trying to get a better view.

'Any moment now,' whispered a young woman to another behind him.

'Maybe he'll spot me.'

'Not you, me. I didn't get dressed up like this for nothing. He'll book me, I'm sure of it!'

There was a sudden disturbance at the edge of the crowd and the mob stumbled back so abruptly that Yozo was crushed against a wall. He heard gasps and shrieks, then angry shouts above the women's shrill voices.

'You – clear off. What do you think you're doing?'

'The boss will be out any moment. Get him out of here!'

'Hey,' a rough voice shouted in a thick southern accent. 'Aren't you one of those cowards who were fighting up north?'

Sensing a fellow northerner in trouble, Yozo forced his way through the bodies, shoving and elbowing people aside, trying to see what was going on.

Standing with his back against the side gate of the Corner Tamaya was a tall, bony figure, staring fiercely around. He looked like a tramp, scrawny and unkempt, with a scar down the side of his face and a couple of swords stuck prominently in his sash. Guards were beating their way towards him, but when they got close to him they drew back and stood, legs apart, sticks in hands, watching the man warily. They were the real cowards, Yozo thought.

'On your way!' shouted one, taking a swing at the man, who grabbed at the guard's stick, twisted it out of his hands, then hurled it contemptuously into the street.

'What were you doing in the Corner Tamaya?' yelled another, aiming a kick at him. 'You're a thief, a cowardly thief!'

The crowd had been watching, silent and cowed. Then a woman squealed, 'Leave him alone!' Voices rose, uncertain at first, then louder, until everyone was shouting, 'Leave him alone! He hasn't done anything wrong. There's one of him and ten of you. Let him be!'

A clog flew from the crowd and hit one of the guards on the back. The guard swung round threateningly, then turned and whacked the man's forearm with his stick.

The man's face darkened. 'Coward, you say,' he said

quietly, his hand on his sword hilt. 'We'll see who's a coward.'

But before he could draw his sword the guards had jumped on him and pushed him against the wall. One punched him in the stomach and another twisted his arm behind his back, shouting obscenities in his face.

Yozo could see by the man's bush of hair that he belonged to the Commander's Kyoto militia; but he was a fellow northerner nonetheless. Shoving people aside, he dived into the mêlée. He landed a punch hard on the ear of the guard who was holding the northerner, then swung round as another guard loomed towards him and sank his fist into the man's fleshy stomach, knocking the air out of him. As the big guard crumpled, Yozo hurled himself on to a third man, knocking him to the ground with such violence he tore off the sleeve of his silk jacket, then lashed out with the side of his foot and felled a fourth. The northern soldier too was fighting like a demon and had brought down a couple more of the guards.

'Let's get out of here,' he shouted, grabbing at Yozo's arm. But as Yozo tried to follow, he lost his grip and the guards, who had scrambled back on to their feet, closed in around him. The northern soldier turned and Yozo could see him struggling to get back, until he was swallowed up in the crowd.

Yozo cursed. He'd managed to do exactly what he'd promised Marlin he wouldn't – get into trouble. If the guards arrested him, they'd discover he was on the run, Marlin and Otsuné would be punished and the plan to rescue Enomoto would be ended before it had even begun. He had put his hand on his dagger and turned to face his assailants, when there was a piercing screech.

'Stop that, right now!'

Silence fell as a steely-eyed crone, sheathed in black from head to toe, bore down on him. She had a crinkled, malevolent death mask of a face and a shiny black wig perched on her head and was flailing her cane. Yozo flinched as the stick cracked down on his skull. She had raised her arm to hit him again when there was a rustle of silk.

'Auntie, Auntie. I know this man.'

Yozo pulled himself free of the guards and swung round. Women in gorgeous kimonos with painted faces had emerged from the house and were standing in the entranceway. Right at the back, almost hidden from view, was a delicate figure, tiny and exquisite. Her hair was in an ornate coil and she wore a kimono that shimmered voluptuously in the sun, but beneath the finery Yozo knew her. It was Hana.

In the hush every word rang out clearly. 'He's one of my staff – a terrible troublemaker – and I take full responsibility. Guards, let him go.'

The guards fell to their knees, bowing. 'Yes, madam,' they grunted. 'Sorry, madam.' They stood up and backed off, muttering curses.

'It's Otsuné's cousin from the countryside,' Yozo heard Hana say to the old woman. 'I promised I'd keep an eye on him.'

She stepped forward and waved her hand dismissively at Yozo. 'You – the maids will take you to my rooms. Stay there and behave yourself until someone comes with orders.'

As the maids ushered him away, Yozo caught a glimpse of a huge figure coming out of the main entrance on stubby legs. The man turned towards him and Yozo thought he caught a glint of recognition in his bulging eyes. Then the man climbed into the palanquin and the porters heaved it on to their shoulders, groaning, their faces purple and the veins standing out on their foreheads.

As the palanquin moved away, a thick finger prodded open the bamboo blind at the back and the beady eye reappeared. He was staring at Hana.

The blind remained open as the palanquin carved a path through the bowing crowd and careered into the distance with its train of liveried servants scampering behind.

29

Yozo stood awkwardly at the entrance to Hana's luxurious living room. In the soft light that filtered through the paper screens that walled one side of the room, he could see that the floor was covered in trays of half-eaten food, broken chopsticks and over-turned sake flasks – debris from an extraordinarily extravagant banquet. Incense had been thrown on the brazier and the scent suffused the room, a complex blend of aloe, sandalwood and myrrh. Yozo recognized it – it was the fragrance that wafted from Hana's sleeves.

So this is where she belongs, he thought, bemused. While he could be perfectly at home on board ship or in a fort or on the battlefield with a rifle slung on his back, here, in a sea of hangings, drapes and kimonos, he felt distinctly out of place. Once he might have been able to afford a woman such as this, but now, in his current straitened circumstances, she was way beyond his means.

But there was something poignant about the place, too. Luxurious though it was, he knew she couldn't leave. The courtesans of Europe might have chosen their profession but she was trapped here, like a bird in a golden cage.

He prowled up and down. He should be outside on the street, he thought, frowning, searching out comrades, not lingering in a prostitute's parlour. Yet still he stayed. After all, he told himself, he had to thank Hana for intervening and saving him from arrest. But there was another bond that held him too, to do with Hana herself.

Something else was bothering him – the toad-like man he'd seen climbing into the palanquin. He remembered the fear on Hana's face when she'd heard the bell toll the previous afternoon. Could it have been because she knew she would have to spend the night with him? Looking around the room, Yozo saw that the cushions in front of the gilded screen were squashed flat as if a huge body had lain on them. He punched his fist into his hand and grimaced, picturing the fellow he had seen enjoying himself here in Hana's boudoir.

A couple of steps took him across the room to the sleeping chamber. He stared at the pile of bedding in the corner – finest silken damask, red crêpe with black velvet borders, heavily scented. Kimonos hung on the walls and on racks and there was a sword rack pushed to the side of the room, but he saw with relief that the futons were scattered around the floor as if a courtesan and her attendants had slept there, not laid out side by side as they would have been for a courtesan and a guest.

Something metallic was poking out from under a kimono. It was a box, not lacquered or inlaid with ivory like the kind a client would give a courtesan, but a plain metal box such as soldiers carried. He had one himself. It was a shock to see it amid the perfumed silks of Hana's sleeping chamber. She must have had a husband or lover or brother or father who had been in the war and had sent it back, he thought. He turned away. The war was behind him and he wanted to keep it that way. Stifled by the swathes of fabric, the quilted kimonos, the perfumes, creams and powders, he hurried back to the reception room.

Sitting cross-legged on the brocade cushions, he picked up a long-stemmed pipe. The toad-like man had looked at him as if he knew him, he thought. He was sure he had seen him somewhere before too, though he couldn't for the life of him think where. Then a faint whiff of opium smoke wafted through the paper screens and in a flash Yozo remembered.

Opium. It had been nearly seven years before, when he and his comrades had been shipwrecked on their way to Holland and had

had to spend fifteen days in Java, in the port of Batavia, the most diseased, fever-ridden place he'd ever known. Yozo had been out one night with Enomoto and Kitaro when they'd lost their way and ended up in a maze of alleys reeking of spices, opium and sewage.

They had been stumbling through the darkness along a particularly noxious back street when a door had opened and a girl had burst out and run straight into him, sending him staggering against a crumbling wooden wall. In the glare from the open door, he had caught a glimpse of a white face with slanted eyes and sharp cheekbones, lit with a yellow light. The girl's mouth was open, contorted with fear, and her pupils huge.

He had been picking himself up when a crowd of men burst out, dragged the girl to her feet and hauled her, screaming and kicking, back inside. Yozo, Enomoto and Kitaro had taken one look at each other and were about to go to her rescue when a dark shadow appeared, filling the doorway. It was a man as bulky as a sumo wrestler, with a small head and eyes that disappeared into folds of puffy flesh, more like the overlord of a Japanese yakuza gang than any local man. The girl too, Yozo realized now, had looked Japanese.

'What's going on?' Yozo had shouted.

'She's my property.' The man had a high-pitched, tinny voice. 'This is a private matter, no need to trouble yourselves. Thank you for your help, gentlemen.' As the door slammed shut they had heard screams from inside and sounds of beating and Yozo had realized as he turned away that if he hadn't blocked the girl's path she might have escaped.

Much had happened since then and Yozo had almost forgotten the incident. But now he remembered, as clearly as if it had been yesterday, the yellow glare falling from the open door and lighting up the fetid alley, the woman's pale frightened face, the gleam of the man's eyes. It had been dark and Yozo had barely glimpsed his face, but it had been so distinctive he could picture it still. He had grown fatter and more bloated since then, but it was the same man.

Thinking back, Yozo remembered that they had reported the incident to the Dutch authorities in Batavia; but once he and his friends had found their way out of the maze of alleys they'd realized that they'd never be able to locate the house again. The authorities had told them it was in a part of town that decent people steered well clear of and that the area was rife with criminal gangs engaged in everything from opium trading to trading in women. Japanese women in particular were in great demand, they had heard, to be sold as concubines to wealthy Chinese merchants. There were murders there too and they were advised not to venture that way again.

Yozo picked up a piece of charcoal, held it to the bowl of the pipe and puffed until the tobacco glowed red, thinking hard. It was best to say nothing to Hana. He had no proof and, even if he had, there was nothing she could do about it.

He blew out a plume of smoke. He would have to keep his eyes open, though. If no one else was prepared to shield her from harm, he would make sure he did.

30

Hana paused outside the doors to her rooms and took a breath. She knew plenty of men and Yozo was just another, she told herself sternly, and that was all there was to it. Only it was not, not at all.

She remembered the shouts and scuffling as she had come out of the house a little while earlier, how she had seen Ichimura's bush of hair bobbing about in the middle of a mob of hoodlums and gasped in horror as he had disappeared under a barrage of whirling arms and topknotted heads.

Then the next moment Yozo had been there. She hadn't even had time to wonder what he was doing there but had watched, breathless with admiration, as he dispatched the thugs with calm efficiency, delivering punches here and kicks there like a martial arts master. And now – unless he'd run off – he was waiting for her here, in her rooms.

Timidly she slid open the door. Yozo was sitting cross-legged, smoking a pipe. His eyes lit up as he saw her and she shut the door and knelt opposite him. He had smoothed his hair and tidied his clothes and was quite transformed from the rough street fighter she had seen a few moments earlier. She took in the contours of his face, his direct gaze and strong mouth. He was looking rather stern.

'I thought Otsuné and Jean told you to stay out of trouble,' Hana said teasingly, trying to keep her voice light and playful.

'You saved my skin,' he said, returning her gaze steadily.

She sighed. In her luxurious quarters, surrounded by lavish hangings, with damask cushions neatly arranged beside lacquered tobacco boxes and a pile of futons visible through the double doors in the sleeping chamber, he could have no more doubts about what she was. 'So my secret's out,' she said at last. 'I so much hoped you would never find out what I do.'

'You certainly live in great splendour,' he said, raising an eyebrow. 'I've never seen such luxury. You must have plenty of admirers, so many that you can pick and choose.' He refilled his pipe, turning the plug of tobacco over and over in his fingers until they were stained brown. When he spoke again his voice was low. 'But doesn't it worry you that there's such a heavy price to pay? I saw the way that man looked at you as he left. You don't even know who he is, yet you let him fondle your body. How can you bear it?'

Hana recoiled as if he had hit her.

'None of us has any choice in our lives,' she retorted, her voice shaking. 'Not you either. Courtesans are not like other women, we're another breed. Maybe I wasn't always so but I realize it now. And I am not ashamed of what I do.' She drew herself up. 'Anyway, you're wrong. I do know who that man is. His name is Saburosuké Kashima and he's rich, far richer than you'll ever be.'

Yozo scowled. 'Rich, you say? Do you know where his money comes from?'

'He's a merchant with a huge trading empire.' Hana tried to keep her voice defiant but it wavered uncertainly. He was looking at her in a way that made her feel uncomfortable.

'For all you know he might be a money lender who sends thugs to beat people up when they don't pay him back in time; or he might trade in opium or women.' Yozo paused. 'I think I came across him once before, in Batavia. If I'm right, he may be dangerous.'

Hana took her fan from her obi. 'There are bad men all over the Yoshiwara who come here to hide from the law. I'm not such an innocent as you seem to think. And anyway, I'm perfectly safe here in the Corner Tamaya. Auntie and Father would never let anyone harm me – they've invested too much in me.'

Her voice trailed off as she realized she had never talked like this to anyone before. Men paid her to take an interest in them, not tell them about herself. But Yozo didn't seem interested in her body so much as how she led her life. Suddenly she was touched by his concern. 'I'm meant to be able to choose who I sleep with – and I always have, until now. But Saburo's different. If Auntie can make money out of forcing me to sleep with him, then she will, and I'll have to.'

She leaned towards him. 'It was Saburo's first visit, and I was lucky. He fell asleep and slept like a baby all night.'

Yozo tapped out his pipe and spread his hands on his thighs. They were tanned and muscular, a working man's hands. Hana reached out and put her hand on his. 'But thank you for caring what happens to me.'

He put his pipe down, sprawled on one elbow and fixed his eyes on her, propping his head on his hand. There was something about him – even the way he held his body – that was different from any man she'd ever known. He was dressed like a serving man in borrowed clothes – she recognized the clothes Otsuné had given him the previous day – and his face was scarred and sun-tanned like a farmer's, yet he carried himself as arrogantly as a prince.

Hana was used to men falling at her feet. She could make herself whatever they wanted her to be – their lover, their confidante, their mother; that was what they paid her for. But with Yozo she knew she couldn't play-act. She had assumed she could bewitch any man, but with him she found herself a little in awe. He seemed to see through her mask to the child inside. She was not even sure if her famed beauty had the slightest effect on him.

'Where did you say you'd met Saburo?' she asked.

He shook his head. 'It doesn't matter.'

'It wasn't in Japan,' she said. 'It was somewhere else. Have you been . . . outside Japan?'

She stared at him, wide-eyed, beginning to realize what it was that made him seem so different. No one she knew had ever dreamed of leaving Japan. That was where foreign sailors came from and where Otsuné's Jean came from. Yozo too had something of that quality of belonging somewhere else, of knowing things she didn't know and being part of a world she couldn't even imagine.

'You said you would tell me everything,' she whispered, moving closer to him. Her arm brushed his and she felt a tingle of excitement.

He stared into the distance for a while, then picked up his pipe again, turning it over and over in his hand. 'You know the saying: "A nail that sticks out must be hammered in"? People think we're polluted, me and my friends, because we've been abroad and mixed with people like Jean. They say we're spies or traitors, not true Japanese.' He smiled, but it was a sad smile.

'I don't think that,' she said. 'But have you been to Jean's country? I'd like to know what it's like, the place where he comes from.'

Yozo sighed. 'It's beautiful,' he said slowly. 'The capital, Paris, is almost as big as Edo, but the buildings are made of stone, not wood, and they're so high it makes your neck hurt to look at them. Even the sky is a different colour, softer and paler.'

Hana frowned, trying to imagine it. 'And the people,' she said. 'Do they look like Jean?' She thought of Jean's huge body, his strange-coloured hair, coarse skin and startling blue eyes, and put her hand over her mouth. 'The women too? Do they have black hair like us, or are they like Jean?'

Yozo was gazing into the distance as if he was somewhere far away. 'But in a way they're right,' he said softly, as if he was speaking to himself. 'I'm not a true Japanese. I don't belong here any more, I've been away too long. This is a closed world and I'm not part of it. I've seen too much, I know too much, I ask too many questions.'

Hana wanted to tell him that she understood, that in the Yoshiwara she too was an outsider, she didn't belong here either.

'Where do you come from?' she asked. 'Where is your home and your family?'

'Gone, all dead. Yours too, I suspect. I wasn't always a poor soldier and you weren't always a courtesan. You don't belong in the Yoshiwara at all, do you? You said it yourself – we've all had to find ways to survive.'

He sat up, looking at her intently, and she noticed a fleck of gold in his brown eyes. Then he took her hands and raised them to his lips. Hana shivered, feeling the touch of his mouth, then quickly drew back. Her body belonged to Auntie. Even to be alone with Yozo was a transgression. If anyone caught them she would be beaten and she shuddered to think what they would do to him.

Yozo was frowning too. 'Men pay for this privilege,' he said. 'But I can't afford even this.'

Hana tried to move away from him, to stifle the yearning that burned inside her, but she seemed to have lost all control over her limbs. IShe looked up at him and he took her face in his hands. As his lips touched hers, it seemed right and complete, like the fulfilment of a dream.

She ran her fingers across his face and stroked his smooth cheek, then took his hand, feeling the calluses that edged his palm.

'This hand has seen fighting,' she said softly.

'Remember what I told you,' he said, stroking her hair. 'I'll always be here to protect you.'

Hana put her arms around him, feeling his body hot against hers. Their lips brushed again and she closed her eyes and let herself dissolve in the shock of desire his touch awakened in her.

Outside, the corridor was silent. With a mad recklessness that was like a reaching out for freedom, she let her body melt into his and their lips closed in a kiss so intense it took her breath away.

31

The morning was hot and sultry and Yozo was lounging in Hana's sleeping chamber in the Corner Tamaya. He ran his fingers through her hair, which tumbled in a glossy cascade across the pillowy futons, and thought the gods must have taken him under their protection. A few days had passed since the fight and he still couldn't believe how much his life had changed.

Their snatched moments together were intensely sweet, all the more so because they had to be so surreptitious. He loved her fragrance, the softness of her skin when he gathered her up in his arms and held her. To the outside world she was a famous beauty; but he knew that with him she could be herself.

Outside, wild geese were flocking and the first bottle gourds were blooming along the walls of the Yoshiwara. Summer was coming to an end. After so much disaster – the unwinnable war, the desperate battles in the burning heat – Yozo had finally begun to forget the horrors he'd seen and look towards the future.

They still hadn't made love. He knew he had her heart, but her body was reserved for other men. The fact that he could never spend a night with her tortured him – yet for all the obstacles that surrounded them, he was happier than he could ever have dared imagine.

He hadn't forgotten his mission to free Enomoto and Otori and that too was beginning to fall into place. The northern soldier he had helped, Ichimura, had joined him along with two comrades he'd tracked down, Hiko and Heizo, and they were doing their best to locate their imprisoned comrades.

Whenever he came for his morning visits, Hana dismissed the maids and closed the doors of the sleeping chamber, leaving them open a crack so she could hear if anyone was approaching. Kawanoto, her young attendant, whom she had taken into her confidence, had promised to keep watch and warn them if Auntie was on her way.

Now Hana lay on her side, smiling up at him.

'Is it true? Has Saburo really gone?' he asked.

'He didn't come back even once. Auntie told me he'd sent a message saying he'd gone to Osaka on business. Of course, I told her how disappointed I was.' She smiled mischievously.

'He'll be back,' said Yozo. 'But we'll deal with that when it happens.' He kissed her nose, smelling the scent of her hair, feeling it brush against his chest as she nestled against him.

'I loved seeing you in western clothes yesterday,' she whispered. 'You looked so handsome.'

'Auntie's very pleased,' Yozo said. 'All thanks to you.'

Hana had persuaded Auntie that what the Corner Tamaya needed to give it the edge above the other houses was an interpreter for the wealthy westerners who were beginning to arrive at the Yoshiwara. Before, unless they'd been brought by Japanese colleagues, they'd always had to go away again, despondent because they couldn't communicate with the girls – except, that is, for the foreign sailors, who weren't interested in talking and headed straight for the lower-class brothels along the back alleys. Otsuné's cousin, Hana had told Auntie, could speak the westerners' languages and, with him as interpreter, the Corner Tamaya would be able to attract a far higher – and better-paying – level of clientele.

'So Tama had her first western clients last night,' Hana said.

'There were two of them, Englishmen. Tama wanted to know if they needed an extra girl as well, or a boy, but I told her I couldn't ask Englishmen a question like that.' He laughed. 'I told her we have to encourage them to come back, not scare them away.'

'Englishmen must be very strange,' said Hana, laughing too. 'I thought they came here to enjoy themselves.'

'They gave her an excellent tip, so Tama was pleased, and they've already booked her again for tonight, so they must have been satisfied.'

In the distance a bell began to toll, booming out from the temple at the far end of the boulevard. Hana started and looked up at him.

'We have so little time together – and always in the morning,' she said wistfully.

'I'll find a way to take you away from all this,' he whispered, kissing her hair.

He stood up, pulling his robe around him. It was time to leave. He was taking a last lingering look around the sleeping chamber when he noticed something had changed.

On the small household altar in the shadows to one side of the room were fresh offerings and a photograph with candles burning beside it. The metal box he'd noticed before was there too, behind the photograph.

Seeing it gave him a shock like a physical blow. In the few days they'd known each other, Yozo had not said much about his life before they met and Hana hadn't either. He had talked about his journey to Europe – though he knew that to her it was more like a fantasy – but he'd skirted around the war in Ezo and what he'd done there, and he'd never asked about her past or how she'd come to be in the Yoshiwara. Yoshiwara women never talked about their past; as far as their clients were concerned, their lives had begun when they arrived there. With Hana he had an intimacy which her clients could never dream of, but nevertheless he had not thought to ask her who or what she had once been. But now all this untold history seemed to close in around him, threatening to crush their cocoon of happiness.

He stepped towards the altar. He was reluctant to see the face in the photograph – he had a superstitious feeling he might recognize it – but he also felt an uncontrollable curiosity. The picture was faded and yellowing, curling at the edges, and it was difficult to make it out in the candlelight, but it was clear enough for Yozo to see the broad forehead, the piercing eyes and the thick hair swept back.

A chill ran down his spine and his throat constricted. Just as he'd started a new life, just as he'd thought the war and its horrors were behind him, this face had returned to haunt him. He swallowed, hearing the roar of gunfire in his ears, feeling the heat of the blazing town, and rounding a corner in a ruined street to see this face looming before him. For there could be no doubting it: it was the Commander.

He stared at the picture, stifled by the incense and candle smoke. There could be only one reason why it was here in the room of this woman who had captured his heart: she must be the daughter or the sister or – most unthinkable of all – the widow of his enemy. He should leave now, he told himself, with no explanation. He had no right to be here. But then he remembered Saburo and the dark street in Batavia. Saburo would be back soon, and he couldn't let Hana fall into his hands.

'This man – who is he to you?' he asked, his voice thick. 'Is he your brother? Your father?'

'My husband.' Her words were like a stone falling into a lake, sending ripples into the silence. 'Did you know him?'

He clenched his fists, feeling himself break out into a sweat. He couldn't lie to her, they'd become too close. But he knew that if he told her the truth – that he had killed this man – he'd lose her for ever.

He hesitated, wondering how to reply. 'Everyone knew Commander Yamaguchi,' he said finally.

'Please keep my secret,' she said urgently. 'My husband was a rebel, like you, and a famous one. If anyone knew, I'd be ruined. The men that come here are all southerners.' He heard the panic in her voice.

He nodded. There was a long silence.

When she spoke again there was relief in her voice. 'I know he was a great man and a great warrior; everyone was in awe of him. My parents told me how lucky I was to be given in marriage to such a man. But I was always afraid of him. It's a terrible thing to say, but I was happy when he left for the war. But then I ended up here, in the Yoshiwara. I've been so afraid that he'd come back and find me here and kill me.'

She moved the photograph and candles aside and lifted down the box. 'Then Ichimura brought me a letter from him and this box. At first I didn't know what I should do; but I realized it was my duty to mourn him. I knew you might see the photograph and recognize him but there's no one else alive now who can pay respect to his spirit. His last wish was for his mementoes to be buried in the family tomb in Kano and I'll do that. He was harsh and cruel, but he was still my husband.'

She opened the box. 'It's strange, but I feel as if I never really knew him. He wrote a poem and when I read it, I was touched by it.'

She took out a small scroll and unrolled it. Yozo was back in Ezo, seeing Kitaro's body in the moonlight and bursting into the Commander's rooms. He could see the Commander's handsome face and the brush in his hand and hear him saying sardonically, *'Your death poem. Have you written your death poem yet, Tajima?'* The first line of the Commander's poem had burned into his mind. He recognized the confident brushstrokes as he read the words:

> Though my body may decay on the island of Ezo,
> My spirit guards my lord in the east.

Somehow the picture hadn't been enough to convince him that the Commander really was Hana's husband. But now as he saw the poem he knew it was true: they were one and the same.

'I'm not even sure he's dead,' she whispered, rolling the paper up and putting it back in the box. 'Ichimura left Ezo long before the last battle and didn't see him fall. I always have the fear lurking at the back of my mind that he might not be dead after all, that he'll come back and find me.'

As she spoke, Yozo realized that he was the one person in the world who knew for sure what had happened to her husband.

'I have a secret too,' he said hoarsely; but as he spoke he realized he couldn't tell her that he had shot his own commanding officer, that he had killed the Commander. No matter how she felt about her husband, it was too dreadful a crime to confess.

'I . . . I fought in the last battle. I was there, I saw him fall.' He shook his head. 'Don't ask me to tell you any more. He's dead, believe me, I know he's dead.'

She put her arms around him and he buried his face in her hair. 'Let's not talk about it any more,' she said. 'It's over. We're here together now.'

32

Hana stood at the door of the Corner Tamaya, bowing to the last of her clients as he turned into the boulevard, then made her way back to her rooms, her mind still buzzing with the conversation she had had with Yozo the day before.

There was so much she would have liked to ask him – how her husband had died, for a start, and what had happened to his body; but she knew she would never be able to. She had seen the pain on Yozo's face; it was obvious he could hardly bear to think about the war. She should be grateful that he had told her as much as he had, she thought.

She didn't even know how well he had known her husband, only that he had been present when he died. They must have been fighting shoulder to shoulder. But the one thing she could be sure of was that her husband was dead. A burden had been lifted from her shoulders, now that Yozo knew her secret. She was no longer alone – and no longer in fear of her husband. With Yozo's help she would find a way to escape and they would go back together to her house, to Oharu and Gensuké.

She would find a way to smuggle Yozo into her sleeping chamber that night, she told herself, hide him in the futon cupboard, perhaps. The thought of it made her laugh out loud. She knew he was far too proud, he would never agree to something so ignominious.

While the maids bustled around, clearing the dishes and folding the futons, she went to the altar and lit the candles and incense and laid out fresh offerings. Hearing footsteps, she looked up eagerly, thinking it was Yozo arriving for his morning visit; but then her face fell as she realized it was not his rapid stride but a shuffle. Pulling her robe around her, she ran into the reception room.

A moment later there was a cough outside and Auntie hobbled in in a cloud of tobacco smoke. Hana looked at her in surprise. The old woman was in a plain cotton robe as if she had dressed in a hurry, without any make-up or wig. She had a strange gleam in her eye. She went over to the alcove and straightened the scroll, studied the shelf of tea ceremony implements and shifted the whisks and bamboo spoons around, then knelt beside the tobacco box and started to refill her pipe.

'How long have you been with us, my dear?' she enquired in her ancient croak. 'More than half a year, isn't it? I've grown so fond of you, as if you were my own daughter.'

Taking the kettle off the brazier, Hana filled the teapot and nodded politely, wondering what Auntie was leading up to. It wasn't like her to be so friendly.

'From the moment I saw you I always knew you'd do well,' Auntie said. 'You've really brought the Yoshiwara back to life. It's nearly as glorious now as it was in its heyday, when I was the star courtesan, celebrated across the country – not quite as glorious, of course, but nearly. And the Corner Tamaya is its most famous house, entirely thanks to you. No other house can boast a courtesan with anything like your charms. You're booked up for months. We're very pleased, my dear.'

She leaned forward. Her face was withered but Hana could see the fine bones under the ruined skin and picture the beautiful woman she had once been.

Auntie wasn't showing any signs of being about to leave. She called to the maids and gave them a scolding, then sent Kawanoto out to get a menu from one of the vendors, puffing energetically on her pipe all the while, then took a sip of the tea Hana offered her. If she didn't go soon, Hana thought despairingly, the morning would be over and there'd be no chance of Yozo visiting that day.

Then Auntie took a long draw on her pipe, puffed out a cloud of smoke and sat back on her heels. 'I wanted to tell you the news as soon as your clients had gone. I knew you'd be excited at such extraordinary good luck. But you deserve it, no one more than you.'

Hana sat up, staring suspiciously. Auntie always came to the point straight away; whatever it was she had to say, it couldn't be good.

'I must say, I'll be sorry to see you go,' said Auntie.

Hana had stopped breathing. Whatever could Auntie mean? Could it be that she was planning to cancel Hana's debt and give her her freedom? She would never dream of doing such a thing. No, something else was going on.

'I know you'll miss us too,' Auntie continued. 'Of course, you'll need to pack up and get ready, but there'll be plenty of time to make the arrangements and give you a good send-off.'

Someone must have offered to buy her freedom, Hana thought; but in that case why didn't Auntie just come out and say so, instead of being so evasive?

'It'll be a wonderful occasion. Saburo's going to close the Yoshiwara for the night and throw the biggest party anyone's ever heard of.'

Hana looked at her uncomprehendingly. 'Saburo . . . ?'

'Yes, you've caught the biggest fish in the country, the one all the girls were after. All these years he's been such a playboy. He's always said he was looking for the perfect woman and now, it seems, he's found her at last. I'm not surprised, mind you, with your talents and looks. He's going to throw a huge party for you when he gets back from Osaka.'

'You mean . . . Saburo's made an offer and you've come to ask whether I agree?' Numb with horror, Hana could barely frame the words.

'My dear girl, you have to move quickly if you want to do

business round here. If we hadn't agreed straight away he might very well have looked elsewhere. He's the most desirable man that's ever passed through the Yoshiwara. Remember, Father and I have nothing but your best interests in mind. You're just a young girl, you have no idea about the world.'

For a moment, Hana was dumbstruck. Then the words burst out before she could stop them. 'You mean you've sold me to Saburo? But . . . but you can't do that.'

Auntie's smile froze. She had that glint in her eye that reminded Hana that no matter how glamorous and famous she might think she was, she was still just a possession. 'I can do anything I want, my girl,' she said smoothly. 'Don't forget, you haven't paid us back a single copper *mon* yet. You owe us a great deal of money and your debt is getting larger by the day. But don't worry, we've worked it all out – how much you could make for us by staying here and how much we'll get if we accept Saburo's offer. Saburo is a generous man and he's determined to have you.'

Her face changed and she gave a bland smile. 'It's for your own good, my dear. We're thinking of your future.'

Hana swallowed hard. She couldn't imagine anything more dreadful.

'No need to worry your head over it,' said Auntie dismissively, rising to her feet. 'You don't even have to have other clients any more. I've cancelled all your appointments.

'And don't imagine you might slip away,' she snapped as Hana opened her mouth to protest. 'You're far too valuable. Till Saburo comes to collect you, you'll stay right here in your rooms. We'll make sure you have all the food and sewing materials and paper and books you could possibly want. Oh, and that Yozo – I've told the men he's not to bother you. You can have a lovely time, reading, sewing, practising tea ceremony, getting ready for the day when Saburo comes to claim you.

'Father's already settled everything and taken a deposit. You're Saburo's property now.'

Hana sat for a long time after the door had closed and the

footsteps had shuffled away, too stunned even to weep. Then, as the full meaning of what Auntie had said began to sink in, she stumbled into her sleeping chamber, buried her face in her futons and sobbed till she thought she could have no more tears left. Just as she'd had a taste of happiness for the first time in her life, she'd lost everything. Sold to Saburo! It was a fate more terrible than she could ever have imagined. Even Yozo couldn't save her now.

Autumn

秋

33

The typhoon season had come and gone, the trees were changing colour and the leaves were beginning to fall. In the mornings frost sparkled on the Yoshiwara's roofs and wooden walkways and paving stones. It was a time of cool air and brilliant blue skies, although along the alley where Otsuné lived the sun barely rose above the meagre houses.

Sitting with Marlin in Otsuné's little house, Yozo sighed and took a puff on his pipe. He was tired of exile, of this small square of five streets inhabited by painted women and outlawed men, with its nightly influx of drunken pleasure-seekers. He was impatient to get back to the real world.

'I have news!'

The door flew open and Ichimura burst in, his hair sticking out wildly around his head. Since the fight outside the Corner Tamaya he had become a regular visitor.

'Admiral Enomoto,' he said panting, kicking off his sandals and throwing himself down on the tatami beside Yozo and Marlin. 'We found him, and General Otori too!'

Yozo leaned forward, listening hard, a grin spreading across his face.

'They're not in Kodenmacho Prison after all.' Ichimura snatched up a cup of sake and gulped it down. 'They're in a prisoner-of-war camp in the castle grounds, inside the Hitotsubashi Gate – the Place of Disciplinary Confinement, they call it. There are five camps with a couple of hundred men in each, dreadful places, all of them.'

'So you saw Enomoto and Otori?' demanded Yozo.

'No. I heard all this from Eijiro, one of our men. He grew his hair to make him look like a doctor and fooled the guards into letting him in.'

'But how are they?'

'He says they're in reasonable health, a bit thin, but in good spirits.'

'And the prison, what's it like, what's the layout?' Marlin butted in in his deep grumble, his heavy brow creased in a frown.

'It's a terrible place, Eijiro says, filthy and infested, and there is not much food – rice and soup, that's all. And it stinks. The lower ranks are crowded into a long hall with two rows of tatami mats, one man, one mat. Some of the men are wounded and a lot more are sick, but at least the admiral and the general have their own room. Eijiro is going back today with food, blankets and medicine, as much as he can carry.'

'We've got to get Enomoto and Otori out, and as many of the others as we can.'

'That won't be easy. The castle grounds are well fortified and guarded, with massive walls. But there are rumours that the admiral and the general are to be transferred to Kodenmacho Prison quite soon.'

Yozo put down his pipe and leaned forward.

'Do you know when?'

'Within ten days. Eijiro's doing his best to find out more.'

'You know there's an execution ground at Kodenmacho Prison,' said Marlin. He sat like the master of the house, topping up the sake cups, poking the glowing embers in the brazier and handing round dried rice crackers. Yozo took a mouthful of sake and raised an eyebrow.

'You've been in the prison?'

'We French officers worked for the shogun when we first came to Japan. We went everywhere and saw everything.'

'Well, they won't execute them behind closed doors,' said Yozo. 'That's not the way we do things here, nor in your country either.' He knew that well enough; he'd seen the guillotine in action in Paris. 'If they're planning executions they'll do them in public, as a warning to the people, and they'll stick their heads on the spikes on Japan Bridge.'

'We'll just have to make sure that doesn't happen, won't we,' said Marlin, getting up and going to Otsuné's work area. He emerged a few moments later with a roll of paper and a brush and handed them to Ichimura.

'They'll be taking them from Hitotsubashi Gate to the prison.' Spreading the paper on the floor, Ichimura put weights on the corners, ground some ink and started to draw a rough map. 'They'll have to take the Tokiwa Bridge across the inner moat then go straight down here through Kanda,' he went on, drawing a line to mark the main road. 'They're loyal to the shogun down there, loyal to the death. If we attack the procession they'll be with us. We can count on them.'

'We'll need to get a message to Enomoto and Otori,' Yozo said.

'Enomoto gave himself up,' Marlin said, waving a large finger. 'He may not want you to free him. He may consider it a matter of honour to go to his death with his head high. He's a proud man.'

'Then he's wrong,' said Yozo brusquely. 'If we free him, it will be a major blow to the new regime. A lot of northerners will gather round him and it will give the resistance a new lease of life. I'll spring him whether he wants it or not.'

'You're on the run yourself, don't forget that,' said Marlin. 'You'll end up with your head on Japan Bridge alongside Enomoto's.'

'That's a risk I'm ready to take,' said Yozo, reaching for the sake flask and topping up the men's cups. 'We'll need to check the exact day and the route the procession will take. They'll be expecting an ambush and will probably make a last-minute change of plan, so we'll need to take that into account too. What weapons do we have?'

'The militia headquarters is sealed off and under guard, but I sneaked in one night,' Ichimura said. 'I picked up Dreyse needle guns, Minié rifles, handguns and some serviceable swords and daggers.'

'Good man,' said Yozo, slapping the youth on the shoulder. He'd be glad to get his hands on a rifle again, he thought.

The men sat in silence for a while, sipping sake. Yozo tapped out his pipe and kneaded a plug of tobacco in his fingers, frowning. Marlin shifted and cursed, then stretched out his long French legs, massaging his knees with a big hand.

'So what's going on in the city?' he asked at last. 'There've been rumours around here about a pawnbroker and a suspicious death.'

'Oh, that.' Ichimura grinned. 'Every time you go to the barber, it's all you hear.'

'You, go to the barber, with that hair?' Yozo asked.

'Well, OK, every time I go to the bathhouse. You'd think people would have something better to talk about.' He leaned forward. 'Rat poison,' he hissed. 'The pawnbroker got ill all of a sudden and his hair began to fall out, then he started bleeding from the nose and ears and died within hours.'

'Nasty way to go,' grunted Marlin.

'His wife, was it?' Yozo asked.

'No one knows. He was a mean old fellow. There were a lot of people who would have liked to see him dead. It could have been someone who owed him money and that he was putting pressure on to pay up, or a gangster he cheated. Anyway, the police are on the case. I'll keep you posted.'

He gave a cheerful high-pitched laugh and Yozo grinned at him. Sometimes he forgot how young Ichimura was.

After Ichimura had left, Yozo and Marlin sat together, puffing on their pipes. Yozo tipped his head back and emptied his sake cup, enjoying the sensation of the hot liquid in his throat. He could feel the sake warming his cheeks and loosening his lips, making the world seem a gentler place.

'You have your doubts about this rescue operation, I can see that,' said Marlin, looking at him hard. Since they'd been in the Yoshiwara the Frenchman had grown plump and sleek, like a well-fed cat. It was obvious he was happy to be back with his woman and not in any hurry to be on the road again.

'I know it's a hare-brained plan but we have to do it,' Yozo said. 'We owe it to Enomoto and Otori. But you don't have to come, Jean; in fact we'd be better off without you. You're too conspicuous.'

Marlin nodded. 'I'm ready to come with you if you want me to. But you're right – it won't do you any good to have a hulking Frenchman drawing attention to himself.'

'And you have to keep yourself safe for Otsuné's sake.'

'She's a good woman, none better,' said Marlin, nodding his head thoughtfully. 'But it's not just that it's a risky enterprise – you've never been one to baulk at taking risks. It's Hana, isn't it?'

Yozo nodded. He knew he had to do whatever it took to save his friends, but he hated the thought of Hana falling into Saburo's hands, all the more so because he'd promised to protect her. And the dreadful secret that he had to keep from her, that he was guilty of her husband's death, bound him to her all the more strongly.

'Otsuné says they're keeping a tighter watch on her than ever,' said Marlin. 'It sounds to me as if Auntie's planning something.'

'She's been like a prisoner ever since that pig made his offer,' said Yozo. 'They're determined to make sure she doesn't slip out of their grasp. I visit her whenever I can and I pick up a lot of news in the kitchens. Saburo is due back very soon.' He clenched his fists as he thought of Saburo and the harm he might do Hana.

'Brute force won't work, my friend,' Marlin said. 'There'll be the Corner Tamaya lads to deal with as well as Saburo and his thugs if we try to get her out openly. We'll have to use cunning.'

Yozo frowned, thinking of how closely guarded Hana was.

'There'll be the feast to end all feasts when he shows up. That's when Auntie will let her out of her rooms. She'll have to get dressed up to take part in the . . .' He twisted his mouth, hating to say the words.

'The ceremony of union.'

Yozo nodded. 'Saburo's going to take over the Yoshiwara for the whole night. If we can create enough chaos, there should be a chance to get her out.'

But what if the day that they were to free Enomoto turned out to be the day of Saburo's feast and he had to choose between them?

Yozo rubbed his eyes and shook his head. He couldn't imagine what he would do then.

34

The day had hardly begun, yet Hana's rooms were already full of women – maids sweeping, dusting and piling up bedding, and attendants crowding around, exclaiming over the lacquerware, tea ceremony utensils and sumptuous kimonos Saburo had sent. Hana was sitting still, trying not to think about the evening ahead, when she heard shrieks of excitement, the tinkling of tiny bells and childish feet racing along the corridor. The door burst open and Chidori and Namiji stood side by side, plump hands clapped over their mouths, eyes wide, their huge sleeves flapping like butterflies' wings.

They scampered across the room to the paper screens that partitioned off the balcony and pushed them back so that light poured in, picking out the red and orange autumn leaves arranged in the vase in the alcove, and falling on the gold-painted walls, the delicate shelves, the hanging scroll and the trunk full of belongings packed up ready to go. Suddenly seeing all these familiar things in the glare of day, Hana realized with a dreadful sense of certainty that Saburo would take her away from the Yoshiwara and she would never see any of them again.

The children threw themselves down on their knees on the balcony and peered up at the men in loincloths and blue-dyed work jackets with hammers tucked in their belts who clambered around outside, stringing lanterns along the eaves. Hana didn't have to look to know that every lantern was painted with the characters 'Saburosuké Kashima'. Loincloth-clad figures shinned up ladders propped against the cherry trees, fixing paper blossoms to the branches until the street was a sea of pink and white, as if spring had come again. Every corner was alive with voices and laughter, the jangle of shamisens and the sound of singing.

She closed her eyes and pictured Yozo's face, his broad forehead, clear brown eyes and full, sensual mouth. He had come to visit just the previous day, after making sure no one was around.

Not long after Auntie had issued her prohibition against him coming to her rooms, Tama had declared haughtily that he was the only person she could possibly trust with messages to Hana and thereafter made sure she had a message for her at least once a day. He had become part of the Corner Tamaya now, he had told her, and was there most evenings, ushering in foreigners, and the ordinary clients too enjoyed talking to him. He had even become friends with her old favourite, Masaharu, despite the fact they had been on opposing sides in the war. The servants too knew him well and often entrusted him with messages for Hana. He knew the rhythms of the house, the times when it was throbbing with people and the times when it was empty.

Hana had found a pretext to send the maids away and for a few precious moments they had been alone together. Wrapped in his arms, she had clung to him like a child and pressed her head against his chest, feeling his warmth and the beating of his heart, sure this was the last time she would ever see him.

'Don't be afraid, this is not goodbye,' he had said, drawing back and looking at her, wiping away her tears. 'I told you I would protect you and I will, I'll keep my word. I'm doing all I can to find a way to get you out of here, I promise you.'

She had looked at him incredulously, suddenly hearing what he was saying.

'You mean . . . ?'

'During the banquet, when everyone's drunk or in an opium stupor, there'll be a chance for you to slip away. I'll be somewhere near by to help you.'

Hana had taken his hands and pressed them to her lips, shaking her head. 'No, no! It's madness, it's far too dangerous. It's not just Saburo, there'll be guards everywhere, and even if we managed to get out of the banqueting hall the Great Gate will be locked.'

'Jean freed me from a bamboo cage surrounded by a battalion of soldiers. If he could do that for me, I can get you to safety too. And there'll be others to help us. I'll find a way.'

He had taken her in his arms and held her close and she felt him run his fingers through her hair and the warm touch of his mouth on her forehead and cheeks. Then their lips met and she kissed him greedily. For a moment all her troubles faded away and she forgot everything in the intensity of being with him.

'If I could escape, I'd go anywhere with you,' she had breathed, allowing herself a moment of wild hope.

'I'm a fugitive,' Yozo whispered. 'How can I ask you to share such a life with me?'

'All this means nothing.' She looked around at the glimmering gold screens and the scrolls, the tea ceremony utensils and the kimonos spread on racks. In the months she had been trapped in her rooms they had come to seem like shackles tying her down. 'It doesn't even belong to me. Auntie would claim most of it as her own.'

Their faces were so close their breath seemed to mingle and she had reached out and gently touched the scar that marked his cheek. His skin was warm and dry beneath her fingertips and she could feel the stubble on his chin.

'Please be careful,' she had said. 'I know they won't hurt me – I'm worth too much to them alive – but I'm afraid for you.'

'I'm not so easy to kill,' he had said, smiling, and pulled her close to him again and stroked her hair. In the distance she could hear the rattling of the screens in their frames, clogs clattering raggedly along the road outside, autumn insects shrilling. If she was safe anywhere in the world, she thought, it was here in his arms.

Then there were voices approaching the room and he had had to slip away. Left alone, she had shed tears. It seemed too cruel to have found such closeness, only to have it torn away.

She knelt in front of the tarnished bronze mirror on the mirror stand and stared at herself. This face that men desired so much – all it had brought her was unhappiness. She had committed the very folly that Otsuné and Tama had warned her against – she had lost her heart, hopelessly and completely. If she had not, perhaps she could have just gone with Saburo, been glad of his wealth and thought of something else when he lay on her. But she knew now that she could never accept such a life.

The shadows of the candlesticks crept slowly across the floor. Time was moving on, bringing her closer and closer to the moment when she would have to face Saburo. Again she remembered the touch of Yozo's lips on hers, the feel of his firm body, and the tender things he'd said to her.

'I wish you weren't going,' said Kawagishi. She turned away, pretending to busy herself with the tubs of make-up, and brushed her hand across her face. 'Maybe one day I'll meet someone like Saburo too,' she whispered, sniffing.

'I'd take you with me if I could,' Hana said, and meant it.

'Saburo must be richer than anybody in the whole world,' said Kawanagi. She reached out a thin finger and touched the sleeve of a kimono thick with gold thread, a hungry look in her eyes. To these girls, Saburo's wealth made him irresistibly attractive. They didn't care that he was old and fat, they didn't notice his small eyes and bulbous cheeks, all they saw was riches. Hana had captured the man every girl in the quarter desired – he had even bought her her freedom – and they seemed bewildered that she was not more excited at her good fortune.

Hana looked at them. Kawagishi's face was pale and pinched and Kawanagi was painfully thin. They both looked beaten, as if they had long since given up hope, as if they knew from bitter experience that it was woman's lot to suffer and it would be foolish to expect anything more of life. Hana frowned. That was not her destiny, she told herself sternly, and she must do all she could to take her fate into her own hands.

'He must have a huge house,' said Kawanagi.

'He probably has lots of houses,' said Kawagishi wonderingly. 'He'll have a house built specially for you in the grounds of his main mansion.'

They both looked at her, wide-eyed, as if they couldn't begin to imagine such bliss.

'You'll be his favourite concubine, just think of that, and have his children,' said Kawanagi, a smile lighting her thin face. Hana tried to smile in return, but she was so weighted down with foreboding it was hard to pay attention to their chatter.

'He's bringing his friends tonight,' added Kawagishi. 'One of them might take a fancy to you, Kawanagi!'

'Or you, Kawagishi,' said Kawanagi.

'Or both of us,' they chorused with peals of laughter.

Even sulky Kawayu had come to visit, though Hana suspected she was just hoping to profit from Hana's triumph. After a hard night servicing clients, her hair was like a bird's nest and she had a shabby unwashed gown tied roughly around her. She gave off a sour odour as if she had rushed out without bothering to bathe.

'Ever since you came you've been Auntie's favourite,' she said, spitting out the words. 'Auntie's always bragging about you and I certainly can't imagine why. There can't be any other reason Saburo would pick you.'

'Saburo knows quality when he sees it,' observed Tama mildly. 'A big spender like him only comes once in a generation.' Hana smiled at her gratefully.

Tama was the only person who was not sunk in gloom, eaten up with envy or burbling with excitement. She was like a cat sitting over a mousehole, poised and still.

With no make-up and a plain cotton gown carelessly wrapped around her big body, there was no hiding the fact that Tama was a heavy-featured peasant girl, but she still exuded glamour. She sat, legs folded under her, smoking pipe after pipe, dispensing advice. Maids ran in to serve tea, a troupe of geishas scurried in to discuss which dances they should do that evening, then jesters arrived to check the order of entertainment and the maids lined up, asking which kimonos to wear.

'Men are foolish creatures,' Tama continued. 'Remember that Shojiro, when you first came, Hana, the one who thought he could get away with visiting another courtesan as well as me? Chidori spotted him as he was sneaking out of the Matsubaya and we held him down and snipped off his topknot, didn't we, Chidori!'

Hana made an effort to smile. She knew Tama was trying to take her mind off the coming ordeal.

'And those Englishmen,' Tama added, winking at Hana. The very thought of the Englishmen was usually enough to make the girls laugh until their stomachs hurt. 'To start with, all they ever said was, "Oh, I couldn't do this, oh, I couldn't do that!"' She crinkled her face and drew her head back in an expression of outraged disapproval. 'They were a bit old to start learning, but I gave them a few lessons anyway and, would you believe it, there's no stopping them now. Mind you, I always make sure they have a good bath before they come anywhere near me. They say in their country they only bathe once a week. Imagine that! Anyway, they must be satisfied because they've sent their friends along. But it's the Frenchmen I like. They'll try anything.'

Chidori bounced in from the balcony and pirouetted in the middle of the floor, red sleeves swinging.

'Watch,' she piped. 'This is the dance I'm going to do tonight.'

She lifted her chubby arms, pouted seriously and took a step or two, then stopped, ran over and put her arms around Hana.

'I'll miss you, big sister,' she said earnestly in her little-girl squeak. 'I wish you weren't leaving.'

Hana bent her head to hide her tears as the door opened and Otsuné appeared, carrying an enormous bundle. She smiled reassuringly at Hana then put her bundle down and started laying out combs and crimping irons and opening tubs of wax and pomade, filling the room with musky smells. Tama turned languidly to the attendants.

'Kawagishi, Kawanagi, Kawayu – and you, Chidori and

Namiji. Be off with you, to my rooms now. Time to get ready. I'll be along in a moment.'

Chidori opened her mouth to complain but Tama frowned and shook her finger and the little girl filed out behind the others. Tama dismissed the maids too and the room fell silent as Otsuné took a curling iron from the brazier and began to tug and stretch Hana's thick black hair.

'Auntie's on her way: there's not much time,' she said.

Hana swung round to stare at her.

'We need to make preparations if you're to get out of here tonight.'

Hana's heart began to thump. Now she realized why Tama had been sitting so quietly with such a strange look on her face. Yozo had kept his word.

'You must make sure no one – especially Saburo – suspects anything,' Otsuné whispered. 'Act happy and excited, make him think you're thrilled to be his concubine, that you've been waiting for him eagerly – you know what I mean.'

Hana nodded breathlessly. 'That's not difficult. I do it every day with every client.'

'And when I give a signal, be ready to leave,' said Tama.

'What sort of signal?' Hana gasped.

'You'll know when you see it. But first we have to put Auntie off the scent.' Otsuné bent over Hana's hair again, applying curling irons as footsteps came hobbling along the corridor and Auntie shuffled in wearing a shabby gown, her face lined and sallow and bare of make-up.

She had a long scroll of paper in her hand and brushes tucked into her sash and was mumbling to herself, 'Thirty lacquered trays, thirty soup bowls, thirty small square plates, thirty shallow oval dishes . . .' Her jaw dropped as she saw the empty room and she gave a squawk of disbelief.

'What's happened? Where is everyone? This is the most important day in the history of the Corner Tamaya. They should all be here, helping Hana get ready.'

'Auntie, Auntie,' gushed Tama. 'Thank goodness you've come. Those foolish girls were fighting about who would sit near Saburo and who would get the best kimono, the one with the gold chrysanthemums on it. Then Kawayu accused Kawagishi of stealing her clients and started pulling her hair and pushing her around. I think she might have torn her kimono sleeve.'

'That Kawayu, not again,' said Auntie with a grunt, pursing her lips. 'We really should get rid of her.'

'They were making such a commotion, I sent them all to my rooms.'

'You're quite right. Hana needs peace and quiet to compose herself before her performance tonight.'

Hana sat silently, hoping Auntie wouldn't notice the strain on her face.

'I've quietened them down, Auntie. You couldn't have done any better,' said Tama in challenging tones.

'We'll see about that,' said Auntie, rising to the bait. 'This is no time for fighting.' And she barged out of the room with Tama at her heels.

Otsuné and Hana held their breath until the footsteps had faded into the distance, then Otsuné dug into her bundle. Underneath the hairpins and strings of turquoise and coral was a pile of faded clothes, neatly folded. She thrust them into Hana's hands.

'Quickly, put these on,' she hissed. While Otsuné kept watch, Hana ran to the sleeping chamber, hid behind a screen and stripped to her red silk underskirt. She pulled on a pair of narrow-legged indigo trousers such as a peasant woman or an apprentice would wear and tucked the underskirt in as smoothly as she could. She fumbled with the drawstring of the trousers, her hands shaking so much she could hardly tie the knots, then realised with a shock of horror that they were on back to front and hastily tore them off, turned them round and put them on again. Then she put on an over-blouse, feeling the scratch of the rough fabric against the delicate skin of her breasts, slipped on an underkimono and a kimono on top of that, entirely covering the skimpy cotton clothes underneath, and scurried back to the reception room. She could feel the trousers catching in her skirts and twisting around her legs, threatening to trip her.

'Do they show?' she whispered, twirling around, trying to see herself in the mirror. 'Don't they look bulky?'

'You can't see a thing even now and once you're properly dressed no one will notice them at all,' Otsuné said calmly.

All the same, Hana's heart thumped and her breath came in shallow gasps as she realized what a risk they were taking. To play with a man like Saburo was madness. He had bought her for a huge sum of money, she was his property; there was nothing to stop him killing her if he so desired. But he wouldn't, she told herself. She was too valuable an investment and her looks offered a sort of protection; he wouldn't want to damage such beauty. Yozo was another matter, though. It made no difference how brave he was or how skilled a soldier; Saburo had far too many body-guards for him to fight them all.

Otsuné put her arm around her.

'Don't worry,' she said. 'Even if Yozo doesn't come for you tonight and you have to leave with Saburo, he'll find you and he and Jean will rescue you. You can trust Yozo. Jean too.' Otsuné held out a purse.

'No, no, I have money,' said Hana, her voice shaking.

'Take this too, take all you have. Hide it in your sleeves, anywhere you can.'

Hana bit her lip and closed her eyes. She had to remain calm, whatever happened.

'For long life and safe travel,' said Otsuné, tucking the purse along with an amulet into Hana's sleeve. Hana took a deep breath and settled down in front of the mirror, feeling the cotton trousers rough against the inside of her thighs, while Otsuné took the curling irons off the brazier and set to work in earnest on her hair.

35

From her rooms on the upper floor Hana heard the creak of a heavy palanquin being set down and a large body easing itself out, accompanied by pants and groans and grunts of 'Imbecile! Over here, hold still! What do you think you're doing?'

She had been hoping something might happen to stop Saburo arriving, but it seemed there was to be no escape. She heard Auntie and the maid calling out a welcome and footsteps lumbering across the house, past the bottom of the staircase, to the grand reception room. Doors opened and shut, guests filed in and she heard the whisper of maids' feet as they slipped to and fro with trays of food and drink.

Wafting in through the paper screens from the street outside came the twang of shamisens, the beat of drums, the warble of high-pitched voices and the clatter of clogs. Parties were starting all over the Yoshiwara. Saburo had hired all five streets and his guests could wander from house to house enjoying music, dance and dinner and sleeping with whomsoever they pleased, at their host's expense.

Night fell, filling the room with shadows, as Hana knelt with Chidori and Namiji, awaiting her call. Her mouth was dry and her heart thundering. She caught a glimpse of herself in the mirror and saw that, instead of Hana, Hanaogi was there, looking back at her like an old friend. She felt a sudden surge of confidence. Hana might be afraid, but Hanaogi was the equal of anyone.

Otsuné had excelled herself. Hana's face was perfectly painted, her eyes sloe black, her lips crimson petals in a snow-white face, and framed by her kimono collars, one blue with a design of maple leaves, another red with a tracery of gold. Her hair was gathered into a towering glossy creation and on it was a crown dripping with gold ornaments, with strings of turquoise hanging beside her face. She felt the weight of her many-layered kimonos and heard them rustle as she moved. Underneath them all the rub of rough cotton reminded her of the job she had to do.

The little girls looked up at her, their eyes huge. They were as splendidly dressed as she, and as nervous. She took a couple of hairpins out of her hair and gave them one each.

'For good luck,' she said. 'Wear these and you'll be great courtesans.'

By the time Auntie sent for her the party was well under way. Waiting outside the banqueting hall, Hana could hear the swish of dancing feet, drunken shouts and guffaws of laughter. She drew herself up proudly. She would give them all a show they would never forget.

The doors opened and there was a hush. She stood for a moment so they could look their fill, then slid her bare foot out from beneath the heavy kimono skirts. Gasps rippled through the crowd and there was a scattering of applause and cries of 'Hanaogi!'

Saburo lay sprawled on brocade cushions on the floor with one arm on an elbow rest, his broad face mottled and purplish. If anything he was even larger than she remembered him. As she met his gaze, inclining her head graciously, she wondered what went on behind that heavy brow and self-satisfied leer and why he had gone to so much trouble to purchase her. Was she a trophy to add to his collection or did he have some other plan for her? He narrowed his eyes and she saw desire burning there and something else that sent a shiver down her spine, something cruel.

Swinging her train behind her, she glided across the room and knelt in front of him. Tama was next to him, in a magnificent black overkimono with an obi heavy with gold and silver embroidery tied in an enormous knot at the front. She passed her a red-lacquered saucer brimming with sake and Hana offered it to Saburo with a bow. The ceremony of union – three sips of sake each from three cups – was over in a moment, but as she took the last sip she felt as if she had crossed a barrier from which she would never return.

Swallowing her panic, she bowed and smiled to the guests. Half the government was there, their faces flushed, raising their sake cups in a toast to the newly joined couple. Scattered over the small tables in front of them were dishes piled with sea urchin eggs, bowls of bonito entrails and slices of squid, carp skeletons with heads and tails intact, slabs of auspicious crane sashimi and rice mixed with clams, a famous aphrodisiac.

The geishas had started dancing again, not the decorous dances that were performed at the beginning of a feast but a wilder, more frenetic dance, driven by the insistent beat of the drums.

Masaharu was on the other side of the room with Kaoru close to him, pressing her knees against his, topping up his sake cup and laughing at his jokes. Hana caught her eye and Kaoru gave her a poisonous smile. Seeing Masaharu's fine-boned young face, Hana remembered the nights they had spent together and felt a pang of sadness. How simple everything would have been if only Masaharu had taken her as his concubine – but then she would not have met Yozo. The heavy-browed young government official who had sworn he couldn't live without her threw Hana a lovelorn glance. If he had wanted her that much, she told herself, he could have ransomed her. But in the end another man had bought her freedom. Saburo's heavy cheeks and the folds of fat under his chin were sticky with sweat. She leaned towards him.

'Where have you been all this time?' she scolded playfully. 'Your work was so important you couldn't come and visit me even once?' She pouted. 'I was beginning to think you didn't care about me any more.'

He flapped his fan and enveloped her wrist with a clammy hand.

'You're mine now, my pretty,' he said, narrowing his eyes like a frog with a fly in its sights. 'I can't wait for all this to be over. I can tell you like naughty games.'

His grip tightened and she felt her willpower ebbing and a spasm of fear tightening in her stomach. Tama put her hand on his damp thigh.

'You've missed a lot of gossip while you've been away,' she said silkily, glancing at Hana out of the corner of her eye. 'Do you remember Chozan of the Chojiya across the road? You'll never guess what she did.'

'I'm sure you're going to tell me,' said Saburo, turning lazily towards her.

'That playboy Sataro – the one who was so keen on her, the son of the rich merchant – she was sure he would marry her if she could convince him she loved him. She thought and thought about how best to prove it, then do you know what she did?'

Saburo shook his head.

'She wrote him a letter telling him she was going to cut off the top joint of her little finger to prove her love – then did it. You can't imagine the fuss and the mess. She fainted, of course, and the tip went flying out the window. Then she realized what a silly thing she'd done.'

'So did he marry her?'

'Of course not. Who wants a girl with no tip to her finger?'

'You know what they say,' said Saburo, glancing at Hana slyly. ' "The courtesan's biggest lie is 'I love you.' The client's biggest lie is 'I will marry you.' " '

Tama was launching into another funny story when Auntie clapped her hands. 'Our honoured patron, Saburo-sama, has arranged a special treat for us tonight. Come in, Chubei, don't be shy!'

Chubei was kneeling in the doorway in his wide-sleeved cotton jacket, hands on the ground, bowing. The Corner Tamaya's chef, he was famous across Edo, and Hana knew him well. He was a kindly man, short and tubby, with a shiny pate and fleshy hands that were always immaculately scrubbed. His one flaw was a weakness for sake and today, as usual, his cheeks were unnaturally flushed. Weaving slightly, he padded across the room and knelt in front of Saburo while white-jacketed apprentices erected a low table and set a couple of large wooden chopping boards on it.

Saburo licked his lips and took a swig of sake and Hana topped up his cup with the warm amber liquid.

'Chubei,' he bellowed. The chef quailed under his gaze. 'Have you forgotten my special order?'

The chef swung round and clapped his hands and a couple of apprentices lugged in a wooden bucket, taking care not to spill a drop of water on the tatami, while the guests sat cross-legged at their tables, watching intently.

The chef tied back his sleeves, then, with the air of a showman, reached in and pulled out a fish, a bloated creature covered in mottled black and browny-orange stripes, with a white underbelly. It was the ugliest fish Hana had ever seen. He held it up in the air and it thrashed violently, spraying water around, opening and closing its small mouth. Tiny teeth glistened inside and its belly was covered in spikes.

'Fugu,' said Saburo, his face cracking into a huge smile. 'Blowfish.'

'Tiger fugu,' Chubei corrected him primly, 'the best there is. If I may say so, it costs a fortune, especially at this time of year.'

'A feast for a rich man,' said Saburo, beaming contentedly. 'And his friends, of course.'

'You ordered three, your honour. One is already prepared. We have sake with dry-roasted fugu fin ready for you.'

'All in good time,' said Saburo. 'Let's see you cut this monster first.'

'We often prepare fugu in front of our diners but it's the first time I've ever done it in a banqueting hall,' Chubei said, a little nervously. Hana watched uncomfortably. Tama was supposed to be in charge of the proceedings but somehow Saburo had taken over.

'Isn't it poisonous?' she whispered.

'What a child!' said Saburo. 'Not if it's properly prepared. It's the king of fish. But don't you worry your pretty head, it's not for you. This is a dish for men! Except for the shogun, of course. He wasn't allowed to eat it in case it killed him – though in the end we managed to get rid of him without the help of fugu. Isn't that right, gentlemen?'

Hoots of unruly laughter filled the room. Hana had forgotten that they were all southerners here.

'Hanaogi-sama is right though, your honour,' Chubei said modestly. 'Only the most skilled chefs can prepare fugu properly. It's a very delicate job and easy to make a mistake. You just have to brush the liver with your knife and the whole fish is tainted.'

'Dicing with death,' Saburo said, rubbing his fat hands together. 'That's what makes it exciting.'

'There are a lot of deaths every year,' said Chubei. 'But not at the Corner Tamaya. I've been serving fugu for years and I've never lost a customer yet.' He leaned forward. 'Did you know that they're the only fish that close their eyes? When you kill one, it closes its eyes and makes a crying sound, like a child.'

The apprentices had laid out knives and two trays, one labelled 'poisonous', the other 'edible'. Holding down the thrashing fish with his left hand, Chubei took a long knife and brought it down with a thunk, cutting the tail off with a single blow. A moment later the fins and mouth too were lying alongside the quivering body. It had all happened too fast to hear whether or not the fish made any noise. The carcass heaved and the gaping hole where the mouth had been opened and closed convulsively.

'Bravo!' the guests shouted. 'What a master!'

Chubei sliced the mouth in half, scraped the board clear and put the fins in the tray marked 'edible'. Saburo leaned forward, his eyes gleaming, as the chef drew his knife along the spine, eased it between the tender flesh and the skin and peeled the skin back.

Hana noticed that his hand was a little unsteady and wondered uneasily how much sake he had had. There was a ripping sound as Chubei tore the skin off in a single piece, transforming the gleaming fish into a lump of inert flesh, then gutted it and wrenched out a shining, jelly-like sack.

'The liver,' he said, putting it on to the tray marked 'poisonous'.

'Female,' he added, pulling out the ovaries and putting them too on the 'poisonous' tray, along with the skin and eyes. He cut the clean flesh into slices so thin they were almost transparent and arranged them on a round plate, overlapping like the petals of a chrysanthemum.

'Chrysanthemum, flower of death!' Saburo was beaming and licking his lips. 'Who wants to be the first to try?'

Hana remembered the white chrysanthemums displayed at her grandparents' funerals and shivered. This was not a good time to think about death.

She broke apart a pair of chopsticks, took a few slices and dipped them in soy sauce. Saburo opened his large mouth, closed his eyes and put his head back and she placed the morsel delicately on his tongue. He savoured it slowly, rolling it around his mouth, then sucked in his lips with a smacking sound.

'A hint of poison,' he said, beaming. 'My upper lip is going numb, yes, and my tongue. And I have a distinct tingle right here. Feel! It's going hard.'

He grabbed Hana's hand, pressed it against his bulging groin and gave an ecstatic sigh followed by a belch. In the background the guests laughed obsequiously.

'What a sensation. Have some, gentlemen, have some. We're going to have fun tonight!'

The white-jacketed apprentices ran up from the kitchens with plates of blowfish and Kawanoto and the other attendants arranged slices of the delicate flesh on small plates and distributed them to the guests.

'Bring on the fugu fin sake,' shouted Saburo. 'Time for some games! Let's get our clothes off!'

*

Whenever Saburo forced a drink on her, Hana had covertly tipped it away. It was important to stay sober, to be ready for whatever was to come. But he insisted she try the blowfish fin sake and watched closely as she removed the toasted fin, inhaled the aroma and lifted the cup to her lips.

'Down it, all of it!' he said fiercely.

The sweet sake had a faint toasty taste. She put the cup down and felt warmth creeping through her limbs as her head began to swim. The room seemed to stretch away into the distance and the clamour of voices faded to a dull echo, like a far-off din of bells. She felt as if she was floating and tried to raise her arm and couldn't. Her lips and tongue grew numb, her eyelids heavy and an ache of desire stirred in her loins as the potent liquor worked its magic.

Saburo reached out a plump hand and grabbed her kimono collars, pulling her face close to his. The smell of his sweat and the moist heat of his large body overwhelmed her as his cheek brushed hers, but the rub of cotton against her skin shocked her back to her senses. She must not allow him to grope beneath her clothes, no matter what. He was tugging at her voluminous skirts, panting hard, when shamisens began to thrum and drums to beat and a singer launched into an erotic ballad. Saburo raised a bleary eye to see what was happening and Hana gathered up all her strength and pushed his hands away.

The blowfish fin sake was taking effect. Cheeks flushed and loins on fire, a couple of the guests were already grabbing at the girls. Others had started a game of forfeits. The attendants and geishas were well practised and it was nearly always the men who lost. At first the loser had to empty a cup of sake but then the game changed and the forfeit became an item of clothing. The men tore off their sashes, then their robes and under-robes, with those in western clothes doing better. By the time Masaharu had removed his lounge jacket, collar, necktie and waistcoat, some of the others were down to their loincloths. Hana,

Tama and Saburo watched, refusing all demands that they join in.

Then the men started clapping their hands and shouting 'Chonkina!' Shamisen and drum started up a rhythm and the attendants and geishas rose to their feet and formed a circle, moving like sleepwalkers in a slow, swaying dance. The music stopped and the girls froze in their tracks – all but small, smiling Kawagishi, who was visibly staggering. While the men cheered and laughed and clapped their hands, she took off her underkimono and stood unsteadily in her red silk underskirt, the brown skin of her body contrasting oddly with her white-painted face. Sweat slicked her small young breasts.

Soon the room was awash with bodies. Kawagishi slumped, totally naked, against a flabby-faced paunchy fellow, giggling helplessly while he mauled her then pushed her over on to her back, while Kawayu, sullen no longer, rolled about with the youthful government official, Hana's one-time devoted admirer, emitting loud groans as he ripped off his loincloth and mounted her.

Hana watched his scrawny buttocks rising and falling and his skinny back quivering. No party she'd been to in the Yoshiwara had ever descended to such levels of abandon. It made her all the more afraid of Saburo's power and his appetite. He was pretending to be drunk but she could see that he wasn't. He was keeping a steely eye on her.

The guests and the women were rolling among piles of discarded clothing when Chubei slipped in and whispered something to Saburo.

'Yes, of course, you fool! Bring it in!' barked Saburo. A moment later Chubei returned, panting and red-faced, and placed a small dish in front of him. It was heaped with livid chopped flesh.

'The liver, your honour,' he said, pressing his head to the floor obsequiously. 'I knew you'd ask for it.'

Saburo ran his tongue around his lips. 'Just what I need, a drop of poison. Just a touch, a little chill, a hint of numbness. I want to feel my mouth go numb and my prick come alive. That will put some spice into the evening.' He turned to Hana and pulled her nearer to him. 'Then we can join in the games!'

36

The kitchens were hot, crowded and noisy, full of maids rushing in and out and apprentices chopping. Women crouched in front of stoves, blowing on the charcoal embers till they glowed, sending clouds of smoke puffing up to the blackened rafters. In his rough cotton trousers and indigo blue jacket, Yozo could have been any of the men who worked in the Yoshiwara. There were plenty hanging around, waiting to help unsteady guests when they left, even carry them to the gate if necessary, chatting about how much sake they would buy with their tips.

'I wouldn't mind trying fugu liver myself.' Chubei raised a cup of sake unsteadily to his lips and gulped it down, spilling drops across his plump fingers and down his stained white jacket. His cheeks had turned dark red and his shaved pate under the thick roll of his headband was shiny with sweat. 'It's supposed to be a real thrill. Tasty too, they say. Sweet, oily, creamy.' He tapped the edge of the tray marked 'poisonous', heaped with sinister-looking chunks of fish, and gave a solemn shake of his large head. 'But I'm not one for dicing with death.'

'Me neither,' said Yozo dryly. 'It's a game for rich men.'

Squatting in a corner, he tapped his heel on the earthen floor and breathed out hard, trying to hide his impatience. Not long had passed since Chubei had taken the blowfish liver in to Saburo. Saburo would probably eat just enough to make his lips tingle and his tongue go numb so that he could enjoy the frisson of playing with death, like most connoisseurs; or, if he wanted a

284

bigger thrill, he might taste a little more to set his genitals tingling too. But there was also the chance he might overdo it. Every time there was a noise from the banqueting hall Yozo jerked round, but nothing ever seemed to happen.

Above the clatter he heared shouts and laughter, the beat of drums and the thrum of shamisens. He grimaced and clenched his fists. He couldn't bear the thought of Saburo's hands on Hana's body. He had been waiting for the chance to smuggle her out of the Yoshiwara for so long but now the moment had come he realized just how much could go wrong. But the plan just had to work.

He thought of the last conversation he had had with Hana and remembered her bright eyes, her laughter, the curve of her cheek and the feel of her soft hand in his. A woman like her should not be in a place like this, let alone be forced to pander to a creature like Saburo. He smiled to himself. If Enomoto or Kitaro had been here, or any of his other companions from his European days, they would have told him he had gone soft, that a man's place was with his comrades, and he would have agreed – till he met Hana.

'It's a mighty aphrodisiac, fugu liver.' The tips of Chubei's ears had flushed purple in the lantern light. 'Rhinoceros horn has nothing on it, nor ginseng root neither. You should see what they're getting up to in there – and that's just the fugu fin sake. That old slug wouldn't share the liver with anyone. I'd give a thousand *ryo* he's worried about satisfying our Hana. He's probably afraid he won't be able to perform. Rich or not, I hate the idea of that old fox making off with her. We all do. If anything happened to stop him, none of us would raise a finger.'

Yozo glanced at him sharply, wondering if the chef suspected anything. Everyone knew he took messages to Hana. He stared at the other men with their skinny legs and leathery faces, roaring with laughter at some joke, and wondered how much they knew too.

'You wouldn't believe the tip the old boy gave me,' Chubei was saying. Smoke filled the room and the lids of the cooking pots rattled. All across the quarter, people seemed to have gone entirely mad. The street was full of clogs clattering feverishly, shrill voices and shrieks of wild laughter and squeaks and grunts as if people were coupling like animals in the road. Yozo drummed his heel on the floor, scowling. Everything depended on being ready and seizing the opportunity when it came. It would have been easier by far to have been back on the battlefield, he thought. He'd have to apply all the lessons he'd learned there. But then he remembered the blazing ruins of Hakodate and the Commander's face looming in front of him and shuddered.

The doors of the banqueting hall burst open. 'Help! The master's poisoned!' people were yelling as the whole place erupted into chaos.

Yozo sprang to his feet. He had hardly dared hope the old man would be stupid enough to overdose on blowfish liver. He couldn't stop a grin of sheer exultation flashing across his face. Then he frowned and checked that his dagger was firmly in his sash. It was time for action.

There was a whimper behind him.

'Not . . . Not my fault.' Chubei seemed to have shrivelled inside his bulky chef's jacket. His face was grey and he was gripping the edge of the counter, his cheeks quivering.

Father burst through the front entrance in a cloud of stale tobacco smoke, his cotton jacket half off his shoulders, his spongy belly hanging over his sash. Yozo cursed silently. He hadn't expected him to appear so soon. Everyone else might be drunk, but not Father. He would be keeping an eye on Hana. She was, after all, his most valuable investment.

'What have you done?' he bellowed. 'You've ruined us.'

'It's nothing to do with Chubei,' Yozo said brusquely. 'Saburo ordered the liver and ate it. He's not going to die. He's given himself a scare, that's all.'

Father's jaw dropped and he gaped at Yozo as if he couldn't

believe anyone would dare answer him back. Yozo returned his gaze. The other men were racing towards the banqueting hall. Scowling, Father swung round.

'Get back here, all of you. Shut the doors. We need to keep this quiet. Tajima, you're a smart fellow, you come with me.'

'It could be the drink. Alcohol exacerbates fugu symptoms,' said Yozo carefully.

'We'd better get a spade just in case,' Father grunted.

Yozo looked at him questioningly.

'We've got to dig a hole and bury him up to his neck,' said Father. 'It's the only remedy. The coolness of the soil draws out the poison.'

Holding a lantern, he waddled off along the dark hallway, low to the ground like a sumo wrestler, panting noisily, moving fast for such a heavy man. Yozo followed a couple of steps behind. He paused at the door of the banqueting hall. The stench of smoke, burnt candle wick, stale tobacco, sake and vomit spilt out, as thick as a wall. Half the candle stands had toppled over. Luckily the candles had gone out before they could set the place alight, otherwise the house would have gone up like a tinderbox.

Keeping behind Father, Yozo strode across the room, treading on soft damp flesh in the gloom. Naked men and women sprawled on top of each other, arms and legs splayed, or crawled around feebly, fumbling through heaps of clothes. Glancing round, he noticed Masaharu in the shadows at the side of the room. He was the only one who seemed to be still fully dressed. For a moment their eyes met. Yozo looked frantically for Hana, but she was nowhere to be seen. Auntie was running to and fro, withered hands pressed to her head, her malevolent old face glaring like a devil mask in the candlelight.

'Father,' she wailed. 'Thank the gods you're here. Do something, fast! We'll never trade again if this gets out.'

Gruff voices bawled, 'Fool! What are you doing?' 'Get out of the way!' 'Open the screens, give him air!' 'No, keep them shut, keep him warm!' On the other side of the room Saburo's bodyguards were jostling each other, crowding shoulder to shoulder in their silken livery, peering down at something on the floor.

As Father and Yozo pushed between them, Yozo heard Hana's voice gasping, 'Saburo-sama, Saburo-sama!' Father held up his lantern.

Yozo stared down at him. Splayed on his back like a giant cockroach, legs and arms twitching, was the man he'd seen on the street that night in Batavia, the monster who'd traded in opium and kept women prisoner. Saburo's eyeballs were bulging as if they were about to burst out of his head, his mouth gaped open and saliva dribbled across his rolls of chin and down his sumptuous black silk collars.

His eyes found Yozo's face and he gave a distinct flinch as if he recognized him too, then his body went rigid. He was wheezing as if struggling to catch his breath.

Hana was on her knees next to him, her hands pressed to her mouth. She looked up at Yozo with huge eyes. Her face was white under the thick make-up. Tama was next to her. She seemed perfectly composed but there was a tic in her cheek and an odd gleam in her eye. Yozo had a sudden suspicion that they had goaded Saburo into eating more than he should have. It would not have been difficult.

'I told him to stop,' Hana whispered, her voice shaking. 'But he wouldn't. He kept eating more and more. He wanted me to have some too, but I refused.'

'He kept saying, "You think I'm not a man?"' Tama said to Father. She was careful not to look at Yozo. 'Every time we begged him to stop he ate more. Then he started complaining his feet were cold.'

Yozo knelt beside Saburo and lifted his hand, his fingers sinking into the spongy flesh. Saburo's arm was stiff, his skin clammy, and a sour stench seeped from his pores. When Yozo managed to find a pulse through the rolls of fat, it was sluggish and faint. Some of the guests and guards were beginning to groan and there were panic-stricken shouts of 'My feet. My feet are cold.' Yozo wondered whether Chubei's knife could have tainted one of the three fish, or one might have been particularly potent. It happened sometimes.

'We need to get him into the ground,' Father barked. 'Fast, or we'll lose him. Tama, get Hana out of here.'

Tama took Hana's arm and pulled her to her feet. As the guards stepped back to let the women pass, Hana's legs seemed to give way under her. Yozo sprang forward but Tama glared at him, hooked her arm around Hana and dragged her out of the room with a rustling of silk.

'Tajima, get the men digging,' said Father. 'Round the back of the house, away from the road, where no one can see. And tell them to keep it quiet.'

A couple of the guards were looking at Yozo strangely. He guessed they had seen him move towards Hana and had recognized him from the fight they had had a few months earlier. The last thing he needed now was trouble.

Stepping hurriedly across the bodies and piles of food he bumped into Masaharu, picking his way towards the door. The southerner's collar was askew and his shirt was hanging out of his western trousers but Yozo could see he was totally sober.

'I'm leaving,' Masaharu grunted.

Yozo met his eye. He hardly noticed the broad vowels of his southern accent any more. He'd had plenty of time to get to know him in the months he'd been working at the Corner Tamaya. He knew he was a man he could trust.

'Good idea,' he said. He touched the amulet in his sleeve and prayed that the gods would be on his side.

37

As Yozo sprinted out of the Corner Tamaya, he nearly ran straight into Saburo's gaudy palanquin. It loomed across his path, casting a huge shadow, as if Saburo himself were standing there like a ferocious guardian deity, arms extended, stopping him from leaving. It seemed a bad omen, but he pushed the thought out of his mind.

Coming out on the street, he looked around in astonishment. It was packed with people, clapping their hands and weaving in and out between the cherry trees in intertwined circles with a great clattering of clogs, as if they intended to dance till they dropped. Men in carnival masks with twisted mouths and staring eyes bobbed about, grotesque faces looming out of the darkness.

Yozo looked about him sharply till he spotted a movement in the shadows beside the house. There were two small figures there, bundled in work clothes with their heads and faces wrapped around with scarves.

Masaharu came out a moment later, a slender figure outlandishly dressed in a western-style overcoat. He too glanced around quickly then strode off, keeping to the edge of the road where the crowds were thinnest, towards the gate at the end of Edo-cho 1. The two figures slipped timidly from the shadows and followed after him, heads bowed like servants. They were dressed like youths but, from the way they carried themselves, shoulders softly bowed, scurrying with tiny steps in their straw sandals, it was obvious they were women. To Yozo's eyes all three seemed dreadfully conspicuous. He walked a little way behind, keeping watch, glancing round every now and then, but the revellers seemed too drunk to notice.

Everything seemed to be going according to plan when suddenly there was a bang as the door of the Corner Tamaya flew back hard in its grooves, followed by gruff voices and heavy footsteps, and two large men stepped out from behind Saburo's palanquin, their shiny pates and stiff topknots poking above the crowd. Yozo caught the sheen of silken livery and recognized the bull neck and narrow eyes of one and the fox-like face of the other. It was the guards who had looked him up and down in the banqueting hall.

He dodged into the crowd of sticky, dancing bodies, feeling the swirl of movement all around him. He hadn't expected anyone to come after them so soon. He knew all too well what Father and Auntie would do once they discovered their most valuable courtesan had gone. They would round up every man in the Yoshiwara and every gangster in the district and send them out to search the marshes till they found her. Any accomplices would be tortured and Hana would be tied up, brought back to the Yoshiwara, beaten and probably killed. He grimaced at the thought. He would just have to make sure that didn't happen.

The guards made for the back of the house. They would be expecting to find him there, instructing the Corner Tamaya lads where to dig, and would discover all too soon that he wasn't. No matter what happened, no matter what he needed to do to prevent it, he had to stop them coming in search of him and running into Masaharu's two 'servants'. He had to make sure Hana was not caught, even if it cost him his life.

A youth staggered up against Yozo and threw an arm around his shoulder, his breath reeking of sake. Dangling round his neck was a comic mask with a puckered mouth and a foolish expression. It was the perfect disguise.

'Lend me that,' said Yozo, pulling it over his head. The youth, flushed and bleary-eyed, reeled off, too drunk to notice.

Fumbling with the strings, Yozo tied on the mask and pushed between the swaying people to the edge of the crowd. Masaharu was well ahead of him by now, turning on to the grand boulevard. Flutes tootled and drums banged feverishly and the crowd danced faster and faster. The sweet smell of opium smoke drifted from the splendid teahouses and even the Chrysanthemum Teahouse was quiet and dark as if the guests were lost in poppy-fuelled dreams.

Peering through the eye holes of the mask, Yozo saw the large ugly guards rounding the corner of Edo-cho 1 towards him. They were scowling furiously, shoving people aside, leaving drunkards sprawling in their wake.

At the end of the grand boulevard was the Great Gate, lit with red lanterns. Usually there were visitors pouring in and out, but today Saburo had taken over all five streets and the massive doors were barred and bolted. The tattooed gatekeeper was at his post outside the guard house, along with a hefty figure Yozo recognized with a surge of relief – Marlin. He caught a glimpse of Masaharu too, just arriving at the gate, and saw that his two charges were with him. As Yozo watched, the gatekeeper left his post and walked quickly towards the small side gate in the shadow of the willow trees. Behind him Yozo could hear the indignant shouts of revellers. The guards were closing in on him.

He felt for his dagger. He had to put them out of action before they got any closer to the gate, and it had to be done quickly and cleanly, without drawing anyone's attention to them. There would be no room for mistakes; he would have only one chance. He would have preferred to challenge them to a fight, of course – man to man, in an honourable way – not hide behind his mask and take them by surprise, but it was too risky to start a brawl. In the dark no one would notice a couple more bodies on the ground.

He pushed his way towards them through the dancing crowd. For all their fancy uniforms he could see they were nothing but gangsters. The bull-necked man was barging in front, glaring around. Invisible behind his mask, Yozo lurched into him, staggering as if he were drunk. He felt the heat of the man's flesh and smelt his sweat and the sour stench of his blood as he drove his dagger hard into his stomach. He twisted the knife sharply to stop the flesh gripping the blade, then wrenched it free.

The man's eyes widened and he reeled, arms flailing. Blood trickled from his mouth and he crumpled, keeling over on top of the fox-faced guard who was behind him. The fox-faced man too crashed backwards and his skull hit the paving stones with a crack.

There was a moment's silence then a yowl of 'Fool! Get off me!' as the guard tried to push clear of his comrade's huge body. Yozo lunged for the man's throat and felt his dagger slicing through bone. The guard made a gurgling noise and was silent.

The scuffle had taken only a few seconds and made barely a ripple in the crowd. Yozo wiped his dagger on his sleeve and tucked it back in his sash. The deed was done, though not as cleanly as he had wanted.

He pulled off his mask, tossed it aside and sprinted for the gate, trampling over revellers and knocking them out of his path. Unless he was very fast indeed, he would miss the chance to slip away unnoticed. Masaharu and his two followers had already gone through.

Yozo paused to salute Marlin, suddenly realizing that this could be the last time he saw him. He looked at his overhanging brow, deep-set eyes and square jaw covered in bristles, remembering his face peering down at him through the open door of the bamboo cage and the weight of his hand on his shoulder, holding him back, that night when he had been about to attack the Commander. He pictured Marlin, arms and legs sticking out of his rough peasant's clothes, pushing past the southern guards and the foreign sailors and swaggering straight through the

Yoshiwara's Great Gate and along the boulevard, his head poking up above the crowds. The Frenchman had saved his life again and again and had been a true friend to him – perhaps the best friend he'd ever had.

Marlin thrust a sword, a gun and a bag of ammunition into Yozo's hands. 'Be careful,' he said. 'There'll be a lot of people out there looking for you. More, once tonight's deeds become known.'

Yozo nodded. 'I'll miss your company,' he said, and he meant it. 'I'll be back when all this is over.'

'We'll meet again,' said Marlin. 'Enomoto, Otori, all of us. And we'll see the shogun back in his castle. You remember what Kitaro used to say: "One for all, all for one." '

Yozo laughed and shook his head sadly, remembering Kitaro and his love for Dumas's famous novel, all those years ago in the West.

'Long live the shogun!' he said. 'I'm in your debt. I'll find some way to repay you.'

'It's enough that we're friends.'

Yozo held out his hand western-style and Marlin shook it, then slapped him on the shoulder.

The gatekeeper was standing by the small side gate, glancing over his massive tattooed shoulder, holding his stave and grimacing fiercely. Yozo bowed. He knew he risked severe punishment for letting them through. Unexpectedly a grin flashed across the gatekeeper's face as Yozo darted past him.

Outside, palanquins lined the crooked road that wound across the Moat of Black Teeth and up to the Japan Dyke, which rose like a wall, black against the night sky, with lights flickering along the top and here and there a bonfire sending up a shower of sparks. Clouds scudded across the moon. The lantern-lit street had been so bright Yozo hadn't even noticed it was full. Now it cast a cold light on the great wall of the Yoshiwara and the stalls and willow trees outside it.

Most of the bearers were asleep, curled under the shafts of their vehicles. One splendid, rather official-looking palanquin was drawn up right at the gate. Masaharu was pacing up and down in his western overcoat. He pulled out a purse and pressed it into Yozo's hand. Yozo tried to push it away, then changed his mind and tucked it into his waistband. He opened his mouth to thank him but Masaharu raised his hand, his face stern.

Yozo bowed. A few months ago he would never have imagined he might come to admire and even like a southerner. 'I hope we have the chance to meet again,' he said.

'I'll make sure we do,' said Masaharu. 'Good luck.'

Otsuné was beside him, dressed in indigo work clothes. She had pushed her hood back and Yozo could see her sweet, round face and the thin lines that wrinkled her pale brow. She was smiling, blinking away tears. She gripped Yozo's arm.

'Be quick,' she said. 'We'll do our best to make sure no one suspects anything.'

She and Marlin had become like family to him and it was a wrench to say goodbye. He bowed, wishing he could give her a hug, like a Frenchman would, but he knew she would have been shocked if he had.

Hana was in the palanquin, her legs tucked under her. She was still wearing white make-up and her oval face was luminous in the darkness. She stared at him as if she could hardly believe he was there, and stretched out her hand. Yozo took it, feeling its softness. He looked at her and she smiled. That moment – having Hana there, safe and close to him – made it all worthwhile.

'You always said you would protect me,' she said, 'and you have.'

'I'll protect you for ever,' he said. He listened hard. There was no one coming after them, no footsteps thundering towards the gate, no shouts on the other side. Impossible though it was to believe, they really had done it.

Masaharu and Otsuné had already slipped back through the gate. Now it slammed behind them and the bolts slid into place. The sounds of music and dancing grew muffled and distant.

Yozo strode ahead as the bearers carried the palanquin across the moat and up the curved slope to the road that ran along the top of the Japan Dyke. Hiko and Heizo were waiting there in the shadows and took their places, loping along behind it, Hiko a hulking figure in his grubby uniform, Heizo small and powerfully built with a bullet head. Yozo grinned when he saw them, glad to have these plain-speaking fellow soldiers with him.

For a moment he stopped at the Looking Back Willow and gazed down at the Yoshiwara, half hidden in the trees below them. With its twinkling lights, music, shouts and laughter, it was like an earthly paradise, but he knew there was violence and cruelty behind the glamour and brilliance.

In front of him the road stretched long and dark. He turned his back on the Yoshiwara and headed into the night.

38

Hana awoke with a start, aware that the jogging and swaying of the palanquin had stopped. The last thing she had heard had been the creaking of wooden panels and the wind whistling across the marshes as she was carried away into darkness.

Curled up in the cold cramped box, her legs squashed under her, she wriggled her toes, trying to get some feeling back into them. Panicking for a moment, she wondered where she was, then everything that had happened that night came flooding back. Nightmarish images filled her mind – Saburo's bloated face as he lay dying, the press of the crowds, the masked faces leering, and the terrible fear that someone would recognize her. She had wanted to run as fast as she could but she had had to force herself to walk slowly, as if she was not in a hurry at all.

Shuddering, she remembered Saburo's fat hands and toad-like eyes, his heavy body resting against hers as she dropped pieces of blowfish liver into his mouth, and how he had started gagging and complaining that his feet were cold. She remembered running to her rooms and tearing off her kimonos, terrified someone would burst in and see her, and suddenly finding herself outside on the street for the first time in months, feeling every eye staring at her. She could almost feel Father's stick thwacking down on her back and his knife pricking her throat, and a shiver of horror ran down her spine.

She heard a temple bell tolling the hour, a watchman's even

tread and the dry clack as he banged his sticks together. Then the door slid back and Yozo was standing outside in the dusky light, his steady gaze and calm smile clear in the moonlight. Behind him, shadowy houses lined a street so narrow she could hardly see the stars between the eaves. She was back in the real world. It was big and cold and dark but she knew that with Yozo there everything would be all right.

'Where are we?' she asked, her voice startlingly loud in the silence.

'In the East End,' said Yozo. 'Edo is the shogun's city still, for a while, at least. We can't stay at an inn tonight. You're too well known and news might get back to the Yoshiwara. We'll stay with the widow of one of our comrades. We can trust her to say nothing. I'm afraid the accommodation will be humble, very different from what you're used to.'

She laughed shakily.

'I'm not so grand as you think. Before I arrived at the Yoshiwara I was just like everyone else. I've lived most of my life without fine food or fancy kimonos.'

But even as Hana spoke, the enormity of what she had done was beginning to wash over her. She'd left behind everyone and everything she had come to care for – Otsuné, Tama, Kawanoto, her spacious rooms, her precious kimonos, her hangings and all the beautiful gifts clients had given her. She tried to push away the thought, but she couldn't stop the knot of fear in her stomach. She bit her lip. She had nothing now, only what she'd managed to bundle up – a cotton kimono, her husband's box and the scroll box with his letter. She would have to go to Kano, she reminded herself, and place them in the family tomb. She owed him that much.

And at least she had money – Otsuné and Masaharu had seen to that, and she also had money of her own.

Conscious of the outlandish young man's clothes she was wearing, she wound her scarf round her face, pulling it up over her nose to hide her make-up. There was a movement at her feet as a rat scuttled past and she remembered the last time she had been in the city, when she had met Fuyu. The place looked even more desolate now, as if all the occupants had fled.

The bearers pointed them to a modest house with potted plants along the edge of the wall where a young woman hurried out, rubbing her eyes, bowing and smiling. She led Hana and Yozo through shabby rooms which smelt of damp to a small chamber tucked away right at the back and brought a pan of hot water and a bag of rice husks. While the woman laid out bedding and sleeping robes, Hana scrubbed off every last vestige of make-up, then took out the combs and ribbons that held her hair in place and combed and combed until it swung long and loose like a silky black curtain. She looked at herself in the mirror. Hanaogi was gone for ever and she was Hana again.

'It's not much of a place, I'm afraid, but at least you'll be safe.' Yozo was kneeling at the side of the room, watching her. He had laid his swords on the sword rest, where he could reach them, and put his gun beside the pillow. In the Yoshiwara he had had to play the part of a servant but now he too was himself again. He seemed older, more serious; he was a soldier, and a high-ranking one. When he spoke to Hiko and Heizo, there was a ring of authority in his voice that Hana found rather thrilling. There was something else too, an edge of excitement. He was free, back where he belonged.

'I'm in as much trouble as you are – more, in fact. You have Father and the Yoshiwara men to worry about but I have half the southern army after me.' He sighed and rubbed his eyes. 'But let's not think about that – not now when I have you to myself.'

In the light of the candle Hana could see his smile, his strong face and expressive eyes. She had never seen anything so beautiful. Craving his touch, she leaned towards him as if she'd lost all will power, as if her body was no longer hers to command.

He took her hand and raised it to his lips and she closed her eyes. She was trembling, almost afraid of the feelings that were sweeping over her. In all her time at the Yoshiwara, she had never known how much she held back, how much she kept a part of herself hidden, protected. Love had been something that was bought and sold, arousing pleasure had been her work. When she had whispered sweet nothings in her lovers' ears, they had known she said the same to every man. It had always been a game. But this was utterly different.

Yozo pulled her towards him and kissed her. The touch of his lips sent a shock leaping through her and she felt her body arch towards his as she gave herself, all of herself, up to him.

'I've waited so long,' he whispered, his voice hoarse. He ran his fingers through her hair and stroked the back of her neck and she felt the warmth of his breath as he kissed her eyes and nose. Then he opened her robe and found her breast, cupping it, rubbing his thumb across her nipple, and she felt pleasure like a slow-burning fire rising in her belly. He kissed her greedily, insistently. There were only the two of them, the darkness, the small room, the embers glowing in the brazier, the silence.

She had never known such tenderness. His touch, so gentle yet so arousing, filled her with pleasure more intense than she had ever known. She heard herself moan as he ran his hands and lips across and between her breasts to the tender skin of her stomach, until every pore was tingling. Stroking her thighs, he licked lower and lower until his tongue found the neatly trimmed triangle of hair and he buried his nose in it, nuzzling like a cat, then licked lower still, lapping up the juices which welled there. Helpless under his touch, she groaned as a long aching spasm swept over her, throbbing in her belly and running like a flame to her throat.

Then he was beside her. Hungrily she ran her hands across his chest and muscular back, burying her face in his smooth skin, inhaling the scent of his hair. She pulled him on top of her, felt the touch of stubble as his face brushed hers, the hardness of his body, the pounding of his heart.

'You,' he whispered as they moved together, faster and faster. And then she was floating, drowning in sensation as a sweet numbness overtook her, filling her belly, creeping up her spine, surging to her fingertips and the root of her tongue. She heard him groan and felt him heavy on top of her.

They lay for a long time in each other's arms, then looked at each other in wonder. This was not the only night they would have, there would be many more. It was the beginning of a new life.

39

In the morning the young widow brought breakfast. She pushed back the screens and Hana and Yozo ate in silence, gazing out at the tiny garden – a couple of rocks and a knotted pine tree, bathed in autumn sunshine. Hana had put on the cotton kimono she had brought with her from the Corner Tamaya and tied her hair back in a simple knot.

It was her first morning of freedom. The great city was at her feet, she could go anywhere and do anything she wanted. She was far enough from the Yoshiwara that Father would never find her now. No one even knew who she was. Wrapped in her winter clothes she would be entirely invisible.

She'd already decided where she wanted to go. She'd always known. She'd thought about it so often – the big house, with its garden of bamboos and pines, its stone lantern, moss-covered rocks and small pond. The maples would be in full blaze by now and Gensuké would be wrapping the shrubs in straw for the winter. She would take Yozo with her. She smiled, imagining his excitement as he saw the house for the first time.

She turned to look at him and saw he was staring abstractedly at the garden. She'd been so thrilled, planning everything she'd do with her new freedom, that she'd forgotten the city was not safe for him. In the Yoshiwara he had been hidden from their southern overlords but now he would have to be cautious. He met her eyes and looked at her questioningly, drumming his fingers on the worn tatami. He was frowning and she wondered what was on his mind.

'I'm afraid I have to leave for a while,' he said. 'I have business to take care of.'

Hana started, shocked. It was the last thing she had expected to hear.

'I told you about my friends, Enomoto and Otori. Today's the day they're being transported to Kodenmacho Prison. It's our only chance to rescue them.' He took her hand in both of his and held it. 'I know you understand. It's a matter of life or death.'

Hana blinked hard. She hadn't expected their farewell to be so sudden or so soon. Yozo put his arms around her and pressed his lips to her forehead.

'Why didn't you tell me before?' she whispered.

'I didn't want to spoil our night together. Anyway, there's no need to worry. We've thought our plan through carefully, in detail. I'll be back by evening and I'll have Enomoto and Otori with me.'

For all his words, Hana knew that he was taking a huge risk and might well end up in prison himself, or even at the execution ground. But she was a samurai's daughter and a samurai's widow and she couldn't stand in his way. She could feel his excitement and realized he wasn't doing this just for Enomoto and Otori. He'd been cooped up in the Yoshiwara so long, playing the servant, being polite and deferential; now he was outside he was longing to be back in the thick of things.

A tear trickled down her cheek. He brushed it away, then smoothed a long strand of hair that had fallen across her face and tucked it behind her ear. She closed her eyes, feeling the warmth of his fingers on her skin.

'Wait for me here,' he said.

She shook her head.

'I've been wanting to go home for so long. I'll wait there.'

'To your house?' Yozo's face darkened. 'But . . . it belonged to your husband.'

'He was never there,' she said. 'Most of the time I was on my own, just me and the servants. It was my home, not his, and it's your home too now. It's in Yushima, not far from the river, near Korinji temple.' She pictured the street, the river, the temple, and the great house with smoke hovering around the eaves. Just saying the names gave her a warm feeling.

'There's something else.' He was staring at the garden and she realized he hadn't heard a word she'd said.

'What is it?'

'I have to tell you about your husband – about how he died.' There was a look on his face that frightened her.

She leaned forward and put her hand on his thigh. 'I don't need to know,' she said firmly. 'I only need you to come back safely.'

Outside, a cicada shrilled, breaking the silence. He shook his head and drummed his fingers on the tatami again.

'I told you that I saw your husband fall, but I didn't tell you why.' He took a deep breath. He was avoiding her eyes. 'I . . . killed him.'

Hana drew back. 'You? Not an enemy?' she gasped.

The room had become very quiet. The widow came in to take away the breakfast trays and they sat in silence till she had gone. Yozo was looking fixedly at the garden still, his shoulders slumped. Hana wanted to tell him that she didn't need to hear any more but he held up his hand, frowning.

'He had my friend Kitaro killed.' His voice was so quiet she could hardly hear it. 'I vowed to avenge him but I had to wait until the war was over – and I knew it was a crime to kill one of our own commanding officers. But in the end, when I saw my chance, I didn't even stop to think about it. It was in the last battle and we all knew we were going to die anyway. I came face to face with him on a deserted street in Hakodate and he taunted me again and I shot him.' He had a strange light in his eyes as if he were back in that distant wild place, seeing it happening all over again. 'I have nightmares about it still. I couldn't bring myself to tell you until now, I was sure you'd hate me for it. After all,

Commander Yamaguchi was your husband, no matter what you felt about him.'

Hana stared at him, wide-eyed. She knew that it was not a crime but a sacred duty to avenge the death of a comrade and that men often killed other men. Her husband had boasted about how many men he'd killed, including his own soldiers; and if he'd come back he would have killed her too, so in a way Yozo had saved her.

'I just couldn't keep it hidden any longer,' he said. 'I didn't want there to be any secrets between us.'

She took his hand and held it in both of hers. 'It doesn't change anything for me – for us,' she whispered. For some reason his confession made him even dearer to her.

'Can you forgive me?' he asked, turning to look at her.

'There's nothing to forgive. The only thing I need is for you to come back safely.'

He pulled her to him and held her close, then drew back, gazing at her as if he never wanted to take his eyes off her again, and slowly straightened his shoulders. 'Your house is where the militia barracks used to be. Ichimura stays near there, and that's where Heizo and Hiko and I are meeting him. I'll go with you and make sure you get there safely.'

She rested her cheek on his shoulder and kissed his neck, then ran her hand across his face, tracing his cheek, his nose and chin, the laughter lines at the sides of his mouth, his smooth thick hair. She wanted to tell him that she would pray that nothing terrible would happen, but she couldn't form the words. She realized now that he wasn't expecting to come back.

'You said you'd protect me,' she whispered. 'Don't forget that.'

'You have my word,' he said, bowing solemnly.

They hurried through the city, Hana keeping a few steps behind. As they crossed the square in front of Sujikai Gate, Hana remembered the women she had seen there, painted and powdered, ready to sell themselves to any man for a rice ball. Smells of waste and rotting food hovered above the Kanda river as they found a boatman to pole them back to the jetty near her home.

All too soon they came to the wasteland she had run across when she was fleeing the soldiers. There were mulberry bushes planted there now, a few bright yellow leaves still clinging to the branches. She knew the moment when they would have to part was very close but despite her sadness and her fears for Yozo, to see this place she knew so well was comforting. She was going home at last.

Tears sprang to her eyes when she saw the familiar wall with its tiled top and moss sprouting between the stones. Yozo stopped at the gate and stared at the name plate, frowning.

'Seizo Yamaguchi,' he read.

Hana wanted to hug him then and tell him that she loved him, that it made no difference to her what he had done, that it only made her feelings stronger. She wanted to beg him not to leave on this perilous mission – but instead she steeled her heart and reminded herself that she was a samurai, smiled and blinked away her tears and wished him luck as demurely as any wife.

Yozo took her hand and pressed it to his lips one last time, then turned back towards the river. She kept her eyes on him, his broad shoulders, his two swords at his side. He looked back once and smiled, then disappeared from view.

She pushed open the gate, barely aware of where her feet were taking her, still dazed by everything he had told her. But she knew it didn't change anything for her. Those grim days when she had been Commander Yamaguchi's wife were over long ago and her heart belonged to Yozo now. Fervently she prayed that he would come back unharmed.

Then she looked around, suddenly seeing where she was. She had been away nearly a year now. There was moss between the paving stones and drifts of fallen leaves heaped against the walls. The garden was rank with weeds and the great cherry tree had grown even bigger. The house was sadly dilapidated, with moss sprouting on the roof and tiles missing here and there, more like the haunt of foxes and badgers than a place where people lived. But it was still the same house and the same grounds. She saw smoke seeping from the eaves and walked faster, thinking how happy Oharu and Gensuké would be to see her, and how surprised.

The great door at the front was closed and bolted. She pushed at it but it wouldn't budge. There were swathes of cobwebs hanging from the lintels and under the eaves and piles of mouldering leaves in the corners. She went round to the family door at the side of the house and wiggled it open and stepped over the threshold, blinking, her eyes stinging from the smoke that swirled around in the darkness inside.

In the threads of light that pierced the slits between the closed rain doors, she could see the cavernous interior, the massive smoke-blackened rafters and the tatami-matted rooms disappearing into the shadows. She smelt charcoal smoke and food cooking and thought with a surge of anticipation that Oharu must be in the kitchen, preparing lunch.

Then she saw a movement in the gloom. There was a figure sitting cross-legged at the hearth, holding a pipe.

There was a thump as her bundle fell to the ground and her hands flew to her mouth to choke back her cry of shock.

For a moment she thought she must be seeing a ghost but the man was too solid – the broad shoulders, the arrogant thrust of the chin, the oiled hair hanging loose and thick and glossy.

Her knees buckled and she gasped as if she were drowning. She wanted to turn and run but her legs wouldn't carry her. She had to hold on to her senses, she told herself, keep her wits about her. How could Yozo have been so dreadfully wrong?

For there could be no doubt about it, no doubt at all. It was her husband.

40

Commander Yamaguchi looked older and thinner. His face was gaunt and his skin, which had been exquisitely pale, had become leathery. His hair too, which had once been as shiny as black lacquer, was streaked with grey. He had dark shadows around his eyes and the crease between his eyebrows had deepened into a scowl. He looked at Hana in silence, then ran his eyes slowly over her from her feet to her face.

Her legs seemed to bend of their own accord and she fell to her knees with her palms on the floor of the entranceway and pressed her face to her hands.

'So it's you,' he said, and she recognized his softly menacing tones and brusque peasant dialect. 'You've been travelling. And now you turn up in this unseemly kimono with your bundle, like some vulgar street person. It wasn't much of a homecoming for me, with no wife to greet me and take care of me.'

She trembled, speechless, and huddled up as small as possible on the cold earthen floor.

'Have you lost your voice? Aren't you going to say you're pleased to see me?'

'I thought . . . I thought . . .'

'You were supposed to take care of the house. Why weren't you here?'

She took a breath. 'S-soldiers . . .' She could barely form the words. 'Soldiers came to the house . . . To kill me – because I'm your wife. I . . . I had to flee.'

'You're a samurai and you're afraid of death? Your duty was to defend this house.'

Hana's guilt hung over her like a miasma and her breath came quick and shallow. Out of the corner of her eye she saw her bundle on the floor, where she had dropped it, and remembered the box, her husband's box. Perhaps if he saw it, it might soften his heart. Perhaps he would understand why she had done what she had done.

'I thought you were dead,' she breathed.

She groped for the bundle and put it on the tatami in front of him and fumbled with the knots, her hands shaking as she opened the carrying cloth. There was the plain metal soldier's box and the wooden scroll box next to it. She remembered opening them in her rooms at the Corner Tamaya, reading the letter and the poem again and again, then putting the boxes and the photograph on the altar there. She'd wept for him, forgotten the harshness and the beatings, remembered only that he had been her husband.

He started back as if he in his turn had seen a ghost and stretched out a trembling hand. His hand was thinner, bony, the knuckles larger.

'Ichimura brought them,' she whispered, looking up at him pleadingly. She remembered the effect it had always had when she'd looked at men in that way, through her lashes. 'I read your letter. I mourned you. I was going to take them to Kano and bury them, as you wanted.'

He prised the lid off the metal box and stared inside. She was startled to see that his eyes were swimming with tears.

'My whole life,' he muttered. 'And it amounts to this, just this. The war lost, the cause defeated, everything I believed in – gone, all gone.' He sat back on his heels and gave a long shuddering sigh. 'I should have died with the others. What kind of world is this to be alive in?'

He groped for his pipe and tapped it slowly on the edge of the tobacco box. The sound echoed in the silence. She held her breath, watching, waiting. Then he narrowed his eyes and looked at her.

'You're different,' he said. 'Come here.'

Her heart pounding, she knelt opposite him and he gripped her chin with his finger and thumb, pinching it so hard it hurt, and stared at her face, twisting her head this way and that. His eyes seemed to peel away every layer, as if he could read her whole story, everything she had done, everywhere she had been, every man she had ever slept with; as if everything – the night she had spent with Yozo, everything – was blazoned on her skin like a tattoo. She squeezed her eyes shut, remembering Father holding her face in just that way. Then he thrust her away so hard that she fell backwards on the tatami.

'Something's changed,' he said, with a scowl of disgust. 'You even smell different. You used to be a foolish little creature, but you're not now. You've learned disobedience. It's written all over you.'

He paused, then looked hard at her again.

'You've learned how to think. You argue, you tilt your head, you look at me through your lashes. You've learned how to play games, how to make men like you. You're not my modest wife any more, are you?'

Hana knew what was coming and there was nothing she could do or say to stop it. Her husband gave a snarl of revulsion. 'You've been in the Yoshiwara. Isn't that it? You've become a prostitute. How many southerners have had use of that body? You belong to me and you gave yourself to our enemies! You've shamed me, you've shamed this house.' He had turned dark red with rage.

As he said the word 'Yoshiwara', Hana knew she was doomed. He would kill her. He had to, it was the law.

She squeezed her hands together, feeling her heart pounding and the blood rising in her head. If only Yozo would come. If anyone could save her, he could. But he wouldn't know what had happened until it was too late.

'Don't try and deny it,' the Commander bellowed, his face black. 'A woman called Fuyu came. She told me everything.'

Fuyu. The name was like a slap in the face. Hana jerked upright, shocked out of her stupor, suddenly furious. She was not going to kneel in silence any longer. In the past she'd accepted that this man was her lord and master and had obeyed his orders and taken his beatings without complaint. But he was right. She had changed. He no longer had dominion over her spirit. Let him kill her. She would have her say first.

'Fuyu's a procuress,' she shouted. 'How dare you believe her and not me? She sold me.'

The Commander ran his hands through his hair, making it stand out like flames around his face. 'You answer me back?' he roared. 'How dare you! You think it makes a difference whether it was your choice or not? No one wants a Yoshiwara woman as his wife.'

He cracked his knuckles and she quivered, remembering how he used to crack his knuckles before he hit her, then he stood up. She flinched and curled into a ball and put her arms around her head as she felt his foot thudding into her ribs and back and thighs. He waited till she sat up then hit her around the ear so hard she fell to the ground, stunned. Slowly she picked herself up and he hit her again.

The room was spinning, her ears were ringing and her head was aching so badly it was hard to think. She felt bruised all over; but he had done worse in the past, far worse. She straightened her back and stared at him defiantly. She would die proudly, not cowering and begging for mercy.

'You don't even weep,' he said, more softly this time. 'You've lost all shame. Get the mat. You know the procedure.'

She stood up and brushed herself off and limped to the kitchen. She heard the screech of metal on stone and knew he was sharpening his sword. Oharu was standing at the stove, stirring a pot as if she would never stop, with Gensuké crouching in a corner. They shrank back and looked away, mute with fear, as she came in.

Rolled in the corner was the straw mat that Oharu used to lay out radishes and persimmons to dry. It was dusty and mouldering and when Hana picked it up it left a mound of tiny dead insects on the floor.

She took it outside, her husband striding behind her. He had tied back his sleeves and tucked his swords into his sash.

'Over there,' he barked.

Hana felt the sunshine warm on her head. The day had never seemed so beautiful. The sky was dazzlingly blue and branches canopied the house, dappling the roof with gold, orange and brown leaves. She walked around the stone lantern and the pond, through the pine trees to the clearing behind the storehouse, where no one could see them.

'Here.'

She unrolled the mat and knelt with her back to him, holding her head high. But despite her resolve not to let him see her fear, she felt herself shaking and her teeth chattering. Her breath came short and shallow and she knew with each one that it might be her last.

'Say your prayers.'

The ground was cold and the stones cut through the thin straw into her shins. A breeze spun through the fallen leaves and made her shiver. A crow settled nearby and stared at her with a beady eye, then opened its big black beak and gave a harsh caw, startlingly loud in the stillness. It was a lonely sound, an omen of death.

In the Yoshiwara she had tasted life and love. If she had never left this house she might have lived to be old but she would never have known life. She had no regrets, she thought. She remembered Yozo and their night together. She'd never before known such intense happiness or felt so complete. She wished only that she could have seen him one more time. She smiled, holding the picture of him clear in her mind. She would die thinking of him.

There was a scrape of metal and she knew it was the last sound she would ever hear. She closed her eyes.

41

The idea had been to follow the procession to the point where the road narrowed, kill the guards and break Enomoto and Otori free. The southerners would think they'd wiped out the resistance and wouldn't have employed enough guards, the cage bearers would run away, and the bystanders, who hated the southern upstarts, would join in the fight alongside Yozo and his friends. That was the plan, at least, though whether it would work out quite so easily in practice was another matter.

But Yozo had survived plenty of hare-brained schemes in the past and he would survive this one, he told himself. He had to. He had a woman now that he cared for; he couldn't continue to risk his life any longer. His mind was still on Hana and the conversation they'd had. He'd needed to make peace with himself, knowing that he might not survive to see Hana again, but he'd feared her reaction when he told her that he had killed her husband. She had been so calm, so forgiving, and he admired her all the more for it. Now he could focus on what he had to do – to free Enomoto.

As he pushed through the mulberry bushes, making for the willow trees and shacks along the riverbank, he noted every detail of the way back to the great house where Hana would be. He wished he had his trusty Snider-Enfield, lost in the last battle. As it was, he would have to make do with the Colt and the sword which Marlin had thrust into his hands as he was running out of the Yoshiwara; unless, that is, Ichimura had found some usable weapons in the militia's arsenal.

At the jetty Heizo and Hiko were leaping out of a boat while the ferry man counted his coins. Yozo grinned as they saluted. Ichimura appeared, stumbling along the embankment, dragging a kitbag clattering and bouncing behind him. He was wearing dark blue leggings and a coarse jacket like a workman and had plastered his hair down so he wouldn't stand out in the crowd. He was grinning exultantly. He put his hands to his mouth and shouted something but the wind took away his words. Then as he got closer he shouted again. Yozo froze as he heard what he was saying. 'The Commander's back! He's not dead!'

'The Commander?' Yozo repeated, trying to swallow. The day suddenly felt darker and colder. 'You don't mean . . . You can't . . . Commander Yamaguchi?' There was a prickling at the back of his neck and a terrible constriction in his throat. 'He's still alive? But he can't be.'

Ichimura came up to Yozo, panting.

'I saw him with my own eyes, sir,' he said blithely. 'Yesterday. He lives near here. I told him our plans and he told me not to be a fool. The war's over, he's trying to avoid arrest. He's not planning to do anything to draw attention to himself.'

But Yozo no longer heard. He had turned cold as he realized what deadly peril Hana was in. But he had shot at him, he thought, had seen him fall, had looked back and seen him lying in a pool of blood. There had been blood on his jacket, blood on the ground. How could he still be alive?

Then Yozo himself had been captured. He'd heard nothing of the Commander after that, nothing all the time they'd been in the Yoshiwara until Ichimura had appeared with his damned box, which had only confirmed in his mind that he was dead. He groaned. How could he have been so wrong? And now he'd sent Hana home – to her death.

He stared around in horror, hitting his head with the flat of his hand as he realized the enormity of the choice he had to make.

There was Enomoto, his friend of many years, brilliant, gallant Enomoto, whom he admired and loved like a brother. His whole life and training – the samurai code that had been instilled in him since birth – had taught him that the most important quality for a man was loyalty to the cause and to his comrades. They would give their lives for you; you would give your life for them. He knew there would be no second chance to rescue Enomoto and Otori and that if the plan failed they would go to their deaths. How could he even think of betraying them?

But then Hana had come along and changed everything. He realized now that she mattered to him more than anything in the whole world. He would give up anything for her, even his honour and the respect of his comrades. All those years in the West had changed him more than he'd imagined possible – and once he'd made this choice he knew he could never look back.

He grabbed Ichimura's bag and ripped it open. It was bulging with rifles, but they were old and rusty and a bulky weapon would just slow him down. He kicked the bag aside.

'Wait here,' he barked.

'There's no time, sir. We have to go.'

Heizo, Hiko and Ichimura were staring at him as if he'd gone mad. They all probably knew about his meetings with Hana. He had done his best to keep them secret but the Yoshiwara was a small place and rife with gossip and Hanaogi, after all, had been the most famous courtesan of them all. All the men must have been jealous of him.

And if they'd guessed what was on his mind he knew what they would think – that women were fine for recreation, but to put personal feelings before duty, to put a mere woman before the need to rescue his brothers-in-arms, was totally crazy.

He shook his head. It was a terrible choice to have to make but he'd made his decision. There was no question about it. He had to save Hana.

'I'll join you later,' he said brusquely.

'But, sir . . .'

But even as Yozo started running he knew that he was almost certainly too late.

Marlin had drilled them to move at the double and now his training came into its own. He sprinted back towards the streets of dank samurai houses on the other side of the mulberry field, retracing his path as carefully as he could, but with each step the grey-tiled roofs and stone walls seemed further away. As if in a nightmare, he ran and ran yet seemed to make no progress at all. He cursed as he realized with a surge of blind fury that he was heading in the wrong direction.

Finally he found the high wall and the gate and pushed it open, grimacing as it screeched noisily in its grooves. There was the big house with its gloomy entrance porch and smoke drifting from the eaves, just as Hana had described, across a gravelled court-yard with paving stones, a well and a huge cherry tree.

Crows cawed, insects twittered and Yozo heard voices from the street outside, but inside the grounds all was silent. He glanced around, then squatted behind the tree and loaded his gun, wish-ing he'd had a chance to try it out.

If the Commander discovered Hana had been in the Yoshiwara, he would kill her. Samurai had to execute their wives if they found them committing adultery, let alone engaging in prostitution, and the Commander's fierce nature made it certain he would cut her down immediately, especially once he realized she'd been with southerners. If Yozo tried to stop him it would be he who was committing an offence, not the Commander.

His only hope was that she might have delayed him. She wouldn't have pleaded for mercy, she was too proud for that, though she might have tried to persuade him that she had been visiting her family. But the Commander would see through that quickly enough. He had only to look at her and he would know. Everything about her – even the way she carried herself – made it obvious that she was a woman used to stirring men's desire.

He had to think fast. If the Commander was going to kill her, he would do it outdoors, out of sight. But where could that be?

Yozo ran across the courtyard, looking for patches of moss to deaden his footsteps, scowling as his foot slipped and gravel crunched under his straw sandals, then reached the house and caught his breath in the shadow of the wall. The place was silent. He skirted a landscaped garden with a pond and a stone lantern, then peered around and saw a squat white-painted building – the storehouse. As he edged along the side of it he heard the scrape of metal and his blood began to pound.

Hardly daring to breathe, he looked around the corner and drew back sharply. Hana was kneeling like a statue, facing the wall, her hands small and white in her lap. She was wearing the plain blue kimono she'd put on that morning. Her hair had come loose and hung in strands around her face, though Yozo could glimpse the soft white skin at the nape of her neck. She was deathly pale but her face was composed and she sat very straight. As Yozo saw the graceful line of her back he felt a surge of pride that she held herself with such dignity. Then he saw that her cheek was bruised and swollen and had to clench his fists to stop himself shouting in fury.

The Commander loomed over her, legs spread apart, hand on his sword hilt, ready to strike. He was thinner and greyer than when Yozo had last seen him, but he was no ghost. He had tucked up his skirts, tied back his sleeves and put on a steel-fronted headband as if he was going into battle. His eyes were narrowed and his mouth set in a look of implacable determination.

Yozo knew that if the Commander so much as moved his hand, his sword would be out of its scabbard and Hana would be dead in a single sweep of the blade. He cocked his pistol. The click was startlingly loud in the silence but the Commander didn't seem to hear it. He looked deep in thought.

Raising his gun, Yozo crouched and took aim. The gun was old and he didn't know how accurate it was and the Commander was so close to Hana he was fearful he might hit her; but there was no time to do anything else. Grunting with determination, he pulled the trigger. There was a deafening bang and a plume of flame.

Through the smoke he saw the Commander leap back, stumble and put out his big swordsman's hand to stop himself falling. The bullet rammed into a wall, sending out an eruption of earth and stones and dust.

Yozo cursed. He had startled the Commander and thrown him off his stride but he hadn't put him out of action.

The Commander jerked round and saw Yozo and a look of astonished recognition flashed across his face. His eyes bulged in their sockets, he roared like a lion at bay and his whole body seemed to convulse with rage. His face blackened as if he was about to explode and he swept his sword out of its scabbard and swung it in an arc that glittered in the sun. If Hana had been in front of him it would have sliced her open from waist to shoulder.

But she was no longer there. At the sound of the shot she had started violently, and as the bullet whistled past the Commander's face, sending him staggering, she twisted round and saw Yozo. She scrambled to her feet, pulled up her skirts and ran to the corner where Yozo was poised, his gun raised. For a moment their eyes met. Hers were huge and white, like a frightened deer's.

'Get behind me,' he whispered urgently. 'Quickly.'

He pulled the trigger again but this time the Commander was ready. With a curl of his lip he stepped aside and swung his sword. Yozo stared in disbelief as the Commander split the bullet clean in half. The shards veered off to each side of the gleaming blade and slammed into the wall, kicking up more earth and dust. The sword glinted in the sun, unmarked.

Cursing, Yozo threw down his gun, but the Commander was already on top of him, yelling a war cry, sword raised in both hands over his head. Yozo wrenched his own sword out just in time to parry as the Commander's blade came slashing down. Steel clanged deafeningly on steel as the blades scraped together, sending out a shower of sparks. The impact drove Yozo to his knees.

He sprang up and they glared at each other, swords at the

ready, as they edged back and forth, each daring the other to be the first to strike.

After the months in the Yoshiwara Yozo was out of practice and his sword was not the best. He knew the Commander's weapon. It was legendary, the work of a famous swordsmith. The Commander must have given it to Ichimura when he realized the war was lost and Ichimura had brought it to the house. For a moment Yozo was struck by the dreadful sadness of it all. He and the Commander had been on the same side, fighting for what they believed in, and now, as once before, they were reduced to fighting each other. For a moment he wanted to throw his weapon down. The Commander was a relic of a lost age and fighting with swords was a dying art. Yozo had had his revenge once and had been haunted by it ever since. It seemed wrong to have it again. But then he remembered Kitaro lying dead on the lonely Ezo plain and thought of the bruises on Hana's face and his resolve hardened.

'So it's you,' the Commander said. 'Yozo Tajima. I can't escape you. Wherever I go, you're there.' He had a spark in his eye, a dancing madness that Yozo recognized.

'Let her go, just let her go,' said Yozo. 'We'll leave Edo, we'll go to Ezo, you'll never see us again.'

'You tricked me once, Tajima, you caught me off guard with your treachery. But now we'll finish off what we began in Ezo, only this time you'll be the one that dies – you and your whore.'

Yozo was a fine swordsman but he knew the Commander was entirely ruthless and without pity, which made him almost invincible. He remembered how he'd boasted that the blade of one of his swords had rotted away from all the human blood that had soaked it.

He knew he had to be the first to strike. The razor-sharp blades could slice through flesh like a knife through silk. A single blow was all it would take to cut a man's arm or leg off or split him in half as easily as the Commander had sliced through the bullet.

Yelling at the top of his voice, Yozo leaped forward, swinging his sword. There was a clang as the Commander parried. Yozo spun on his toes, turned his sword and slashed again, then gripped the hilt with both hands, raised it over his head and brought it whistling down. The clang and clatter of steel were deafening. But the Commander anticipated his every move and easily parried each blow. As they drew apart, Yozo lunged again, taking the Commander off guard, and drove his blade deep into the soft flesh of his shoulder before he had a chance to leap back. Blood spread in a huge stain across the Commander's torn jacket but he didn't wince, just glared at Yozo as if he hadn't even noticed.

Then he grinned. His eyes sparkled and he laughed that arrogant laugh of his. He yelled as he charged forward, swinging his sword savagely. He danced to and fro, skirts flying, nimble as a deer, striking from every possible direction. His blade was like a razor, flashing in the sunlight as it swished through the air. Yozo was driven against the wall as he desperately tried to block his strokes, knowing that all it needed was a single stroke and he would be dead.

The Commander closed in, bringing his blade down fast and light, again and again. Reaching out to parry a blow that seemed to come from nowhere, Yozo stumbled. He leaped out of the way but not far enough and the blade sliced his cheek. The sudden pain made his eyes water and he felt his face wet with blood. He gritted his teeth and swung his sword again and again, trying to fend off the barrage of blows, but then the Commander's blade sliced down and he felt a stinging pain, nauseatingly sharp, in his left arm. He reeled, exhausted. He was panting, covered in sweat, his chest heaving and his breath puffs of steam in the autumn air.

The Commander stood over him, his sword raised for the kill. He was grinning. He had barely raised a sweat and Yozo realized he could have finished him off long ago. He'd been playing with him like a cat plays with a mouse, for sport.

Back to the wall, Yozo waited for the blow. But instead of bringing his sword down and finishing him off, the Commander stood poised, like a statue, as if he wanted to draw out his own enjoyment of the moment.

Yozo stared at him, wondering why the Commander didn't strike. It was almost as if he was giving him a chance – as if he wanted to die.

Suddenly Yozo was blind with rage. If he was going to die he would take this demon with him. As the Commander stood gloating, he yelled, 'For Kitaro and Hana.' Gripping his sword in both hands, he turned the point upwards and rammed his blade deep into the layers of silk that covered the Commander's stomach. He felt it glide smoothly through his spine.

With the last of his strength he pushed until he was sure his sword had pierced the Commander right through, then twisted it and wrenched it out and prepared to strike again.

The Commander's eyes widened and he staggered suddenly. Yozo expected him to fall but instead he gave a screech of pure hatred that sent a shudder jarring through Yozo's skull. Perhaps he was not human at all, perhaps it really was impossible to kill him, and, as if in proof, the next moment the Commander's sword was swinging down. Yozo saw it coming, slanting towards him like a ray of sunlight. He tried to dive out of the way, raising his sword to parry, but he knew it was too late. The Commander had won. They would go to heaven or hell together.

Then there was a clang and the sword flew out of the Commander's hand, wheeled in the air and thudded harmlessly to the ground a little way away. Dazed, Yozo looked up. A blade had appeared from nowhere and deflected the blow.

The Commander swayed. Blood gushed from his stomach and mouth and he staggered again, then his knees folded and he toppled to the ground, sending leaves whirling around him.

He stared up at Yozo and the faintest of smiles crossed his face. His lips twitched. Yozo leaned forward, trying to catch his words.

'You fought well. You've done me . . . a favour.'

He gave a sigh. Slowly the light in his eyes faded and his head rolled heavily to one side.

42

With the clash and clang of steel ringing in her ears, Hana had raced into the house and snatched her halberd from its ledge above the lintel. She'd come running out again to see Yozo with his back against the wall and her husband standing over him with his sword raised, his lips curled in a triumphant smile. She'd seen Yozo twist round with sudden ferocity, tilt his sword upwards and drive the blade into her husband's belly, and the crazed glint in her husband's eyes as he brought his sword down for the final blow.

Before she had time to think, she'd braced herself, swept her halberd in a great arc and lashed out at the falling sword with all her might. She'd felt the two blades crash together and staggered under the impact, clinging desperately to the haft of her weapon as it was nearly wrenched from her hands. Then with an almighty effort, with more strength than she'd known she possessed, she had turned the lethal blade in its course and thrust it aside.

Now she stared at the tall man sprawled on the ground, blood pumping from his wounds. Dust and leaves spun in the air. She watched, her breath loud in the silence, as a yellow leaf wafted down and settled on his hand.

She had been so sure she was going to die herself, she had already said goodbye to the world. But now that she knew she was going to live, everything looked so beautiful it brought tears to her eyes. The walls of the storehouse were dazzlingly white in the sunlight, bamboo swayed and rustled in the breeze and the scent of woodsmoke filled the air.

She stared at this man she had dreaded for so long, almost afraid his eyes would spring open again and he would sit up and stare at her. His face was composed and peaceful, more than it had ever been in life. She had thought she would never see him again – but she had, first alive, now truly dead.

Yozo heaved himself to his feet, resting his hand on the wall to steady himself. He was pale and covered in blood and sweat and dirt and his hair had come loose and hung around his face.

'Wait,' he said, raising his hand as Hana ran over to him. He wiped his blade on the corner of his jacket and slid his sword back into its scabbard, never taking his eyes off the dead man. 'I'm going to make sure you don't mourn a third time.'

He picked up his gun, still lying on the ground where he had dropped it, knelt and pressed it to the dead man's head. Hana put her hands over her ears. She too wanted to be sure he didn't rise from the dead ever again. But Yozo was looking at her husband's face and put the gun down again without firing it.

'He deserves respect,' he said solemnly. 'He was a great warrior, a warrior of the old school. We'll give him a proper funeral and take his ashes to Kano and bury them there in the family tomb along with his box.'

Hana knelt beside him and reached out her hand shyly and put it on his thigh.

'It's over,' he said quietly. 'In the end he won. There was no way I could ever have beaten him. He wanted to die: he let me kill him.' He seemed almost sad.

'It's true. There was no place for him in this world.'

He looked at her and smiled, then winced and put his hand to his face. There was blood trickling from the livid slash along his cheek. 'You're a warrior too. You saved my life.'

'No, you saved mine,' she said softly. 'I was sure I was going to die. I never thought you'd come back in time.'

He took her hand and she felt the warmth of his palm on hers.

'There was never any doubt in my mind that that was what I had to do. When I heard the Commander was alive I couldn't think of anything else. Only you, and the peril you were in.'

He raised her hand to his lips. She loved the way his smile began in his eyes, then moved to the corners of his mouth till his whole face was smiling.

'I disgraced myself,' he added. 'Or so Heizo and Hiko and Ichimura think. I betrayed my friends.' He paused, then sighed. 'Anyway, it was a crazy plan. They may have saved Enomoto and Otori but I doubt it. They're probably all in Kodenmacho Prison by now.'

'Come inside,' she said. 'We need to wash your wounds and bandage them.'

But Yozo was looking at the Commander's body again.

'It's finished,' he said, 'his era, the era of warriors. All that battling and fighting, all the hatred of north for south.'

He stood up slowly and took Hana's hand. 'I got to know Masaharu quite well in the Yoshiwara. He's a good man. There are others like him in the government. I know they were our enemies but they've won now, there's no disputing it, and we'll have to get used to it. They're bumpkins, those southerners, they've got no culture and no style, but they're idealistic. They want to look to the world outside Japan, and Masaharu knows there are very few of us who've actually been there. It makes sense to use our skills and knowledge, not keep us locked up for ever. We need to look to the future, not back at the past.'

The past. The previous night Hana had been sitting with Saburo, then jogging along in the palanquin through the darkness. It was hard even to think about now, it seemed so long ago. All her adult life she'd known hardship – with her husband, then at the Yoshiwara. But now as she looked at Yozo she knew that the future would be quite different. She didn't know what they would do or where they would go, but whatever they did she knew they would be together.

'You told me about your house,' said Yozo, 'but I haven't even seen it yet. Aren't you going to take me inside?'

As they walked through the early-morning sunshine, through the fallen leaves, across the grounds, it felt as if they were at the beginning of a new life. They turned the corner and there was the house with its tiled roof and wooden rain doors and smoke coiling out from under the eaves. Hana looked at it and knew she was home and that no one would ever threaten her again. Then she took Yozo's hand and led him inside.

THE END

Afterword

Hana and Yozo are fictional but the historical events which form the underpinning of *The Courtesan and the Samurai* are as close to the truth as I could make them, including the story of the fifteen youths who were sent to Europe, Enomoto's last-ditch attempt to reinstate the shogun and the desperate battles in Ezo. The shipwreck in Batavia and the lunch with Alfred Krupp, as well as the *Kaiyo Maru*'s long journey back to Japan, are all true. And, of course, the Yoshiwara really existed.

In real life, Enomoto (whose full name was Takeaki Enomoto) escaped execution, not through any plot by his friends but thanks to his own passionate idealism. This is what happened. Before the last battle, when it was obvious that the northerners had lost, he sent the precious volumes of naval tactics he had brought back from Holland to the commander of the southern forces, saying that his country should have them no matter what happened to him. After his surrender, many leading men in the government (which consisted almost entirely of southerners) demanded his execution, but others argued that he should be spared because he had shown such patriotism. As the fictional Masaharu realized, very few Japanese had been to Europe or had any knowledge or understanding of the West and Enomoto was recognized as being particularly brilliant.

In the end he spent two and a half years in Kodenmacho Prison, until January 1872, when Emperor Meiji issued a pardon for those who had fought on the shogun's side. Enomoto was immediately given a government posting in Ezo, by then renamed Hokkaido. He went on to become a vice admiral in the fledgling Japanese Imperial Navy, then special envoy to St Petersburg, and was finally awarded the rank of viscount, one of only two northerners to be so honoured. He died in 1908 at the age of seventy-two.

A real-life Yozo would undoubtedly have had a career as brilliant as that of many of the fifteen young travellers, though those who had joined Enomoto in his rebellion against the new regime had to wait until they were pardoned, in 1872. One went on to become deputy director of the naval academy, some were given leading positions in government ministries, one became the empress's physician and another became surgeon general.

After his two and a half years in prison, Otori (whose full name was Keisuké Otori) became president of the Gakushuin peers' school (akin to Eton), and later ambassador to China, then Korea. He created an archive to preserve the memoirs and accounts of those who had fought in Ezo on the shogun's side and had a monument built in Hakodate to the many northern soldiers who perished there. It can be seen to this day.

Hakodate is as cold and snowy as ever. I was there one December to research this book and experienced for myself the dramatic scenery and savage cold and the unpredictable winter weather, with snow storms blustering up in minutes out of what had been a clear blue sky. Of the Star Fort only the five-pointed battlements and the moat remain, along with the graves of some of the leaders and a museum housing relics and uniforms.

I also took a three-hour train ride across the peninsula to see the *Kaiyo Maru* – for, after more than a hundred years underwater, she was discovered on the sea floor in 1975 and salvaged and reconstructed in 1990. She now stands proudly on the waterfront at Esashi, a beautiful sight with her three masts and huge funnel. Inside, her Krupp cannons are lined up at the gun ports and there are display cases containing all the items that have been retrieved – western and Japanese swords, pistols, Dutch knives and forks, straw sandals, combs, fans, lunch boxes, coins and hundreds of cannonballs. The weather is so atrocious it's not surprising that she went down. Trying to take a photograph of her with frozen fingers I was driven by the gales right across the dock.

The Commander's Kyoto militia is modelled on the Shinsengumi, the shogun's notoriously ruthless police force which patrolled Kyoto and went on to fight alongside the last of the shogun's troops in Ezo. Commander Yamaguchi is inspired by the great hero and leader of the Shinsengumi, Toshizo Hijikata. The Commander's death poem is his. The real Hijikata was not from Kano and there's no record that he ever married, though he was famously popular among the women of the Yoshiwara. He was killed in the last battle in Hakodate at the age of thirty-four and his grave is there.

The French officers who were evacuated from Hakodate were sent back to France. The Japanese government called for them to be court-martialled and executed but the French populace and government were so impressed with their gallantry in sticking by their men that they were not even put on trial. Captain Jules Brunet ended up a general and chief of staff of the French army and in 1881 and again in 1885 was awarded medals by Emperor Meiji, probably at the instigation of Enomoto who by then was Navy Minister.

Sergeant Jean Marlin really did stay behind when his fellow officers went back to France – though what he did and why he stayed are my invention. He died in 1872 at the age of thirty-nine and is buried in Yokohama International Cemetery.

Like Hana and Otsuné, many young women of families loyal to the shogun, particularly those from the lower ranks of the samurai class, found themselves on the streets with no one to support them when civil war broke out, and ended up going into prostitution. The inhabitants of the Yoshiwara in *The Courtesan and the Samurai* are fictional but the names of the streets and brothels (including the Corner Tamaya) are real and the gate-keeper was always called Shirobei.

At the time of my story the Yoshiwara had been in decline, but when the southerners took power they patronized it and for a while its fortunes rose. New licensed districts were created and the government even built a Yoshiwara for westerners and named it the New Shimabara after the Kyoto equivalent of the Yoshiwara. Seventeen hundred courtesans and two hundred geishas moved there from the Yoshiwara but westerners didn't patronize it; it seemed they preferred to keeep their pleasures sur-reptitious and it soon closed down.

In 1871 fire destroyed much of the Yoshiwara. It was rebuilt with western-style buildings, some as tall as five storeys high, and the streets were widened to prevent fire spreading so easily. The Yoshiwara shown in old photographs dates from after this and looks quite different from the way it must have when Hana was there.

Japan was rapidly becoming part of the wider world and this had a devastating effect on the old ways of life, including the Yoshiwara. Foreigners condemned the buying and selling of girls as a form of slavery and in 1872 the government, concerned with how Japan appeared in the eyes of the world, passed the Prostitute and Geisha Emancipation Act, freeing the young women and cancelling their debts. Many, however, had no other way of making a living and the Yoshiwara brothel owners simply renamed the houses 'rental parlours' and continued to operate. Prostitution was made illegal in Japan after the Second World War and it went underground.

The Five Streets are still there, clearly marked on the map of Tokyo, though they are now lined with what are euphemistically called 'soaplands', with ferocious-looking bouncers outside. The marshland is gone and the Japan Dyke has been levelled and become a road, but there is still a rather bedraggled Looking Back Willow where the zigzag road begins that leads into the Yoshiwara, and until recently there were courtesan shows, where actresses dressed as courtesans served sake to nervous-looking men. When I was there I visited the local graveyard at Jokanji Temple and saw the vault stacked with shelf upon shelf of small urns, holding the ashes of thousands of unfortunate girls who were buried there, most in their early twenties.

Some ten years ago I spent several months living among the geishas of Kyoto and Tokyo to research my book *Geisha: The Secret History of a Vanishing World*. This experience was of enormous help in enabling me to imagine what life in the Yoshiwara must have been like. While the geographical Yoshiwara is a pale shadow of its past glory, its legend continues. It still exists in stories of the period, woodblock prints and photographs, through which we can imagine ourselves back in the *ukiyo* – the floating world.

Lesley Downer
February 2010

Bibliography

History is written by the winners, and never more so than in the case of the revolution that came to be known as the Meiji Restoration. Hana, Yozo and their friends were on the losing side and, as a result, the stories of the fifteen young adventurers who went to Europe and of the last desperate battles in Ezo are far less widely known than the exploits of their southern contemporaries. Nevertheless, the story as I tell it is largely based on research and historical fact.

My primary resource for the story of Enomoto and the Ezo Republic was the accounts in newspapers of the time – *The Japan Times Overland Mail*, *The Hiogo News* and *The Hiogo and Osaka Herald*, all of which started publishing around 1860 and provide detailed accounts of the battle for Ezo. They tell a totally different story from the version as reconstructed after the fact by the winners. These newspapers use the terms 'northerners' and 'southerners' for the opposing forces and make it clear that western observers were unsure for some time which side was likely to prevail or provide the more stable government. There are also accounts in *The Illustrated London News* with illustrations by the artist Charles Wirgman and by an officer of HMS *Pearl* who was present as an observer in Hakodate at the time of the battle.

Another important source, telling the story from the point of view of the 'Kyoto militia', is Romulus Hillsborough's *Shinsengumi*, listed below.

For those who want to read more about this fascinating period, here is a short bibliography.

The Yoshiwara

de Becker, J. E., *The Nightless City or the History of the Yoshiwara Yukwaku* (ICG Muse Inc., New York, Tokyo, Osaka & London, first published 1899)

Segawa Seigle, Cecilia, *Yoshiwara: The Glittering World of the Japanese Courtesan* (University of Hawaii Press, 1993)

Segawa Seigle, Cecilia, et al, *A Courtesan's Day, Hour by Hour* (Hotei Publishing, Amsterdam, 2004)

You might also enjoy:

Bornoff, Nicholas, *Pink Samurai, The Pursuit and Politics of Sex in Japan* (Grafton Books, London, 1991)

Dalby, Liza, *Geisha* (University of California Press, Berkeley, Los Angeles, London, 1983)

Danly, Robert Lyons, *In the Shade of Spring Leaves: The Life and Writings of Higuchi Ichiyo, A Woman of Letters in Meiji Japan* (Yale University Press, New Haven and London, 1981)

Downer, Lesley, *Geisha: The Secret History of a Vanishing World* (Headline, 2000)

Hibbett, Howard, *The Floating World in Japanese Fiction* (Oxford University Press, London, 1959)

Screech, Timon, *Sex and the Floating World: Erotic Images in Japan 1700–1820* (Reaktion Books, 1999)

Seidensticker, Edward, *Kafu the Scribbler: The Life and Writings of Nagai Kafu, 1879–1959* (Stanford University Press, Stanford, California, 1965)

Hana's favourite romance, *The Plum Calendar,* is partially translated in:

Shirane, Haruo (ed.), *Early Modern Japanese Literature, An Anthology, 1600–1900* (Columbia University Press, New York, 2008)

Ezo

Beasley, W. G., *Japan Encounters the Barbarian: Japanese Travellers in America and Europe* (Yale University Press, New Haven and London, 1995)

Bennett, Terry (ed.), *Japan and the Illustrated London News: Complete Record of Reported Events, 1853 to 1899* (Global Oriental, Folkestone, 2006)

Hillsborough, Romulus, *Shinsengumi: The Shogun's Last Samurai Corps* (Tuttle Publishing, Tokyo, Rutland Vermont, Singapore, 2005)

Satow, Ernest Mason (translator), *Kinse Shiriaku: A History of Japan from the First Visit of Commodore Perry in 1853 to the Capture of Hakodate by the Mikado's Forces in 1869* (Japan Mail office, Yokohama, 1873, facsimile published by Kessinger Publishing)

Steele, M. William, *Alternative Narratives in Modern Japanese History* (Routledge, London, 2003)

Books on the period in general

Meech-Pekarik, Julia, *The World of the Meiji Print: Impressions of a New Civilization* (Weatherhill, 1987)

Naito, Akira, *Edo, The City that Became Tokyo: An Illustrated History*, illustrations by Kazuo Hozumi, translated, adapted and introduced by H. Mack Horton (Kodansha International, Tokyo, New York, London, 2003)

Nishiyama, Matsunosuke, *Edo Culture: Daily Life and Diversions in Urban Japan, 1600–1868* (University of Hawai'i Press, Honolulu, 1997)

Seidensticker, Edward, *Low City, High City: Tokyo from Edo to the Earthquake, 1867–1923* (Alfred A. Knopf Inc., New York, 1983)

Shiba, Goro, *Remembering Aizu: The Testament of Shiba Goro*, edited by Ishimitsu Mahito, translated by Teruko Craig (University of Hawai'i Press, Honolulu, 1999)

Diaries of Victorian travellers of the period

Alcock, Rutherford, *The Capital of the Tycoon, Volumes I and II* (Elibron Classics, 2005, first published 1863)

Cortazzi, Hugh, *Mitford's Japan: Memories & Recollections 1866–1906* (Japan Library, 2002)

Satow, Ernest, *A Diplomat in Japan: The Inner History of the Critical Years in the Evolution of Japan When the Ports were Opened and the Monarchy Restored* (Stone Bridge Press, 2006, first published 1921)

Samurai films/DVDs set in this period

When the Last Sword is Drawn, directed by Yojiro Takita, 2003
Gohatto, directed by Nagisa Oshima, 1999
Twilight Samurai, directed by Yoji Yamada, 2002
Hidden Blade, directed by Yoji Yamada, 2004

And a stunningly beautiful post-modern film set in the Yoshiwara

Sakuran, directed by Mika Ninagawa, 2006

A website on the Yoshiwara

www.oldtokyo.com/yoshiwara.html

And a ship

Anyone fascinated by the *Kaiyo Maru* should make a trip to Portsmouth to see HMS *Warrior*, which was built in 1860, at almost exactly the same time: www.hmswarrior.org

About the Author

Lesley Downer's mother was Chinese and her father a professor of Chinese, so she grew up in a house full of books on Asia. But it was Japan, not China, that proved the more alluring. She lived there for a total of some fifteen years.

She has written many books about the country and its culture. To research the bestselling *Geisha: The Secret History of a Vanishing World*, she lived among the geisha and little by little found herself being transformed into one of them. Her first novel, *The Last Concubine*, was set in the women's palace in the great city of Edo, a harem-like complex, home to three thousand women and only one man – the shogun. It was shortlisted for the 2008 Romantic Novel of the Year Award.

Lesley has presented television programmes on Japan for Channel 4, the BBC and NHK. She lives in London with her husband, the author Arthur I. Miller, and still makes sure she goes to Japan every year.

Also by Lesley Downer

Non-fiction
Madame Sadayakko: The Geisha Who Seduced the West
Geisha: The Secret History of a Vanishing World*
The Brothers: The Hidden World of Japan's Richest Family
On the Narrow Road to the Deep North

Fiction
The Last Concubine

*Published in the United States as Women of the Pleasure
Quarters: The Secret History of the Geisha

For more information on Lesley Downer and her books, see her
website at www.lesleydowner.com